Praise for *New York Times* bestselling author Jill Shalvis

"Hot, sweet, fun and romantic! Pure pleasure!"
—#1 *New York Times* bestselling author Robyn Carr

"Shalvis thoroughly engages readers."
—*Publishers Weekly*

"Shalvis' writing is a perfect trifecta of win:
hilarious dialogue, evocative and real characters,
and settings that are as much a part of the story as the hero
and heroine. I've never been disappointed by a Shalvis book."
—*SmartBitchesTrashyBooks.com*

Praise for *New York Times* bestselling author Leslie Kelly

"Sexy, funny and a little outrageous, Leslie Kelly is a must read!"
—*New York Times* bestselling author Carly Phillips

"Leslie Kelly introduces characters you'll love spending time with,
explores soulmates you'll dream about, open honest sex
and a hero to die for."
—*RT Book Reviews* on *Naturally Naughty*

"[Kelly is] the perfect blend of sass and class!"
—*New York Times* bestselling author Vicki Lewis Thompson

ABOUT THE AUTHORS

JILL SHALVIS

New York Times and *USA TODAY* bestselling and award-winning author Jill Shalvis has published more than fifty romance novels. The four-time RITA® Award nominee and three-time National Readers' Choice winner makes her home near Lake Tahoe. Visit her website at www.jillshalvis.com for a complete booklist and her daily blog.

LESLIE KELLY

New York Times bestselling author Leslie Kelly has written dozens of books and novellas for the Harlequin Blaze, Temptation and Harlequin HQN lines. Known for her sparkling dialogue, fun characters and steamy sensuality, she has been honored with numerous awards, including a National Reader's Choice Award, a Colorado Award of Excellence, a Golden Quill and an *RT Book Reviews* Career Achievement Award in Series Romance. Leslie has also been nominated four times for the highest award in romance fiction, the RWA RITA® Award. Leslie lives in Maryland with her own romantic hero, Bruce, and their daughters. Visit her online at www.lesliekelly.com, or at her blog, www.plotmonkeys.com.

Bare Essentials

NEW YORK TIMES BESTSELLING AUTHORS

JILL SHALVIS
&
LESLIE KELLY

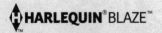

HARLEQUIN®BLAZE™

Recycling programs
for this product may
not exist in your area.

ISBN-13: 978-0-373-43040-6

BARE ESSENTIALS

Printed in U.S.A.

CONTENTS

To Wanda,
You held my hand on this one, and I'll never forget it.

And to Birgit Davis-Todd,
For always being there when I needed you.
Thanks, ladies, and here's to many more....

Jill Shalvis

NAUGHTY BUT NICE

Prologue

Ten Years Ago

THE LINE OF CARS heading out of the Daisy Inn was long but giddy. After all, it was prom night. The night of hopes and dreams. The night of spiked punch and lost virginity. The culmination of high school, where one was to have the time of one's life.

Unless you were a Tremaine, of course.

In the town of Pleasantville, Ohio, the only thing worse than being a member of that family was being a *female* member.

Cassie Tremaine Montgomery, an extremely female Tremaine, looked over at her date. Biff Walters. Hard to imagine any mother disliking her newborn son enough to name him Biff. But his name had nothing to do with the reason why Cassie had agreed to go to the prom with the tall, blond, gorgeous—but stupid—football star.

No, the reason had everything to do with his graduation present from his daddy—a cherry-red Corvette.

Since Cassie had a love affair with all things expensive and out of her reach, the convertible had been irresistible.

"Hey, baby," Biff said, catching her eye and putting his big, beefy, sweaty paw of a hand on her thigh. "You look hot tonight."

How original. *Not*. So she was blond and five foot ten, with the stacked body of a *Playboy* model—she'd been that way since the age of thirteen. Which meant men had been drooling over her for four years now. Added to that was the fact that while the men in her family were bastards—some quite literally—the women were all tramps. No exceptions. There was a rumor it even said so in the law books.

She could live with the stigma, or get the hell out of Pleasantville. The town didn't care much either way.

Unfortunately as a kid, the second option had never been viable. She and her cousin Kate had grown up learning that lesson all too well. Cassie's mother, Flo, otherwise known as the town vixen, had long ago guaranteed her daughter's fate by cheerfully seducing as many of the husbands in town as possible.

By default, Cassie was as unpopular—or popular if you asked the men—as her mother.

Which burned her; it always had. So Flo had a weakness. Men. So what? Everyone had a weakness. At least her mother's was basically harmless.

"Wanna go to the lake?" Biff asked hopefully.

Ugh. The lake was the typical make-out spot just outside of town. Tonight it'd be crowded with overeager guys toting their dressed-to-the-hilt dates, if they were lucky enough to have coaxed them out there.

Not for her, thank you very much. Cassie didn't share her mother's weakness for men, and never would.

"Of course you want to go, you're a Tremaine." Biff laughed uproariously at that. His fingers squeezed her thigh and moved upward, leaving a damp streak on the designer silk dress she'd secretly purchased at a thrift store.

"All the Tremaine women love sex." He was confident on this. "The wilder the better. It's why I asked you to the prom.

Come on, show me what you've got, baby." Leaning over, he planted his mouth on the side of her neck, smearing beer breath over her skin.

Smiling when she wanted to puke, Cassie backed away and combed her fingers through the hairstyle she'd spent hours copying from an ad in *Cosmo*. Fine price she was going to pay for wanting a cruise through town in a hot car. Now she had to figure a way out of the rest of the night. "What's the rush?"

"This." Biff, panting now, put his hand on his erection to adjust himself.

Oh, good God, men were ridiculous. The smell of beer and sweat permeated the car's close quarters. "Biff, they didn't let us buy beer before the prom, remember? We got carded."

"I know." He looked extremely proud of himself.

"So why do I smell it on you?"

His grin was wide, wicked and stupid. "Jeff had a twelve-pack in the bathroom. He gave me half."

Six beers. Cassie wasn't afraid of much, and God knows the town thought her a brainless drunk in the making simply because of the misfortune of her genes but, contrary to popular belief, she was very fond of living. "You drank them all?"

"Yeah." They pulled out of the inn in a show-off peel of tires. The car swerved, making Cassie grab the dashboard with a gasp.

"Don't worry, baby." He sent her another ridiculously dumb grin. "I drive better under the influence."

Right. Damn it, graduation was only a week away. Freedom loomed like a rainbow over her future. Seven days and she was outta this one-horse town and she wasn't going to ever look back. She was going to show the world she could be someone. Someone special.

But she had to be alive to do it. "Biff, pull over."

"Now, baby—"

"Stop the car," she said through her teeth. If he called her baby one more time she was going to scream. And then she was going to make *him* scream.

"Watch this." He stomped on the gas and whipped into the oncoming traffic's lane to pass a slower car. "Woo-hoo!" He craned his neck to look backward, flipping his middle finger at the driver as he came back into the right-hand lane with one second to spare before causing a head-on collision. "Bitchin'!"

"Biff." Cassie's fingernails, the ones she'd so carefully painted candy-apple red, dug into his dash. "I—"

"Ah, shit," he said at the same time Cassie heard the whoop of a siren. Flashing lights lit up Biff's face as he swore the air blue.

They pulled over. When Cassie saw Sheriff Richard Taggart coming toward them, all she could think was *Thank God.* He'd just saved her from a car accident. Or at the very least, a wrestling match with an idiot.

Biff was still swearing, and Cassie couldn't blame him. The sheriff wasn't exactly a warm, fuzzy sort, though she did trust him despite his being a tough hard-ass. She trusted him because he was the only man she knew who hadn't slept with her mother, and therefore the only man she knew worthy of her respect.

He came to the driver's window. Tipped his hat back. Switched his gum from one side to the other. Calmly and quietly assessed the situation with his sharp, sharp eyes. "You kids heading anywhere special?"

"Are you kidding? Look at my date." Biff leaned back so the sheriff could see Cassie. "I got me a Tremaine for the night."

The sheriff looked at Cassie. Something in his eyes shifted. "The lake, huh?" he asked.

Biff just shot his idiotic grin.

The sheriff shook his head. "Get out of the car, Biff."

"But Uncle Rich—"

"Out of the car," the sheriff repeated. "You won't be driving again any time soon. I can smell you from here."

"Ah, man—" Biff started to whine, but sucked it up when the sheriff glared at him.

"Start walking home, little nephew. Before I arrest you for Driving Under the Influence."

Biff slammed out of the car like a petulant child and without so much as a backward glance at Cassie, whose panties he'd wanted to get into only five minutes before, started walking.

Fine. Cassie tossed her hair out of her face and did her best impression of someone who didn't care what happened. But her heart was pounding, because though she was grateful he'd pulled them over, suddenly she felt...nervous.

That was ridiculous. He was rough and edgy, ruled the town with an iron fist, but he was also fair. A pillar of the community.

No reason for her to feel anxious. After all, what would he do now? He'd probably just make her walk home, too. Yeah, that worked for her. The entire evening had been a bust anyway. She had no idea why she'd thought dressing up and going out with the most popular jerk—er, *jock*—would be fun.

"Cassie."

"Sheriff."

"Don't you dress up nice."

He was staring at...her breasts? That didn't seem right. Cassie managed to keep her shock to herself. "I—yes."

"You think the dress changes what you are?" he asked softly. "Or who you are?" His gaze ran over the black silk, which had been designed to make men beg for mercy. She'd loved it when she'd found it, she'd loved it all the way until this very second, but now she felt like hugging herself.

"Get out of the car."

She didn't move, and he leaned in. "I can make you," he said silkily. "In fact, I'd like that."

There was no one around. Not that anyone would have stood up for her if there had been. No doubt the people in the cars driving by figured she'd done something to warrant the sheriff pulling her over. Chin high, Cassie got out of the car. Casually leaned back against it. Tossed her head. Played cool as a cucumber. "What can I do for you, Sheriff?"

"What can you do for me?" He stepped close. So close she could see the lights from his squad car dancing in his eyes. Smell his breath. Feel his hips brush hers. She wanted to cringe back, wanted to panic, but no way in hell was anyone in this goddamned town ever going to see her panic.

"What you can do for me, Cassie, is rather complicated, though being Flo's daughter…"

"You…know Flo?"

"Intimately."

He was aroused. And he had been with her mother. Odd how that felt like such a betrayal. But she was very careful not to react because it was one thing to mess with a stupid eighteen-year-old punk driving his brand-new car. It was another thing entirely to mess with a fully grown, aroused man with a badge. Fear threatened to paralyze her but she tossed her hair back again. "You must have mistaken me for my mother then."

"I don't make mistakes." He lifted a hand.

It hovered in the air between them for a long moment, while Cassie held her breath. When she released it, his fingers danced along the very tops of her breasts, which were pushed up and out by her dress. His breathing changed then, quickened, and she realized he was no different from his nephew at all. The knowledge that any man, even this one, could be turned into a slave by his own penis was disturbing.

Skin crawling, she slapped his hand away. "Unless you're

going to arrest me for having the poor judgment to go out with your idiot nephew, our business here is over," she said with remarkable calm. "Get out of my way. I'm walking home."

"I can give you a ride. Maybe Flo is home. Maybe the two of you would be interested…"

She shivered at the obvious innuendo. He wanted the both of them together. And why not, right? After all, a Tremaine was a Tremaine.

How did her mother stand this? Seducing men at the drop of a hat because she could? Cassie understood Flo enjoyed the power of bringing a man to his knees with lust, but Cassie would rather bring a man to his knees with pain. A direct kick to the family jewels would do it.

But this wasn't the man to do that to. Keeping her smile in place, she pushed past him. "Sorry, Sheriff. Not in the mood tonight."

Her heels clicked on the asphalt as she started walking. *Don't follow me, don't follow me.* She felt him watching her every step of the way, until she turned the corner.

Only then, when she knew she was truly alone and out of his sight, did she break stride and start running. No one stopped her. No one cared enough to.

Down Magnolia Avenue to Petunia Avenue, and then finally she turned off onto Pansy Lane. For the first time she didn't stop to sneer at the ridiculous flower names of the streets, and instead ran down the driveway of the duplex she'd shared all her life with her mother.

Her aunt and cousin lived on the other side. Kate would be a huge comfort right now, the voice of calm reason, but she'd still be with her date from the prom. Probably having the time of her life.

Cassie didn't go inside the house. Didn't want to face her mother, who would get misty-eyed at the sight of Cassie all over again. They both knew Cassie was leaving, and soon. The day she graduated, if possible. She had a life to find.

And someday she'd come back here and show them all. She'd come back driving a fancy car. She'd live in the biggest house on Lilac Hill, just because she could. And...oh, yes, this was her favorite...she'd get the sheriff. Somehow, some way.

But most of all, she'd...become someone. Someone special.

She went around the side of the duplex to the backyard. Kicked off the Nine West pumps she'd saved all last month for and dug her toes into the grass. Tipping back her head, she gauged the distance she had to jump in the dress wrapped around her like Saran wrap.

And took a flying leap for the rope ladder. In her skimpy black dress, she shimmied up the tree and landed in the tree house that had served as her and Kate's getaway all their lives.

It was cramped. And musty. Probably full of spiders. It'd been a long time since she'd needed to be alone, but she needed that now. Desperately. She was close—far too close—to losing it, when losing it was not an option. Ever.

Opening the small wooden cigar box she and Kate kept hidden, she took out her private and personal vice and lit it. A cigarette. It helped steady her nerves. There was also her diary, and Kate's, inside the box. She reached for hers.

Leaning back against the trunk of the tree, she studied the stars, mentally reviewing the list of things she wanted to accomplish with her life before she scribbled them into her diary. Kate would get a kick out of the fancy-car goal, she was sure of it.

When she was done writing, she leaned back and watched a falling star, and though she would have denied it to her dying day, she wished.

She wished that life would get better soon as she got the hell out of Pleasantville.

1

SHERIFF SEAN TAGGART—Tag, as he was commonly known—
had eaten, showered and was sprawled naked and exhausted
across his bed when the phone rang.

"Forget it," he muttered, not bothering to lift his head. He
didn't have the energy. God, he needed sleep. He'd been up
all night helping a neighboring county sheriff chase down a
man wanted for two bank robberies. Then this morning, before he could so much as think about sleep, he'd had to res-
cue four stupid cows from the middle of the highway. He'd
also wrestled a drunken and equally stupid teenager out of a
deep gorge.

Then he'd delivered a baby when the mother had decided
labor pains were just gas so that she'd ended up stranding herself thirty-five miles from nowhere.

Now, though it was barely the dinner hour, he just might
never move again. He lived alone on a hill above town. Not
on Lilac Hill like the rich, but in a nice, comfortable, sleepy
little subdivision where the houses were far apart and old
enough to be full of character—aka run-down. His place was
more run-down than most, which was how he'd afforded it.

Renovation had come slow and costly, so much so that he'd

only gotten to his bedroom and kitchen thus far. But it was his, and it was home. After growing up with a father who ruled not only the town with an iron fist but his kid as well, and no mother from the time she'd left for greener pastures when he'd turned eight, having a warm, cozy home had become very important to him.

Truth be known, he was ready for more than just a home these days. It wasn't his family he wanted more of, as he and his father had never been close. How could they be when they didn't share the same ideas, morals or beliefs, and to the older Taggart, Tag was little more than a disappointment. Regardless of the strained relationship with his father, Tag felt he was missing something else. He was ready for a friend, a lover, a wife. A soul mate. Someone *he* could depend on for a change, instead of the other way around.

But right now, he'd settle for eight hours of sleep in a row.

The phone kept ringing. Turning his head he pried one eye open and looked at it. It could be anyone. It could be his father, ex-sheriff, now retired, calling to tell Tag how to do his job. Again.

Or it could be an emergency, because if life had taught Tag any lesson at all, it was that just about anything could happen.

"Damn it." He yanked up the receiver. *"What?"*

"Dispatch," Annie reported in her perpetually cheerful voice. Off duty she was his ex-fiancée and pest extraordinaire. On duty, she was still his ex-fiancée and pest extraordinaire. Not long after becoming engaged, they'd decided they were better co-workers than co-habitors, and they'd been right. Tag could never have taken her eternal cheerfulness in bed night after night.

"Heard you didn't even kiss Sheila good night after your date," she said. "I'll have you know I went to a lot of trouble to set that up. You've got to kiss 'em, Tag, or you're going to ruin your bad-boy rep."

He groaned and rolled over. "God, I hope so."

"I just want you happy. Like I am."

She was getting married next month to one of his deputies, which was a good thing. But now she wanted him as almost married as she was. Sighing would do no good. Neither would ignoring her—she was more ruthless than a pit bull terrier. "If it's any of your business, which it's not, I didn't kiss Sheila because it wasn't a date. I didn't even want to go in the first place—" Why was he bothering? She wouldn't listen. Rubbing his eyes, he stared at the ceiling. "Why are you calling?"

"Know why you're so grumpy? You need to get laid once in a while. Look—" As if departing a state secret, she lowered her voice. "Sex is a really great stress reliever. I'd give you some to remind you, just as a favor, mind you, but I'm a committed woman now."

Tag wished he was deep asleep. "Tell me you're not calling me from the dispatch phone to say this to me."

"Someone has to, Tag, honey."

"I'm going back to sleep now."

"You can't."

"Why not?" He heard the rustling of papers as Annie shifted things on her desk. He pictured the mess—the stacks, the unfiled reports, the mugs of coffee and chocolate candy wrappers strewn over everything—and got all the more tense. "Look at the computer screen in front of you," he instructed. "Read me your last call."

"Oh, yeah!" She laughed. "Can't believe I forgot there for a moment. There's a stranger downtown, driving some sort of hot rod, causing trouble. We've received calls on and off all day, complaining about the loud music and reckless driving."

He opened his mouth to ask what had taken her so long

to say so, but bit back the comment because it wouldn't do him any good. Back on duty whether he liked it or not, he rubbed his gritty, tired eyes and grabbed for his pants. "Theft? Injuries?"

"Nope, nothing like that. Just the music and speeding."

"Speeding?" He'd given up sleep for speeding? "Why didn't...hell, who's on duty right now...Tim? Why didn't he take care of this earlier if it's been a problem all day?"

"Seems Tim stopped off at his momma's for some pie after lunch and got sick. Food poisoning. He's been bowing to the porcelain god ever since. Poor guy, bad things like that don't usually happen here in Pleasantville."

Since he'd had plenty of bad things happen to him right here in this town, the least of which was caving in and hiring his ex on dispatch, Tag just rolled his eyes. "If nothing really bad could happen, why can't I manage a night with some sleep in it?"

"Because we all love your sweet demeanor too much. Now get your ass up. Oh, and careful out there, okay? Don't do anything I wouldn't."

Which was damn little and they both knew it. "Yeah, thanks," he muttered, looking for more clothes. He jammed on his boots, yanked on his uniform shirt and grabbed his badge.

With one last fond look toward his big, rumpled, very comfortable bed, he shook his head and left.

Halfway to downtown Pleasantville, his radio squawked. "Got the license plate and make for ya," Annie said, and rattled it off.

"Sunshine-yellow Porsche." Tag shook his head at the idiotic tourist who'd probably taken a wrong turn somewhere and ended up in Pleasantville. "Shouldn't be hard to find. Owner's name?"

"Let's see, it's here somewhere...Cassie Tremaine Montgomery."

Not a tourist. Not a wayward traveler lost by accident. Not by a long shot.

Cassie Tremaine Montgomery.

She'd belonged here once. Though now, as a famous lingerie model, she was as far from Pleasantville as one could get.

He might not have ever met her personally since he'd been several years ahead of her in school, but her reputation preceded her. A reputation she'd gotten—according to legend—by using men just like her mother.

If he remembered correctly, and he was certain he did, Cassie had been tough, unreachable, attitude-ridden and... hot. Very hot.

And she'd been practically run out of town after her high school graduation by rumors. They'd said she was pregnant, on drugs, a thief. You name it, someone in town had claimed she'd done it. Hell, even his loser cousin Biff had plenty of wild stories, though Tag had no idea how much of it was true given Biff's tendency toward exaggeration. He'd never expended any energy thinking about it.

But now he was sheriff and she was back, stirring up trouble. Seemed he'd need to think about her plenty.

He saw her immediately, speeding down Magnolia Avenue in her racy car, with a matching racy attitude written all over her. Blond hair whipping behind her, her fingers tapping in beat to the music she had blaring.

Knowing only that things were about to get interesting, Tag turned his cruiser around and went after her.

GET WHAT YOU CAN, honey. Get what you can and get out.

Cassie Tremaine Montgomery smiled grimly as she remembered her mother's advice on life and took Magnolia Avenue at a slightly elevated speed than was strictly allowed by law. She couldn't help it, her car seemed to have the same attitude about being in this town as she did.

In other words, neither of them liked it.

As she drove downtown throughout the day, running errands, people stopped, stared. Pointed.

Logically, she knew it was the car. But the place had slammed her into the past. People recognized her. People remembered her.

Had she thought they wouldn't? Hadn't Kate warned her after she had been back in town recently to close up her mother's house? Good old Pea-ville.

There was Mrs. McIntyre coming out of the Tea Room. The Town Gossip hadn't changed; she still wore her hair in a bun wrapped so tight her eyes narrowed, and that infamous scowl. She'd maliciously talked about Cassie and Flo on a daily basis.

But that was a lifetime ago. To prove it, Cassie waved.

Mrs. McIntyre shook her finger at her and turned to a blue-haired old biddy next to her. That woman shook her finger at Cassie, too.

Well. Welcome home. Cassie squashed the urge to show them a finger of her own. She couldn't help it, this place brought out the worst in her.

But she wasn't here to reminisce and socialize. God, no. If left up to her, she'd have never come back. There was nothing for her here, nothing.

Kate was gone. She'd marched out of town hand in hand with Cassie all those years ago, each determined to make something of themselves.

Kate had done spectacularly in Chicago, with her specialty ladies' shop, Bare Essentials.

Some would say so had Cassie. But that she could afford to

buy and sell this sorry-ass town was little satisfaction when just driving through made her feel young and stupid all over again. Two things she hadn't felt in a very long time.

Everyone in Pleasantville had assumed she'd grow up the same as the trouble-loving Flo. Destiny, they'd said. Can't fight it.

And if you counted going off to New York and becoming one of the world's most well-known lingerie models following her destiny, well then, that's what Cassie had done.

Now she was back. Not by choice, mind you. Oh, no. She passed the library. And yep, there was the librarian standing out front changing the sign for tonight's reading circle. Mrs. Wilkens hadn't changed a bit, either. She was still old, still had her glasses around her neck on a chain and…was still frowning at Cassie.

Cassie had spent hours at the library looking for an escape from her life, devouring every historical romance novel she could find.

Mrs. Wilkens had always, always, hovered over her as if she was certain Cassie was going to steal a book.

Oh, wasn't this a fun stroll down memory lane. With a grim smile, Cassie drove on. She passed the old bowling alley, the five-and-dime, the Rose Café.

Pleasantville had a scent she'd never forgotten. It smelled like broken dreams and fear.

Or maybe that was just her imagination.

There was sound, as well. Other cars, a kid's laughter…the whoop of a siren—

What the hell? Craning her neck in surprise, she looked into the rearview mirror and saw the police lights. Her heart lurched for the poor sucker about to get a ticket. A serious lead-foot herself, Cassie winced in sympathy and slowed so the squad car could go around her.

It didn't.

No problem, she'd just pull over to give it more room. But the police car pulled over, too.

And that's when it hit her. *She* was the sucker about to get the ticket.

"Damn it. *Damn it,*" she muttered as she turned off the car and fumbled for her purse. She hadn't been pulled over since…prom night.

All those unhappy memories flooded back, nearly choking her. She hadn't given thought to that night in far too long to let it hit her like a sucker punch now, but that's exactly what it did. Her drunken date. Then dealing with the sheriff, who'd been one of the few men in town she'd figured she could trust.

She'd been wrong, very wrong. No man was trustworthy, hadn't she learned that the hard way? Especially recently.

But after all the terror she'd been through in the days before she'd been forced back here, Cassie wasn't going to get stressed about this. She'd find her wallet, explain why she was in such a hurry, and maybe, just maybe, if she batted the lashes just right, added a do-me smile and tossed back her hair in a certain way, she'd get out of here ticket-free.

Please, oh please, let there have been a new sheriff in the past ten years, she thought as she finally located her wallet in the oversize purse that carried everything including her still-secret vice—a historical romance. Pirates, rogues, Vikings… the lustier the better. She hadn't yet cracked the spine on this latest book, but if the sheriff saw it she'd…well, she'd have to kill him.

"Damn it."

No driver's license in the wallet. Oh, boy. Her own fault, though. In getting ready for the club she'd gone to several nights ago with friends, she'd pulled out her license and stuck it in her pocket so she wouldn't be hampered by her heavy purse.

And she hadn't returned it, not then, and not in the shocking events since. "Damn it."

"You said that already."

Lurching up, Cassie smacked her head on the sun visor, dislodging her sunglasses. Narrowing her eyes at the low, very male laugh, she focused in on...not Sheriff Richard Taggart, thank God.

No, Richard Taggart would be in his late fifties by now. Probably gray with a paunch and a mean-looking mouth from all the glowering he'd done.

The man standing in front of her wearing mirrored sunglasses and a uniform wasn't old, wasn't gray and certainly didn't have a paunch. In fact, as her eyes traveled up, up, up his very long, very mouthwatering body, she doubted he had a single ounce of fat on his tall, lean, superbly conditioned form.

Not that she was noticing. She worked with men all the time. Fellow models, photographers, directors...and while she definitely liked to look, and sometimes even liked to touch—on her terms thank you very much—this man would never interest her.

He wore a cop's uniform and a sheriff's badge, and ever since prom night she had a serious aversion to both.

Not to mention her aversion to authority period. "I don't have my license," she said, dismissing him by not looking into his face. Rude, yes, but it was nothing personal. She might have even told him so, if she cared what he thought, which she didn't.

"No license," he repeated.

What a voice. Each word sent a zing of awareness tingling through her every nerve ending. He could have made a fortune as a voice talent. His low, slightly rough tone easily conjured up erotic fantasies out of thin air.

"That's a problem, the no-license thing," he said. Having clearly decided she was no threat, he removed his sunglasses, stuck them in his shirt pocket and leaned on her car with casual ease, his big body far too close and...male.

She took back the whole voice-talent thing; he should go bigger and hit the big screen. She didn't need her vivid imagination to picture him up there as a romantic action-adventure hero.

Without the uniform, of course.

Obviously unaware of the direction her thoughts had taken, he nodded agreeably at her lack of inclination to apologize over not having a license. But one look at that firm mouth, hard jaw and unforgiving gaze, and Cassie knew this man was agreeable only when it suited him.

A car raced past them, a blue sedan with a little old lady behind the wheel. "Hey," Cassie said, straightening and craning her neck to catch the car vanish around the corner. "That lady was going way faster than me!"

"Mrs. Spelling?" He shrugged and tapped his pen on his ticket book. "She's late picking up her grandkids."

"She's *speeding,*" Cassie said through clenched teeth.

"Well, you were speeding first." He cocked his head all friendly-like. "And you're not carrying your ID because...?"

Because she'd left New York in a hurry. That was what happened when three incredibly shocking things occurred all at the same time.

One, she was being stalked. The man doing so had been a friend. That is, until she'd declined to sleep with him—which is when it'd turned ugly. Seems that if he couldn't have her, he wanted her dead.

Her agent, her friends and her fiercely worried cousin had

all insisted she get the hell out of Dodge—and since Cassie was rather fond of living, she had agreed. What better place to disappear than in a town that had never seen her in the first place?

Two, her mother had decided to sail around the world with her latest boyfriend. She would be away indefinitely, which meant she'd left Cassie a surprising and early inheritance. That Cassie had been forced to come back to Pleasantville to take care of that inheritance coincided with her need to vacate New York for a while.

The third shocking thing wasn't life-altering, but had bothered her enough that she'd dreamed of it for the past several days. Kate had found their high school diaries and the ridiculous lists they'd each made that fateful night in the tree house after their disastrous prom. Lists that included their childish wish for revenge on a town that had always spurned them. Cassie's was inspired, if a bit immature, and she eyed the sheriff again, remembering what she'd written.

1. Drive a fancy car, preferably sunshine-yellow because that's a good color for me.
2. Get the sheriff—somehow, some way, but make it good.
3. Live in the biggest house on Lilac Hill.
4. Open a porn shop—Kate's idea, but it's a good one.
5. Become someone. Note: this should have been number one.

Amusing. Childish. And damn tempting, given that she had already nailed number one. Maybe that's all she'd ever accomplish, driving a fancy yellow car, but one thing she'd come to realize in her most interesting career, she had a zest for life.

She wanted to live.

But if anyone thought she wanted to live *here,* they needed to think again. She'd rather have an impacted wisdom tooth removed. Without drugs.

She took off her sunglasses and immediately wished she hadn't. The glare of the sun made her squint, and she hated to squint. She also felt…exposed. The way she hadn't felt since her very first day of kindergarten, walking in with a big smile that slowly faded when all the other kids and their mean moms had stopped to whisper.

Tremaine.

White trash.

Daughter of a tramp.

Wild child.

At age five, she'd had no idea what those whispered words meant. But even then she'd recognized the judgment, so she'd simply lifted her chin to take the verbal knocks. She did the same now. "I don't have my license because it's not in my purse," she said, refusing to explain herself to anyone in this town. Including a cop. Especially a cop.

"Hmm. I hadn't realized Cassie Tremaine Montgomery was famous enough to not need ID."

"You know who I am."

His lips curved. "I've seen the catalogs. Interesting work you've gotten for yourself."

"Those catalogs are for women."

"With you in silk and lace on page after page?" He shook his head, that small smile looking quite at home on his very generous mouth. "Don't fool yourself. Those catalogs are scoured from front to back by men all across the country."

"Is that why you pulled me over? You wanted to meet me in person?" Disdain came easily for any man with authority, especially this one. "Or is it because I'm driving an expensive and brightly colored sports car?"

"Contrary to popular belief," he said conversationally, "cops don't necessarily have an attraction to all cars painted red or yellow. What we do have, however, is an attraction to speeding vehicles."

"And this has to do with me because...?"

"Because you were speeding," he said in that patient—and incredible—voice that told her he thought she was the village idiot, not the other way around. Then he straightened and waved his ticket book. "The question now is, were you going fast enough to warrant reckless driving."

Cassie never gaped, it went against the grain, but she did so now. "You've got to be kidding me."

As he had before, he leaned in, resting his weight on his arm, which lay across her open window. It wasn't a beefy arm, or a scrawny one, but somewhere in between, more on the side of tough and sinewy.

Again, not that she was noticing. He was probably a jackass, as Richard Taggart had been. He was probably prejudiced against anything different from his small-town norm. He was probably mean-spirited and stupid, as well—most men that good-looking were. For the second time she considered going the batting-the-eyelashes route. It would work. She'd been rendering men stupid with her looks for a very long time now.

In that spirit, she put her saucy smile in place to butter him up. His slate-blue eyes went as sharp as stone. He wasn't going to fall for the saucy smile, damn it, so she let it fade. "Look, I wasn't reckless driving. And you already know who I am so the license isn't really necessary."

In front of them, an older couple started to cross the street. Cassie ignored them until they stopped and stared at her, then started whispering furiously to themselves. Recognition came sharply to Cassie—they'd run the drugstore years ago, where she'd done her best to prove to the town she was just as wild as they thought by purchasing condoms regularly. "Oh, forget it," she said on a sigh. "Just do what you have to do."

"Which would be what, do you think?"

Well, hopefully it wouldn't be to make her get out of the car so he could try to feel her up. "You could let me go."

He smiled at that. A slow, wide smile that had her heart skipping a beat. "But you were speeding."

"Maybe I'm in a hurry to get out of here."

"Wouldn't be the first time, so I hear."

Now what would he know about her fast exit after graduation? She took another long look at him, squinting through the bright sun to see his name. *Taggart*. Oh, my God. "You're…"

"Sheriff Sean Taggart. You can call me Tag, most do."

Suddenly she could hardly breathe. She couldn't have managed a smile to save her life. Pulling back, she stared straight ahead out her windshield. "You're Richard's son."

"That would be correct."

It wasn't bad enough she'd had to put her entire life on hold because some jerk had decided if he couldn't have her, he'd terrorize her. Or that she had to be here while her life was on hold. No, she had to run into her old nightmares to boot. That, added to her current nightmares… God, she needed a cigarette.

Too bad she'd quit smoking five years ago. "Just give me my ticket then."

He was silent for so long she broke her own code and turned to look at him. Silent—still, even—but not idle. His eyes reflected all sorts of interesting things, mostly curiosity. "You know my father."

No. Her mother had known him. Cassie had just hated and feared him. "The ticket?"

"Now you're in a hurry to get your ticket? What's up, Cassie?"

The sound of her first name in his incredibly sensuous voice seemed so...intimate. "Like I said, I'm in a hurry to get out of here."

"Are you on your way out then? Already?"

She opened her mouth to remind him that was none of his business but her cell phone rang. It was Kate.

"Did you get there yet?" came her worried voice across the line. "Are you okay? How is it? You run into anyone we know? Talk to me."

Cassie stared up at the tall, dark and intensely handsome sheriff. "Kate, your timing is something."

"Oh, honey. Who is it? That mean old Mrs. McIntyre? Mrs. Wilkens? Because if it is—"

"As a matter of fact," Cassie said, slowly smiling as her and Tag's gazes locked. "It's Sheriff Taggart."

"Is that old fart still sheriff?"

"No, Tag here is Richard's son." When her gaze ran down the front of him, slowly, across his broad shoulders and what looked like a very promising chest and flat belly, over his trousers, which lovingly cupped powerful thighs and everything in between, then back up again, he lifted a daring brow, then gave her the same slow perusal.

Good, she thought in triumph. He *was* just a man after all, a man run by the equipment between his legs. A man who'd possibly forget to write that ticket due to the fact her little yellow sundress not only matched the car she'd bought herself last year but also accented the body she'd been well paid for over the years.

"Cassie," Kate said into her ear. "I worry about you there, all alone."

"I'm used to being alone." Funny how that worked. She was surrounded by people all day long and yet it was true. She was utterly alone.

"I mean because of your stalker."

Cassie's stomach tightened with the fear she pretended not to feel and glanced at Tag, who was unabashedly eavesdropping. "I'm safe enough here." *She hoped.*

"The guy slashed all your tires in the hopes of leaving you stranded, remember?"

"I do."

"And then he ruined two photo shoots—"

"I remember all of it, Kate."

"I'm sorry, of course you do. Okay, subject change. You going to be okay facing what Flo left you?"

That had been a shocker. That her mother had actually come out on the winning side after all, after always being considered the town joke. Seems the men in her life had come through, over the years gifting her a prime piece of real estate downtown, an amazing turn-of-the-century house on Lilac Hill overlooking town, and supposedly some other equally valuable things she needed Cassie to take care of. Cassie still couldn't believe it.

"Cassie?"

"I'm okay, Mom," she said, and accomplished what she'd wanted. Kate laughed.

"Call me back."

"Oh, I will." She clicked off and tossed the phone into the back seat. Then looked at Tag. "So…"

Tag looked right back. "What do you mean, you're safe enough here?"

"It's considered rude to eavesdrop."

"Talk to me, Cassie."

Oh, *right*. Terrified as she might be in the deep dark of night, she'd rather face the boogeyman bare-ass naked before asking this man for help. "If I do, can we skip the ticket?"

Now he laughed and, good Lord, she hoped that wasn't a

weapon he used often because just the sound could make a grown woman quiver with delight. She was fighting doing just that—uniform or not—when he flipped open the ticket book and started writing.

2

TAG ACTUALLY MANAGED a night of uninterrupted sleep, mostly due to the fact that he'd turned off the ringer on his phone and had shoved his pager beneath the couch pillows.

Not being on call did wonders for his mental health. What hadn't done wonders for that same mental health had been his dreams.

X-rated dreams about Pleasantville's latest visitor. He doubted they'd sprung from the photographs in the lingerie catalog he'd received in the mail and had perused over dinner. Photographs that showed every perfect inch of the body that belonged to one Cassie Tremaine Montgomery.

Lord, she was stacked. All long, tanned...lush. With the wild mane of sun-kissed blond hair and come-hither mouth... man, she was sure built like a goddess.

A tempting goddess, for certain. But luckily, not his type. A woman like Cassie was trouble, and on top of that trouble, he imagined she'd be high maintenance.

Tag was done with high maintenance, done with people needing him to take care of every little thing. The next time he let a woman into his life—and there would be a next time—it was going to be for keeps. She was going to be a sweet, quiet little thing who lived for him.

Yeah. *He* was going to be the high maintenance one for a change.

But as he showered, it wasn't the quiet little woman that came into his mind. It was Cassie. As in his dream, her cynically lit eyes were hot with passion, her mouth wet from kissing him, and her amazing body wrapped around his. Not only wrapped, but soft and pliant and so ready for him she would explode when he plunged into her.

Now *there* was an image to make a shower nice and steamy and his body hard and achy. Nothing he couldn't take care of by himself. But that wasn't what he was looking for.

Once the hot water turned cold, Tag got out, slipped on his uniform pants, and reluctantly put Cassie out of his mind. Even more reluctantly, he pulled his pager from beneath the couch cushions.

His father had called—again. He'd probably heard about the tri-county arrest, the one in which it had taken the authorities—including Tag—three days to apprehend the suspect. Yeah, ex-sheriff Richard Taggart probably wanted to make sure Tag knew *he* would have done it in one day.

Well, hell. So he wasn't like his father. So he didn't believe he had to bully the town into obeying the law. *Hallelujah.* But it'd be nice if just once, just one damn time, his father could acknowledge Tag's success.

Tag ran a hand through his wet hair and bit back a sigh as he strode through his very quiet house to the kitchen, where he poured himself a bowl of cereal.

"Note to self," he said to no one in particular. "The little wife will make me a hot breakfast every morning."

Soon as he found her.

The phone rang. Not surprisingly, it was Annie.

"Hey, boss, get your sweet ass up. We're short-staffed. Turns out Tim didn't have food poisoning, it was the flu, and half the staff is out."

"Any bright yellow Porsches out there speeding this morning?" he asked.

"Just one."

And he was just in the mood for it, too. He slipped into his uniform shirt, grabbed his badge and hit the road.

He found her immediately, cruising downtown, rolling through a four-way stop where he'd cleaned up more accidents than he liked to remember. Pulling her over, he strode up to the driver's side of her car and had to laugh at the look of fury on her beautiful face.

"Let me guess," Cassie said through her teeth. "You haven't met your ticket quota yet for the week."

"Careful, or I'll think you like me." He grinned when she snarled. "Did I mention yesterday that the speed limit is enforced here? As well as the *full stop* sign, which by the way, means you're supposed to come to a full stop. It's a ticket if you don't."

She rolled her eyes and tapped her red-lacquered-tipped fingers on the wheel, the picture of impatience. "I'm in a bit of a hurry."

"You know, you'd get farther with honey than vinegar," he said, pulling out his ticket book.

"I save the honey for someone who'll appreciate it."

Well, she had him there. She could bat her pretty lashes and flirt all she wanted, he was pretty much fed up with the tactic. No way could she bowl him over with those sexy green eyes and walk away. Nope, he was far tougher than that.

Maybe he wasn't big city. Maybe he had only the badge and his training behind him, but he was his own man and he knew what he wanted.

And okay, he wanted her. He was red-blooded, after all. But

a quick affair to let off some steam wasn't enough for him, not these days. Slumming around no longer appealed. He wanted for keeps. The real deal.

Nothing about Cassie was the real deal.

"Meow."

This came from the passenger seat, on which sat the biggest, fattest tabby he'd ever seen. "Well, hello," he said, and when the cat climbed all over Cassie to get to him, obviously using nails for leverage if Cassie's hiss was any indication, he obliged it by reaching in and scratching beneath the chin.

A loud rumble filled the car.

Cassie narrowed her eyes at the purring cat. "Look at that, the Daughter of Satan likes men. What a surprise."

"Daughter of Satan?"

She sighed. "Sheriff, meet Miss Priss. Miss Priss meet—" She glared at the cat when it growled at her. "Oh, never mind, you're so huffy and snooty and rude you don't deserve an introduction."

"Funny," Tag said. "I would have said the same thing about her owner."

"I don't own this cat, and I'm never huffy. Snooty and rude, most definitely. But not huffy."

Despite the fact he didn't want to acknowledge his dreams hadn't been as good as seeing her in the flesh, his gaze gobbled her up. She was wearing white today. White tank top, white mini skirt, white leather boots. It seemed almost sacrilegious, all that virginal color on that mouthwatering body. *Down, boy.* "Why doesn't your cat like you?"

"It's not my cat, it's my mother's. Apparently they frown on felines on cruise ships, so she left the thing for me to take care of, along with—" She sent him a look designed to wither. "Why am I telling you all this?"

"Because I'm irresistible?"

For one moment she let her guard down and laughed. Her entire face softened, and he stared at her in shock. My God, she was beautiful like that, he thought, and wondered what it would be like to see her happy, really happy.

But then he took back the thought. He didn't care what she looked like happy; he'd prefer to see what she looked like from the back, heading right out of town. "Let me guess… you're on your way out of here."

Now her frown was back, on those perfectly glossed lips. "I wish." She flipped her hair out of her eyes and lifted a shoulder. "I think you might be stuck with me a little bit longer. Hope you can handle it."

"The question is, can your car insurance handle it." He opened his ticket book and she sputtered, making him laugh again. "Why do I get the feeling that not many have crossed you?"

"Why do I get the feeling you don't care?" she muttered.

When he'd handed her the second ticket in as many days, she grabbed it, tossed it over her shoulder into the back of her car and took off, her hair flying in the wind, her cat back in the passenger seat. The two of them were frowning, two obnoxious females thrusting their chins out against the world.

HONEY, do what you got to do. The blazes with anyone else. Cassie heard Flo's voice in her head clear as day. More rarely she heard Edie's voice, Kate's mother, and for all intents and purposes Cassie's Mom No. 2. It seemed Cassie's bold-as-brass lifestyle leaned more toward Flo's advice than Edie's.

She wondered if hearing voices meant she was going crazy, or just that Pleasantville was getting to her. Both, she decided, and stripped out of her clothes, fingering through the things she'd brought, looking for some comfy pajamas.

She was a clothes hound and, thanks to her job, had collected many beautiful things. They were a comfort to her, the silk and lace, and proved, if only to herself, she was no longer poor.

Poor had meant longing, yearning, helplessness, and she hated all three. She would never long, yearn or be helpless again.

She thought of her little stalking problem—the slashed tires, her ransacked apartment, the threatening letters—and shivered.

Well, *hopefully,* she'd never feel helpless again.

In her suitcase she came across a tin of cookies her agent had given her. Cookies were a rare treat for a lingerie model, but since she'd canceled work for the entire summer, she tore into them and grabbed her book.

The Savage Groom. Maybe some good old-fashioned French Revolution period lust would clear her head. At least she could afford her books now instead of sneaking into the library and past the haughty Mrs. Wilkens for them.

"Chocolate," she moaned out loud and stuffed another in her mouth. Happy and cozy in imported silk, a fattening cookie in one hand and a book in the other, she flopped back on the bed and let herself relax for the first time in too long. "Two days, two tickets and a pounding headache. That's got to be some kind of record, even for me."

Another weight hit the bed and Cassie lifted her head. Her gaze collided with the slanted yellow one of Miss Priss. "You."

"Meow."

Cassie tried to shoo her off, but the cat wasn't only annoying, she refused to budge, letting out that terrible wail she had.

"Meow."

"Hey, I just fed you…" When had that been? "Yesterday." Oh, man, good thing she wasn't a mother. Just as she opened her mouth to apologize, the cat turned in a circle, presented her behind and sat within an inch of Cassie's nose.

"Eww, *move*."

Miss Priss did. She moved closer and, claiming half the pillow with her big, fat, furry body, she began to clean herself. Her private self.

"I am *not* sharing a pillow with someone who licks her own genitalia."

Miss Priss didn't seem to agree, and with a bolt of ingenuity, Cassie grabbed the spare pillow and threw it at the cat, who landed with a hiss on the floor. Leaning over the edge, she smiled smugly. "Stay."

"Mew."

That was an "I'm sorry" mew if she ever heard one. Damn it. What was she doing, snapping at a cat? Wasn't that like kicking a puppy? With a regretful sigh, she reached out a peace offering in the form of a cookie, and—

"Ouch!" Yanking back her scratched palm, Cassie sat up. "That's it. Go play on the freeway."

"Mew."

"Oh, fine." She got up and fed the ingrate. Then, using both pillows now, she settled back on the bed against the headboard.

The sound of a roaring truck ruined her peace, and she went to the window. The trash truck. Now there was a job. The guy on the back of the truck hopped off at her neighbor's house and hoisted the cans. He had a slouch and a gut and... and it was Biff. In an instinctive gesture she backed from the window. Assessed how she felt.

And grinned. There had to be some justice in the world if she—a Tremaine—was living on Lilac Hill and Biff—former star football player—was collecting her trash.

She called Kate, who'd appreciate the irony.

"Kate, Biff is the trash guy," she said when her cousin

picked up the phone. "And he's not even the driver. He picks up the trash."

"Perfect job for him, I'd say."

Oh, yeah, she could count on Kate. "I'm sprawled on the most luxuriously silk-covered bed in a luxurious bedroom surrounded by the most amazing, luxurious house. Can you believe it? My mother lived like a queen after I was gone." And because it felt good, so good to relax, she arched her neck.

"My God," Cassie murmured.

"What? A spider?"

She stared at herself in the mirror framed above the bed. She'd seen the mirrors before now, of course, but they were still a shock. She studied herself dispassionately. Her body was barely covered in azure-blue imported silk, showing off her full breasts and the belly that didn't look quite as flat as it should for a lingerie model. With a grimace, she tossed the cookies aside. "No, it's just this place. The garage is full of furniture from the duplex and my mother has mirrored ceilings."

Kate let out a startled laugh. "Well, we always knew Flo wasn't a prude."

Funny how even though Cassie knew exactly who and what Flo was—a woman unable to resist a man, any man at all—when it came right down to it, it was hard to picture her own mother having sex on this bed and enjoying the view from above. "You realize I'm on Lilac Hill, right? *Lilac Hill.* My fancy neighbors would have a coronary at the secrets this bedroom holds."

"I imagine that was part of the fun for her."

Ever the voice of reason, her Kate. Despite Kate's own demons, she'd always helped Cassie see things differently. And more importantly, she made Cassie smile. "Flo did enjoy a good scandal. But Lilac Hill, for God's sake." The place that as children they'd stared at enviously, fantasized over. "I feel like I fell down the rabbit hole."

"You deserve it," Kate said with a sudden fierceness in her voice. "Both of you. You've worked so hard all your lives, and now Flo is sailing the Greek Islands and you're a world-famous lingerie model. You both paid your dues for so many years. You're supposed to enjoy this."

"But I miss work." Cassie sighed. "The photo shoot I bailed on this week was in the Bahamas."

"Which is where your stalker was going to meet you. Isn't that what the last threat said?"

Yes, but she didn't want to go there. She *so* didn't want to go there. "So I'm here. In a house my mother never paid for."

"Of course she did. She loved…who was it—Mr. Miller the banker, right?—and he cared enough about her to give it to her. Just like Mr. McIntyre, who left her that building downtown." She laughed. "I bet Mrs. McIntyre is spitting nails over that."

"Oh, yeah. If looks could kill, I'd be six feet under. Which reminds me." Cassie took a deep breath. "I have some ideas." She sat up because she had to be careful how she phrased this. After all, Kate was a Tremaine, which meant that like Cassie, she had more pride than sense when it came to accepting help. "You said you were ready to open another shop."

"I said I *wanted* to open another shop, I never said I *would* open another shop. Successful as I've been in Chicago, I don't have the money for that yet."

"I know. But I do."

"I'm not taking any more of your money. I just paid back the start-up loan you gave me for the first Bare Essentials."

"I'm not talking *money,* per se. I want you to take the building, the old men's store that Flo inherited from horny old McIntyre."

"No."

"Kate."

"Cassie."

Cassie had to laugh at Kate's calm annoyance. "Stop it. I have an ulterior motive."

"If you want a new toy, all you have to do is ask. We just stocked up."

"Hey, I still have Mr. Pink that you bought me for Christmas and I just loaded up on batteries, thank you very much."

Miss Priss leapt back onto the bed, and with one long daring glare, she settled at Cassie's head.

"If I wake up with a fur ball lodged in my throat, you're dead meat," Cassie told the snooty cat. "And you," she said to her cousin, "will you listen to me for a moment?"

"You got one minute. Fifty-nine, fifty-eight, fifty-seven... you'd better hurry."

"Should have been a comic, Kate. Listen, I want you to have the building because it feels right. I don't know what to do with it, and it's just sitting there going to waste. Besides, it's right downtown. Right smack in the middle of downtown... are you following me here?"

"Let me see if I am...you see Bare Essentials, basically a very naughty ladies' store—"

"One which sells a most excellent dildo, I might add."

"Thank you. You see Bare Essentials fitting right in with the Rose Café and the five-and-dime."

"Why not? This town could use some spice."

"More than having their wild child come home?"

"Hey, they made me this way. Come on, say yes. It's on our lists of things to do..."

"Cassie." Kate laughed. "Those lists were written by bitter teenagers."

"So?"

"So…it's not that easy. I was just there, I don't want to move back to that place any more than you want to be there."

Cassie flopped back on the bed and stared at herself in the ceiling mirror. Her agent had cleared her schedule for the entire summer and it was only early June. The police and her friends had convinced her that a low profile would be best.

She knew that to be true. No matter her outwardly brave facade and joking, cynical manner, she hated the fear, the terror. Because of it, she sat in Pleasantville with no one but a mean old cat for company and nothing to do but pay her moving violations.

Oh, and stare at the sheriff's ass. It was a mighty fine ass, but that simply wasn't enough. Especially since he wasn't so much as slightly interested in her.

How long had it been since a man hadn't fallen in a pool of saliva at her feet? Didn't matter; unlike her mother, she had no need for a man to fall all over her.

"Cassie?"

"I'll get the shop going for you," she said rashly. "Come on, Kate. Opening a porn shop in Pleasantville. It doesn't get better than that."

"Bare Essentials, which is doing exceptionally well by the way, is *not* a porn shop." Kate sniffed.

"I know that. But everyone here will think it is." Glee leapt wildly within her. This idea just got better and better the more she thought about it. "This is inspired, truly inspired. I can keep myself from going crazy and—"

"Oh, honey. You *are* going crazy, I knew it. Maybe I should come back—"

"—and I can shock this mean-spirited old town while doing it. Mrs. McIntyre. Mrs. Wilkens. All of them. No, don't you dare come back. Unless of course, you want to. I can do this. I want to do this."

"Are you sure?"

"Absolutely. I can't just sit here and hide, Kate. I just can't. Otherwise every shadow, every little thing, makes me jump."

"Have you informed the sheriff about why you're really there?"

"Of course not. I'm fine. I just need to do something and this is perfect. What do you say?"

"You can't just give me the building. If we do this, it's as a team. And, damn, revenge on that godforsaken town sounds really good. Too good."

Cassie knew she had her. And if she did so in part because Kate was worried about her, then she was willing to play that card, because though she'd eat a stick before admitting it, she was worried about herself, too. "So then…?"

"Yes," Kate said. "Yes, let's do it. Partners?"

"Partners," Cassie vowed.

ONE WEEK—and another ticket—later, Cassie was still jerking awake at night, certain her stalker had found her. Just last night she'd opened her mouth to scream at the weight holding her down, only to find Miss Priss sitting on her chest. The cat she could handle.

She had also handled the town—by snubbing her nose every morning at her fellow shop owners on Magnolia Street. Specifically, anyone and everyone going in and out of the Tea Room right next door, most of the waitresses at the Rose Café, and anyone else who stopped to point and whisper.

This didn't include the Downtown Deli across the street, mostly because the deli was new, and therefore the legend of Cassie Tremaine didn't live there. And also because Cassie had discovered a weakness for pastrami on rye, along with the thirtysomething owners Diane and Will. Silly Diane and Will, they actually seemed to like her.

Cassie's building had been cleared of old debris and cleaned. They still had to paint, refloor and decorate, but that was the fun part. Since she was the one in town at the moment, she would handle most of that, happily. She loved to decorate and organize, and loved to paint. Which was a good thing, as Kate was notoriously bad at it, and was never offered a paintbrush.

She and Kate had spent hours teleconferencing over the stock for the store, with Kate sending naughty sample after naughty sample. The UPS girl, a very cute little thing named Daisy—only in Pleasantville—had continuously asked what was in all the boxes she kept delivering. When Cassie had finally broken down and told her—Daisy was simply too sweet for both this town and its gossip mill—Daisy had nearly swallowed her tongue.

In spite of it all, or maybe because of it, Cassie felt like a little girl at Christmas. One night, during a wicked early summer storm, she sat in the deserted building, surrounded by boxes and Miss Priss.

The cat hadn't relented—she still hated Cassie—but she refused to be left home alone. If Cassie did leave her at the house, she paid for the mistake dearly as Miss Priss wasn't above leaving "deposits" to show her annoyance. Yesterday it had been in her slipper, which Cassie had unfortunately put her foot into, so she'd caved like a cheap suitcase and took the damn cat wherever she went.

Rain beat against the windows of the building, while thunder and lightning beat the sky. She'd lost power about thirty minutes ago, but undeterred, she'd lit a lantern. In her mind's eye, she could *see* the store, envision the displays, the music, the lights—everything laid out the way she and Kate had planned—and the work was so therapeutic, she didn't want to stop. Unafraid—a nice change—she sat alone on the floor making copious notes to share with Kate during their next phone call.

Bare Essentials. Even the name was perfect, and she jotted a note to talk to Kate about what type of sign they should have made to hang out front. Everyone in town would assume the worst, of course, and to make sure she fulfilled those thoughts, the shop would carry a variety of items for shock value alone. Maybe they could create an interesting window display with cock rings and anal plugs....

Time flew by as she opened boxes, spread the samples out this way and that, made notes, even tried some things on.

Miss Priss had long ago fallen asleep in a box. Outside, beyond the shuttered windows, traffic had dribbled to nothing.

Cassie, wearing a simple, basic black camisole—the design was so exquisite, she absolutely loved it—was sitting on the floor with the last box. She pulled it close and opened it. Inside she found a note from Kate. "Think the lovely patrons of Pleasantville will like these?"

Cassie grinned as she laid out a selection of body jewelry. She could see the looks now, especially when the Pea-ville matrons were confronted with nipple and clit rings.

Cassie herself had once had her belly button pierced, but it had gotten in the way of certain photo shoots so she'd let it grow in.

But a nipple ring...if she wasn't such a chicken when it came to pain she'd have the real thing. Since she never would, that left the clip-on variety. She opened up a package that held a pretty, delicate-looking silver hoop, slipped a spaghetti strap off one shoulder and bared a breast. With her fingers she plucked her nipple into a hard bead and applied the jewelry.

With a hiss, she let out a slow breath. It was a clamp of sort, but surprisingly, it didn't hurt at all. And looking down at herself, she had to smile. "What do you think, Miss Priss? Pretty hot, huh?"

. "Does my vote count?" .

With a scream, Cassie leapt up, instinctively reaching out for a weapon as she did. That she grabbed Big Red—her nickname for a twelve-inch long, three-inch thick, glow-in-the-dark red dildo—didn't matter. The sucker was heavy and she could wield it like a baseball bat no problem.

"Whoa, just me."

In the back of her mind she recognized that incredibly sexy voice.

Not her stalker.

Not a Joe Blow off the street.

But dangerous, none the less. And she was standing there in a camisole with her faux-pierced nipple hanging out. Keeping hold of Big Red with one hand, she used the other to cover her breast. "You."

"Me," the sheriff agreed, partially stepping out of the shadows into the meager light let off by the lantern so that she could see just his face. His sharp eyes scanned everything, including her, while his long, rangy body remained utterly still. "I thought this building was supposed to be empty and I saw the light. Had a few complaints."

"Let me guess. Mrs. McIntyre?"

"Among others."

"I'll bet. How did you get in?"

"You have a bum door. It's locked but not shut all the way."

"Look, the place is mine, no one in this bitter old town can say otherwise, so if you're thinking about giving me another ticket—"

"Another ticket." God, that voice of his. "Gotta tell you, Cassie, I wasn't thinking ticket when I first saw you." He shifted closer. "Have you done anything illegal lately?"

As he asked, his gaze ran leisurely over her, making her very aware of how she must look standing there holding a big, fat dildo and her own breast. "Uh…"

"Other than indecent exposure, that is?"

"Indecent?"

He cocked his head and looked her over good, his eyes eating her up. "Actually, that's a matter of opinion."

She could feel her other nipple tighten; she told herself she was cold. Which didn't explain why the silk between her legs suddenly felt as soft and incredible as a man's touch.

As he still stood in the shadows, she couldn't see what he wore, but she imagined him in his uniform, and it hardened her against him despite the fact that he looked good enough to eat.

But the expression in his eyes as he drank in her scrap of black wasn't a cop's look. It was a man's.

And something within her tingled. Lord, he was something, all rough-and-tumble ready. He'd make a nice diversion, wouldn't he? If he wasn't such a cop.

Go for it, honey, said Flo's voice in her head. *Get what you can and get out.*

Standing there, he was tall, dark and shockingly, overtly sexy. It wouldn't be hard to "go for it." But beneath that laidback, easygoing facade, he was tough as nails, and she knew it.

She'd never been shy about her own sensuality, but unlike Flo, she refused to let it run her life. Flo couldn't resist a man.

And yet Flo had always brought men to their knees. Cassie liked that part. But something told her the big, bad Tag wouldn't be easy to control. Bottom line—if she couldn't be in charge, she never dallied.

Never.

Still, the summer loomed long and empty in front of her.

If nothing else, surely she could get him to take care of her tickets...

Grab everything they'll give you, Flo would say right now. *Grab it and walk away.*

Tag's hot, hot gaze ran down her body, making her stomach quiver, making her forget the tickets. His gaze settled on Big Red. "Cassie, what were you going to do with that thing?"

Just his voice made her thighs clench. "Big Red? Did you know he glows in the dark?"

He lifted a brow. "What else does he do?"

He can drive you crazy, she thought, and let out a wicked smile.

3

Oh, yeah, Tag thought. No doubt about it, Cassie Tremaine Montgomery had a smile capable of rendering a grown man stupid. The outfit didn't hurt, either.

Or lack of outfit.

Did she have any idea how she looked standing there in the glow of the lantern wearing…what the hell was that black thing anyway? It had wispy little straps that would be easy to nudge off with one fingertip, or a single touch of his tongue. One already hung off her arm. The bodice was sheer, except for the lace roses that strategically covered her nipples.

Or nipple, since the one was hidden from his view not by the lace flower but by Cassie's own fingers. The sheer black slid over her belly and ended very high on her hips, with just a scant little strip disappearing between her thighs, where he imagined it was held together with a few strategic snaps.

His teeth itched to see how quickly he could undo them.

Which was bad, very bad. Even worse, just seeing her fingers on her own bare breast was enough to turn his insides quivering. She was touching herself, had been touching herself when he'd walked in. She wore a nipple ring and was handling the biggest dildo he'd ever seen. If there was a man in the world strong enough to not be brought to his knees by that image, Tag wasn't him. "Cassie, what are you doing here, dressed like…that?"

"Haven't you heard?" She seemed utterly unconcerned by her near nudity. He had to admit, he'd never seen a more mouthwatering, luscious body in his life. Covering it should be a crime. And if he was to believe even one quarter of the stories he'd heard about her, she apparently didn't have a problem with *un*covering it.

"We're putting a new store in this building," she said.

"We?"

"My cousin Kate and I. Bare Essentials. It's a bit of a secret what we're selling."

"Why?"

"It's going to be a…ladies' shop."

"Ah. You want to shock the good people of Pleasantville."

"Oh, yeah, we do. You caught me playing with some of the merchandise." She hefted the dildo in her free hand. "Think the good ladies of Pleasantville will admit to needing one of these bad boys?" She ran the tip—the very large, red, bulbous tip—across her collarbone.

His heart nearly stopped.

Down her stomach.

Riveted, he stood there practically panting.

"Hmm." She pursed her glossed lips. "That reminds me." The dildo dipped below her belly button. "We'd better sell batteries, too, don't you think? I'd hate to force some shy thing into the hardware store with this bad boy."

It wasn't often Tag found himself speechless. Or with an uncontrollable erection while on duty. "Your strap. It's…" He held her gaze as she stepped closer. Unable to stop himself, he reached out to slip a finger beneath her fallen strap, slowly bringing it back up. The material dragged over the breast she was covering with her hand making her other nipple tighten all the more. Her breath caught at that, he heard it, and it caused his own to do the same. Beneath his fingers he felt her warm, soft skin. Almost unaware, he'd dipped his head to hers. He didn't have far to bend. She was a tall woman, which he'd just discovered was an incredible turn-on. Lying down, they'd be chest to chest, thigh to thigh, and everything in between would line up so damn perfectly....

She tilted her head slightly, too, and his jaw brushed her long hair. A silky strand clung to the slight stubble on his cheek, and he stilled to keep it there.

She moved again, lifting her head so that they were mouth to mouth, breathing each other's air, which turned out to be the most erotic thing he'd ever experienced.

She licked her lips, and they were so close he felt the brush of her tongue against his lips. "Mmm," she whispered. "It's a night for this, don't you think? A night for a memorable kiss."

With a groan, he parted his lips and slid them to hers. Hot. Wet. Heaven. She opened for him and as his tongue lightly caressed, she gave in with a hungry sound that sent his every rational thought skittering out the door. Because it was quiet and relatively dark, and because he couldn't think with her so close to him, he gave in to the hunger. Her lips parted farther and the kiss deepened into an explosive, frantic, lush mating of mouths and tongues. And for one glorious moment they connected—lost, wild, clinging—until she shifted a fraction to stare at him with eyes satisfyingly full of hunger and passion.

He still had his fingers entwined in her camisole. Beneath them her skin felt like silk. Hot silk. The taste of her was still on his tongue—forbidden passion and the promise of head-banging, toe-curling sex. No doubt, he had to get her covered before this got out of control, but the material of her lingerie stuck to the hand she held over her breast.

Slowly, still holding his gaze prisoner in her own, she pulled her hand free, giving him a devastatingly thorough glimpse of that silver hoop on her puckered nipple. Utterly unable to help himself, he lifted his hand and ran the pad of a finger over the mouthwatering tip. The hoop danced, her breast quivered. And every bit of saliva in his mouth dried up. In that moment he knew he was out of control, that at the slightest invitation from Cassie, they would be naked and rolling on the floor.

Then she let the material cover her breast, and he managed to take a breath.

"Thanks," she whispered.

He would have whispered something back but he was still facing that whole speechless problem. Both nipples were hard, clearly defined. The one he'd just covered now had the clear outline of a circle around it, and picturing her placing that ring on herself all over again, he groaned.

"It's not real," she said softly. "It's just a clip-on. I was just—"

"Trying on the merchandise. I know."

"I have more. We have one for a guy." She ran a finger down his chest, past his belly to the top button of his pants, which she toyed with, making his already straining erection painful. "Want to try it on? I can do it for you. You put it—"

"Cassie."

She actually smiled. "Chicken?"

"No." He let out a careful breath and caught her wandering fingers in his. "But I am on the very edge. Tease me another second and I'll prove it to you."

"Maybe next time, then."

"Yeah." His knees were actually knocking. Shocked at how much he wanted her, when she wasn't what he wanted at all, he pulled away, closer to the lantern. He needed to see things clearly, damn it, he needed the electricity back on. The dark was lending an intimacy to this little episode that he didn't need. He opened his mouth to say his goodbyes, maybe even offer an apology for barging in on her, for giving in to temptation, but Cassie had backed away, too.

No longer were her eyes open and warm. No longer was her body loose and relaxed. Instead she stood there staring at him as if he was the lowest form of life.

"What?" he asked, his head still spinning from their kiss.

She pointed at him with the dildo. "You're on duty."

Hadn't he already said so?

"I…hadn't really realized…you're in uniform."

Confused, he glanced down at himself. "Usually, this shirt is a turn-on for women," he said, thinking to tease because he was at a loss to understand her.

Not that he wanted to. No, what he wanted…well, *that* was as dangerous as understanding her.

"I'm not your usual woman," she said.

Wasn't that the truth.

"I'm not turned on by bad attitude and authority."

"Bad attitude?" He had to laugh. "I thought that was you."

Wrapping her arms around herself, she turned away, but not before he caught a quick glimpse of her own confusion. Her own pain. It stopped him in his tracks. But then he caught more than that. He caught a good look at the back of her, and nearly had heart failure.

There *was* no back to her outfit. It dipped down in an open scoop far past her waist, so low that if she so much as shifted he was going to get quite the view. There the outfit would have resembled a pair of hot shorts, except the words "hot shorts" were too conservative. In any case, the scant material divided the most delicious-looking butt cheeks he'd ever seen.

"You've done your civil duty," she said in a voice as cold as the south pole, which was in such direct opposition to that hot body he could only stand there gaping like an idiot.

"I'm not breaking and entering," she said. "I'm not speeding. There's really no need for you to be here."

Well, that much was true. As a cop he had no need to be there. But he glanced at his watch and was rewarded by the time. "I'm off duty."

She peered at him over one creamy shoulder and he lifted his wrist to show her. "It's five minutes past midnight, which was when my shift ended."

"A cop is always a cop."

Why was she so angry? Risking life and limb he came close again, reaching out to touch her cheek. "I'm just a man." A man who would die for another kiss.

She shifted away. "A *cop*."

Her skin had been warm. Soft. And he wanted more, but she was still backing away. He snagged her hand, knowing she was far too proud to look weak and to try to pull free. "I don't take my work home with me, Cassie. When I'm standing here with you like this, I'm not working."

She let out a laugh he was sure she meant to be harsh, but it came out more as a question, making her seem...vulnerable.

But why? Why was she wary of him? Was it him as a man or as a cop? Either way, his gut clenched.

She wasn't as tough as she wanted to be, and that was a huge shock. He thought he'd had her pegged; knowing he might be wrong about her was more than a little unsettling. Knowing that this hard-as-nails, gorgeous woman could be vulnerable did bad things to his resolution to stay away from her. With a little tug, he brought her closer still. Now he could smell her, all warm and clean and sexy female. His body went to war with his mind. His mind wanted to know more about her. Not his body; no, that part of him just wanted to haul her close. "Someone in a uniform hurt you," he guessed.

She lifted a shoulder, neither denying nor confirming, and

a part of him actually ached. "I'm sorry," he said, and found himself startled to realize he meant it.

She lifted that shoulder again. "Don't be *too* sorry, Sheriff." She lifted the red dildo. "I was going to tease the hell out of you with this bad boy."

He stared at it, felt his mouth go dry again as his penis jerked to hopeful attention. "You could still try."

The smile on her lips didn't meet her eyes. "Nah. The fun's gone." She stared pointedly at his hand on hers until he let go. "Good night, Sheriff."

"Good night, Cassie."

She waited until he got to the door. "You might think of me tonight," she said softly. "I'm taking Big Red home, along with a pack of batteries."

He groaned, and in tune to her low, satisfied laugh, he let himself out.

Two weeks after her arrival, Cassie was still keeping herself busy. She was in charge of readying the store, while Kate handled the inventory, getting lots of beautiful, sexy lingerie from her business partner and designer Armand.

Cassie made more calls to Kate, did more cleaning and painting. There was more delivering by Daisy in her UPS outfit and sweet smile.

It should be illegal to be sweet and innocent in Pleasantville.

Cassie had the Bare Essentials sign made, and the day it went up was fun. It gave her great satisfaction to stand directly beneath it and pretend she didn't see the commotion it caused.

Up and down Magnolia Avenue, which had been designed for pleasant foot walking, people came out of the woodwork and stared.

"They're talking," Daisy whispered. "About...you."

"Always." Cassie looked at her. "I'm sure you've heard the stories."

"Well, sure. You're a legend."

Cassie laughed. "A legend, huh?"

"No, really. You're a homegrown hero come back to her roots. You made something of yourself."

"I made *something,* all right." But Daisy didn't smile, and Cassie had to wonder…was she just imagining all the malicious curiosity? Her gaze met Mr. Miller's widow from across the street, where she stood just outside the deli. *Frowning.*

Nope, definitely not imagining it. But…she did have to admit, most of the negative energy was coming from the older generation.

Maybe that was simply because Cassie hadn't been around long enough to taint the younger one.

Since no one dared ask, she put up another sign, this one in the window, saying they'd open for business in two weeks.

"Two weeks?" Still wearing her apron, Diane came out from the Downtown Deli and stood under the sign. "Cool. I'm not sure what you're selling, but I have a feeling Will's going to love it."

Cassie stared at her as Diane simply smiled and walked away. But then she shook it off. She had work to do.

Two weeks in which to get the place ready to go. It would be a challenge for both her and Kate, but they were up for that. For Cassie, she needed something to keep her mind off her career, off the trouble that had brought her here.

Off the sheriff.

Because really, who would have thought such a man could melt bones with a simple kiss? A simple touch? But there had been nothing simple about either his kiss or his touch. She'd underestimated him, that was certain, and it wouldn't happen again.

Unless it was on her terms, of course.

Those terms were simple. If she could keep the control, if she could drive him crazy and walk away, then perfect.

Otherwise, she wasn't interested.

Time to get back to work. *Work.* Not really a decent description for what she'd been doing because she'd actually been enjoying herself, all the way down to dressing the part of a co-owner of a ladies' shop. She'd pulled out all the stops in that department, wearing some of the more outrageous clothes she'd collected over the years.

Take today, for instance. Her halter top had nothing but three straps across her back and her leather pants looked as if they'd been spray-painted on. After all, everyone expected the daughter of Flo to look a certain way—why not give it to them?

"Excuse me."

"Yes?" Cassie turned around on the sidewalk and faced a woman. She was dressed simply in jeans and a sleeveless blouse, little to no makeup, and looked to be around thirty. There was a two-year-old clinging to her hand. "Can I help you?"

"Are you going to sell…" The woman blushed a little, and bit her lower lip.

Cassie sighed. "Let me make this easy for you. Bare Essentials will be a fully stocked women's store. If you're embarrassed to ask for it, chances are good that we'll carry it."

The woman nodded, then laughed at herself. "I'm sorry. My name is Stacie Harrison. I've been wanting to introduce myself."

Probably wanted to satisfy her curiosity about the new harlot in town. Behind Stacie, literally hanging out of the Tea Room, were Mrs. McIntyre and her sister Mrs. Hampton. Their mouths were turned down in disapproving frowns. Cassie lifted a hand and waggled her fingers at them.

"Well, I never," one exclaimed.

"Really? You never?" Stacie tsked. "That's just a shame, ma'am."

Both of them let out a collective gasp and, with daggers in their gazes, vanished back inside.

Cassie turned and stared at Stacie, who giggled. "Are you insane? They're going to make you miserable now."

"No one can do that but me," Stacie said calmly.

Whatever. Stacie's social suicide was none of her business. Cassie had a shop to open. She was doing this, and people needed to just get used to it. Turning to enter her shop, she stopped when Stacie put a hand on her arm.

"Did you know we're neighbors? I live three doors down from you on the hill. I made you cookies last week but my ex-husband—the jerk—called and annoyed me, and I ended up eating them all myself. With Suzie here—" she smiled down at her toddler "—I haven't had a chance to make another batch."

"You…made me cookies."

"Yes." She smiled brightly. "My ex is a surgeon, you see. And he was boinking the X-ray tech. But the good news is I got the house."

Cassie let out a startled laugh.

"Anyway," Stacie went on, "I like to cook off my stress. I was going to bring them to you, maybe sit down with a glass of iced tea or something, and talk."

"I don't drink iced tea."

"Oh, well, that's okay." Stacie smiled. "Water would have worked."

What the hell was this woman's angle? "If you want to see the inside of Flo's house, all you have to do is ask. You know what? I'm thinking of conducting tours." She could make a fortune. Too bad it wasn't money she needed.

Stacie looked confused in the face of her sarcasm. "Flo? Who's Flo?"

Right. "You don't know my mother?"

"Should I?"

"She lived in the house before I did."

"Oh. I saw her a few times but I'm sorry to say I didn't have the pleasure of meeting her. And…" She looked around to make sure they were alone. "You know, I always wanted to live there, up on the hill, but to tell you the truth, now that I'm there I'm realizing it's awfully quiet. I'm going stir-crazy."

Uh-huh. The ex-wife of a surgeon. Mother of…a very sticky-looking kid. Bored? Cassie didn't believe it. Not in Pleasantville. No, the town she knew like the back of her own hand didn't breed nice, compassionate people. It bred smallness. Meanness.

And she was here to repay that in kind. "I've got to get busy."

"Sure. I'm hoping to bake again tonight. If I do, I'll stop by tomorrow."

"Uh-huh." Maybe Cassie should give tours of just the *bed-room,* show everyone the mirrored ceilings. *Wait.* Maybe they should *sell* mirrors to put on the ceilings!

"See you tomorrow then." Stacie smiled. "I'm glad we met."

Before Cassie could process the words, Stacie walked away, swinging her daughter's hand.

She was glad they'd met.

But how could that be?

CASSIE SPENT THE rest of the day and the next readying the interior of the building. She'd been working on it all week, paying for manual labor when she had to, using high school seniors who were grateful for the cash.

And who didn't remember her from her youth.

She was sure their parents did, and wondered what they thought of Cassie now, paying their sons to do work for a Tremaine.

Then wondered why she cared. She *didn't* care. Not one little bit.

Oh, damn them all anyway. It burned like hell that she'd never accomplish that last thing on her list. In this town's eyes, no matter what, she'd never become *someone*.

And it burned even more that she thought about it.

It angered her enough to forego the cheap labor for the day and to do it all herself. The boys seemed quite disappointed when she'd told them to go. Cassie wasn't sure if that was because of the cash she paid them, or her overalls, under which she wore a comfy, but very skimpy, crop-top.

Didn't matter. They were gone and she was alone. Contrary to popular belief, she was very capable of hard work. She loved hard work.

The alone part was a little unnerving since she wasn't exactly here in town for a picnic. But surely she was safe.

She really wanted to think so. She *had* to think so.

She stood on a ladder, paint splattered across the front of her designer cargo overalls, enjoying the paint fumes, when her cell phone rang. She unclipped it from her belt and let out a happy smile at the Caller ID. "Kate, my love, you should see this delicious shade of pink I found. It simply screams 'come in, you must buy a new sex toy.'"

"I'd love to see it. How does next Friday sound?"

Cassie's grin widened. "You're coming!"

"I'm coming," she agreed, but with a surprising lack of enthusiasm. "I can't miss the grand opening, now can I?"

Cassie set down her brush and backed down the ladder. "What's the matter?"

"Nothing."

"*Kate.*"

"Can't a girl just call her favorite cousin?"

"I'm your only cousin. Spill it. Does it have anything to do with that guy you saw when you were here? The one you won't tell me about?"

"Jack? No."

"Then what?"

Across the miles, her cousin sighed. "You remember how before you left, you arranged to have all your mail forwarded to me for the duration?"

"Yes." Cassie's heart kicked into gear. "So no one could locate me through the postal service while I'm here. What's the matter, are my bills piling up?" Her mouth was suddenly dry. "You were going to just send them on to me, and—"

"It's not your bills."

"Too many magazines, huh?" *Oh, God.* Please don't let it be what she feared.

"It's not the magazines, either. Though I am enjoying *Playgirl,* thanks."

"Okay." Cassie pulled off the painter's cap and let her hair fall free. She sat on an unopened five-gallon can of paint and unhooked one side of her overalls for freedom of movement. "Let me guess..." She was surprised at how fast her pulse could race. "You got a letter from him."

"He's not happy you've vanished from the face of the earth, Cass. He's scaring me."

He was scaring her, too. *Peter.* One of the first men she'd met when she'd gone to New York. He was a photographer, and he'd taken her first publicity shots for a price she'd been able to afford—a date. They hadn't slept together because unlike Flo, Cassie had her own personal standards, which included never sleeping with a man when business was involved.

So they'd become casual friends. And as Cassie's career had

boomed, she'd done her best to get Peter jobs. Occasionally, while between relationships, he'd drink too much and try to tell Cassie she was the one for him. She always gently turned him down, knowing his next girlfriend was right around the corner, and she'd always been right.

Their friendship had sustained.

Until now.

Now, he was her stalker.

Cassie shivered. Though she was not a woman to let fear run her life, this guy truly got to her. Enough to have uprooted everything.

Hard to admit she'd been stupid enough to actually trust a man. And look what it had gotten her. He'd taken her away from her career, away from her life, and sent her back to a town she was fairly certain wasn't ready for her. Wouldn't *ever* be ready for her.

"He says he's never going to stop looking for you, Cassie," came Kate's stressed voice. "You're the only one for him, and if he can't have you, he says no one else can, either."

Okay, now her heart was ricocheting off her ribs. She'd known he'd never really recovered from the last dumping by that waitress/actress-wannabe.

And this time, unlike the others, he couldn't seem to wrap his mind around the fact Cassie wasn't interested in him that way.

Not only not interested, but good and truly scared. He'd broken into her place. Touched her things. Left her a threatening note on her mirror in her own lipstick. *You're mine.*

Then he'd vanished. Which is why the police hadn't been able to get to him. Which was how she'd ended up with a restraining order, and then landed herself here. "I'm okay here, Kate. I never talked about my past with Pete."

"Are you sure?"

"What do you think?"

Her cousin actually let out a relieved little laugh. "Yeah. How silly. Thinking you'd open up and tell someone about yourself. Much less open up to a *man*."

"He has no idea I'm not a native New Yorker. Even all those years ago when I first got started, he had no idea."

"Okay, but I'm still coming. I want to see you. It's been too long. And I want to do more to get the store ready—the opening will be a thrill. Can't miss that, or the chance for some good old-fashioned revenge. And then there's my mom's house. I have to take care of that situation. I talked to Flo and I'm going to stay in her half of the duplex, since Mom is renting out her side."

"And you know all of Flo's old furniture is in my garage. We'll haul it out for you when you get here."

"Which won't be until Friday so I'd feel better if you'd tell someone there what's going on."

Cassie snorted. "Who am I going to tell, someone in the Tea Room?"

"How about the sheriff?"

"I'll see you soon, Kate."

She sighed. "Love you, Cass."

"Love you, too." Cassie clipped the cell phone back onto her belt and stared sightlessly across the future Bare Essentials. Kate was worried.

And damn it, so was she. Big time.

4

ON CASSIE'S WAY HOME that night she made a trip to the library. For nostalgia's sake, she told herself, moving directly to the small paperback section at the back. It smelled the same and, oddly comforted by that, Cassie sank into one of the beanbag chairs that had surely been in the same spot since the flower-power sixties. How many hours had she sat in here, inhaling one historical romance after another, lost in a world that had always been a better world than hers?

"Oh, Barry, stop. You're making my knees weak."

What? Cassie craned her neck. Behind her, in the doorway to the backrooms, stood Mrs. Wilkens whispering into a cell phone.

"I know you're my husband, you silly man. But I told you, we can't have phone sex until my break." She grinned.

The old lady with the severe white bun and pursed lips *grinned*. At her husband. As he gave her phone sex.

Cassie had entered the twilight zone.

"Call me later," Mrs. Wilkens whispered. "Yes, I'll bring home another romance novel, don't worry. Some new ones just came in…. I love you, too." She slipped her cell phone into her pocket and then went very still when she saw Cassie.

Who didn't quite know what to say. A definite first. "You... you have *phone sex?*" she managed to say.

"Romance readers have a sixty percent better sex life than nonreaders," she sniffed. "If I'd known you were coming, I'd have put out some more books for you."

"You'd have..." Cassie narrowed her gaze, suddenly transported back in time. Every time she'd sneaked into the library, she'd always found a stack of new books seemingly waiting just for her. It had been her own little miracle. Her oasis in a life of hell. "You..." Oh, my God. *"You."*

Mrs. Wilkens nodded. "We had the same tastes. And it seemed to keep you off the streets."

"But...I thought you hated me."

Mrs. Wilkens smiled, her face softening. "You thought everyone hated you. Hang on, I'll find you some books."

Oh, yeah. She'd definitely entered the twilight zone. But Mrs. Wilkens came back with three books Cassie had been eager to read. Unbelievable.

When she finally left the library and drove home, she sat in her car for a moment, staring up at the big, dark house on Lilac Hill, wishing she'd thought to leave every light burning.

"Meow."

"Yeah, yeah." With one last apprehensive look at the dark walkway, Cassie got out of the car, reached for the cat and got hissed at for her efforts. "Fine. Walk. Hope there aren't any dogs out here."

Miss Priss lifted her chin and leapt from the car like royalty, leading the way with her head held high.

Cassie had to admit, the attitude helped. When she imitated the cat and threw her shoulders back, head up, she felt better. Invisible. Or was that invincible?

She just wished she had claws like Miss Priss, on the off chance she needed them.

But no one jumped out and yelled boo.

There was, however, a package on the porch, which gave her one bad moment. She opened it, pretending her fingers weren't shaking as she did so, and found the most incredible-smelling batch of chocolate cookies. Her mouth watered—mostly because she'd skipped lunch.

"What do you think, Miss Priss? Poisonous? Or delicious?" When the cat didn't so much as look at her, Cassie took a tentative bite. "Mmm."

She'd been walking through the decadent house flipping on all the lights, munching on cookies for dinner, when the knock came at the door. Cassie opened it and found the woman from town standing there, minus the toddler.

"Hi, remember me? Stacie?" Stacie grinned at the cookie in each of Cassie's hands. "Oh, good. You're enjoying the goodies I made."

"They're heaven," Cassie admitted. "I have no idea how I'll fit into my work clothes in the fall, but thanks."

Stacie smiled. "No problem."

Cassie nodded in what she considered a friendly, neighborly manner, not that she'd ever had any neighbors to be friendly with. When she'd lived in this town growing up, she hadn't been allowed to talk to her neighbors—except for Kate—as in the house on one side of the duplex had lived a man who'd sold drugs, and in the other the resident had a police record a mile long.

In New York, she'd never even seen her neighbors.

So she didn't have a lot of experience to go on here. She waited for Stacie to get to the bottom of her visit. To tell her what she wanted.

But the woman just stood there. Cute as a button. Still smiling.

"Uh…" Cassie offered a half smile. "So…"

"This is where you invite me in for a drink," Stacie said helpfully.

"Oh." Cassie looked over her shoulder and wondered if she'd cleaned up after herself. "Well…"

"That's okay." Stacie reached out and squeezed her hand. "We can work our way up to that. But you could do me one little favor."

Here it was.

"Tomorrow's opening day of the carnival."

"Carnival."

"Don't tell me you don't know about Pleasantville's annual carnival! The one to raise money for arts in the schools. Held at the beginning of every summer."

Oh, Cassie knew all about the carnival. She'd sneaked her first beer at the carnival. Her first cigarette.

Lost her virginity.

Oh, yeah, she had a whole host of whoopee memories from the annual event. "Let's just say I'm not particularly fond of it," she said carefully.

"Oh."

Stacie looked so disappointed, Cassie sighed. "What's the favor?"

"I'm going to be sitting in the dunking booth. Thought you'd come by and say hi. Since the divorce I haven't socialized very much and…" She lifted a shoulder and let out a little laugh. "And it's been a bit lonely, you know?"

Friends. Is that what Stacie wanted? Ha! Obviously she hadn't been listening to the town gossip lately. As for lonely… ah, hell. "Yeah, fine. I'll stop by."

Stacie's entire face lit up, and before Cassie could blink she was enveloped in a hug. "See you tomorrow," Stacie whispered, and then she was gone.

Leaving Cassie with one more thing to think about.

PLEASANTVILLE'S ANNUAL carnival brought out the best and the worst in the general population. There were clowns, games, crafts, rides and enough junk food to keep the town in stomachaches for the rest of the year.

There were also whiny kids, grumpy parents, the occasional drunk and a slew of trouble-seeking high school kids out to score.

Not to mention the heat. Dark had fallen and yet at nearly ninety degrees, the temperature hadn't.

Not exactly the way Tag would have chosen to spend a Saturday night. He wasn't on duty, not officially anyway, but they were still short staffed due to the flu, and he knew his presence would help.

The music pulsed loud, as well as all the hooting and hollering from the rides and games. Pulling his shirt away from his damp skin, he strode up and down the aisles thinking of how he'd *rather* be spending his evening.

In front of ESPN. With air-conditioning.

No, scratch that. In the arms of a woman. Yeah, now there was a way to pass time. His nice, quiet, sweet, loving woman, whose entire life would center around him and his needs. And though she'd be quiet, she wouldn't be shy. No way. She'd be wildly passionate and erotically sensual.

She'd greet him at the door wearing his opened shirt and nothing else but a smile.

Now there was a fantasy.

He strode down a row of games, then around a corner to another aisle, stopping to gulp down a large lemonade. People had shown up in force tonight to support their schools, but few had found this area yet. He could see straight ahead to the dart game, where all one had to do was pop three balloons to win a prize.

A woman stood there. There were women all over the

place, but this one, dressed to kill in her jade-green haltered sundress, stood out. She was concentrating fiercely, her back to him as she threw back her arm, aimed...and missed.

He knew that long, slim back. Those blond waves tumbling over straight, proud shoulders. Those long, long legs that could wrap around a man and—

"Shit," she muttered, and shoved a hand into her pocket. That she came out with another buck surprised him, as her skirt appeared to have been painted on.

Several women passed Cassie, each of whom stopped to stare at her, then kept going, laughing unkindly. Tag frowned and opened his mouth to say something but Cassie flipped them off and went back to shooting.

It made him grin.

And suddenly he was incredibly glad he'd come. Still grinning, he sauntered up to the booth and leaned a hip against it as he turned casually toward her.

She didn't even glance at him, just accepted her new darts from an awed-looking, pimply-faced teenage boy and aimed again.

Two balloons in a row, bull's-eye. Pop. Pop.

"One dart away for the big prize," the boy told her with a huge, dopey smile on his face. "You have to hit all three to get the—"

"I know what I have to do." She threw the dart.

"Close," Tag said conversationally when she missed by a mile. "But no cigar."

Oh, she noticed him now. Narrowed her very incredible, very green, very expressive eyes on him. "You distracted me."

He lifted his hands. "Hey, you didn't even see me until just now." Slipping a hand into his pocket, he came out with another buck. "But here. Try again, on me."

"I'm not taking your money." She slapped down her own dollar. "Back off, you're in my space."

"Backing off." But he didn't. She smelled too good, looked too good. He wasn't going anywhere.

She didn't even notice. In fact, she appeared to forget about him as she took aim. And this time hit her target. Then did it again.

"One more time," the kid said, ever so helpfully, and Cassie lowered the third dart and glared at him. He took a step back. "Sorry. I just know how bad you want this pretty teddy bear here."

"Teddy bear, huh?" Tag tucked his tongue into his cheek as she aimed and once again missed her third and winning shot. "I gotta tell you, I never really pictured you as a teddy bear type, Cassie."

"Oh, she wants it really bad," the kid offered as Cassie grated her teeth. "She's already put at least ten bucks on it."

"Is that right?" Tag looked at Cassie and lifted a brow. "You need something cuddly to sleep with at night, Cassie?"

She sighed. "Is there a reason why you're standing there staring at me?"

"Well…" He scratched his jaw and looked her over, from the long neck he suddenly wanted to nibble on, to the breasts nicely outlined behind her halter, down her curved hips and mile-stretch legs. Her toenails were hot pink tonight, and she wore a silver toe ring, reminding him of the nipple ring. Was she wearing it now? "You are something to look at."

With a roll of her eyes, she slapped down another buck and went back to the task at hand. Aimed. Let it rip, and Tag had to admit, she knew what she was doing.

Pop. Pop.

Two balloons down.

"Only one to go," he offered.

Her hand lowered, and she shot him a withering look. "Don't talk."

He smiled and waited until she aimed again. "You know, if you want the teddy bear that badly, I could win it for you."

"I'll win it myself, thanks."

"Oka-a-ay," he said, and watched as she missed.

She swore with impressive skill, then dug into her pocket again. Came up empty. Swore some more.

"My offer still stands." He smiled when she bared her teeth at him. "If you're interested. I'll win it for you."

"Sure you will."

He put a hand to his chest. "Your doubt wounds me. But you should know, I was all-city dart champ."

Cocking a hip, she crossed her arms over her chest. "Really."

"Really."

"So you'll win me the teddy bear."

"Just said so, didn't I?"

She studied him, then let out a little laugh. "Okay, cocky man, what happens then? After you win?"

"I hand you the prize."

"And?"

"And…" He let out a slow, wicked grin, both because he could taste victory and because she was so incredibly hot. And fun. That was the shocker. He was having fun with her. "And in return, *you* give *me* a prize."

Her eyes narrowed to little slits. "Which would be what exactly?"

"I don't know yet. I'll think about it." He slapped down a buck, accepted his three darts. Aimed.

And was stopped by a hand on his arm. He looked into deep green eyes that held a world of knowledge. "I don't want the teddy bear."

"Liar," he said softly, and hit the first balloon. "But that's okay. The bear will look good on my bed." He hit the second balloon.

Pop.

She tossed back her hair. Looked at him with fire-spitting eyes. Then caved. "Okay, damn you, I want the bear." Her fingers dug into his arm. "Name your price."

They weren't touching—other than her fingernails digging into his biceps, that is—but their mouths were only a fraction apart. Hers was all glossy and smelled like peaches.

He loved peaches.

Their breath comingled, and with a sharp stab of lust he remembered exactly how good those lips tasted. He wanted another taste. "My price?" He lifted the third remaining dart. Weighed it in his hand. "A kiss."

A laugh escaped her. "Just a kiss? You don't aim very high for yourself, do you?"

"On the contrary…" He narrowed his gaze, studied the distance to the remaining balloon. Hefted the dart. "I know exactly what I want. And I'm not afraid to get it." Turning his head, he shot her a last look. "How about you?"

"I know what I want."

"The teddy bear." He smiled. "But I've discovered I want it, too." He aimed, but before he could throw the dart she stopped him.

"Fine," she said.

He set down the dart. "Fine what?"

"You want me to say it?"

"Yep."

That earned him a roll of her eyes. "If you win the bear, I'll give you a kiss for it. Okay? Right here, right now."

"Oh, no," he said with a shake of his head. "Not right here."

"Where then?"

"Where I say."

She looked him over. Wanted to tell him to go to hell, he could tell. "You have twenty-four hours to claim it, big boy, or all bets are off."

"Deal." He leaned close and she tilted her head back, away from him. Lifting a finger, she wagged it in his face. "Gotta win it first, ace."

He arched a brow, then showed her he was just leaning in to grab the dart.

She crossed her arms and didn't offer another word.

He smiled and tossed the dart.

And won the girl the bear.

Handing it to her, he grinned and said, "You're welcome." He watched as she turned away and buried her face into the bear's neck, her arms hugging the thing tight. Because suddenly his throat was tight as well, he cleared it. "So… Are we going steady now?"

"In your dreams." She huffed off, a vision in her little sundress, her blond hair flying everywhere, arms wrapped around the huge bear.

The kid running the booth watched her go. "That was amazing, dude."

"Yeah." But all Tag could think about was his prize. And it was walking away.

So he did what any red-blooded, aroused man would do. He followed her.

CASSIE STALKED through the carnival, glaring at any man who so much as looked at her. And there were plenty. Women looked, too, if her itchy shoulder blades were any indication. Good. Let them look at bad-ass, no-good, trouble-seeking Cassie Tremaine.

The high-heeled sandals had been a mistake, she thought

now, because she couldn't really motor in the them. *Should have worn tennis shoes.*

Had she even packed tennis shoes?

"Cassie."

Oh, that voice.

"Cassie, wait up."

Nope. She kept walking, smiling as though she was the queen of the ball, as if the sexiest, most obnoxious man she'd ever met wasn't striding behind her.

He'd won her the teddy bear. Not only that, her heart had gone all pitter-pattery watching him do it. Unacceptable, really. She had no need for a man doing something she was capable of doing for herself. She wasn't like her mother, damn it.

She had no need for a man, period. Never had. Not knowing who her father was, having never had a positive male role model, having never had men do anything but drool when they looked at her, she supposed she had a rather low view of men in general, but not one had ever proven her wrong. Not yet anyway.

At least Tag wasn't wearing his uniform. Maybe that was the trouble, she thought now. Because without the uniform she obviously couldn't be trusted to remember she didn't like him.

The carnival wasn't that big, and before she knew it she was in the parking lot. Good thing she'd gone and dunked Stacie before going for the teddy bear, because she was good and ready to leave now.

But not to go home. Home was dark and lonely, with only a grumpy cat waiting for her. And nightmares of Pete finding her.

The night was still and hot. She'd give just about anything for a cool breeze. And that's when she decided.

The lake.

It wasn't a very far walk, and her feet were tougher than

they looked. She wanted to see the lake by moonlight, and what she wanted, she got. She started off, hugging the teddy bear, not listening in the least for Tag's footsteps. But even if she had been, they weren't there to hear.

Good. He'd gone away. Just as she wanted.

Bastard.

The moment she stepped off the road and onto the little sandy beach, she set down the teddy bear—careful that it didn't get covered in sand—and kicked off her sandals. Her toes dug into the wet sand and she nearly moaned at the cool pleasure of it. *This*. This is what she'd needed. She walked to the water, letting it lap at her ankles.

Alone. "His loss," she told the moon.

"Not yet, it's not."

She was not going to scream, jump, or give any sign that he'd nearly scared her right out of her skin. Again. Calmly, with a little smile on her lips, she turned. "What are you doing?"

"Collecting my prize." He stepped close, so very close that she could see the moonlight dancing in his eyes. Could feel the heat of his big, tough body.

Tensing, Cassie waited, because she wouldn't welsh on her promise. She'd pay the price. She held very still, waiting to be grabbed. Groped. Conquered.

But he did none of the above, just stepped even closer, careful not to smash her toes.

"What—"

"Shh," he said before sliding his arms around her and putting his mouth to hers. She should have known from their earlier encounter he was different. There was no grabbing, no groping, no conquering. Nothing even close. Yes, his arms were strong and firm, but also loose enough she could wriggle free if she wanted to.

She thought about it for all of one second. He was tall, powerfully built, and smelled like heaven. It wasn't often she stood in a man's embrace with every thought draining out of her head, but it happened now as his hands cupped her face, almost reverently, tipping her head for better access.

Oh, yes, better access was good. So good she arched against him. The sound he made low in his throat caused a mirroring one in hers.

At that, the kiss went instantly explosive. His tongue slid home. He hauled her body up against his. And still, she didn't want to be free. The opposite, she realized dimly, snaking her arms around his neck to hold on tight.

With the touch of her fingers on the back of his neck, he groaned, a very erotic sound, and nibbled at her lower lip.

Ohmigod, was all Cassie could think, and then she couldn't have repeated even that. Her knees wobbled; her heart rammed against her ribs as they practically ate each other alive. This… this—whatever it was they were doing to each other—was far more than she had bargained for, and still it wasn't enough. She wanted more. She, a woman who never wanted more from a man. Never.

It took her a moment to realize he'd released her, and that she stood there weaving like a drunk.

"Thank you," he said very politely, in direct contrast to the way he was breathing as if he'd run five miles. Uphill. "That was…"

"Yeah." She licked her lips, tasting him on her. "That was…" Craving his mouth back on hers, she licked her lips again.

He made another rough sound, almost a growl. "Unless you want to extend that price you negotiated, don't."

"Don't…?"

"Don't look at me as if I'm the first one who's ever kissed

you stupid. Don't stand there weaving weakly with lust… Ah, hell. Don't even breathe. Yeah, that should do it." He turned from her, shoved his hands through his hair and stared out at the lake.

Shocked, she looked at him. Really looked at him—at his stiff shoulders, his rough breathing—and knew he was as out of control as she was.

And how annoying was it that she no longer wanted him just so that she could cross another item off her revenge list. She wanted him because…well, just because. "It got a little out of hand, that's all."

He shot her a look of disgust over his shoulder. "You think?"

"Yeah."

Before she knew what he was about, he turned, lifted a hand and caressed her cheek. "So it wouldn't, couldn't, happen again, right?"

She barely caught herself from closing her eyes and sighing at the surprising tenderness of his big, warm hand. "Of course not."

"Liar," he whispered softly. Before she could snarl at him for that, he walked away.

5

Two DAYS LATER Tag still couldn't get that kiss out of his head. It went with him to work, to play, to bed…and that's where it was the worst. Bed.

He wanted Cassie there with him, he couldn't deny that. He wanted her badly.

But why? She was bad attitude personified. She hated everything about him, his life, his job.

So what did that say about him, being so undeniably attracted to her?

That he was sick, very sick.

But knowing it didn't stop the desire, so that when he walked into his office after a day from hell, desperately in need of coffee and some time off, and saw her standing there in front of his receptionist, his gut took a hungry leap.

He told himself it was simply because she exuded sex appeal and it had been…well, longer than it should have since his last sexual experience.

It was the outfit, he decided. She wore a microskirt the color of a field of daffodils, and a matching zippered crop-top, out of which came two spaghetti straps from what he assumed was a bathing suit worn beneath. Her hair had been piled on top of her head, with strands tumbling free to her shoulders.

And then there were her legs—long and toned and bare except for a pair of strappy sandals.

"I was just wondering if the restraining order I took out in New York protects me here," she was saying, and all Tag's lusty thoughts flew right out the window. "Because I've received some more threatening mail and—"

"What restraining order?" Tag asked, moving close. "What threatening mail?" She smelled like coconut oil. He loved coconut oil. Ordering himself not to notice her scent, or to picture what she was obviously dressed for—sunbathing—he looked into her green, green eyes.

"If you don't mind, I'm having a conversation with your receptionist," she said. "A *private* conversation."

Roxy, who'd been working at the station since his father had been sheriff, shot him a sympathetic look, then turned back to Cassie. "You do have a restraining order already in place? In New York, you said, right? Can you give us the details?"

Cassie glance sideways at Tag. "Us?"

"Well, the sheriff here is really good at what he does," Roxy assured her. "He can help protect you—we just need to know what's going on. We'll need to know who the restraining order is for, what specifically, and any other pertinent details for our records."

"Such as why you didn't tell me when you first hit town," Tag said lightly, not feeling light at all.

Cassie picked up the purse she'd set on the counter. "You know what? Never mind."

"But—" Roxy made a frustrated sound when Cassie pivoted away and headed toward the door.

"Thanks anyway," Cassie called over her shoulder.

Not even her curvy little ass could sidetrack him now. With

one last glance at Roxy, who lifted her shoulders to indicate she knew as much as he did, he followed Cassie.

Who gave no indication that she even noticed.

"Cassie," he said as she strode out of the station and into the early evening.

Her heels clicked on the asphalt. Everyone she passed took a good long second look, both men and women. Some started talking. Cassie didn't so much as look at a single one of them.

"Cassie," he said again, but as she was having no part of him, it left him following her like some damn puppy dog. But she'd tweaked his curiosity—and concern—and if there was anything more dogged than a curious, concerned cop, he didn't know what it was.

At her car, she opened her purse. Slid on sunglasses.

"Cassie."

Pulling out her keys, she opened her door, and would have slid inside if he hadn't put a hand on her waist.

Going still, she stared down at his hand, which looked large and imposing on the paler, softer skin of her very tantalizing middle. "I paid the debt the other night," she said very quietly. "We're even, remember?"

With a rather unprofessional oath, he dropped his hand. "Do you think I care about that?"

"You've got a penis, don't you?"

He sucked in a slow careful breath because something about her stoked his temper every time. "You wanted the teddy bear, I won it for you."

"Thank you, Mr. He-Man. And I paid your price."

"That's right," he said, keeping his voice even with effort. "End of story."

"Then why are we still talking about it?"

"Because you brought it up!" Lord, she could try the patience of a saint. He took a deep breath. "I want to hear about the restraining order. About your threatening mail."

"Yeah, well that was a private conversation and you were eavesdropping." But she seemed less hostile now and he forced himself to relax.

Forced himself to be the calm cop he knew he was. And once he did that, he had to admit it bugged the hell out of him that she thought he'd insist on more "payment" for that damn teddy bear.

Had she really never met a guy who didn't want something from her? He knew she didn't have a father around—never had. He knew what Biff had wanted from her. But what about others? Hadn't there been others? Anyone who'd just been there for her? Given her attitude, he had to doubt it. That thought unsettled him to the core, and if the kiss hadn't so rocked his world, he might have spared a moment to feel guilty he'd asked her for that much.

Then he realized something else, that she was avoiding looking at him, and when he took a good look, he saw why.

She was uncomfortable around him. Interesting. If she'd paid the debt, and it was as over as she'd said, why wouldn't she look at him? "Cassie, talk to me." He paused. "Please."

With an exaggerated sigh, she tipped her head and looked skyward. "You know me. Wild Cassie Tremaine. I go looking for trouble. Just ask anyone."

"Pleasantville isn't Mayberry," Tag said. "We have our fair share of village idiots." With his cousin leading the pack.

"Surely you've heard the stories."

"And I sincerely doubt any of them are true."

Her gaze jerked up to his. Oh, yeah, he'd managed to surprise her. Had no one ever believed in her?

"I'm just having some trouble with an obsessed guy, that's all," she said finally.

"A fan?"

"Sort of."

This he didn't like. He imagined, given her chosen occupation, she faced similar problems all the time. That she actually needed a restraining order was deeply disturbing. "How serious is the trouble?"

She lifted a shoulder and didn't look at him.

"Serious enough for a restraining order." He turned her to face him, left his hands on her bare upper arms because he wanted her unsettled enough to talk. "I can find out with or without you, but I'd rather you tell me."

"It's not that big of a deal." She shrugged him off. "I'm safe here. Nothing bad can happen in Pleasantville, right...*Sheriff?*"

"Do you have a thing against all cops or just me?"

"Oh, definitely all cops, but especially second generation ones."

It wasn't the first time he'd wondered. "You know my father."

"I grew up here, didn't I? Right here in good old Pleasantville, where, like I said, nothing bad could ever happen." Her laugh didn't convince him, but mostly because it wasn't humor in her eyes now but...hurt? If he had to guess, he'd have said plenty of bad things had happened to her, right here in Pleasantville.

"Look, I just...had a long night last night and got a little spooked. Okay?"

"I can't imagine you being spooked for anything less than a good reason."

"I know. I'm so tough I'd scare away the mob."

She didn't look so tough right now. "Cassie. You're scaring me."

"Look, Pete's just a typical guy. He thought he could have

something I didn't want to give him, and he's pissed. He'll get over it."

"Pete. A...lover?"

She ripped off her sunglasses, her eyes gleaming. "None of your damn business. Now if you'll excuse me, I'm headed to the lake for some time alone."

"It's going to be getting dark soon."

"Thanks, Einstein."

He looked into the open convertible. Miss Priss lay asleep on the passenger seat, next to a picnic basket and a book. *"The Rogue's Kiss?"* he asked in surprise, staring at the historical romance novel with the half-naked guy on the cover.

"Do you think underwear models can't read?"

"You read...romance?"

"Shockers, isn't it?"

What was shocking was the layers to her. Who'd have thought Cassie Tremaine would have a romantic side?

She sank into the car, started it. "Unless you didn't meet your ticket quota for the week, back off. I'd hate to run over those toes on my way outta here."

Risking it, he held open her door. "Is that why you're in town? To get out of the limelight for a while to avoid this guy?"

"I'm in town opening—"

"Bare Essentials. Yeah, yeah." He gripped the hand that would have slid on her sunglasses again. "I'm not buying that anymore, Cassie. You're here because you're scared. How long are you staying?"

"Until I feel like hitting the road again. Now move."

He did, only because he felt the tremble in her fingers and it shocked him. Vulnerability? He'd seen a flash of it before and dismissed it because it was unthinkable. The smart-ass, tough-as-hell Cassie couldn't be vulnerable.

Or was she? He couldn't help but feel that he'd missed something about her. That there was more to the tall, incredibly beautiful, distant woman than she wanted everyone to see.

He watched her peel out of the parking lot, heading toward the lake. It frustrated him that he'd been unable to figure out who the hell she really was.

He went back inside the station, thinking maybe he'd just try harder.

Roxy looked at him with a raised brow. "What's up with the lingerie lady?"

"I haven't a clue."

"You'd better get one."

"Why do you say that?"

"Well…" Roxy glanced at the door, a worried look on her face. "I know people like to whisper about her behind her back, talk about her like she was the wild child from hell all those years ago…"

"And?"

"And I think it was just that…talk. I think she's got guts, coming back here. She holds her head up like it doesn't matter what people say, but…"

He sighed, because Roxy was always like this, always had to be coaxed out of her stories. "But?"

"But she's scared, Sheriff. A woman like that, who's been through so much…she doesn't get scared easily. And yet she is."

Tag thought about that as he changed out of his uniform. As he promised himself pizza and a beer. But then the funniest thing happened.

His car drove to the lake, just as the sun took its final dip beneath the horizon. Bypassing the popular swimming hole, he drove around to the east side, where a quiet bay surrounded by trees and growth made a more private area.

It was where he'd kissed Cassie only a few nights before.

He parked next to the only other car around, a sunshine-yellow Porsche.

It was open and unlocked, and he shook his head. She should be more careful. He stopped to stroke Miss Priss, who stretched, purred, and went right back to sleep on the passenger seat. "If only your mistress was as easy to please," he said, then headed off on the trail down to the beach.

The night was a dark one already, with just a few silvery clouds. The heat from the day hadn't begun to fade, which was why the sound of the water hitting the shore in gentle waves made him yearn to dive in.

The small bay was deserted—unless he counted the sexy mermaid playing around in the water. She popped up about twenty feet out, her back to him. Her long wet hair clung to her shoulders, which gleamed in the meager light. Tipping her head back to the night sky, her eyes were closed, and on her face was an expression he'd never seen before.

Contentment.

Then she bent to dive deep. For a second he had the magnificent view of her backside, and the small patch of wet material dividing the most perfect set of buns he'd ever seen.

Then she was gone.

He stared at the water, waiting for her to surface, and she didn't disappoint. She came up only about five feet out now, and facing him. "I already ate the picnic," she said, treading water.

"I'm not hungry." For food, that is.

Still treading water, she studied him, only her elegant neck and face showing. "You coming in?"

And have that long, sleek, wet body within reach? Slowly he shook his head. "That would be a bad idea."

"No bathing suit, huh?"

"No."

"That can be fixed." She reached behind her back for a moment, then flung something that landed at his feet.

He scooped up two tiny triangles and some string, dangled it from his fingers. Her bikini top.

His mouth went dry.

Then something equally wet hit him in the chest. Catching it with his other hand, he held up...her bottoms. This time it wasn't just his mouth that reacted. "What are you doing?"

"Treading water. Naked." She smiled the smile of an angel.

And if he could have, he would have laughed. *"Cassie."*

"You sure say my name a lot. Don't worry, slick. Your virtue is safe with me. I just thought I'd put us on even playing ground. You can strip down and come in now."

Hallelujah, cried his body.

Holy shit, cried his mind.

Good thing his mind was in control, barely. "You want me to come in. Without my clothes."

"Unless you want to get them wet."

"I want to talk about your visit to the station. What the hell is going on?"

Instead of answering, she floated on her back for a moment before executing a perfect back somersault. At the flash of generous breasts, then flat belly, then...he nearly swallowed his tongue. Tan lines. She had lots of tan lines.

He loved tan lines. Christ, just shoot him now.

"Are you coming?" she asked when she surfaced.

Nearly in his pants. "About the restraining order—"

"I'm tired of shouting."

"So you'll talk to me if I come in."

"You're quick, Tag."

"Uh-huh." He didn't believe her. "Why are you being... nice?"

She blinked at that.

"Is it because I'm not in my uniform?"

Now those eyes chilled and she dipped down to her chin. "Your uniform has nothing to do with this."

"Really?" Ripping his T-shirt over his head, his hands went to the buttons on his Levi's. To hell with being stoic. To hell with restraint. To hell with not taking what he wanted when it was being offered to him. "Then why do you only talk to me when I'm out of it?"

"Because I don't like it?"

He undid his first button, watching her watch him very closely, the desire unmistakable. Good. She wanted him, too. They could scratch this itch and get it the hell out of their way. But he wanted to hear her say it, wanted to hear that she wanted him as much as he wanted her.

"You look hot." She splashed him, just a little.

And he opened another button. "You want to watch what you start, Cassie."

"Oh, I'm watching." And she was. She hit him with another splash.

Another button.

More desire.

"Get in the water, Tag. Cool off." With that, she allowed the very tips of her breasts to break the surface.

His eyes narrowed into dangerous slits as he kicked off his shoes and socks.

Then shoved off the rest of his clothes.

And my, oh, my, Cassie thought, her body humming already, he looked amazing naked. She splashed him again for the sheer pleasure of watching water running down his big, strong, sleek form in little rivulets she suddenly wanted to lick off. Broad, tanned shoulders, hard chest tapering to a narrow waist, powerful legs…and what lay between those thighs made her breath catch. "Coming?"

"Oh, yeah."

Oh, yeah. With any luck, they'd both come.

She needed this, she decided. She deserved it. And afterward, she'd feel better. More relaxed. They could go back to ignoring each other. But damn, he looked good strutting into the deliciously cool water without so much as a wince, never breaking eye contact, until, a few feet from her, he vanished into the water.

With the lack of a moon, she couldn't see where he was headed, but she wasn't stupid. Braced and ready, she let out only a cool smile when he surfaced again, slowly, confidently, only a fraction of an inch in front of her.

He shook his hair back. Water ran down his jaw. A jaw she suddenly wanted to touch. Strange, that urge. Sex was a tool and only a tool. A stimulus. A muscle relaxant. A great way to guarantee a good night's sleep.

Nothing more.

So this urge to be tender bugged the hell out of her. Forget tender. She wanted hard and fast, and then she wanted him gone. To facilitate the matter, she put her arms over his shoulders, letting him do all the work to keep them afloat.

It also slid their bodies in direct contact. Chest to chest, thigh to thigh, and everything in between. And oh, baby, was there a lot in between. Her nipples brushed the light hair on his chest. His legs entangled with hers. And his erection… Mmm, she slid it between her legs, loving the feeling of having him there. He was hot, pulsing. Huge. And it wasn't easy to keep her eyes open on his, to keep her thoughts straight, when her entire body had melted so that she had no bones left.

"Cassie." One large hand danced down her spine, cupped her bottom and pressed her against his hot, hard body as he supported her weight. "I'm ready to hear about the restraining order," he said very quietly, keeping them above water with no apparent effort.

"I…" He had his hand on her ass, his penis between her legs. "Um…" Her heart was pounding dully in her ears. Her nipples had long ago pebbled to hard, needy beads. And between her clenched thighs she was creamy. Rational thought escaped her and he hadn't done anything yet. "What?"

He let out a slow, knowing smile.

Damn him and his unbearable control. Well, she had enough left to know she had to destroy it. Sinking her fingers into his hair, she shifted even closer so their mouths were just touching. "So. You really want to…" She wrapped her legs around his waist, thrilling to his quickly indrawn breath. "Talk?"

Now both hands held her bottom, hard, his fingers squeezing. She was so close to him they'd melted together. And because she'd spread her legs wide, wrapping them around his waist so satisfactorily, the tip of his penis…oh, yes, nearly slid home.

Nearly. Because he held back. Everything. "You want me?" he asked, his voice rough and serrated, his mouth so close to hers, but not close enough. His hands still gripped her bottom, holding her slightly away, so that his wonderfully hot, hard, huge erection only teased the very center of her universe.

"I think that's fairly obvious," she answered.

"Then talk to me."

"Uh…"

Looking fierce and hot, and so damn sexy she wanted to gobble him up in one bite, he stroked her again. This time his chest lightly brushed her nipples, and she could barely breathe.

"Maybe you skipped the birds and the bees lesson," she

said. "But you should know, talking has little to do with wanting you."

He looked down at her breasts, two hard, aching points brushing against his chest, and groaned. Slowly he lifted her up a little, dipping his head so he could rub his jaw across the very tips. "Can Pete find you here?"

No, she wouldn't talk about this, even if he'd forced a pathetic, needy whimper from her throat.

"Cassie?" Another little stroke with his not-so-little penis. Her entire body quivered, dancing on the very edge of an orgasm she wanted with all her heart.

"Can he?" he growled.

She stared down at his mouth, wanting it on hers. At the look, he groaned low and deep. His fingers, still supporting her, glided farther down her backside and dipped between her legs. Unerringly found her flash point.

Unable to help herself, she thrust against him and he groaned again, the sound melding with hers. She'd never had an orgasm without purposeful, calculated thought before, and yet here she was, quivering on the very edge without a thought in her head other than...*more, please, more.*

They weren't very far out in the water. Not too far to miss the fact that her cell phone was ringing. She stared at the spot where she'd left it while he stared at her.

"You get a lot of calls?" he asked hoarsely.

"Very few now that I'm off work." She closed her eyes, then jerked them open when she felt his mouth slide over hers in a far too brief kiss.

Bending his head, he sighed and rubbed his jaw lightly over her breasts, making them both moan again. "Get it," he said and with one last perfectly aimed stroke with his fingers, gently unwrapped her legs from around him. "It might be important."

Walking out of the water, feeling him alongside her, Cassie wondered at the amazing control of the man. She wondered how he'd gotten that way, and—

And all else fell from her mind as she scooped up the phone from her towel. She'd missed the call. But the caller had a New York area code that didn't belong to her agent. And then the phone rang again...same number. "Hello?" she said.

"Hello, Cassie," said Pete. "I'm here and you're not."

Cassie looked up into Tag's face and felt the blood drain from her own.

6

"You haven't called," Pete said in a congenial voice. "Even though I know you had some…car trouble before you left. Why didn't you call, Cassie?"

Very aware that Tag stood less than a foot away, still as gloriously naked as was she, Cassie didn't say a word. Pete's voice gave her goose bumps, as did his casual reference to how he'd slashed her tires.

"We're friends," he went on. "*Friends,* Cassie. And we're so much more than that, too. Did you know I haven't come to find you, not because I couldn't, but because I wanted you to come find me?"

His words disturbed her, made her feel sick. She'd liked this man, had let him into her life, and that her instincts had been so far off, so wrong, cut deeply.

"We belong together, you know this," Pete said in her ear. "We were meant to be. I'm going to make it happen."

Her skin crawled. "No—"

"Yes." His voice hardened. "You can't treat me this way, Cassie, vanishing from my world like this. It's not okay. Friends don't do that to one another."

"Friends." Suddenly she felt cold, so very cold, and she grabbed for something to cover herself. That it happened to be

Tag's T-shirt didn't stop her; she shoved it over her wet head and body, then wrapped her free arm around herself. "Funny you use that word. I don't have any."

"Cassie." His voice was low now, conciliatory, quick to soothe. "Just tell me where you are, I can make it all up to you."

He was insane. And she hadn't seen it until it had been almost too late. "Don't call me again, Pete." She clicked off, tossed the phone down by her sandals, and stared off into the night, telling herself he still had no idea where she was or he'd have come for her by now.

Tag came up beside her. He was still looking at her with his sharp, probing gaze, still naked and apparently unconcerned about that fact. She knew male models, tons of them, and had never seen a man so comfortable in his own skin. He was beautiful, and the way he looked at her...in another place and time she might have been tempted to let herself weaken for him.

Who was she fooling? She *had* weakened for him, had very nearly trusted him with anything he wanted to do. Good God, what was wrong with her? He was a sheriff, of all things, a man with authority and power over her if he so chose, and more than that, he was his father's son. No doubt Sheriff Sean Taggart couldn't be trusted any more than Richard could be, and yet she'd nearly...

He pulled his jeans over his still-wet body but didn't fasten them. He looked like a Greek god standing there next to her, staring out into the night.

Until he turned to look at her. Those eyes of his weren't a god's. They were a cop's. "Pete."

"Yes."

"Another threat?"

"He's upset because he can't find me."

"Well, thank God for small favors." When she didn't answer, he sighed, put his hands on her and pulled her close. That her body wanted to be even closer felt like a betrayal. "You're not going to ask me for help," he guessed.

"No."

"Then I'm going to ask you." He shook her lightly until she locked gazes with him. "Let me help you, Cassie. *Please.* Let me do this for you."

"I don't need—"

"No, you don't *want.*" His hands slid up her arms, cupped her face. "You're independent, I get that. You're proud. I get that, too. But you're not stupid. You need help. We're friends, if nothing else, and—"

"Oh, no." She let out a short mirthless laugh and backed up. "Not you, too."

He narrowed his eyes. "What, is the word *friend* a trigger word for you?"

"I'll admit, we're…almost lovers. Sparring partners, maybe. But not friends." When he stepped close again, she took a shaky breath because her heart suddenly and inexplicably hurt. "We're not. We'll never be that."

She saw surprise flash across his features and, damn it, hurt, too, but that wouldn't stop her. It was a dog-eat-dog world and she had to stay on top. "A man can't be a woman's friend, not—"

"That's bullshit."

"—when—" she continued coolly while shaking like a leaf inside. "Not when all he wants is sex."

He stopped cold, stared at her. She could see the shock in his eyes. Then he pulled away, turned his back.

Oh, yeah, she'd hit the mark that time. He felt guilty as hell, and that should have been tremendously satisfying. But the victory felt hollow.

"I'm sorry," he said.

"It's nothing personal."

"Like hell." But he merely slid his hands into his pockets. "You came back here to Pleasantville to hide. That's fact. You came here even with bitter childhood memories because you knew one thing...you knew you'd be safe."

"You don't know a single truth about my past."

"I would if you told me."

She wasn't going to tell him anything.

"Fine," he said angrily. "I'll have to guess then, and you have no one to blame but yourself if I'm wrong."

"You've already heard what I was like."

"I have." He looked over his shoulder at her, his eyes dark and intense. "But as I've already told you, I think the truth is radically different."

He didn't believe the gossip. So what *did* he believe?

"You were right to come here." He still looked toward the lake. "You'll be safe. You'll come to the station and let someone know if you feel Pete has managed to track you."

"Yes," she told his sleek, still-wet back. The back she'd wanted to touch, wanted to put her mouth to.

She'd tell him anything if he'd go away and leave her be, with her burning eyes and burning throat. "I'll come to the station if I need help."

With one short nod, he bent, scooped up her towel and tossed it to her. He looked at her for a long, long moment, then his lips curved slowly. Solemnly. "Be careful, Cassie."

And then she was alone. Just as she'd wanted.

WELL, HELL, Tag thought, stretching out in the hammock in his vast front yard, studying the stars. He'd certainly learned a few things about himself at the lake tonight, hadn't he. And none of it was anything to be particularly proud of.

First, he'd apparently proven to Cassie that all men were

scum. Every one of them. Not that she hadn't apparently already formed that opinion, but he'd definitely enforced it.

What had come over him? Lust, he admitted. A red haze of lust.

She was being stalked for crissake, and what had he done? He'd stripped down to his birthday suit like a hopeful high school kid and dove into that water without a single thought.

Oh, yeah, he deserved her disdain, every ounce of it. But she hadn't deserved his momentary lapse in judgment.

Well, he could fix that much at least. On his way back from the lake he'd gone to the station and done what he could for her, not that she'd appreciate it. He'd arranged for drive-bys at her house. He'd alerted his deputies to the possibility of trouble. And he'd put in a request for a copy of the original report and the restraining order.

She wouldn't thank him, he knew that, but at least he had his head on straight now and wouldn't be distracted from what he had to do.

He wouldn't. No matter how glorious she looked nude, swimming like a mermaid beneath the stars, her satiny skin glistening like a feast as she frolicked unselfconsciously. Her body—a mind-blowing study in curves and feminine delights—was perfection, and he'd seen every bit of it tonight. Rock-hard mauve nipples made for sucking. Rounded hips begging for his hands to grip tight. Long, tanned legs, and the treasure in between that had made his mouth water with hunger.

Just the thought could bring him to his knees, so he stopped thinking.

But he didn't stop dreaming, not that night, and not the next.

He did, however, a few days later, take his weekly phone

call from his father, something he would have gladly skipped if he'd only put in Caller ID as he kept meaning to.

"You feeling better?" Tag asked him, knowing his father had been suffering from rheumatory arthritis, and knowing the man would never admit it.

"I'll live, unfortunately. You keeping the streets clean of stupidity, son?"

Tag let out a silent sigh and rubbed his temples. "What do you think?"

"I think I shouldn't have retired. Heard Cassie Tremaine Montgomery is back in town. The slut."

Tag went utterly still. "She left here right after high school. What was she, maybe seventeen? Don't you think you're being a little harsh?"

"What do you know about it? You were at college when she left. Trust me. Keep your eye on her."

That didn't seem to be a problem. What *was* a problem was the fact that he wanted to keep more than his eyes on her. He wanted his hands, his mouth and his body on her, as well.

"What's happening at work?" his father asked.

"The usual," Tag said. "Just a D.U.I. at the moment."

"Any ongoing cases?"

"Nothing I can't handle."

"Sure?"

Tag counted to ten. "Positive."

"Okay, then. I've got to go."

"Sure. But in case you were wondering, I'm fine."

"I know you're fine. If you weren't I'd hear about it. It's work I want to know about. You'd best be doing a good job, upholding our family name."

Or what? Tag wondered wearily. He'd swing his authority around like a belt? He rubbed his temples. "I'll talk to you next week."

"You haven't been out to see me."

Tag hadn't, that was true. He hadn't been able to take the hour or so of verbal abuse he'd no doubt have to sit through before being dismissed like a worthless underling.

He bit his tongue on the harsh words he wanted to say. He wouldn't act like his father. "I've got to go, Dad." Hanging up the phone, he gave in to a brief moment of self-hatred for not telling his father to just go to hell.

Pretty pathetic. Thirty-two years old and he still had a deep desire to have a picture-perfect family life with warm, loving people around him.

Or one loving person. The one he hadn't found yet—his fantasy wife. The thought made him huff out a mirthless laugh because he was no closer to finding her than he was to really living in Mayberry, U.S.A.

KATE ARRIVED, and Cassie had to admit she'd never been happier to see anyone in her entire life. Her cousin hadn't changed at all; she was still the voice of calm reason to Cassie's wild heart.

Physically, they were opposites as well, and Cassie had always admired Kate's long, thick dark hair, her perfect heart face, her sweet smile. Although she hated people thinking so, Kate was sweet everything, and being around her calmed Cassie's restless soul in a way few others could.

On Kate's first night back in Pleasantville they stayed up late, sitting on the floor of the nearly ready Bare Essentials, gorging on pizza and M&M's, going over the plans for their grand opening.

Maybe it was the bottle of wine they shared, or maybe it was simply the sheer delight of seeing each other after too long an absence, but they laughed and talked and listened to music until well past midnight.

Cassie had to give her cousin credit. Kate let Cassie keep the conversation safe. Meaning they talked about Kate. Bare Essentials. And gossiped happily about the people in Pleasantville.

Then the clock struck one and Kate's smile faded as she studied Cassie. "You know I love you, right?"

Ah, hell. "Yep." In case Kate wanted to talk serious, she cranked up the radio to ear-splitting level.

Kate simply lifted that superior brow Cassie was certain had intimidated hundreds of others. "You could tell me anything," she yelled over the music. "You know that."

"I'm fine."

"Yeah." Kate put her hand around her mouth and shouted, "So fine you have purple bruises beneath your eyes." She flicked the radio off. "Delicate ones, of course, because you're the only woman I know who could skip makeup and eat junk food for a week and still look amazing. But I know you, Cassie." She softened her voice and reached for her hand. "Whether you like it or not, I know you're not okay."

"Kate—"

"You haven't asked for your mail." She reached into her purse and came up with a handful of letters. All addressed to her. All from Pete. "You should be giving these to the local authorities."

"The authorities here know about him." Deciding she was done with this conversation, Cassie stood and stretched, and caught sight of a car pulling up out front.

Not just any car, but a police squad car. Damn it.

She tucked Pete's letters into her purse and turned with her hands on her hips as one tall, dark and sinfully fine-looking Sheriff Sean Taggart entered the building with a casual nonchalance that made her every hormone stand up and quiver.

Take what you can, honey, and spit the rest back out. Cassie thought about what Flo would say and had to admit there wasn't much to spit back out when it came to Tag.

Not exactly a comfort.

"Fancy you showing up out here," she drawled slowly though her heart had started racing at just the sight of him. She hadn't seen him since that night at the lake when he'd stripped down and showed her he was one pretty remarkable male specimen. When she'd accused him of only wanting sex. When she'd nearly succumbed to temptation and let herself lean on someone. *Him.*

Kate's head was swiveling as she looked back and forth between the two of them. "I take it you two know each other."

Tag just stared at Cassie, and she sighed. "Kate, meet Sheriff Sean Taggart. The man who single-handedly tripled my car insurance rates."

"Well, then." Kate smiled and held out her hand. "Nice to meet the rare person who can get the best of my cousin." When Tag nodded, then looked back at Cassie, unmistakable trouble in his gaze, Kate grabbed her purse. "Oka-a-ay. I'm thinking now is a good time to get some shut-eye."

"Kate—"

"I have a feeling you're in good hands," she whispered, then hugged Cassie tight before she vanished.

"You scared her off," Cassie accused.

"If she's related to you, she's no more scared of me than she would be of a kitten," Tag said evenly.

"Why are you here?"

"Because of the five complaints logged about the volume of your music."

"I turned it down." She turned her back. "I'll behave now. You can go."

"I'll just wait while you lock up."

"Oh, I'm not leaving yet." She bent to stroke Miss Priss. "I have some stock to go through, and—" She squeaked in surprise when he whipped her around to face him.

"Damn it to hell," he muttered, staring down into her face.

"Damn what to hell?" she asked, pure frost in her voice.

Her shoulders were stiff in Tag's hands, but it had just come to him. The problem he'd been stumbling over since she'd strode into town.

Yeah, he wanted her, just as she'd accused. But he also... *liked* her. More than that, he wanted her to trust him.

She didn't, not even close, but she would. He was suddenly quite determined about that.

"You know what I think?" he asked her softly. "I think your kick-ass demeanor, as well as the job that's made you so famous, is all a front."

She stared at him as if he was crazy. "What?"

"Beneath all that wild sensuality and come-hither smile designed to make grown men beg, you're all talk."

"Excuse me?"

"You just stroked the cat. I saw you."

"So?"

"So you claim to hate that cat. You claim to hate this town, and yet here you still are. Oh, yeah, I'm on to something all right. You're not nearly as untamed and uncaring as you want people to believe, not even close." Sure of himself, he smiled. "In fact, you're just one great big fraud."

She let out a disbelieving laugh. "You have no idea what you're talking about. I'm as out there as they come, just ask anyone."

"Not buying it. You're all talk, Cassie Tremaine Montgomery. All talk."

"You think so?" She grabbed a box off a shelf, tossed it to the floor, then kneeled down to riffle through it. "I'll show you talk." She lifted a set of handcuffs. "I have a set of these in my bedroom. Waiting for the right evening, the right lover."

He nearly swallowed his tongue, and instead lifted a shoulder. "So what? I have a pair on me all day long."

A sound of frustration passed her kissable lips as she tossed the handcuffs over her shoulder and pawed through the box again. With a cry of triumph, she help up a small plastic package holding...

He gulped hard.

"A clit ring," she said. "I have one of these, too."

"Are...you wearing it now?"

Her triumph faded, and with a growl she tossed it over her shoulder to fall next to the discarded handcuffs, leaving him to give a silent thanks because he doubted he could have handled remaining so calm, cool and collected if she'd showed him a clit ring.

On her clit.

Just the thought made him break a sweat.

Cassie dove back into the box, and this time came up with a small white leather pack and a smile that went right to his crotch.

Lord help him, he'd opened Pandora's box.

"Know what this is?" she asked in a sultry voice. "A portable vibrator. For the woman on the go. It fits into a pocket or small purse."

Oh, man. He leaned back against the wall, crossed his arms and forced himself to yawn. She would not goad him into a physical relationship, not when she still believed he wanted her only for sex. Nope. He wouldn't touch her.

At his feigned boredom, she sputtered. "You think I wouldn't use this to make myself come?"

He just lifted a brow.

Still on her knees, she shot him a look of pure daring, which in truth started his heart pumping, even before she lifted her denim skirt, revealing a tiny patch of red satin masquerading as panties. Pulling out the small white vibrator, she turned it on, smiled the very smile of the devil, and ran it over her thigh before settling it directly between her legs.

"Mmm," she whispered, letting her head fall back on her shoulders. Her eyes closed as she slowly moved the vibrator up and down and back again.

Her breath came quicker, and so did his. "Cassie—"

"Shh." Her hips started pumping in tune to her hand.

His own hands fisted.

"God. This is so much better than a fumbling man."

He'd show her fumbling.

"Oh, yeah…" The vibrator hummed. Her hand moved faster.

She moaned softly.

Up and down.

The red satin became wet, he could see it.

And Tag nearly sank to the floor. "Cassie—"

Her mouth fell open, her tongue came out and wet her lips. Her breath caught and she went still, so utterly still… then shuddered as she let out a little helpless cry, lost in her own pleasure.

Tag didn't move a muscle, he couldn't.

After a moment she opened sleepy, sated eyes and smiled. "Definitely much better than a man." With a click she turned off the vibrator and let her skirt fall back down.

Before she could riffle through the box again, his brain started functioning, barely, and he came forward. "Uncle," he said hoarsely, hauling her to her feet. "I get it. You're not all talk. And you're killing me. Lock up, you're going home."

"I suppose you think you're going to tuck me in and sing me a lullaby."

"No. You're going home alone."

"Suit yourself."

No mistaking her anger that he hadn't fallen at her feet in a boneless mass of need, but no one had ever wanted her for anything besides sex, and he refused to fit into the same mold as all the other assholes in her life.

"Got your keys?" he asked calmly, as if he couldn't have hammered steel with his raging erection.

She pocketed the vibrator and shot him a long look, definitely noticing the problem behind his zipper. "I have my keys." She patted the vibrator. "In fact, I have everything I need, thank you very much."

Fine. She was pissed at him, nothing new. But it was satisfying, despite the burning need of his body, to see the shock in her eyes that he wasn't going to try to get into her very wet panties.

And he would hold firm. At least for tonight.

7

WITH KATE IN TOWN to help get Bare Essentials going, Cassie felt free to give in to impulse.

And impulse had her eating whatever she wanted—screw her agent telling her to remain thin—which included a daily sandwich by Diane at the deli. Impulse had her going to the library for more of the books she sucked down every night—and teasing Mrs. Wilkens about her phone sex.

And impulse sent her back to New York for her agent's birthday party bash.

Going back had nothing to do with work. Nothing to do with needing something from her apartment. Or even wanting to see her friends.

Neither did it mean that she missed New York, because actually, surprisingly, she hadn't given it that much thought.

She just needed…out.

And she made no mistake about it, she knew exactly why she needed out. Tag.

She still couldn't believe he'd sent her home alone after she'd teased herself into a feverous pitch in front of him. Granted she hadn't shown as much skin as she had at the lake, when she'd worn nothing *but* skin…but she'd masturbated right in front of him! She knew men, damn it, and knew that watching a woman touch herself was basically nirvana. Heaven on earth. A fantasy come true.

She'd given him that, and still, he'd remained cool as rain. Nearly a week had gone by and she still couldn't believe he hadn't given in to his body's obvious craving.

But he hadn't, at least not in front of her.

Which meant he had far more self-control and restraint than she did, and she had plenty. It startled her, knowing he wasn't the usual puppet on a string. That he had his own mind. Was his own man.

It startled her, and unsettled her. Enough that she told Kate she was going for two days. She needed some action, and New York was where it was at.

Kate wasn't happy, but Cassie easily distracted her, mostly because Kate was busy with other projects such as working at the local theater—the Rialto—not to mention she had her own problems with the sexy Jack Winfield. And he *was* pretty damn sexy, so Cassie could understand the distraction.

In any case, Cassie wasn't worried. She wouldn't be in New York long enough for Pete to track her down. Besides, she had the restraining order. And in the mood she found herself in, she felt invincible.

Or at least, battle ready. *Bring it on, Pete,* she thought testily. *Bring it on.*

Back in the city, she looked up her friends, went to the birthday party, hit a great new dance club afterward, lined up some work for the fall and winter…and by the end of forty-eight hours, was ready to go home.

Home. As in Ohio.

Pleasantville, Ohio. She sat on the plane, staring sightlessly down as the landscape passed her by, wondering when exactly she had started to think of that one-horse, narrow-minded, too small town as her…*home?*

Not good. In the name of distraction, she asked the flight attendant for a deck of cards and tried to occupy herself in a mean game of solitaire, but she kept losing.

By the time she got off the plane, shouldered her carry-on and walked outside, the sun was setting. She put on her sunglasses and looked for Kate, who'd promised to pick her up, and realized she was still carrying the deck of cards.

Maybe she'd get Kate to come over to play a game with her tonight. Then she wouldn't have to stay up late and stare into the mirror above the bed wondering what the hell she was going to do for another long month and a half.

Only there was no sign of Kate. Really, that was no surprise. Cassie had always figured Kate would be late to her own funeral. With a sigh, she found an empty bench and sat, idly shuffling the cards to keep her hands busy.

When a patrol car pulled up, she frowned. Her frown turned to an all-out scowl when Tag rolled down the window. His eyes were hidden behind mirrored sunglasses, his shoulders straining his uniform shirt. Not that she'd admit it to him, but she knew him now, and could read his tension. What had gotten his panties all ruffled?

"Ready?" he asked.

Ready. Maybe that explained the odd tremble in her limbs at the sight of him. "Has hell frozen over?"

His jaw tightened. "You want to be nice to me today, Cassie. I'm in a mood."

"Oh, fine, you're in a mood. Well, just take it on down the road."

"Get in."

"What's the matter? Am I disturbing the peace?"

"Yeah. Mine."

"Kate is going to meet me."

"The arrangements have been changed."

She was going to kill Kate at the first opportunity. "I'd rather walk."

"It's thirty miles and it's going to be dark in five minutes." He sighed. "Let's go."

She would never in a million years be able to explain to anyone, much less herself, why she stood up and got in the squad car.

Without glancing at her again, he put the car in drive and took off. Cassie looked around her with morbid curiosity. "I've never been in one of these before."

"Uh-huh."

She hadn't, but at his sarcastic "Uh-huh" she folded her arms and stared straight ahead. Why had she said that? Why had she just opened her mouth and let something personal like that fly out? She never did that, and she never would again, or she'd cut out her own tongue.

Another rough sigh punctured the air, and his hand went to her thigh. She tensed, but all he did was gently squeeze her. "I'm sorry," he said. "That was uncalled for."

She tossed his hand off her leg. "Whatever."

With a soft oath beneath his breath, he exited the freeway, took a few turns, obviously knowing where he was heading despite the dark, dark night and the fact that there were no streetlights. They ended up on the east side of the lake.

"What are we doing?" she asked.

"Talking."

She stared into his sharp, knowing eyes. "About?"

"You shouldn't have gone to New York this weekend."

"I was in and out. Never saw Pete. He never saw me."

"How can you be sure?"

"I'm sure. Look, he's probably already lost interest."

He shook his head. "It was still foolish. Foolish, danger-ous and *stupid*."

She crossed her arms. "Well, why don't you just tell me how you really feel?"

"Why did you do it?"

"I needed to get away."

"From me?" He seemed too big for the car. His shoulders and chest and arms filled her vision. So did his badge.

She turned and stared out the windshield. "Awfully conceited, aren't you?"

"When are you going to tell me why you're so bitchy when I'm in my uniform?"

"Um, because it's a terrible color on you?"

"Goddamn it, can't you just answer a question?"

She expertly flipped the deck of cards between her fingers. "Sure, when I feel like it."

He got out of the car, came around for her and opened her door.

Cassie looked out over the black water and felt an urge to strip down and swim off all her tension. "You're on duty."

"I left work when I picked you up."

"I want to be alone. I want to go home."

"We're alone here, this is a secluded spot. Please?" He held out a hand.

She stared at that large, work-roughened hand, at his long, well-shaped fingers. If he'd said anything else, if he'd been a jerk and demanded she get out, if he'd just hauled her out himself, she would have been able to tell him to go to hell in a handbasket.

But he'd said please, in that low, husky voice that could charm a nun. Damn him. "I suppose it's hot enough that I could dip my feet in for a few minutes."

"Good. Bring the cards."

"Why?"

His lips curved slightly but he said nothing as she got out

without accepting his help and walked to the empty beach, making sure to walk the walk, to toss her hair, to glance back at him over her shoulder.

Just so he'd remember exactly what he'd turned down the other night. It'd serve him right, she thought, for always so effortlessly making butterflies dance in her belly.

For making her so off balance with just the look in his eyes.

TAG CAUGHT THE WALK. His gaze was pretty much glued to her ass and hips as she swung them all the way down to the water.

He knew she had no plans on letting him get any closer than it took to drive him wild with desire. He understood that, and appreciated the need coursing through him at the sight of her lush body, clad in a hip-hugging, gauzy white skirt and matching sleeveless blouse that was tied beneath her breasts, exposing a good hand span of her midsection.

Added to that dazzling effect was the fact the material gave off the impression of being sheer, that with every movement he was catching peekaboo hints of the soft flesh beneath.

Hell yeah, he wanted her. Badly. But something had happened to him that night she'd accused him of being like every other guy on the planet. Oh, he wanted the sex. He wanted the sex with her. And yet, surprisingly, he wanted more.

And he wanted her to know that. He wanted her to face it, to accept it, because he had the most shocking feeling no one had ever given her more. Ever.

In front of him, she kicked off her shoes and sat on a pile of rocks, watching the water hit the sand. She pulled up her skirt to her knees and leaned back, appearing relaxed and at ease.

Coming up next to her, he took in the gentle rise and fall of her bare stomach as she breathed, and concentrated on matching her calm rhythm. "Remember that night I won that teddy bear for you?"

Still facing the lake, her lips quirked. "I remember."

Hunkering beside her, he studied her beautiful profile. "Do you remember the kiss?"

He was close enough to hear the little catch in her breath as she turned to him. "Is that what you wanted to talk about?"

"No." Sitting, he kicked off his shoes and socks, then took the cards from her hand, shuffled and dealt them each five cards. "Want to play?"

"I'm good," she warned.

"So am I. Poker?"

Her eyes lit with pure trouble. "*Strip* poker?"

"If you'd like."

Her gaze fell to his uniform shirt and she lifted a shoulder noncommittally, but it was enough to decide him. In uniform he made her nervous, not that she'd ever admit it, and he didn't want that barrier between them. "I'd like," he said, and picked up his cards.

"You're going to lose. You'll be buck naked in no time flat, big man."

"If I lose, I'll strip." He lifted his gaze. "And if you lose…"

"I won't lose."

"If you lose…" he repeated, "you have to answer my questions."

"Questions?"

All of which had been met with resistance so far, but he was a patient man. He had this wild, incredible woman alone on the beach with nothing but the water for company, and he was just smart enough to take advantage of it. "You're not afraid of a few questions, are you, Cassie?"

"What about the strip part of the strip poker?"

"If it suits you."

"It's going to suit you." She gestured to her cards. "I'll take two."

"Me, too."

She accepted her cards then fanned them out and showed him a straight. Keeping his gaze locked on hers, he tossed his cards away and peeled off his uniform shirt.

Her eyes flared as his bare chest came into view, and she made no attempt to hide the way she looked him over. "You're in pretty good shape," she murmured. "Considering."

"Considering?"

"Your age."

He barely managed not to sputter. "I'm hardly over the hill at thirty-two."

"Maybe not, but studies *do* prove you are a decade past your prime. But I wouldn't worry too much…" Again her eyes went on a little tour. He wondered if she'd notice he was hard as a rock. "You seem to be holding up. Deal the cards."

Oh, he'd deal. "Holding?" he asked sweetly. He had a full house.

She laughed and slapped down one card. "Hit me once, but don't hold on to your pants, cowboy. It's nearly over for you."

"All talk, Cassie," he said softly, letting out a husky laugh when she shot him a saucy look.

"We already proved I'm not all talk," she reminded him, her voice just as soft. "Or do you need another lesson?"

He dealt her another card and waited while she lifted a sly eyebrow, cocky as hell, so damned beautiful it almost hurt to look at her. "Isn't that something," he murmured.

Distracted with her cards, she didn't look up. "What?"

"You look amazing when you smile for real."

Her smile started to fade and he put a finger to her lips and shook his head. "Don't stop," he whispered. "I'm sorry."

"Don't be sorry," she said, fanning out her cards for him to see. "Just be naked."

She had two pairs. Studying them, he nodded seriously, then exposed his cards.

"Cheater," she said to his full house.

"You know I didn't cheat."

"Yeah. Damn it." A huff escaped her, and she was still shaking her head when she looked into his eyes and brought her fingers up to the knot beneath her breasts. The three buttons came next, leaving the white gauze open but still covering her breasts. "Lucky hand." With a shrug, the material slipped off her shoulders. For a moment she held her hands over her breasts, then dropped them to her lap.

The blouse fell away, and since she wore nothing beneath it but glorious, generous curves, Tag sucked in a careful breath. "You...have to answer a question now."

"I can't believe you're going to stick to that."

"Yeah." Her breasts were white and creamy, standing out in comparison to the rest of her tanned torso. More than anything he wanted to touch. To lean in and nibble. If he kept thinking along those lines, his pants were going to cut off his circulation. "Give me a sec, I'm having a bit of trouble thinking."

Her nipples slowly hardened.

He swallowed hard and forced his gaze above her chin, remembering he'd done this for a reason. "Why do you hate that I'm a cop? Truth."

She looked away. "I'd rather take a dare."

"You going to welsh on me?"

Her eyes flashed hot. "It's no big mystery, really."

"Then tell me."

She wrapped one arm around her bent knees, hunched over—blocking him from the incredible view of her breasts—and started drawing in the sand. "You might remember, I didn't exactly have the most conventional of childhoods."

Not with a mother who'd switched relationships like some

switch shoes. Not with an entire town watching, waiting for her to fall on her face. "I remember."

"You might also remember, my mother was—is—fond of men. We had a lot of them around. For the most part, I hated them all. They were weak and malleable. Led around by their egos. Except one. I thought he was different." Her face hardened. "Turns out he was just like all the other penis-carrying humans. On prom night, he…" She closed her eyes. "He proved it. Asshole."

"And he was a cop?"

"Yeah."

God. Prom night… "Weren't you with Biff?"

Her eyes shuttered and he shook his head. "No, don't clam up, I never believed those stories he's so fond of telling."

"Let's just say Biff wasn't the problem that night."

She'd been seventeen. Underage. Tag's gut twisted. "What exactly happened?"

"Probably nothing as bad as you're thinking. Let's just say we disagreed on what I was willing to put out, so to speak."

"Did he hurt you?"

"No."

Not physically at least. "Cassie."

Another shrug. "You know, to be fair to him, I did have quite the reputation. Being a Tremaine and all. It was no big deal."

She'd been a minor, with someone she'd trusted, when trust had not come easy, and that cop had destroyed that trust. Fury bubbled, but she was looking at him with eyes that dared him to offer sympathy. "We going to play or what?"

Reaching out, he stroked her cheek. "I'm sorry, Cassie."

"Water under the bridge."

"No, it's not."

She let out a little laugh. "I know, a shrink would have a

field day that I still hate a uniform. Sue me." She grabbed the cards, shuffled and started dealing. "Anyway. End of story."

Hell if it was. "Who was it?"

"That's another question, and…" She looked over her cards. "You'll have to win first. Which I don't plan on letting you do." She showed him her three queens. "What do you have?"

A damn pair of twos. He turned his hand to show her.

"Bummer." Her gaze was glued to his body as he stood up and unzipped his pants. When he kicked them off and tossed them to where his shoes, socks and shirt already lay, she grinned. "I have to give it to you, Sheriff. You're a man of your word."

And that appealed to her, he could see that. With his uniform gone, she'd warmed up toward him, in a way that was warming him up, as well.

She'd sat back, resting her weight on her palms behind her. Beneath the glow of the stars, her bare breasts were offered up like a feast. "You're also a man with the most incredible physique." Leaning over, she ran a hand down his chest, swirled it around his belly button, then toyed with the elastic edging of his dark blue knit boxers.

He was already hard. He knew she was trying to seduce him to deflect more questions, and if she hadn't been so incredibly sexy, it might have been infuriating. As it was, he didn't have enough blood left in his brain to be infuriated. "Cassie—"

"My turn for a question," she said softly, her finger just barely under the edge of his shorts. A fraction of an inch more and she'd meet hard, hot flesh. "Ever been in love, Tag?"

It was the last thing he expected her to ask. And with her finger now dipping into his shorts, he could hardly think. "Twice."

Her eyes flickered. *Disappointment?* "Twice?"

"Kelly May Johnson." Oh, yeah, definitely a flicker. Maybe even more.

Interesting, very, very interesting. Enlightened, he took his own finger on a tour, too; ran it up her arm, watching her nipples pebble tighter. "She was so pretty. Dark hair, heart-shaped face, petite little thing." When his fingers ran over one soft shoulder and down her collarbone, she shivered, and slapped his hand away.

"You asked," he reminded her, biting back his grin.

"My mistake."

He brought his finger back to her collarbone and very carefully traced the very top of her breasts. "I was in fifth grade." He laughed when she shot him a look. "She broke my heart at second recess when she left me for Tommy O'Mara."

She grinned. "You were dumped." Her grin went shaky when his finger danced down, down…right between her breasts now.

"And the second?" she asked a bit breathlessly.

He added his other fingers to the one skimming beneath a generous curve over her ribs, his thumb outstretched, just barely caressing the weight of a breast. "I was engaged a while back. Turns out it wasn't love, just temporary lust. It passed."

"I've never been in love," she said, closing her eyes on a sigh at his caress. The rest of her hand slipped beneath the material of his shorts. "I've never mistaken lust for love."

Tag wrapped his hand around her wrist just as she wrapped her fingers around him.

Their gazes met, Tag's admittedly hazy. But he'd just realized something shocking. That no matter what she said, no matter how fierce and cool and wild she acted, she'd never been wanted, craved or needed for anything but the facade she gave people. She'd never been loved for the woman she was on the inside… Cassie Tremaine Montgomery.

Eyes on his, she fisted him. Stroked him. "Oh, yeah," she breathed. "A very nice physique indeed. Are you going to get yours tonight, Tag? Or are you going to just watch me again?"

She wasn't talking making love. She was talking sex. That's how she wanted it, that's all she knew. He understood that now. With sex she could keep it reined in, could control it.

The idea of giving up that tight control terrified her. But she would let go, he was bound and determined about that.

He would show her the way life was supposed to be. That a relationship went two ways. She could give what she wanted, but she would receive, as well. She could allow someone to care for her, even love her. She could share what was on the inside as well as the outside, and she could be safe while doing it.

But then she stroked him again, this time letting her thumb swirl over the very tip of him as she did, and he nearly lost it.

"Good?" she whispered.

He couldn't find his tongue much less use it.

Her other hand dipped into his shorts, too, cupping him, causing him to suck in a hard breath. "Tag? Good?"

"You know it is," he managed.

"I aim to please."

Hmm. She could prove that. Later. But first he had a lot to show her. A whole lot. With a smile, he slid his hands up the backs of her legs to her perfect, edible butt. Gripping a cheek in each palm, he yanked.

With a gasp, she fell flat to her back on the sand. When she went to sit up, he towered over her, still smiling, thrilling to the way she licked her lips a little uncertainly, just before he claimed her mouth with his.

8

WHEN TAG PULLED BACK from her mouth to drag hot, wet, openmouthed kisses down her throat, Cassie watched the stars above his head dance, hardly able to draw a breath.

He continued his exploration, intent but unrushed, which in itself was a new experience for her. Fast, hard, hot sex was pretty much her forte. She had no need, nor yearning, for anything drawn out and complicated. And she especially had no need for morning afters.

Oh, he knew how to use his mouth. And suddenly shortness of breath didn't seem to be her only problem as he worked his way leisurely through her senses, destroying them one by one with terrifying ease.

Somewhere along the way a knot in her belly had developed. It wasn't supposed to be there. This was supposed to be done her way, in her time. "I've...gotta go," she decided, and pushed at him.

Supporting himself on his elbows, still sprawled above her, Tag lifted his head and looked into her eyes. "No more running," he said. "Not from me."

The knot in her belly tightened, but she forced an easy smile. "Surely you don't mean to...here..."

His smile was genuine. And so unsettlingly sexy. "Haven't you ever made love outside before?"

Made love. She swallowed hard. *"Tag—"*

Gently he covered her mouth with his in a kiss that melted her with its sweetness. When he lifted his head, he smiled. "Scared you with that L-word, didn't I?" When she closed her mouth, he cocked his head. "Admit it."

"I'll admit sex is a better term."

"Do you always get your way?"

Now they were bantering, back on familiar ground. She could handle this. "Absolutely. Tag—" Before she could finish, his mouth took hers, and after a moment she forgot what she was going to say. Forgot everything but getting his hands on her again. "Are you going to get to it or what?"

He let out a low laugh, unbearable in its sexiness. "We could." Almost idly, he traced a nipple with the pad of his thumb. She made a small sound, a sound of wanting, desire, and his eyes darkened as he made the motion again. "You're so beautiful, Cassie."

Her heart picked up speed, and was joined by a quickening inside her. The knot in her belly tightened all the more.

Another pass of his thumb over her puckered nipple, and with a low groan, he bent his head, replacing his touch with his tongue.

She nearly died.

She was still trying to recover when he cupped her face in his hands, tipping it up so that she could see nothing but his face, so intent on hers, his eyes shining with promise. He kissed her again, his mouth as firm and hungry as his body, sensual and heated and so deliciously male. Never before had she understood the passion of a kiss, but she was beginning to. It made her knees weak, and she gripped him for support. By the time he lifted his head again, she was dizzy.

"Here." His voice was low, gritty. "Right here."

God knows, there were a million reasons why they shouldn't. And yet, with his hands all over her, with his amazing body on hers, she couldn't remember a single one. "Here," she whispered. "Right here."

The words were barely past her lips before he took her mouth again. Deeper, hotter, then again. And again, yet somehow still leisurely, as if he had all the time in the world. Lowering his head, plumping up her breasts with his hands, he opened his mouth on a pouting nipple, teasing, licking, sucking, and finally nibbling her to a writhing frenzy. Then he turned his mouth to her other side while his hands ran down her body, over her gauzy skirt. "I've been wondering all night what's beneath this," he said hoarsely against her skin.

She opened her mouth twice before she managed to speak. "Why don't you check for yourself?"

With characteristic bluntness, he did just that, then let out a rough groan as he pushed up the material, baring her to her waist. Ran a finger over the edging of her very tiny lace panties. "Pretty." He spread her legs, settling his big body between them. Staring up at her, he dragged the lace aside.

Then bent his head to study what he'd revealed.

Blinking up at the stars, she waited, holding her breath, knowing he was looking at her, open and vulnerable in a way she couldn't remember ever being before. "Did you forget what to do?" she managed to quip. "Because I could—"

He glided a finger over the throbbing spot between her thighs and all words backed up in her throat.

"You could what, Cassie?"

"Um…"

That knowing, talented finger slowly circled, then sank into her before circling again.

Ohmigod. "Uh…"

Another slow, tortuous round of the finger. "You could… use Big Red? Hmm? Your portable vibrator? I don't think so, Cassie. No batteries tonight. Just me."

She didn't miss those batteries one little bit. Arching back, digging her fingers into the sand at her sides, she gritted her teeth to keep from coming. "Are you going to talk all damn night?"

"Maybe," he said with a smile in his voice.

"Just…" She dragged in a breath and spoke through her teeth. "Tell me you have a condom."

"Actually, I have two."

"Thank God," she said fervently.

"But I don't need them yet." He used two fingers now. Around, in, around again, at just the right tempo, as if he knew her body better than she did. He reduced her world to those fingers and the havoc he'd created within her. Oh, yeah, one more time, just one more…but he stopped and dragged a pathetic whimper from her throat.

"Don't worry, you're going to come. Soon as I do what I've been dying to do." He slid off her panties. Used his fingers to spread her open to him. "I'm going to taste you now, Cassie," he whispered against her, and made good on his promise, using his tongue, his lips, his teeth, until she had to bite her lip to keep from screaming.

Then he dragged the most sensitive patch of skin on her entire body into his mouth and suckled her.

She exploded on the spot.

After what might have been a minute, or maybe a year, she blinked the stars above into focus. Managed to lift her head to find him resting his on her belly, watching her closely.

He smiled. "Hey."

"Condom," she demanded.

He laughed and surged up to his knees, pulling one out of the pocket of his pants.

Pushing him to the sand, she grabbed the packet from him and opened it with her teeth. Spitting out the foil corner, she concentrated on her task, sucking in a breath at the feel of him, all hard, velvety steel in her hands. "Mmm, much better than Big Red."

"Cassie," he said in a voice that sounded a little strangled, and she looked into his face. His jaw was tight, his eyes hot, and as she watched, slowly stroking him, he let his head fall back on his shoulders and groaned.

Oh, yeah, power was good, she thought greedily. Bending over him, letting her hair fall across his heated flesh, she kissed the very tip of his penis, eliciting another tortured groan from his lips. Suddenly she found the value of taking her time, and she smiled as she slowly, slowly, rolled the condom down his length.

"You know exactly how badly you're killing me, right?"

"Uh-huh."

Tag, being who he was, managed to let out a tight smile. "I'll get you back for this."

"Promises, promises." Finished, she sat back and let her hands skim over her own body. "Come inside me."

All humor faded from Tag's expression to be replaced with a sheer heat and need that made her tremble anew. Running his hands up her thighs, he held them open, made a place for himself between them, and thrust home.

She cried out, she couldn't help it. She'd never felt so heated, so high, so filled. One stroke and she nearly came. Two strokes, and she did, with another helpless cry as her body became one endless wave of exalted bliss while he continued to move. Then she heard the rough groan torn from

Tag as he came, too, and realized he was trembling, breathing as harshly as she was.

Well, she'd wanted fast, she'd wanted reckless. She'd wanted it over so she could get on with her life.

Only as she blinked the stars above her into focus, as she felt Tag's warm, strong arms surround her, as she felt his mouth nuzzle at the spot beneath her ear, she thought maybe the joke was on her.

Because she didn't feel finished with him yet. The thought made her shiver.

With a sigh, Tag got up.

"What—" The words ended on a gasp as he scooped her into his arms.

"I want a bed," he said, then looked down into her eyes. "With you in it."

"Do I have a choice?"

"Sure. Yours or mine."

SHE CHOSE HERS. It was a matter of control, and in her own space, she thought she had it.

A mistake, a crucial one. Because she was beginning to understand that with Tag, control was up for grabs. She didn't like it, would strategize about it in depth.

Later.

God, he had a mouth. A beautiful, glorious mouth that she couldn't get enough of. It would be humiliating, if he didn't apparently feel the same way. The drive to her house was punctuated by fumbling hands trying to feel more flesh. Stolen kisses. By the time they got there, they stumbled out of the car and made it just inside before he backed her up against the front door.

"Here?" she whispered breathlessly.

"Maybe. Yes." He sucked her lower lip into his mouth.

"I can't get enough of you." In the next instant he deepened the kiss, sliding his tongue along hers as he rocked his hips to match her needy thrusts. "It's only been twenty minutes, how can I want you again like this?"

"It's crazy," she agreed, her mouth busy taking tiny bites out of his neck. "We should just stop." Only half kidding, she pulled back. "Just walk away."

"Hell, no." His voice was rough. So were his hands as he ran them up her arms, holding them over her head against the door. "You want me. Say it."

"I never say it."

His eyes glittered as he ran one hand down her body, skimming his fingers beneath the lace of her panties. And found her drenched. "You want me. Your body is saying it for you."

Before she knew it he had her panties off and his pants open. Getting the last condom on was trickier, but he managed just fine. And then he was sinking into her wet heat, making the breath sob in her throat as he filled her as no one else ever had. "Tag…"

"Wrap your legs around my waist. Yeah…there…*there,* like that." Using the door as leverage, he started to move inside her.

Cassie could have sworn she saw stars again as he thrust into her. She couldn't understand the way she needed him more than her next breath, but she did. When he lifted his head to kiss her again, mating with her mouth the way he was with her body, she started to shudder. Within seconds he matched her, barely holding them upright as he found his own release.

"Damn," he finally breathed, and put his mouth to her throat, nuzzling gently. "You okay?"

She realized she was clinging to him, still humming, still pulsing, and not ready to let go. That horrified her enough to force herself to do exactly that.

Slowly, almost reluctantly, she thought, he let her slide down his body until her feet touched the floor. "I guess there's no need to show you to my bed," she quipped, turning away.

With a hand on her arm, he pulled her back, looked deep into her eyes, making her shiver, making her thighs quiver, making the knot tighten in her belly. "Guess again."

MUCH, MUCH LATER, Tag opened his eyes and stared up at himself in the mirror above Cassie's bed. Flat on his back, he had Cassie facedown, sprawled over the top of him. He had a fistful of her very nice ass in one hand, the other stroking her hair.

Next to the bed, on the floor, was the teddy bear he'd won for her at the carnival.

She'd kept it. He wasn't sure what that meant or why it made him want her again.

But moving seemed impossible. His bones had liquefied since they'd spent the past hour tasting every square inch of each other's bodies. "I consider myself pretty contemporary," he said, watching his hands dance over Cassie's gorgeous body. "But that mirror is rather…startling."

She sat straight up and looked at him from sleepy eyes. "Yeah." She got out of the bed, pointedly looked at the clock, then strode naked across the room to the bathroom and shut the door.

"Gee, Tag, think that was a hint?" he asked his reflection, who smirked.

Oh, definitely, Cassie had gotten what she wanted out of him, and now she was ready for him to go. But was that because she truly was done with him? Or because she was uncomfortable with the intimacy that sleeping over entailed?

With a sigh and a groan, he stood. His legs wobbled with the aftermath of great sex. Staggering a bit, he walked across the room and knocked on the bathroom door. "Cassie? You okay?"

"Why wouldn't I be?"

Well…good question. He himself was feeling pretty damn fine. He leaned against the dresser and pondered this, idly running his gaze over an open book. A diary, it seemed, and before he could stop himself, he read the entry.

1. Drive a fancy car, preferably sunshine-yellow because that's a good color for me.
2. Get the sheriff—somehow, some way, but make it good.
3. Live in the biggest house on Lilac Hill.
4. Open a porn shop—Kate's idea, but it's a good one.
5. Become someone. Note: this should have been number one.

A quick glance at the date explained most of the above— she'd written it ten years ago. Still, far more disturbed than he would have liked to admit, he closed his eyes.

The sound of the book slamming shut had his eyes whipping open again.

"Learn anything?" Cassie asked, still naked. As if she didn't have a care in the world, she strutted that mouthwatering body to the closet, from which she extracted a shocking-pink silk robe and covered herself.

"You've just about got your list handled," he noted, casual as she. "And I've got to give it to you, the yellow car is most definitely a good color for you."

"And let's not forget the house on Lilac Hill."

"Let's not. Interesting goals. But it's the second one that intrigues me most."

"Ah, yes," she said with a little smile. "'Get the sheriff.'"

"Well, you did that, didn't you?"

She was good, but he knew her now, or he was beginning to, and he imagined he saw a flinch in those eyes.

"Oh, yes," she agreed, cool as she pleased. "I definitely did him."

Wasn't she amusing? "So now what?"

"Well, I don't know about you, but I'm going to sleep pretty good."

"Alone?"

She turned away. "Always."

Always. Didn't surprise him. What did was the hurt he felt. "Don't judge me by all the other men in your life, Cassie."

She crossed her arms and arched a brow so high it vanished into her hair. "Meaning?"

"Meaning we're not all scum."

"I don't think you're scum."

"But you don't think I'm good enough to share yourself with."

"I shared."

"Your body," he agreed. "There's more."

"No."

"You know, if you keep harboring your emotions like a miser, it's going to be a lonely life."

"Good night, Sheriff."

"That's it? No talking about it?" He heard his own anger and frustration but didn't care.

"No talking about it."

He nodded. Dressed. Walked to the bedroom door. "Lock up after me." When she didn't respond, he said, *"Cassie."*

"Yeah, fine. I'll lock up after you."

She waited until she heard the front door shut before she went down and bolted it. And only then did she let herself sink into a chair and cover her face.

The damn list. He'd read it, believed she'd slept with him

because of it, and the ironic thing was, she'd finally hurt him the way she'd wanted to in the beginning.

But somehow, somewhere, things had changed. She didn't want him hurt, she just wanted him...to not hurt her.

He didn't know the truth, didn't understand, and he never would.

She couldn't tell him.

How could she? How could she explain she'd made that list the night of her prom, when she'd been little more than a frightened teenager, coming home so destroyed, so determined to leave this town and to come back only for revenge?

How could she tell him the catalyst for that entire event had been his own father?

Simple.

She couldn't.

IT WAS A LIFELONG HABIT of Cassie's that when she felt troubled, she went looking for more. Trouble, that is.

Nothing much had changed in that department. By ten o'clock the next morning she was on the lookout for a good diversion. Not easy to find in a small town, but she hadn't been a wild child for nothing.

By noon she'd recruited Kate, who loved her idea for a "pre" show of the store. A private party, much along the lines of say...a Tupperware party.

Except instead of kitchenware, they'd have it with naughty lingerie and toys.

Always enthusiastic, Kate came up with a list of women to invite, which included—among others— Annie, Daisy and Diane. Cassie came up with...Stacie. She actually didn't expect Stacie to be interested, but by the next night, despite the hastily thrown together party, her neighbor came an hour early, flushed with excitement, waving her checkbook.

Diane was right behind her, grinning from ear to ear. "Hey, babe, let us in."

"You're...early," Cassie said, blocking their way. She couldn't let them in yet, she had a ton to do.

"We came to help." Stacie craned her neck, trying to see around Cassie. "Come on, let us in."

But she wasn't ready. And she didn't need help. She never needed help. Besides Kate would be here any second now, and—

"Don't make us beg," Stacie said. "We want to help."

"Ah, jeez. Okay."

"You know, normally Will pales when I go shopping," Diane said about her husband as she gently pushed Cassie aside so they could enter the store. "But I told him I think you're selling naughty stuff and he got all excited. He actually told me to go for broke." The redheaded thirtysomething grinned like a newlywed, making Cassie actually...*yearn?*

That made no sense, she never coveted what other women had, especially when it came to marriage. Being stuck with the same man every night for the rest of her life, cooking his meals, folding his clothes?

No, thank you.

And yet...she couldn't help but wonder. What would it be like to have a man on your side, forever? For a moment she closed her eyes and tried to picture it. The image she came up with was a potbellied man with a cigar hanging out of his mouth and a remote control in his hand as he lay on the sofa shouting out orders for her to follow.

Pass.

Then the image faded and was replaced with the tall, dark, unbearably sexy Tag. No potbelly. No cigar. Nothing but hot eyes and a hot body, and a voice that assured her she was the only woman on the planet.

Ha! As if that would ever happen. Not after the other night, when he'd misunderstood why she'd had sex with him. When she'd let him misunderstand.

"Oh, Cassie..." Stacie grinned as she looked around. "This is wonderful."

"Oh, yeah, it is," Diane said. And before Cassie knew it, all the work was done. In half the time.

It allowed her mind to wander. Right to Tag. She'd been feeling a little raw ever since he'd left her bed, so she'd been careful to keep her car under the speed limit. She hadn't answered her phone. She'd hidden out in the store with the shades drawn while working.

That Tag hadn't found a way past those barriers only made them all the more important.

And now the shop was filling with women. Young, old, in between—including Mrs. Wilkens!—all curious about the famed Kate and Cassie, and even more curious about Bare Essentials.

But it was the oddest thing...from the moment she'd opened the door to Diane and Stacie, to passing out wine and laughing as the women got a charge out of ordering the most outrageous things of their lives, Cassie never felt one ounce of animosity from any of them.

Not a single one.

Was it really possible Pleasantville had urbanized? Accepted change? Grown up? Well, at least some of it had.

"I think we were a hit," Kate said in disbelief hours later as they cleaned up. "Do you have any idea how much money we made tonight?"

Cassie shook her head, still in shock. "They like us, Kate. They really like us."

"Yeah. We're going to make it, aren't we?"

Cassie looked into Kate's eyes and realized her cousin had been just as unsettled about being in town as she herself had been. "A Tremaine woman always lands on her feet. You know that."

"Sometimes it's a long fall first."

"You deserve this, Kate."

"So do you. I love you, Cassie."

Cassie hated getting sentimental, but she'd never been able to refuse Kate. "I love you, too."

And later, when she left the shop long after Kate had, walking slowly to her car lost in thought, she was *still* marveling at the entire evening.

Until a movement in the shadows on the other side of the parking lot made her glance over.

Her heart stopped.

Her everything stopped.

She could have sworn she'd just seen Pete standing there against the building, staring at her from behind the cloud of his cigarette. But that was impossible. She'd called her agent just that morning and had been told Pete was thought to have gone to L.A. and was probably working under an alias.

Still… She quickly slipped into her car, locked the doors, and took off out of the parking lot, craning her neck to see behind her, but she didn't see him again.

Real or Memorex? She had no idea, and though she wasn't the hysterical type, she drove past her house and headed straight toward Kate's. Her cousin would gladly spare a couch, no problem.

Yet she drove past Kate's, too.

And ten minutes later found herself in front of one certain Sheriff Sean Taggart's house.

9

THOUGH IT WAS WELL PAST midnight, Tag heard the car. He had an ear for such things, and even before his mind dispatched the information on the make and model, his body knew.

He had a feeling his body would always know.

She couldn't see him. On the hammock between two trees in the vast acreage of his front yard, his still nearly full beer balanced on his chest, Tag didn't turn his head to look, but just stayed where he was, studying the night passing him by.

Cassie stayed where she was, too, running the Porsche for a long time, and with each moment that passed, Tag just concentrated on the beauty around him.

He wanted her to go away.

He wanted her to find him.

And then she shut off the engine. Got out of her car. He heard the click-clicking of her heels as she sauntered up his walk toward his porch and wondered what she was wearing to go with those heels.

A sexy little sundress designed to destroy his brain cells?

Skintight, hip-hugging jeans riding so low he'd wonder about the laws of gravity?

He wouldn't look. Why torture himself? It wasn't as if she'd let him have her again. Nope, she'd crossed him right off her list and out of her life.

And he was so fine with that. Hell, he had a list of his own. And she was most definitely not even on it. She wasn't sweet, or even especially kind. She would never put his needs first.

She wasn't ever going to love him, not the way he wanted to be loved.

She knocked on his front door. No soft, timid knock for this woman. Despite the late hour and the fact there were no lights on in the house, she rapped her knuckles against the wood with authority.

"What if I'd been sleeping?" he asked lazily, and let out a not-so-nice smile when she shrieked in surprise.

"Tag...you scared me half to death," she breathed, stepping off the porch, probably sinking her heels into his grass as she came toward him. "What are you doing out here?"

"Well, now, that's my question to you." He didn't get up, didn't even look at her, just kept his head tipped back, staring at the night sky.

"Yeah." She let out a breath, and in it he heard everything he'd heard in her voice. Nerves. Loneliness. Fear.

And damn it, it was that last that got to him. With a sigh he left the hammock and took his first good look at her since that late, late night in her bedroom when she'd reminded him why he should have stayed away from her in the first place. She was wearing silky-looking pants that were indeed doing the gravity-defying, hip-hugging thing. A matching blouse with cutouts teased him with glimpses of her skin. She looked like a million bucks, and if he hadn't known about her humble beginnings, he'd never believe it.

But it was the expression she wore that stabbed right through his resentment in a heartbeat. "What's the matter? Something's happened."

"Oh." She lifted a shoulder. "I was just out for a drive."

Uh-huh. "You're scared."

"Are you kidding?" She let out a laugh and lifted her hair off her neck, tipping her head back and closing her eyes. "I just wanted a piece of the night. It seems cooler here at your house. Do you have anything to drink?"

So they were going to play it that way. Fine. He handed her his still-cold beer. Lifting it in a toast, she tipped her head back and drank. Licking her lips, she looked him over, from his bare chest to his loose sweat bottoms, to his bare feet. "Having trouble sleeping?"

Hell, yes. "No."

"Miss me?"

Hell, yes. "No."

"Why, Sheriff, you lie nearly as good as I do." Setting down the drink, she reached out and ran a finger over his shoulder, down a pec. "Wonder if letting off a little steam might help the both of us."

"Is that what you're doing?" he asked as her finger trailed down his bare belly and toyed with the string of his sweats. "Letting off steam?"

"You have a problem with that?"

His body sure as hell didn't. He'd gone hard at just the sound of her voice. "If that's all it is."

"What else would it be?"

He took another good long look at her. She'd hidden the emotions he'd sensed when she'd first arrived. She was good at that. "I don't know. Maybe you came for...comfort." It'd been just a guess, but he would have sworn she'd flinched.

"I don't need comfort from a man. Never have."

"That's a shame," he said, sucking in a breath when her fingers skimmed up his ribs, danced over a nipple. "You're trying to seduce me."

"Is it working?"

While he pretended to ponder, she glanced at him. Just once, nonchalantly. But it dissipated the sensual haze she always put him in. She *was* scared. She *had* come to him for comfort. He could see right through her, damn it. Did she really think he couldn't?

Whatever she thought, she wanted to keep it to herself. And would try to do so unless he could pry it out of her. "Come inside," he said. She wouldn't talk to him, not now, not yet, not when she was so keyed up.

And hell, he wasn't above letting her blow off steam first, especially if that meant letting her have her way with his body. There were some sacrifices worth the trouble.

Being with her would be one of them.

Silently they entered the dark house. Taking her hand, he led her up the stairs to his bedroom. His bed was huge and unmade, and she walked over to it, dropped her purse to the floor and stared down at his tossed sheets as she unbuttoned her blouse. "I thought of you these past few days," she said.

He nearly did a double take. Had she just…opened up?

"I found myself looking for you as I drove around."

Had she just…said something sweet? Couldn't be. "Probably trying to avoid getting another ticket."

"No." She let the blouse fall to the floor while he soaked up her incredible body. "About that list, Tag…I wrote it a very long time ago."

"I know."

"I didn't even see it again until Kate mailed me my diary a few weeks ago. And while I should admit that after that first ticket, I did briefly fantasize about using you to cross that item off, I never gave it serious thought. I didn't have sex with you because of it." Now she turned and looked at him, the soft truth in her eyes.

And suddenly his throat was thick. She *was* sweet. She *was* kind. "Cassie..."

"I brought you something." In her sheer demibra and silk pants she bent, opened her purse and pulled out a small bottle. "From Bare Essentials. The best body massage oil made." She untied her pants and they puddled at her feet, revealing matching panties. She stepped clear, a vision in sheer lace and high heels. "I've had the stuff in my purse for a week now. I...thought I'd give you a massage."

She was trying to give, in a way he instinctively knew she'd never given to a man before. And while he wanted to demand to know what had scared her, what had caused her to show him a side of her she'd never shown before, he knew better than to push. In her own time, he thought, and moved close. Cupping her jaw, he brought her face up for a kiss that ignited in less than two seconds.

Until she pushed him away. "If you keep that up, you'll miss out on your massage."

"You don't have to—"

"Lie down." She softened. "Please?"

He did as she asked, spreading himself out on his stomach on the bed. He groaned when she straddled him, sliding her long, long legs to his, bending over him so that her breasts teased his back. "Relax now," she whispered into his ear, and then she straightened.

The next thing he felt were her hands, slick with the oil, running over his back, his shoulders, his arms, and he groaned again. Her fingers were magic, alternately strong and soft, digging into his knots, easing them out of his body with attentive care.

When he was the consistency of a wet noodle, she got up. He nearly groaned his protest until he felt her stripping off his bottoms, leaving him bare-butt naked, sprawled on the bed. Then her fingers returned to his body, digging into the muscles of his legs and his feet, then up to his back once again. "Good?"

"Mmm—*hey*—" he yelped when she bit his butt.

"Turn over. I'll do your front."

Oh, yeah, he wanted her to do his front. One area specifically; the area currently digging into his mattress like a steel rod. But first... He kneeled up, grabbed her around the waist and tumbled her down to the bed.

Flat on her back, her body automatically cradling his, she laughed up at him. "We're done with the massage, I take it?"

"We're done with mine." With that, he flipped her over, facedown on the bed. With a smile, he looked at her delicious rear end wriggling as she tried to free herself. Her very sheer panties were riding up, and he took a moment to enjoy the view. "Relax," he whispered into her ear as she'd done to him, letting her feel the length of his body over hers. He lifted up, ran a finger from the back of her neck down her back to the base of her spine, then traced the line of her mouthwatering butt as far as he could. "It's your turn."

"You don't have to—"

"Hush." He stroked the part of her that was already wet for him, just once, and she moaned and arched her hips. So he did it again, outlining her through her panties, keeping up the rhythm she set with her rocking hips. Bending over her, he put his mouth to the very base of her spine and licked her.

With a gasp, she tightened her legs around his hand, as if to make sure he didn't stop. But he had no intentions of stopping, and showed her with his fingers as he continued to stroke in tune with her pumping hips. Faster now, and as he licked and kissed and nibbled his way over a perfect, luscious cheek, she panted and strained, looking so erotic there facedown on the bed he nearly couldn't stand it. He wanted her to come, had to see her come, so he slipped his fingers beneath the panties.

Gripping the sheets in her fists, she whimpered for more. He gave it to her, nudging her over the edge when he sank his fingers into her wet heat.

She came in long shudders.

He'd never seen anything so arousing, and as he slowly brought her down, still stroking her ever so lightly now, still nibbling on her body, he wanted more for her.

When she would have gotten up, or at least turned over, he held her still. "Hold on." Straddling her hips with his legs, he unhooked her bra, letting the straps slip to her sides.

"What are you doing?"

"Giving you a massage."

"But...what about you?"

"You did me already."

"I mean your orgasm."

"Oh, I'll get mine." He poured some oil down the middle of her back, loving the look of it on her skin. "Hasn't anyone ever done this for you?"

"Given me a massage that I haven't paid for?" She buried her face so he couldn't see her expression. "No," she said finally, tenser than he would have liked.

Well, he could fix that. "Come on, relax a little," he coaxed, and ran his fingers down her slim back.

She shivered, but didn't say another word.

"Breathe," he urged when he saw that she was holding her breath. "Come on, deep, long breaths."

Her neck had hard knots that dissipated the last of his frustration at her. Poor baby. What had made her so incredibly tense? The same thing that had driven her here?

Or was it him? He found he didn't like either possibility. Her shoulders were even worse, and he spent long, long moments rubbing her down, firmly, then more gently kneading until the knots were gone. Her skin was so creamy, so silky soft, the pleasure was all his, for he'd wanted his hands on her like this again. As he rubbed and stroked, she was utterly silent, but she was breathing deeply now, slowly, and he could tell she'd decided to relax.

Trust. Had she finally given it over to him? For this moment, at least, and feeling the sweet taste of victory, he got off her, pulled off her panties, and poured more oil into his hands. Then he started on her endless legs. He was a little surprised at how fast she'd given herself over to him, having expected her to protest again by now.

Glad she hadn't, he spend some time on her feet, then made his way up her legs. When he traced his fingers along her perfect and gratifyingly bare bottom, she didn't move. He shifted to her side, pulled the blanket away from her face and…let out a little laugh. He'd done his job all right. He'd relaxed her.

Right into a coma.

CASSIE WOKE WITH the sun streaming in on her face and sat straight up with a gasp. Looking down at herself, her nightmare was confirmed—she was as naked as the day she'd been born. Scented with her own Bare Essentials oil.

In Tag's bed!

Good God, she'd fallen asleep with his hands on her and had slept the entire night through, as if she didn't have a care in the world.

The bathroom door opened and Tag strolled out, fully dressed for work. Well, if that didn't just top the cake for her. Nope, nothing like a uniform first thing in the morning to rev her gut into gear.

Looking as if he didn't have a damn care in the world, either, he smiled at her. "Hey. Morning. There's food in the fridge. Help yourself, okay?"

Speechless, she could only gape when he leaned in and kissed her cheek, smelling like soap, like man, like an incredibly sexy man.

His gaze ran over her very bare form, heated and flared, but he didn't so much as touch her. "Have a good day."

"You…I…" Shaking her head, she ran her hands over her face.

"Not a morning person, huh?" He tsked in sympathy. "I'll start the coffee on my way out."

He got to the door before she found her tongue. "You let me sleep."

"That's what people do at night, Cassie."

"But…you made me come," she blurted. "I didn't make you come back."

"Hmm." He rubbed his jaw. "I guess you owe me."

"I don't want to owe you!"

He lifted a shoulder. "Okay." With a shake of his head, he went through the door. "I'll make that coffee with double caffeine, okay? Try not to see or to talk to anyone before you drink the entire pot."

While she sputtered, he laughed and shut the bedroom door. A few moments later she heard the front door shut, as well, and then his car started.

He'd left her! He'd left her naked in his bed, without so much as a single sign of his anger about last night. He hadn't even looked disappointed. Or frustrated.

She looked down at her body. It still looked pretty damn fine if she said so herself, so it wasn't that. And it wasn't as if he hadn't been interested. She knew an interested penis when she saw one, thank you very much. He'd looked down at her slick, sleek form and gotten aroused.

So why had he seemed nothing but amused by the entire fiasco?

In her world, she knew men. She understood them. Knew what made them tick. As they weren't a particularly complicated species, it wasn't a difficult task.

But she didn't understand Tag, not one little bit.

She hated that.

TAG COULD LIST about a million things he'd rather be doing on his lunch hour than driving all the way out to see his father.

Actually, the most he could think of was *one*.

Cassie. The look of utter disbelief on her face as he'd left her sputtering and rumpled and heart-wrenchingly confused in his bed had brought quite a few emotions out in him.

He'd wanted to stay in bed with her. Had wanted to wake her in the most interesting and erotic of ways. Had wanted to love her senseless, into that same trusting stupor he'd had her in last night.

And then demand to know what was wrong.

A fantasy, of course. Cassie wasn't ready for that. And truthfully, he wasn't sure if he was, either. To take that step would be to bring them closer than just physically. It would imply some sort of a relationship, an emotionally based one.

His next emotionally based relationship was going to be permanent, and he still had his specific vision of what his soul mate would be like.

Just because he'd seen a softer, sweeter side of Cassie did not mean she could cut it, and he knew it.

But damn, she was sexy and arousing and beautiful as hell. Good thing he knew that that alone would never be enough for him. Never.

Grimacing, he made the turnoff to the cabin his father had purchased for himself upon his retirement. It was out in the middle of nowhere, on a windy, remote lake with a rutted road, and Tag swore the entire mile-long driveway.

When he got out of the car, the heat sucked the soul right out of him. Or maybe that was the impending visit he'd been commanded to make. He braced himself for the usual stilted conversation over Tag's lackadaisical sheriffing style compared to his father's tight, unbending one. He'd hear once again what a sorry disappointment he was as a son.

"'Bout time," his father grumbled when Tag knocked. "I could have died waiting for you to drive me to the doctor's office."

"What are you talking about?"

"I fell, Sherlock. Now help me into your car."

Tag glanced down where his father gestured and saw his bare foot. Saw the bucket of ice he'd had it in. Saw the swelling and severe discoloration around the ankle and heel.

"I think it's broken."

Tag stared at his father as he moved in to help support his weight with his own. "Why are you even on it?"

"I had to get the door."

Tag knew he should have felt a wave of sympathy, but he felt only anger. "You mean you waited hours for me to get here instead of calling an ambulance, or better yet, telling me you needed me to hurry? Jesus, Dad." With sheer disbelief, he half carried, half supported his father on their awkward walk to the car. "I can't believe you. How did this happen?"

"I slipped getting out of the boat."

"You could have hit your head."

"I could have drowned. I could have choked on the fish I ate last night, too. It's just an ankle. Now let's see if you can get me to the doctor in a timely fashion."

Tag shook his head and went back for the ice, feeling only

slightly chagrined when his father sucked in a harsh breath as he applied it to the injury. "Stubborn to the end, aren't you?"

"How about you? It takes a near fatal accident to get you out here to see me."

"You wouldn't have died. You're too ornery for that."

His father looked proud of that assessment. "How's town?"

"Behaving," Tag said, getting ready for an argument. They always had one when it came to work.

"Then Cassie Tremaine Montgomery must have left."

"Actually, no."

"Humph." His father leaned his head back and, looking a bit pale, closed his eyes. "Christ, was her mother something. She knew how to screw a man and scramble his brains at the same time."

Tag's heart stopped, then started again with an unnaturally heavy beat. "You dated Cassie's mother?"

"Dated? No."

"You…slept with her?"

"Just like every other man in town. But she was so good, I never cared. She had a way, that woman, of making you feel like the only man on earth. Now her daughter, Cassie…born with claws, that one."

Tag's fingers held the steering wheel so tight he was amazed he could steer the car. "What do you mean?"

"Let's just say she wasn't as friendly as her mother."

Tag got off the freeway, pulled into the hospital parking lot, turned off his car and faced his father, all without reaching over and shaking the life right out of him. "It was you."

"It was me what?"

"The night of her prom. You came on to her. In uniform, no less." He fisted his hands on the wheel instead of his father's face. "What did you do, force yourself on her?"

"Hold it right there, goddamn you." His father grabbed

the front of Tag's shirt. "I'm no rapist, and no son of mine is going to imply so."

Tag shoved him back then got out of the car, leaning against the hood. God. No wonder Cassie could hardly stand the sight of him in uniform. No wonder she was so reluctant to let him inside her.

But why the hell hadn't she told him the truth?

Back to the trust thing, he supposed, feeling incredibly bone-weary. And sad. So very, very sad. Not for himself, but for one hauntingly beautiful, tough-as-hell, seventeen-year-old Cassie.

"Hey, so maybe I let her get to me a little," his father said behind him, holding on to the open door for support. "She was wearing a dress that... *Lord.* Anyway, she put off vibes that told every man out there she was available, but when you came within five feet of her she burned you. Devil woman to the very core, that one."

Sick, Tag shook his head. Waved to an emergency room attendant.

"Aren't you taking me in?"

The only place Tag wanted to take his father was straight to hell. He came around and looked him right in the eyes. "I want you to listen to me very carefully. Cassie Tremaine Montgomery is back in town. I don't know for how long, but she's here. She's welcome. And if you so much as look at her, I'm going to make you wish you hadn't." He waited to make sure that sank in. All he'd ever wanted from this man was to know he'd made him proud, but even that small scrap of affection had been too much for his father to handle.

And suddenly Tag let go of it. He no longer needed it. He

no longer needed anything from his father at all. Knowing that, he turned away.

And figured he'd just learned the one thing that could possibly convince him Cassie would never be able to trust him.

10

AFTER WAKING UP in Tag's bed, Cassie's entire day was slightly off. She ran out of gas. Was rudely stared at by some old biddies at the Rose Café—which reminded her of what Tag had said about this not being Mayberry. She ran out of cat food, and in the grocery store was frowned at by the checkout clerk, then followed to the car by another one, who wanted to know what hours Bare Essentials would be open, because she couldn't wait to get inside and spend money.

Contradictions. Her life was full of them.

In the post office, no one even looked her way, making her quite suddenly realize that not everyone in town was talking about her or staring at her. Which brought her to another shocking thought. Was the entire attitude she sensed here in Pleasantville simply a reflection of her own attitude about the town?

She would have dwelled on that more but had picked up her forwarded mail from the agent and found two more letters from Pete. All of her preoccupation with the inhabitants of Pleasantville flew out the window at this startling reminder that at least one person was dangerously obsessed with her.

At least the return address was Los Angeles, far from Pleasantville, Ohio.

True to form when faced with something that scared her, she refused to think about any of it. She spent the day at Bare Essentials, arranging and rearranging stock on the new shelves and walls, getting more stock delivered by a grinning Daisy, who admitted to wearing crotchless panties—courtesy of Bare Essentials—beneath her uniform. Maybe Daisy wasn't quite as sweet as she appeared to be.

While Cassie and Kate worked, they laughed and talked, and laughed some more, reveling in spending so much time together for the first time since high school. Their laborious efforts seeming a lot more like fun than revenge.

The fun took a downturn when Kate threw her a knowing glance and brought up the subject of Tag.

"You do remember the sheriff, right?" Kate asked, tongue in cheek. She was hanging silk robes according to size on a wooden rack. "The man who's given you three tickets. The man more gorgeous than sin itself. The man who whenever I bring him up you go slightly bipolar?"

"He has that effect on people."

"No, he has that effect on you. And I think you have that effect on him, as well. You going to do something about it?"

"Such as?"

"Such as...I don't know..." Kate opened another box and pulled out more padded hangers. "At least burn up a box of condoms together."

Cassie, who'd just taken an unfortunate sip of soda, choked.

Kate spun around, then laughed. "You liked that one?"

Cassie wiped her chin. "You never used to say such things. What's come over you?"

"We're talking about *you*. And the sheriff. I guess, judging by your reaction, I should have said *second* box of condoms, huh?"

"Kate. Please." She sniffed, acting insulted because she

didn't want to get into this, not when last night was stamped so indelibly in her mind. "We all know I never go back for seconds."

"Yes, but we both know he's different. You're different."

"It's not like that." Scowling, Cassie stared down at the shipment of thigh-high stockings she'd been folding. "I have no idea why we're even wasting our breath talking about it."

Kate put down the hangers and came to Cassie. Took her hands, looked deep into her eyes, which Cassie hated because Kate seemed to see all when it came to her. "We're talking about it because I'm worried about you. I think Pete is a loose cannon, and I like knowing there's someone here who cares about you after I leave. I like knowing you care about him back."

"I don't care about men."

"I know." Kate squeezed her shoulders. "And for the most part, I agree with you. They're scum. But Tag is not, and I think you know it. I think you're scared of that very fact."

"Look, you won't even admit you have a thing for that sexy Jack. You know, the guy who helped you with Flo's furniture. The one you got caught parking with while I was in New York. The two of you are sniffing around each other like crazy. So you tell me who's running scared here."

Kate tightened her lips and went back to hanging silk robes. "I don't know what you're talking about."

"Uh-huh."

Kate placed three more robes in the display, moving very carefully, very purposely, as she always did when she was annoyed. She shot a look at Cassie.

Cassie just lifted a daring brow.

Kate twisted her lips, holding back a smile.

Cassie didn't bother holding hers back, and suddenly they

were both laughing. "We're pathetic," Kate said when she could.

"Yeah. But at least we know it."

They left out the deeply personal stuff after that.

And later, when Cassie went home—where she showered and decided to hell with getting dressed again, to hell with anything remotely related to beauty—she tried to relax.

Which is how she ended up on her couch with a half gallon of double-fudge chocolate ice cream and a spoon, wearing a large, shapeless T-shirt over equally large and baggy sweat bottoms, looking like a fashion don't.

Comfort clothes and comfort food were heaven on earth, she thought, shoving in another mouthful as she sat on the couch with the remote, changing channels at the flick of her attention span.

"Meow."

She turned her head when Miss Priss leapt up to the back of the couch and balefully studied the ice-cream container. "I don't share."

"Meow."

Ah, hell. She held out the spoon and watched the cat curl up at her shoulder and very delicately lap at the offering.

A loud rumbling made her jump until she realized it was coming from the cat. For a moment she seriously went still, thinking Miss Priss must be dying from some stomach ailment, but then she realized the cat was...*purring*.

Apparently Miss Priss liked comfort food, too. "Well, what do you know, common ground."

The cat's eyes were closed in ecstasy as she lapped at the spoon, and Cassie actually felt a melting low in her belly at how cute she looked. She dipped the spoon back into the container for more. "Maybe we can coexist after all, huh?"

At the knock on the front door, cat and woman looked at

each other. "You expecting company?" Cassie asked. "Because I'm sure the hell not." Reluctantly she set down the ice cream and padded into the foyer. She eyeballed the umbrella stand and one of the long-handled umbrellas in it, thinking that if Pete had somehow found her she could crack him over the head with one. Action plan in place, she looked through the peephole.

Stacie stood there, smiling and waving at her.

Cassie nearly groaned. She was *so* not feeling social. She looked like death warmed over...but then again, Stacie was holding an aluminum-foil-covered plate that looked loaded with incredible calories from heaven itself.

Opening the door, Cassie's gaze locked on that plate, so she didn't anticipate the bone-crunching hug.

"Oh, Cassie." Squeeze, squeeze. "You're here!" Stacie pulled back and offered the plate. "I don't know if you realized but we do a cookie exchange every month—me and Diane and Annie and some others—and everyone is still talking about Bare Essentials. About the party you and Kate gave for all of us. We're just so thrilled with what we purchased, we wanted you to have these goodies as a thank-you."

Cassie, in the act of lifting the foil and eyeballing a meringue cookie, went still. "This is from...everyone?"

"Everyone."

"To me. Cassie Tremaine Montgomery."

Stacie laughed. "The one and only. We sent Kate a plate, as well." Her smile faded a little. "That's okay, isn't it? Because actually, they wanted me to invite you to join our cookie exchange, but we thought you might think it was...well, you know, too small-town. Sort of stupid."

"I...don't think it's stupid." In fact, she could hardly talk. She felt overwhelmed by their openness and generosity. "And if I wasn't leaving at the end of the summer, I'd join your cookie exchange. If, um, I could cook."

Stacie grinned and hugged her again. "If you were staying, I'd show you myself. It's fun."

"But I'm not staying."

"I know."

"I'm leaving soon as fall hits. I have some jobs lined up."

"You lead such an exciting life," she said on a sigh. "Well... enjoy. Do you have any plans for the night? Maybe a hot date or something to go with that exciting life?"

Cassie looked down at herself and laughed. "Yeah, hot date. Look at me."

"I am. You're beautiful."

"Stacie, I am dressed like a potato sack. I haven't combed my hair or put on any makeup."

"Really?"

Cassie started to laugh then realized Stacie wasn't. "Maybe you need glasses."

Stacie shook her head, looking suddenly sad. "I mean, I can see you're not dressed for a photo shoot, as you usually are, but my God, most women would kill to like you do right now on their very best day."

From inside, Cassie's phone rang. Stacie smiled again. "I'll let you go. Maybe tomorrow we can catch lunch together or something."

"I..." She stared into Stacie's hopeful face and let out a breath. "I'd like that," she said, shocked to mean it.

She thought about that as she went running for the portable phone, which she kept meaning to put back on its base after she used it but hadn't managed yet. By the time she found the thing, under Miss Priss and her big butt, she was breathless. "Hello?"

Dial tone.

Well, damn she hated that. She set it down and told herself she'd just taken too long to get to the phone and whoever had been calling had gotten tired of waiting.

Only no one ever called her but Kate, who would have called her on her cell phone, not Flo's phone. She shook her head to clear it. She was *not* going to get paranoid.

"Meow."

Cassie sank back to the couch, reached for the ice cream and found it nearly gone. Shocked she craned her head and stared at the cat, who had a fudge mustache. "You are a pig."

Miss Priss started the rumble thing again and shifted closer. Then closer still, until she was in Cassie's lap. Only then did she close her eyes and drift off.

Cassie stared down at the big, fat, lazy cat. "You're shedding," she said. "Ugh. Luckily I don't care about these clothes." Leaving the cat in her lap, she reached for the plate Stacie had just brought, feeling a stab of something that felt uncomfortably like a conscience.

Stacie thought they were friends, and Cassie had never said otherwise.

But what kind of a friend took, took, took and didn't give anything in return? *Couldn't* give anything in return?

"I'm leaving in a month," she told Miss Priss. "Stacie knows that. *You* know that."

Miss Priss opened her slitted green eyes and stared at her.

"I *am*," Cassie said firmly, but her fingers sank into the cat's fur. "And you're going to have to find another person to mooch off of."

The doorbell rang again, and Cassie dislodged the fat cat. Grabbing a fistful of white-chocolate macadamia cookies to die for, she walked back into the foyer, figuring Stacie had forgotten something. Maybe she had another high-calorie offering.

She just wished she didn't feel so…vulnerable. Inexplicably, she felt open in a way she didn't usually allow, and for some reason, couldn't seem to close herself off. A little shaky, needing to be alone to regroup, she stuffed a cookie into her mouth and reluctantly opened the door.

Not Stacie.

"Tag," she said around a mouthful.

"Me," he agreed. He was holding up the doorjamb with his long, rangy body. His legs were casually crossed, his weight on his arm and shoulder, with his sunglasses hanging out the side of his mouth by an earpiece. Then he straightened to his full height, removed the sunglasses from his mouth and used it for his lethal weapon.

A smile.

Only this smile was different than any other one he'd ever given her. This smile didn't quite reach his eyes, and now that she was staring at him so closely, she could see the strain around his mouth, the tension in every muscle so unfairly and perfectly delineated in his damn sheriff's uniform.

And there she stood, holding a fistful of cookies, crumbs down the front of her— Oh, God. Forget the crumbs. Forget that her heart had stopped at just the sight of him. Forget that she could tell something was wrong. She was standing there in baggy, ugly clothes, with her hair piled on top of her head in a ponytail of all things, and not an ounce of makeup on her face.

She felt naked. "This isn't a good time," she said, and started to shut the door on his face.

He simply slapped his hand to the wood and held it open.

"Go away." God, her voice sounded small. She cleared her throat and lifted her chin. "I'm not in the mood for you." She tried to push the door shut but he was still in her way. Refusing to humiliate herself in a battle of the muscles that she couldn't possibly win, she glared at him. "Is there something wrong with your hearing?"

"Not at all." His gaze ran over her face and she wished to God she'd at least put on makeup. Without eyeliner and lipstick at the bare minimum, she knew she looked like death warmed over. And how pathetic was it she still had a grip on a handful of cookies, not to mention the fudge ice cream stain on one breast.

"Cassie, I don't want to force my way in."

"Good. Then go."

"Please. Please let me in."

That low, gravely voice had never failed to knock her knees together and now was no exception. It really ticked her off. "Do I have a choice?"

"You always have a choice, damn it."

She closed her eyes and put her forehead to the wood.

So light she was certain she imagined it, he ran his hand down her hair. "If it's because you're not dressed," he said quietly. "I've seen you like this before."

"Don't remind me." When he reached out and tugged lightly on a wayward strand of hair, she rolled her eyes. "No one sees me without makeup."

"I like you without it. You seem different. Softer. Let me in, Cassie."

"Why?"

"Because we need to talk."

"About last night? I already said I was sorry. I didn't mean to fall asleep on you, but I don't feel like paying you back right now—"

"Maybe another time," he said very softly, and if she wasn't mistaken, he sounded frustrated, as well, "we'll talk about the fact that you will never, ever owe me for letting me touch you. But right now I want to talk about my father."

Everything within her went still and she slowly lifted her head, thinking she couldn't have heard him correctly. "Who?"

"You know who. My father."

11

"YOU MIGHT HAVE TOLD ME you knew him personally," Tag said to Cassie. "Especially since I asked you."

She lifted a shoulder. He'd thrown her off, just as both Stacie and Miss Priss had. He stood there gazing at her from eyes filled with hurt and pain and anger.

And it made her...ache. Damn it, she didn't want to think about this. She cared about him, she did. But it was just the bottom-line basic kind of care. The way she cared about her dentist. Her personal trainer.

Her gynecologist.

Which didn't explain why she felt the inexplicable need to make him understand her.

"Hey." He stepped closer. "You okay?"

"Of course."

"Cassie." His eyes held so much. "Why didn't you tell me my father was the one to hurt you that night?"

He was putting her on the spot. *No one* put her on the spot. And suddenly she couldn't remember why she'd wanted to spare his feelings. Why it mattered what he thought.

She really needed a moment, to think, to regroup. To build defenses against all these damn strings on her heart. "So I knew him. So I've always known him. So what."

"So, you might have told me. Did you think I wouldn't care? That I wouldn't believe you? That I wouldn't want to kill him?"

This was definitely the last thing Cassie wanted to talk about tonight. She didn't want to hear how he'd found out. She didn't want to know how it affected him. She didn't want to do anything but polish off the last of her ice cream.

Alone.

But Tag was looking at her with an expression of sober fury bordering on fear, and she realized it was all for her. Whether she liked it or not, her past had come back to haunt not only her, but him. "He didn't hurt me, Tag."

"Not physically, but you trusted him."

"I don't trust anyone."

"Because of him."

"That would be flattering him."

"Cassie…" A disparaging sound escaped him. "My father and I aren't close. We tolerate each other at best. You wouldn't be hurting me to admit he should have paid for what happened that night."

"I've forgotten all about it."

"Really? Is that why you're gripping the wood so hard your knuckles are white?"

Thrown off, when she was never thrown off by a mere man, she turned her back and stalked through the house. Naturally he followed her, because he was a jerk, because he was an a—

"Cassie." He was right behind her, matching her stride for angry stride. "Stop. We have to talk about this."

She whirled on him at that, right there in the hallway. "Talk? About how your father thought I was as wild and fun and man-hungry as my mother? No."

"Cassie—"

"Don't you get it? He knew how I was. Let's face it, Tag,

everyone knew, so why should he have been any different? I came to terms with that a long time ago about this place."

"Then why did you come back?"

"Well, there was that little matter of living on Lilac Hill," she said sarcastically. "And let's not forget, I couldn't wait to drive my fancy car downtown just to show everyone."

"You've never mentioned that last thing on your list," he said very quietly.

"It wasn't important."

"On the contrary, I think it's the most important one." He stepped closer, then closer still, so they were breathing each other's air, their bodies just brushing. His hand came up, cupped her face, and his thumb traced her jaw in an aching tenderness that made her eyes burn.

"You wanted to become someone," he said. "You even made a note that it should have been number one on your list. What were you thinking when you wrote that, Cassie? That you didn't matter? You did. That you weren't important? You were. You are."

"Stop it." She slapped his hand away. "We both know I wrote that list ten years ago. It doesn't mean anything now."

"It does if you don't believe it, that you are someone."

"Oh, yeah, look at me." She lifted her hands and turned full circle, giving him a good look at the au naturel Cassie Tremaine Montgomery. "I'm someone all right."

He shook his head. "My God, you have no idea, do you? How beautiful you are on the inside, or," he said, holding her arms when she would have fled, "on the outside. Cassie, you're just one big fraud."

She struggled, but he held firm. "Don't be ridiculous."

"No, I mean it." He bent a little, to look right into her eyes. "You honestly believe it's the makeup and the body that sets you apart. You know what else? You honestly think the only thing between us is physical."

"It is."

"I don't mind you wearing me out trying to prove that fact, but one of these days you'll have to face the truth. There's more to us than sex." He let go of her arms, holding her with his gaze.

"No." Unable to stand the empathy and compassion in his eyes, she covered hers. "Damn it, you really caught me at a bad time, Tag. Just go away, okay?"

"I can't. I can't seem to stop thinking about you."

Shocked, she dropped her hands and stared at him, then let out a laugh. "That's funny."

"Really? Why?" He snagged her hand, brought it to his mouth. "Because you think about me, too?"

She would have yanked her hand away but he'd opened his mouth on it and was doing something to her finger with his tongue that made her unable to speak. Then he sucked her finger into his mouth.

Her breath caught. "I…I think about a lot of people."

"Me?"

Still watching her, he bit the pad of her finger, just lightly, but she felt it all the way to her toes. "Maybe occasionally."

His tongue swirled over the pad of her finger before working its way to the inside of her wrist. Her tummy danced. Her nipples beaded.

"Do you want me, Cassie? Right this minute, do you want me?"

She forced out a laugh even as she felt her body weeping for him. "Of course not. You barge in here, you—"

"You're such a bad liar."

Her mouth had been getting her into trouble since the day she'd figured out how to use it, and today was no exception.

"Okay, you're right," she said sarcastically. "Oh, Tag, I want you. I want you to make love to me. All night long—"

His mouth covered hers in a kiss that stole her breath. "I'm going to pretend you meant that," he said when they came up for air.

"You can pretend all you want," she said, daring him, then remembered...daring Tag was not a good idea.

With a triumphant glare of his eyes, he cupped the back of her head with one hand. The other traced a finger over her throat to right between her breasts. "Not aroused at all?"

"Absolutely not."

"And yet your nipples are begging for attention. *My* attention."

"Maybe I'm cold."

"Ah." Nodding agreeably, he swept his big, warm hands down her back, then beneath the material of her too-large T-shirt, spreading them wide on her bare skin. "Let me warm you then, since you're not aroused at all."

His warm, warm fingers lightly ran up and down, causing a shiver when they just skimmed the very sides of her breasts. "Better?"

"Um...yes." She cleared her throat. "Much better, thank you."

"You're not turned on at all, right?"

"Just still slightly chilled, that's all." But a delicious languid feeling had begun to overcome her, and damn if her hips didn't want to arch to his. Just barely, she managed to contain herself, and bit her lip to keep any moans she might feel the urge to utter to herself.

"What was that?" His mouth lightly brushed her ear, causing another shiver. "Was that a...moan?"

She locked her knees together. "Don't be ridiculous."

He cupped her bottom, then gripped her hips to his so that

she could feel how hard he was, and he *was* gloriously hard. His mouth was still doing something mind-boggling to that sensitive spot just beneath her ear and she let her head fall back to give him better access.

"Cassie?"

"Hmm?"

Now his hands slid beneath her sweats, and finding her without anything beneath, he groaned. "Warm yet?"

"Getting there," she murmured, loving the way his fingers cupped and held her butt so that the hardest, neediest part of him was gliding over the softest, neediest part of her.

"But not turned on, right?"

She'd planted her face in his throat so she could smell him better. Realizing she was nuzzling up to him, her eyes flew open. She stared at his tanned, sexy throat. "Uh…no."

He let go of her. Then suddenly her sweats were down around her calves. Before she could grab for them, Tag sank to his knees in front of her. Hands on her hips, he stroked his thumbs over the quivering skin of her belly, then lower. "I'm turned on by you," he said hoarsely, putting his lips to the very top of one thigh. "So turned on I can think of nothing else." Now his thumbs met and together they slid over her mound and slowly, slowly, spread her open to his gaze.

She was drenched.

He looked up into her eyes, his glittering with triumph. "Don't worry, I'm not the kind of man to say I told you so."

"Bastard—" But the word backed up in her throat when he leaned forward and licked her like a lollipop.

"Oh, my…" that was all she managed to get out, sinking her fingers into his hair and holding on tight. It was that or fall.

Then he opened his mouth and took her in with a sucking motion that rocked her world. She couldn't think, she couldn't breathe. She sure as hell couldn't stand, so she crumpled to a boneless heap.

He caught her. They rolled on the carpet like a couple of wrestlers, fighting for space, struggling to remove clothes, biting, kissing, swearing, laughing.

And then he had her flat on her back, arms held over her head. His body, hard and satisfactorily naked, pressed into her. "Still want to fight?"

Slowly she shook her head.

"Want to give me a hint on what you *do* want to do?"

"I saw a condom fall out of your pocket."

He had it on before she could say anything else. She had barely spread her thighs for him when an impossibly powerful thrust sank him inside her to the hilt.

And then she was lost. She was always lost when she was with him, just as, when he stroked them to a simultaneous orgasm in less than five hard strokes, she was found.

How devastating was that?

THEY SPENT the next few nights in the same manner, with Tag attempting to talk to her, Cassie resisting, distracting him with other things—namely her body—and both of them ending up wearing each other out every way but yesterday.

Unfortunately, they couldn't seem to stop. Cassie couldn't seem to stop. The devastating tugs on the strings to her heart just kept getting stronger every single day.

At least she was sure she hadn't seen Pete again, but what she had seen was worse. In the grocery store, no less than four people she recognized but didn't personally know smiled at her. *Smiled.* At the gas station, the mechanic came out and offered to pump her gas—and he didn't want anything for it.

Then she caved and, at Stacie's insistence, went over there for dinner and found her child a messy, sticky delight. She actually got talked into bowling afterwards—*bowling!*—because Stacie had just joined a league. And then, because apparently a weekly bowling night complete with greasy fries and cherry sodas appealed to her in a way she hadn't imagined, she joined the league, too.

Insanity.

Then, when she thought she couldn't get more conflicted, Kate dropped a bomb, saying that already Bare Essentials was such a success that it deserved a chance to become more than a revenge vehicle. She asked Cassie to stay to run it. Permanently. She said Cassie couldn't be a model forever, and she was right. She said Cassie was made for such a thing, and she was right. She said Cassie seemed happier and more content here than she'd ever seen her and…Cassie was deeply afraid to admit that Kate was right yet again.

So why did she feel such an inexplicable weight on her chest? She could hardly breathe because of it. Home alone late one night, she moved through the living room to the den, off of which was a sliding-glass door that led to the surprisingly large, lush, five-acre-long backyard.

There was a lovely wooden deck opening up to that land, on which sat the hot tub that had become her best friend. She needed that friend now as her every muscle was screaming with a tension tighter than she'd felt when she'd been stalked right out of New York.

The water was already hot, and if she'd had any energy left she might have whimpered in gratitude but her head was working on a more important issue.

Her biggest worry of all wasn't the town or the people in it. It wasn't Kate or the store. It wasn't even Pete.

It was Tag.

He wouldn't come tonight—she'd asked him not to. He would want to talk, want to share, want to…well.

She wanted to be with him, but for her, it was all physical. It was, damn it. It had to be, it was all she could give.

But why? cried a very small, very in-the-minority voice in her head. Why did it have to be so shallow, like everything else in her life? Why couldn't it be different? Deeper? More meaningful? *Real.*

Because she didn't know how to do that. She didn't know if she even believed in it.

So physical and shallow it would stay. And while that had been enough for Tag up until now, she was terrified things were changing. She was terrified he wanted more. And if he didn't get more, she was terrified he'd walk away.

At the bare minimum, he wanted to talk about his father. He thought he had to atone for that long-ago night in some way, and of course he didn't.

His father had told him...what, exactly? God, the humiliation of that night hadn't eaten at her in a long time, but it was eating at her now.

She cranked on the jets of the hot tub. Kicked off her sandals. Stared at the water. Had Sheriff Richard Taggart told his son how Cassie had dressed for the prom? What was it he'd said back then... Oh, yes, he'd said she'd dressed like she wanted it.

Had he also told Tag where Biff was heading with her?

And what had Tag really thought about that night?

Why did she care? "I don't," she said out loud, and dropped her pants. Reached for the buttons on her shirt. "I don't care—" But she did, and her voice caught. She cared about all of it. She cared about the store. She cared about the people she'd come to know—Stacie, Daisy, Diane. Damn it, she even cared about the stupid cat.

But mostly she cared about a man she wasn't sure about. With a vicious yank, she pulled off her blouse and stepped into the hot tub, sinking with a hissing breath into the hot bubbling water up to her chin.

Putting her head back on the edge, she stared up at the stars. What if all these feelings were hers alone? What if he was just out for a good time, using her body as she was using his, and after she left he'd happily move on to the next woman?

Oh, God. That thought tore her apart and she put a shaking hand to her mouth. No. No, this couldn't be happening. She couldn't be falling for this place, for the people in it. For Tag.

No. She'd leave, soon as she could. Pack up and go, and if New York still wasn't safe for her, she'd find somewhere else to go, somewhere where there were no strings attached, no—

"Meow." Miss Priss butted her jaw with her stubborn little head.

Which for some reason made Cassie burst into tears.

TAG WORKED LATE, mostly because his head had not been into his paperwork for weeks now and he was helplessly behind.

The extra hours in the quiet station didn't help much. He had too much time to think. And what he was thinking about was crowding around his head, fighting for space.

His father. They hadn't spoken again, and Tag wasn't sure they would.

Then there was Kate, who'd actually called him today to see if he could check on Pete's whereabouts. Tag had been checking daily to no avail. No one had located Pete and he could only hope the L.A. rumor was true.

And then there was one stubborn, ornery, strong-willed, wildly passionate woman he couldn't seem to get enough of. Cassie Tremaine Montgomery. Not his fantasy woman, that was certain, but somehow…better.

She'd asked him not to come to her tonight, and he'd had every intention of keeping himself busy without her. Only there had been something in her voice that had disturbed him, something...lonely. She was hurting, and she was alone.

In spite of all they'd given to each other—and taken—she was still struggling to keep him at arm's length. She still wanted to separate the physical from the emotional. He'd been all for that, until he'd realized he wanted both. He wanted it all.

And he wanted her to know that.

Tonight.

SHE DIDN'T ANSWER the front door, but since the sunshine-yellow Porsche was blinding Tag from the driveway by moonlight, he knew she was home.

The front door was locked. Good girl, he thought, and walked around the side yard to see if he could find her outside.

The swing out there was empty. But from where he stood he could hear the jets of the hot tub, and continued on that way.

He was caught up thinking about the things they could do to each other in the hot tub, so it took him a moment to assimilate what he was seeing.

Cassie sitting in it. Long, wavy hair piled on top of her head. Bubbles surrounding her gorgeous body, hiding it from view.

And she was quietly sobbing her heart out.

"Cassie." He was there in a heartbeat, kneeling on the deck behind her, reaching for her shoulders. "Cassie. Oh, baby."

She jerked at his touch, whirling around and backing away into the center of the tub while doing so, making him realize with the sound of the jets and her own grief, she hadn't heard him approach.

"You," she said in such a way that told him exactly who was at the center of at least some of this.

"Me," he agreed. "Tell me what's wrong."

She wiped at her face. "What's wrong is you're trouncing on my privacy again."

"Cassie." Knowing she was hurting made his heart hurt. "Come closer."

"No."

"Come out then."

"No."

She was still right there in front of him, but she'd suddenly retreated into herself before his very gaze. He had no idea what was going on in her head. And damn if he wasn't very, very tired of that. "Fine. I'll come in."

"Don't be silly, Sheriff. You'd wrinkle your uniform."

Ah, the uniform. The center of every single argument they'd ever had. Well, he was done with that. Done with all of it. Frustrated, he kicked off his shoes.

She craned her neck and stole a peek, probably hoping he'd left. Her eyes widened when his hands went to his belt. "What are you doing?"

"Getting rid of the brick wall between us." He shoved down his pants. Kicked them away with his shoes. Ripped off his shirt.

And stood there in front of her bare-ass naked. "Not a sheriff right now, am I?"

"It's just a shirt. A pair of pants."

"I know that." He put his foot in and refused to hiss out a breath at the hot water. "I'm just not sure you do."

"Put your clothes back on."

"Not until you understand."

"Understand what? That you're butting in where you're not wanted?"

"Understand that I'm just a man. A regular man." He sank

in to his waist and walked toward her, stopping when they were only a breath apart. "A regular man who's falling in love with you."

12

SHOCKED TO HER VERY CORE, Cassie stared at Tag for one long heartbeat before whirling away. Splashing. Trying to move. Damn the water now, because it slowed her down. She needed out. She needed to run. Not because he was a cop. Not because he'd invaded her space.

But because he'd used the L-word.

Not fair. Definitely foul. Definitely hitting below the belt.

Oh, God. She needed air—

Long, wet, strong arms encircled her from behind. Pulled her back against a warm, bare chest.

"Cassie." His mouth was at her ear, his voice low and anguished. "Don't."

She kept fighting him. And as a woman who'd learned to fight very young, she was good. She was fast. She fought nasty.

"No," he murmured, sliding one arm across her front, the other low on her belly. "Shh."

Shh my ass, she thought, and fought harder, satisfied when water sloshed out of the tub, more satisfied when she elbowed him and heard the "Oomph" of his breath whoosh by her ear. But even as she fought, she felt hyperaware of two things.

One, she was naked.

Two, so was he.

And all that nakedness was rubbing against each other—her back to his chest, her butt to his groin—and her anger was starting to turn into something else entirely, something beyond her control, something…something she no longer wanted to run from.

But there was the principle of the matter, she couldn't forget that. He'd betrayed her by adding all this emotion to the pot. "You shouldn't have said that. That you were…that you might be…"

"Falling in love with you?"

Because she'd stopped fighting, he carefully loosened his hold but didn't take his hands off her. They were standing in the middle of the tub, her back to his front, the bubbling water lapping at their hips. She became very conscious of the fact that her breasts were plumped up by his arm, that his other arm lay across the front of her so that his hand rested across the very top of her thighs.

"I didn't say it to hurt you." His arms tightened, as if in a hug. "It's just the truth and I wanted to share it with you."

She stared down at his big, tanned hand spread wide on her softer, whiter skin and recognized that by just his touching her, she felt very female, very special.

Damn him. "Sharing is overrated."

"Yeah, you're right, it can be overrated. With the wrong person, that is." Slowly he turned her around in his arms. Let her look into his face, where she could see the hurt she'd put there.

Her gut pinched. He'd given her so much, whether she wanted to admit it or not. She wasn't that selfish that she couldn't give him something back, just a little something. "I don't care that you're sheriff," she whispered.

"Okay. Define 'don't care.'"

"I mean I'm getting used to seeing you in the uniform,

okay? I'm getting used to it even if it means I can't drive my
car as fast. And..."

"And..."

"And...I guess I should say, I know you're the same with
or without the stupid badge."

"Ah." His mouth lowered to within a fraction of hers. "Are
you sure about that?"

Her breath caught when his body slid against hers. Lord,
he had such a beautiful, hard, sinewy, tough body. "Um..."

"Maybe we should make sure. Tell me, for example, do I
kiss the same with or without the uniform?" He put his mouth
to hers, ripping a helplessly hungry sound from her throat.

At that, he deepened the kiss, dancing his tongue to hers
in a way that made her dig her fingers into his arms and press
even closer to the body she couldn't seem to get enough of.
Obligingly, he leaned into her as the kiss spun out of control,
leaned and leaned until suddenly they both fell back into one
of the double seats of the hot tub, splashing water, laughing a
little, but diving right back into the kiss.

Breaking off for air, Tag put his wet mouth to her ear and
slowly exhaled, making her shiver. Making her want more.
Now.

"Cassie."

"Yeah." A fog of sexual arousal had descended over her
vision.

"Is it the same?"

She sighed. "Fine. Yes, you kiss me stupid with or without
the uniform. Tag...tell me you have a condom in those pants
on the grass over there."

He slowly shook his head, his thumb tracing her lower lip.
"I do, but we're not going to have sex."

She stared at him, feeling a little befuddled. She looked at
the hair lightly decorating his muscular chest. At the line of

that same hair that divided his hard stomach and vanished with the rest of his good parts into the swirling water. Then she watched his tongue slick over his wet lower lip. Oh, God, she wanted him. Wanted him to obliterate all the emotional tension and get right to the physical. "We're not going to do it in here?"

"No." Leaning forward, he put his mouth to her throat and sucked.

Her head thunked back against the edge. "But…" The backs of his fingers brushed over her right breast as he reached up to touch her cheek. But she wanted his fingers back on her breasts. Wanted that so badly she was shaking. "Why not?"

His eyes were all over her, and their hot intensity as he stared at her told he did want her very much, so she could forget the sudden fear that he didn't.

"I want more than sex, Cassie. I want more, and I want it with you."

Her eyes widened, because…oh, God, if he used the L-word again right now—which would be the equivalent to an icy bucket of water being dumped on her hot, hot body—she was going to slug him.

Then probably start bawling again.

"I want you," he said again through very tight vocal cords. "More than I want my next breath, if you want the truth. I want to make love. Then I want to sit here with you in my arms and talk. I want to know why you were crying. I want to know your hopes and dreams. I want—"

"I get it," she said tightly, bitterly disappointed, and crossed her arms. "But I'm not up for that."

"Really? Or are you just scared?"

Her chin came up. "I am not."

"Prove it," he dared softly, his heart in his throat because this felt as though it was the most important moment of his life. He didn't know when exactly, or the where or the why of it, but this woman had become more important to him than anything or anyone else.

And he wanted to show it to her.

"You want me to prove you don't scare me," she said to herself, taking a deep breath that brought the very tips of her breasts out of the water. "Yeah, okay. I can do that." Eyes glittering, she climbed out of the water into the equally steamy night.

For a moment she simply looked at him, naked and gleaming by moonlight, and his chest ached just looking at her. Would she go through with it?

But his Cassie was nothing if not the bravest woman he'd ever met, and slowly her lips curved. "Come here," she said in a sultry voice that matched her body. She led him to the long, wide swing, which had a comfortable cotton cover and more pillows than his own bed. Standing in front of it, she twined her arms around his neck, tipped her head and kissed him. Kissed him with her lips, with her tongue, and when she made that helpless sound in the back of her throat again—the sound that assured him she was every bit as lost as he was—he knew she was kissing him with her heart.

His own opened. Flooded. "That's it," he murmured, stroking his hands down her back. "Oh, yeah, Cassie, that's it. Do you feel it?"

"I feel you. God, Tag, I feel you." One of her legs bent, hooked at his hip so that his engorged penis brushed at the very core of her. Her head fell back and she arched closer. "Please, Tag, please…"

"Oh, yeah." He sank with her onto the swing. "But we have all night."

"We've had all night before."

"This is going to be different. More." He reached out a reverent finger to the tip of one nipple, lightly circling it, watching it bead up tight beneath his touch until it distended out a good half inch, pouting for more. He shivered and brought his other still-wet hand up, dripping water over her skin. Waiting until a small rivulet ran down her breast to the very tip of the puckered nipple before he leaned in and licked it off.

With a little cry, she arched up and did her best to thrust her entire breast into his mouth. But he simply pulled back and repeated the feathery touch to her other nipple. She let out a little mewl, gripped his hair in her fists and held his mouth to her breast.

Tag growled and hauled her into his arms. Her mouth raised to his and he took it, groaning when she used her tongue in a blatant motion that mimicked what she wanted him to do to her. Holding her head, he gentled the kiss, sucking on her bottom lip, licking the corner of her mouth before slowly deepening the connection, making love to her mouth the way he was going to make love to her body.

Panting, she tore free and arched her body toward his. "I'm ready right now."

"Are you?" Holding her gaze, he slid his hands down her body to her hips, and slowly rocked them to his.

"Yes!" Spreading her legs, she managed to get the very tip of him inside her before he gripped her hips with a rough groan. His hands were shaking as he held her still. "Not yet." There was still more. He slid his fingers between her legs and nearly fell to a boneless heap when he felt how hot, how wet she was. It was impossible not to stroke her, not to get caught up in her rhythm.

"Oh, please," she whispered, rocking against him. "Please, Tag."

"Tell me." Laying her back, he looked down into her eyes, at her mouth still wet from his, at the body he wanted to make love to for the rest of his life. He skimmed a hand over her breasts, her stomach, lower. Past her belly button, over her mound so that the tips of his fingers divided slick feminine folds.

Her eyes went opaque and arching up, she cried out.

"You want...this?" His middle finger feathered over her while he took her nipple into his mouth. "Or...this?" He slid that finger inside her now, then added another, while stroking her with his thumb.

"Tag...oh, *Tag*." She couldn't stop saying his name. She couldn't help it, sensations rocked and throbbed and demanded completion. Never in her life had she experienced anything like it. Oh, definitely she'd enjoyed sex, more than maybe she'd like to admit, but always...always, she'd kept her head at all times, even during a climax. And always, she'd been able to walk away.

But right this minute, under his knowing, tortuous administrations and his most amazing fingers, she couldn't keep her head. Couldn't walk away. Could hardly breathe. One desperate mass of flesh, she spread her thighs to take in more of the magic. Her fingers dug into his arms, his chest, wherever she could reach, in an attempt to get a grip, but with his mouth on her breast, his fingers buried in her, his voice echoing in her ears that he was going to make love to her until they couldn't take any more, there was no grip to be found.

"You're so wet," he murmured, his fingers playing in that wetness. "Wet for me."

She couldn't stand it, not the kisses, the erotic words, the careful, knowing strokes. Her muscles started to quiver and she was one heartbeat away from coming when he released her breast with an audible pop and took his fingers away, making her nearly scream.

"Not yet." He came up with a condom and tore it open

with his teeth while his fingers stroked her one last time. Her toes curled.

"Don't come yet," he begged, pushing up onto his knees between her legs. For a moment he just stared down at her, with such heat and affection and need she nearly came from that alone.

"You're so sweet," he whispered.

Well, that was a new one, and it shouldn't have caught her breath, burned her eyes. Shouldn't have done anything but infuriate her because he was effortlessly holding her on the very edge as no one had ever dared to before.

Then, with just one finger he lightly circled her opening, not quite penetrating, bringing back the heat, the need in a flash.

Biting her lip to keep from begging, she arched her hips. His erection bumped just the right spot, and he inhaled sharply, letting her know he was as on the edge every bit as much as she was. The muscles of his arms quivered. His hips pressed forward. His face was tight with need. "Now," he said.

"Finally."

"Let me in, Cassie."

She pulled her knees back, opening herself, more vulnerable with him in this moment than she'd ever been with anyone, her surrender utter and complete. Slowly, so slowly, he pushed into her, his jaw tight, his eyes holding hers as her body closed tightly around him.

At the same time he slid a hand down her belly, put his thumb on her clitoris as he pulled out of her slightly, dragging against her needy flesh, ripping a cry of need out of her as she wrapped her ankles around his waist.

In and out. A stroke of his thumb. In and out again. "Here's the more," he murmured, and thrust inside deep.

She burst right out of herself. Vaguely, she heard his low,

wrenching groan as he found his own release, but she couldn't stop shuddering.

Eventually, she became aware of his wonderful, warm weight. Of the night all around them. Of Tag's lips as he pressed them to her neck. It was shocking how her arms tightened, how she clung, wanting to hold on to this moment forever.

But after a moment he pulled away, obviously not feeling the same need. "I'll be right back," he said, and she nodded, telling herself she was relieved.

Get what you need, Flo had always said.

Well, she'd sure as hell gotten what she needed.

And now, she didn't need anything more.

TAG DISPOSED of the condom and came right back out, but found the swing empty.

He turned in a full circle, his heart thudding because, damn it, he knew he shouldn't have left her when she'd been feeling so open, so raw. He'd felt every bit the same, and had wanted to hold on to her forever, but there'd been the little matter of the condom to deal with.

Still, he nearly sagged in relief when he saw her sitting on the edge of the hot tub, her feet in the water, a towel wrapped around her body.

She'd left another one out for him, which he slid around his hips before sinking to the edge right next to her. He hissed when his feet hit the hot water.

She smiled. "Wuss."

"I am not." But because her smile looked so good on her, he smiled back. "So."

"Yeah." She sighed and splashed with her toes. "So. The dreaded 'after.'"

"You're only dreading it because you promised to cuddle and talk."

She looked as if she'd rather face the electric chair and he smiled again. God, he loved her grumpy, beautiful hide. "Here, I'll make it easy..." He spread out his arm and waited for her to move in close.

She stared at him, rolled her eyes and shuffled close, briefly losing her towel and giving him a bonus glimpse of her breasts. "Hmm, nice," he said, reaching in and stroking a nipple before she managed to cover herself back up.

"You just saw it less than two minutes ago." She fit her shoulder beneath him and shocked him by slipping an easy arm around his waist.

"Honey, the thing with men and breasts...we never get tired of them."

She let out a laugh. "That's pretty pathetic. I've always wondered...don't you men ever get over being a slave to your penis?"

"Afraid not."

She was comfortable, relaxed, swinging her feet and still smiling. He hated to ruin that, but he had to know. "Why were you crying?"

For a brief second she went really still, then sighed and sagged just a bit against him. "It's...complicated."

"So? What isn't?"

She shook her head and her hair clung to the stubble of his jaw. Stroking a finger over his skin, she pulled her hair free, then put her fingers back on his face. "That was amazing, you know. On the swing."

He looked into her eyes and spoke the utter truth. "I've never felt anything like it."

For a second she closed hers. "Me, either." Then she opened those fathomless eyes on his and they were damp. "It's going to sound really pitiful to you, a man who's so confident and respected, but…I've been thinking about this place, about the people in my life." She turned to stare into the water and shook her head. "And much as I would have denied this even yesterday, I…"

"You what? What changed before yesterday and today?"

She glanced at him. "It's pretty hard to admit."

"You can tell me. You can tell me anything."

"I know." She scrunched up her eyes. "I want to be liked, okay?"

When he just looked at her, she visibly relaxed. "I, um…I want people around me who care. I want a home." She let out a disparaging sound. "I know, it's so stupid. But the truth is, I'm falling for this ridiculously opulent house. I'm falling for the horribly spoiled cat that came with it. I'm falling for the steady job at Bare Essentials, where I don't have to take off my clothes and deal with grumpy managers and psycho photographers." She peeked at him. "Don't you dare laugh."

"Are you kidding?" He cupped her jaw, made her look at him, which she did so defiantly his heart ached. "Tell me you left something out of that list you're falling for. Like me. Are you falling for me, Cassie?"

Her mouth opened, then carefully closed. She dropped her gaze and pulled back just enough that his hands fell from her. "I hadn't quite taken it that far yet."

He stared at her profile while that sank in. "I see."

She winced, kicked at the water. "Tag, I—"

"No. You're being honest." He surged to his feet. "And it's late." He needed to go before he did something asinine, such as try to talk her into liking him. Now that would be pathetic. "Good night, Cassie."

He made it to the sliding-glass door before he realized he wore only a towel. Swearing, he dropped it to the ground and turned around, looking for his clothes, and bumped into Cassie who was holding them out for him.

"Thanks." He shoved one leg into his pants but because he was wet and frustrated, he nearly killed himself trying to get the other leg in.

"Tag."

At the soft plea in her voice, he gritted his teeth and looked at her. Ever since he'd known her, her eyes had been filled with intelligence, sharp, biting humor, and not a little cynicism. She'd seen and done it all, and it showed.

Not now. Now all he could see was anguish, and he took a deep breath. "It's okay."

"I never really gave a shit about anyone before, Tag. I mean, I love Kate, I love Aunt Edie and I love Flo, but other than that—"

"I know." And damn him for being such a jerk, because he did. Reaching out, he stroked her jaw. "I know."

"I think about you." She put her hand on his wrist and turned her face into his palm, pressing her lips there. "I can give you that."

"That's nice. It's really nice. But I want more, Cassie."

She closed her eyes. Turned away. "That I can't give you. Not right now."

"When?"

"I don't know. I need some time."

"Fine. I'll call you tomorrow."

"I need more time than that, Tag."

"Yeah." His heart hurt again, damn it. And he had no one to blame but himself. "Right."

TAG SPENT THE NEXT DAY in a rare form of frustration. He knew as he patrolled town that he was being particularly hard-assed, giving out tickets left and right, but he didn't much care. And when his cell phone rang, he barked into it. "What?"

"What's going on today, sweetie?" asked Annie.

"Why aren't you on dispatch?"

"I am."

Sighing, he pinched the bridge of his nose. "Then why aren't you calling me through the radio?"

"Because I wanted to tell you that you're being a jerk, and I didn't think you wanted me to say that on the radio." This was said so cheerfully his head hurt.

"Now I know you're getting laid on a fairly regular basis," she said. "So—"

"*What?*"

"It's all over the gossip train," she said without apology. "So...what's up? You fall in love or something?"

"And why would that make me a jerk?"

"It makes all men jerks at first, until they get used to it. That's why I'm calling, to tell you it's okay and you'll get used to it. So why don't you just come on back to the station and I'll make you some iced tea."

"I don't need any iced tea," he said through his teeth.

"I think maybe you do. Do yourself and the town a favor, hon. Come on in."

13

Bare Essentials opened with the hoopla of a cocktail party attended by nearly everyone in town. Kate was ecstatic. Cassie pretended to be.

Oh, she was beyond thrilled that the store had done well, and continued to do so the week following the opening. It had given her summer purpose while she waited out Crazy Pete. But she'd also done it in good part due to her yearning to hurt Pleasantville. She'd done it for revenge.

But where was the revenge exactly? What had happened? Somehow instead of fulfilling her list and making everyone sorry, *she* was the sorry one. Sorry in love with the life she'd made here.

Thinking about that life made her want more of it. Thinking about that life made her smile.

Smile, for God's sake.

But thinking about Tag made that smile fade. What did she feel for him? Hell if she knew, but she sure felt something. She felt it all the time; when she was sleeping, when she was driving—okay, *speeding,* with a half-hopeful glance in the rearview mirror.

Only Tag never pulled her over.

Kate had told her rumors were running rampant in town.

Supposedly he'd been sullen and serious, so much so that people thought he'd turned into his father. People wished she'd sleep with him again so he'd cheer up.

Well, big surprise, she thought as she got into her car one morning. She *did* want to sleep with him again, wanted that more than she wanted anything, even her old life back.

Because when it came right down to it, she actually *didn't* want her old life back. How scary was that?

Suddenly she realized she'd stopped in front of the police station. Parked. Gotten out of the car and walked inside.

And asked for the sheriff.

She had no answers for him, had nothing to say at all, she just...wanted to see him. Oh, God, that was stupid, she shouldn't have come—

Before she could turn tail and run, he came out of his office, tall, dark and attitude-ridden.

"Cassie." That was all he said. Just her name in that terrifyingly distant tone.

How could he look so damn calm? Her heart was in her throat, her palms damp. She forced a smile and hoped she looked half as cool as he did. "Hi. I just..."

"Yes?"

"Um..." She'd regressed into the village idiot. Damn him for not helping her. "I wanted to see how you were."

He lifted his hands and shrugged. "I'm fine."

"Yeah." Well, hadn't this been one big, fat mistake? "Okay, good. You're fine. All righty then, I've got work..." She moved to the door, furious and sad and embarrassed and needing to kick her own butt all at the same time. "Goodbye, Tag."

He watched her stalk to her car in leather pants and a see-through blouse that had made his body quiver hopefully.

"She looks like she's got steam coming out of her fine ears," Annie said conversationally from behind him.

Steam? He hadn't been able to get past the flash of hurt he'd seen in her eyes. The hurt he'd put there.

"Why are all men jackasses whenever they're hurting anyway?" Annie asked. "Is it because they need to share the wealth, do you suppose?"

He *was* a jackass. Worse. What the hell had he just done, besides let his pride take over? She'd come to see him, something that spoke volumes, and she deserved much more than his cool "I'm fine" crap. All she'd ever asked of him was to give her time. He hadn't bothered to even try.

Well she deserved that time, and his patience, too, and she was going to get it. Even if it killed him. She was worth the wait, and with a little of that patience, she would come around. Because he was worth it, too.

Or so he hoped.

"You going after her, Romeo?"

"I have an hour left on my shift."

"And then?"

"If I tell you, are you going to broadcast it on the five o'clock news?"

"Of course."

Tag sighed. "Yeah. I'm going after her."

"Let's hope she'll have you, boss. Let's hope she'll have you."

Cassie took herself to work as if nothing was the matter. She sat on the front counter preparing the receipts for bookkeeping.

Bookkeeping meaning Kate, of course, who, as the entire accounting department, not only had a head for such things, but was also so completely anal she squeaked when she walked.

Cassie worked steadily, refusing to think about the little visit she'd made on the way over here. "Men suck."

Miss Priss, who sat at Cassie's elbow, occasionally batting

an important piece of paper to the floor, looked up with what Cassie would have sworn was complete agreement on her feline face.

Then she batted yet another receipt to the floor.

"Stop that." Cassie hopped down to get the piece of paper. "Or I'll put you out and let animal control take you away."

Miss Priss yawned, and Cassie had to laugh, but it faded when suddenly she couldn't imagine her life without the damn fleabag. "So what do you think of New York, cat? Think we should blow this pop stand? I do," she said. "Screw living in fear."

But the scarier truth was…she didn't really want to go. "Hey, you know what? I'm not letting any man chase me from where I want to be. Not ever again. And you know what else?"

Miss Priss blinked.

"This is where I want to be. So…stay with me? Here? Forever? What do you say—we can be old maids together."

Another yawn as the cat craned her head and looked at the phone when it rang.

"Baby!"

Cassie pulled the phone away from her ear to stare at it. "Mom?"

"Who else! How's that town treating you?"

"Decently," Cassie had to admit. "I thought you were on a cruise. How's the boyfriend?"

"He's been upgraded to the husband. We got married on a Greek island today."

"What?" Cassie screeched.

Miss Priss fell off the counter.

Cassie just stared into space. "But…but…"

"I know." Flo sighed. "But it's wonderful. Love is wonderful."

"Mom! How could you? You always told me to get what I could from a man and then walk away!"

"Of course I didn't!"

"Yes, you did. You always told me to get out, to leave them hanging." If she hadn't said that, then what had she said?

Flo sighed on the other end of the line. "I said you get what you can, honey, and walk away if it suits you. If what you're getting is love though, I'd grab it and hold on tight."

Holy shit, how had Cassie gotten it so wrong all these years? "Mom?"

"Yes?"

"I'm happy for you."

"Thanks, hon. I'm happy for me, too. He's wonderful. You'll have to meet him sometime. Hey, our sailboat is ready. Love you!"

Click.

Cassie stared out the window, lost in thought about her mother's revelation until she realized Stacie had pulled up and was headed toward the doors of the shop. She knocked on the glass, waving and smiling at Cassie who, still in shock, unlocked the door for her. "We're not open yet. I've got another half hour to get an hour's worth of work done."

"That's what I wanted to talk to you about." Stacie moved in uninvited, grabbing the sign taped to the glass as she went. Turning it around, she grinned. "You won't be needing this anymore."

Cassie looked at the Help Wanted sign she and Kate had put in the window. "Why not?"

"Because help has arrived." Stacie tore it in two and, tossing the pieces in the air, she clapped her hands. "My mom said she'd baby-sit for me when I'm on shift. Oh, Cassie, please say yes. I want to work here, in the coolest store ever, with you."

Cassie shook her head helplessly, laughing a little in the

face of such pure enthusiasm. "But it's a salesclerk position. Have you ever—"

"I've worked at Taco Bell, Dr. Bean's office, Farmer's Insurance and, most recently, the five-and-dime. Plus, I'm a mom, was a wife and therefore also a cook, maid and baby-sitter. Trust me, I can handle this. I can handle anything."

"Can you handle cleaning up the paper you just dumped on the floor?"

Stacie beamed. "Yep."

"Can you then handle sorting the new silk pyjamas that just came in?"

"Double yep."

"Okay, then." Cassie nodded. "You're hired."

"Oh, thank you!"

Cassie braced herself but not in time. She was hauled into a bear hug that went on and on and on.

"You're supposed to hug me back," Stacie said in her ear.

"Oh. Yeah." So Cassie lifted her arms and hugged Stacie back.

"This is nice. You being my friend." Stacie pulled back to smile in Cassie's face. "And maybe someday soon, you'll let me be your friend back."

Cassie opened her mouth, then shut it. Because wasn't that the cold, hard truth? "Stacie, I'm—"

"No." She shook her head. "I'm sorry. That was rude of me. You're not ready to open up and I had no right to say—"

"Yes, you did." Cassie had to marvel at the truth that had just smacked her in the face. "You know, before you got here, I was sitting right there on that counter feeling a little bit sorry for myself. Thinking poor me, I actually like it here, I actually like that stupid cat, I like you, I like this life. Now, it just sounds silly. It's okay to like what I've found here."

Stacie's smile was slow and genuine. "So you like me back?"

Cassie smiled back and felt her heart warm. "Yeah."

"Can I have a raise?"

"Aren't you a riot?"

"I do try. You have some forms for me? I want to make this official."

Cassie moved toward the back office. "I'll have to dig for them. Might take me a few. Just start over there with those boxes on the floor by the second shelving unit. Don't open the front door yet."

"Got it."

Cassie, followed by Miss Priss, walked down the hallway past two disastrous closets she and Kate hadn't gotten to yet, past the bathroom, to the small cubicle they'd claimed as their office. With a sigh she divided a look between Kate's spotless desk to her own cluttered, dusty, overloaded one.

Miss Priss leapt up to Cassie's and plopped her big, fat body down on a pile. Not wanting to admit how much that silly little gesture meant, she said, "One of these days I'm going to get myself organized."

"Really? Will you return my calls and letters then?" came a sardonic male voice she instantly recognized for the shiver it put down her spine.

Pete had found her.

14

CASSIE TURNED to see Pete sprawled in a chair against the wall, looking tall, California-blond and cold as ice. He had her water bottle from her desk in his hand, which he raised in a silent toast. "Well, look at who the cat dragged in," he said. He purposely lifted the water to his lips and, smiling at the lip gloss outline of a mouth on the rim—obviously hers—he put his mouth to that exact spot.

Her heart was beating so hard she was certain Pete could see it, but she smiled and backed into her desk, reaching behind her, patting, searching for the steel, pointed letter opener she knew she had there somewhere.

Instead of cold steel in her fingers, she felt Miss Priss butt her head into her palm.

Useless cat!

Slowly, Pete came to his feet, standing between her and the door. "I still can't believe you hurt me the way you did, tossing our friendship out the window. After all we meant to each other."

"Yeah, being stalked tends to make me a terribly disloyal friend." Okay so she couldn't get to the door, but she could scream.

And yet that would bring Stacie running, she was certain

of it. And what if Pete hurt her? Cassie would never be able to live with that, being the cause of something happening to her new and very wonderful friend.

And they *were* friends, the marvel of that could wash over her even now, strengthen her. She was more than just *that* woman here in Pleasantville. She had people around her who cared, making her and this place a unit. She had Kate; she'd always have Kate. And now she had Stacie, too.

And Tag. Even though she'd hurt him, he cared about her, deeply. She took strength from that, felt herself stand tall.

She needed that extra strength because Pete took a step toward her. "How did you get in?"

"Back door. It was locked, but ajar. Not smart, Cassie."

Damn, she'd done it again with the stupid door.

"I know you told the police I was stalking you," he said. "That nearly killed me, Cassie. I can't show my face in my own hometown. My career is ruined. You did that to me, and I didn't deserve it." With a vicious swipe, he reached out and cleared the credenza of all the stock, boxes and papers carefully stacked there.

In spite of herself, Cassie flinched. "The police will come. They'll take you back to New York and prosecute you."

"Not that I want to disagree with you, but you're wrong. You're alone here. The store is closed and locked. In fact…" He kicked a stack of boxes and sent them flying before looking back into her face with a definite glee. "Scream. Scream all you want. No one will hear you, and even if they did, no one will care. Not about you."

He couldn't know that was her secret weakness. That no one cared. But people *did,* she knew that now, and managed a smile. "You're the wrong one, Pete."

"Here's how this is going to work. You're going to come back with me. Tell the police you were mistaken. I won't take no for an answer, Cassie." He moved toward her and she side-stepped around the desk, putting herself behind it.

"I'm not going back to New York." She wasn't, she knew that now. Oh, she'd go back to model, as long as they'd have her, but this would be her home base. Pleasantville. Bare Essentials. It's what she wanted with all her heart, and if she wasn't about to have the fight of her life, she would have reveled in the sudden epiphany.

Damn it, where was the letter opener? She couldn't see it anywhere, but there was King-Size Kong, the latest, hottest, eighteen-inch-long, five-inch-thick dildo on the market. Kate had ordered it for fun, and hadn't quite yet decided on how to display it. The thing was made of rubber and weighed more than a bowling ball. It even had batteries in it, because Cassie had put them in there to tease Kate about how to stay busy during late-night accounting sessions.

"Are you listening, Cassie?" Like a flash of lightning, Pete leaned across the desk and latched onto her wrist.

Tug-of-warring did no good; the guy was as strong as an ox. And because he was looking at her with a sick hopefulness that said he wanted her to try to fight him, she forced herself to remain calm. "Let go of me."

"I'm not going to ever let go of you again." He lifted his other hand, whether to hit her or to grab her and haul her across the desk she'd never know, because Miss Priss took one look at him towering over her and, with a hiss, swiped him right across the face.

With a howl, Pete dropped to his knees. "My face, my face!"

Cassie hefted the heavy dildo and brought it down on Pete's head.

Just as he crashed to the floor, Tag slammed into the office, looking larger than life and battle ready with his gun out. He took one look at Cassie wielding her weapon, at Pete prone on the floor, and shook his head. "Damn, Cassie."

"Did I kill him?" She came closer, the dildo resting on her shoulder like a baseball bat, ready for another swing.

But he didn't twitch.

"Pete?" She kicked him gingerly in the leg with her toe, and would have bent over him to check for a pulse but Tag stopped her. He'd holstered his gun and had put his hands on her shoulders, making her look at him. "Jesus. I came to talk to you, and Stacie told me she'd heard banging back here and— Are you hurt?"

"Of course not."

Gently he gave her a little shake. "Stop it. You don't have to always be so tough. It's okay to lean on someone once in awhile, damn it."

"You don't want me to lean on you."

"Is that what you think?" His voice had gone a little hoarse as he ran his hands down her arms, linking their fingers. "That I don't want you to lean on me?"

She closed her eyes, a little overcome by all the emotions she'd allowed to swamp her lately—as in the past twenty minutes.

"Cassie?"

"No," she whispered. "I know what you want."

"And that is?"

"Me." That still could make her tremble in amazement and she opened her eyes. "You want me. Not just sex, you want all of me. I'm…getting used to that."

"You are?"

Oh, the things in his voice—the gruff yearning, the hope, the wariness. "Tag, this morning, I realized some things. I realized—"

Pete groaned and Tag backed up a step to put his foot in the middle of his back. "Go on," he said to Cassie.

She looked down at Pete. "Shouldn't you—"

"Tell me."

But Stacie poked her head through the open office door. "I hope it's okay that I let Tag in. I heard the noise and got worried. You wouldn't believe the crowd out here, Cassie. Sheriff, the backup just pulled up outside. I think we should—"

"Cassie?" Kate pushed Stacie aside. "Oh, my God," she whispered, looking at Pete sprawled on the floor, at Tag who was holding him there with a foot in the small of his back. "Oh, my God."

"You already said that," Cassie said.

Two more uniformed officers pushed their way through, followed by Diane and Will and at least half the population of Pleasantville, all of whom tried to fit into the doorway to see what the commotion was all about.

Cassie looked at them and felt none of her usual resentment and anger. They weren't there to see her fail, or to make fun of her behind her back. They were there because they cared, and suddenly she grinned.

"What's so funny?" Kate stepped over Pete. "He could have killed you."

"Nah. I was armed." She lifted the ten-pound dildo from her shoulder and laughed.

Tag frowned and exchanged a worried look with Kate. "Cassie, sweetheart, I think maybe you should sit down." He stepped back from Pete and let one of the deputies haul him out of the office. "Come on." He reached for her, but she danced away, far too full of joy to be contained. *"Cassie."*

Kate said her name then, too, and so did Stacie, but she just whirled around in a circle until she was dizzy, finally collapsing…right in Tag's arms, as he reached out with an oath to catch her.

"Hey, look at that," she said, gripping his shirt, putting her face close to his. "Just where I wanted to be."

His arms tightened on her. "I think this is delayed shock. Let's sit down, okay? And—"

"Nope, not delayed shock." She cupped his face, and right there in front of everyone in her entire world, she sighed. "It's called an epiphany, Tag. I came here to get away, but I also came for revenge. It wasn't going to be pretty. But the oddest thing happened."

"What?" he whispered.

"You," she whispered back. "And Kate. And Stacie. And everyone else. I came for revenge but got something even better. I got you." She raised her voice so everyone could hear. "I'm not going back to New York. I'm going to stay."

Kate grinned. "Yes!"

"Someone's got to keep things hopping." Cassie kept her eyes on Tag, who was watching her very carefully, very intently.

"How do you intend to keep things hopping?" he asked softly. "More stalkings? Another interesting shop? More tickets?"

"Nope." She swallowed, because this is where it got a little risky. Not that she wasn't above risk, but this was the mother of all risks. "I'm going to marry the sheriff."

Stacie gaped, then laughed.

Kate whooped.

Tag went utterly, utterly still. "You're going to marry me."

"Yep." She held her breath. "Because I'm assuming you still love me."

"My love wasn't the love in question," he pointed out, now holding her with a death grip, as if he was afraid she'd vanish.

"No, it wasn't, was it?" She laughed, then kissed him. "But now, no one's love is in question." She bit her lip. "Right?"

"Is that your way of asking if I still love you?"

"A Tremaine would never ask such a thing."

"Hmm." Tag lifted a doubtful brow, then ruined it by shaking his head, cupping her face and kissing her long and hot and wet. Coming up for air, he put his forehead to hers. "I do love you. I always will."

"That's good." She was shaking. *Shaking.*

"It's your turn, Cassie," Stacie hissed.

"Yeah." She took a deep breath. "Okay. Tag…"

"Yes, that's his name," Kate said impatiently. "Damn it, Cassie, just tell him! You're killing us here."

Tag nodded in agreement. "Killing us."

God, he was adorable. How could a man be so hot, so sexy, so absolutely magnificent, and still be adorable? "I love you, Tag. I always will."

"Well, then." His voice was suspiciously wobbly. "What do you say we kick everyone out of here, and…" Leaning forward he whispered a lovely, very wicked suggestion in her ear involving King-Size Kong Dildo and her desk.

Even more wobbly now, she gestured behind her back for everyone to go, her eyes on Tag's as her heart rate kicked into gear. "Lock the door on your way out," she said to them and, with a grin, reached for Tag.

Epilogue

One Year Later

CASSIE LIFTED HER fingers to adjust the blindfold and felt a large, warm hand hold her back.

"Don't touch it."

Despite the warm night, she shivered at the rough whisper. "Then tell me where you're taking me."

"You'll know it soon enough. Nervous, Cassie?"

Her body was tingling in awareness. Not fear, but arousal. "No," she decided, and felt a stroke of work-roughened fingers over her jaw as a reward.

"Almost there," Tag said, and tugged on her hand, making her stumble against him. Taking full advantage of that, his hands molded her body under the guise of supporting her. Her legs trembled—a direct result of his hands dallying on her breasts and between her thighs. Her surrendering sigh was swallowed by his mouth.

Long moments passed until they both came up for air, panting like a pair of hormonal teenagers. Then Tag lifted her, carried her for a moment before setting her down.

On sand.

He pulled off the blindfold. She stood on the beach—*their* beach—by the lake, lit only by the barest of moons.

"Today is exactly one year since you told everyone you were marrying me," he said, tugging her down, laying her back, towering over her as he covered her body with his. Gathering her hands in his, he lifted them over her head and held her still. "But since you haven't done that yet, I thought…"

"You thought…" She was breathless already. And dying for him. She'd have imagined this would have gotten old after one long year together but they still came together every single night as if they couldn't get enough.

She had the feeling she would never be able to get enough.

"I thought it was time," he said. "To set a date."

Her entire body, straining for release only a moment before, jerked with shock.

Taking advantage of her pinned hands, he unbuttoned her sundress until she was bared to him. With a groan, he bent to a breast, worshipped a nipple. "How about Labor Day weekend? I have some time coming—"

"Tag." Unable to think with his mouth on her, she bucked beneath him until he lifted his head. "Tag."

"I know." He kissed her so gently, so tenderly on the mouth it brought tears to her eyes. "It seems silly to need the paper. But I do. I need it, Cassie." He stripped off his shirt, shoved down his jeans. Swept aside her panties.

And entered her. Then went absolutely still as he stared down into her face with so much emotion, her throat closed. "I love you, Cassie. I always dreamed of this, of asking my fantasy woman to be mine forever—"

"Don't tell me I'm your fantasy woman." She gasped when he stroked once, nearly begged for another one. "We…both know I'm not."

"That's what makes this so perfect. You're better than my fantasy woman could ever be." He stroked again and they both let out a helpless hum. "Oh, yeah, so much better."

"Tag…" To make sure he wouldn't stop again, she grabbed his butt and pulled him closer. "Keep going."

"If you say it."

"Tag…"

"Say it."

"Okay." Her eyes nearly drifted shut when he rewarded her with another thrust, but she forced them to stay open. She didn't want to miss this. "I never wanted anyone in my heart, but somehow you wormed your way— Ouch!" She laughed when he bit her lower lip. "Okay, I *let* you in. I wanted you in. I love you. And yes, it's time. I want to be your wife. Marry me, Tag."

"Right now?"

"Yes. But…finish me first!"

His grin was full of both love and wickedness as he rubbed his jaw to hers. "As your heart desires."

"My heart desires!"

Beneath the stars and in tune to the lake's water gently hitting the shores at their feet, he did just that. Gave her everything her heart desired.

★ ★ ★ ★ ★

To Jill Shalvis—a great critique partner, an even greater friend.
Thanks for always being there.

And, as always, to Bruce.
Thanks for the Christmas gifts/tax write-offs.
Research has never been more fun.

Leslie Kelly

NATURALLY NAUGHTY

Prologue

Ten Years Ago

HOLDING HER PINK taffeta dress up to her knees, Kate Jones trudged toward home wishing the ground would open up and swallow her. Live burial seemed better than spending one more night in Pleasantville, Ohio. Her cousin's favorite expression came to mind—*This town's about as pleasant as a yeast infection.*

Without a doubt, this evening would have a place on Kate's list of all-time worst experiences. No, it wasn't nearly as bad as when her dad had died, or when her mom had brought her here to live, a town where their family was treated like dirt. In terms of teenage experiences, however, tonight was bad. Kate had been resoundingly dumped. On prom night no less.

You should have stayed, a voice whispered in her brain.

Kate snorted. "Stayed? After being jilted by Darren McIntyre for Angela Winfield, wickedest witch on earth? Right!"

Cassie wouldn't have run away. No, her cousin would have popped Angela one, kicked Darren where it counted, and told them to stick it where the sun didn't shine. Too bad she'd left early.

She passed another dark house. Its inhabitants were probably cozy in their beds, reflecting on their *pleasant* days. They wouldn't think twice about her trudging in the street. Who'd expect anything else from a trashy Tremaine? Her last name might be Jones, but no one let her forget her mother's maiden name. In spite of being a straight-A student who'd never gotten into any real trouble, people here believed Kate must have hit every no-good branch on her way down the Tremaine family tree.

Turning off Petunia onto Pansy Lane, Kate grimaced for the half-millionth time at the dumb street names. *I'd love a giant bottle of Weed-B-Gone.* She could think of a creeping pest she'd like to zap. Darren.

"Darren's a conceited jerk." Kate knew she shouldn't have gone with him, especially since his mother hated her. But just for one night she'd wanted to be part of the in crowd. She'd wanted to be cool and popular, instead of the nice, quiet girl who tried to disguise her family's poverty by getting good grades and working harder than anyone ever expected.

Tonight at the prom Angela had pawed all over Darren, urging him to ditch Kate and leave with her instead. The whole school knew Angela put out. And despite being a trashy Tremaine, Kate did not. Hmm, such a tough choice for Darren—Angela the tramp from the most respected family in town? Or Kate the pure, from the trashiest one? What was a horny eighteen-year-old boy to do?

He'd left so fast Kate's head had spun.

Kate was nearly home when the rain started. "What did I do to deserve this?" she said as drops hit her face. She was long past the point of caring about her panty hose. Nor did she worry about her makeup smearing—her tears had accomplished that.

The rain was just one more insult in a rotten night.

Spying her family's duplex, she prayed her mother was asleep, and Cassie home in the adjoining unit where she and

Aunt Flo lived. If Cassie was home, Kate would knock on her bedroom wall, which butted right against Cassie's in the next unit. They'd communicated by knocking on it since they were little girls. She'd signal her to sneak out back for one of their late-night gab sessions and fill her in about her lousy prom night.

Then she noticed a parked car out front. When her mother emerged from it, Kate wondered who Edie could have been out with so late. As a man exited she said, "Mayor Winfield?"

Yes, Angela's father. Rich, jolly John Winfield who kept her mother busy cleaning his fancy house on Lilac Hill. Once again the mayor thought nothing of working Edie late in the night, as if she didn't already spend forty hours a week scrubbing other people's toilets. Kate raised a brow as the mayor played gentleman and walked her mother to the door.

Walk away, her inner voice said. But she couldn't. Moving closer, she'd reached the steps when they began to kiss.

Kate moaned. Her gentle mother was having an affair with the very *married* mayor? John Winfield was the patriarch of the town, a family man, father of Angela and of town golden boy, J.J., who'd gone away to college years ago and hadn't returned.

After their kiss Winfield said, "I don't know what I'd do without you. You've made life bearable for me all these years."

Years? Mr. Mayor, the pure saintly leader of Pleasantville, has been having an affair with his cleaning woman for years?

"Here," Winfield continued, reaching into his pocket. "Your paycheck. I'm sorry it's so late, sugar, you know how she is."

A sweet smile softened her mother's face. "I'm okay, John. If she's overspent again and you're in need, I can wait a bit."

Kate shook her head in shock. The phone bill hadn't been paid. They'd had canned soup and tuna sandwiches for dinner all week. And her mother was giving back her paycheck to the richest man in town? Worse...the son of a bitch took it.

Blinking away tears as she acknowledged her respectable, much-loved mother was the willing mistress of a married man, she darted around back. Kate instinctively headed toward the ramshackle tree house where she and Cassie had played as kids, seeking comfort like a child would seek her mother's arms. Kate whimpered as she realized she no longer had that option. Her mother wasn't the person she'd always thought she was.

Looking up as she approached, she saw a glow of light from within and the burning red tip of a cigarette.

Cassie. Kate paused. She simply could not tell her cousin what she'd witnessed in front of the house. Cassie and Kate had long ago accepted the truth about their mothers. Cassie's mom, Flo, was the wild charmer who'd let them have makeup parties at age seven, and bought them their first six-pack. They loved her, no matter what the town thought of her outrageous clothes and numerous affairs. But Edie had been the real nurturing mother figure, the kind one who'd dried their tears and encouraged their dreams.

For Kate, Edie would never be the same. How could she destroy Cassie's image of Edie, too? In spite of her outward toughness, Kate knew Cassie would be very hurt by this. As hurt as Kate had been. So no, she couldn't tell her. Not now. Maybe not ever.

"Kitty Kate, you down there?"

Wiping away her tears, she climbed the rope ladder. Inside the tree house, Cassie's golden hair was haloed by candlelight. "Hi."

"Hey." Cassie took another long drag of her cigarette.

"Got another one?" Kate sat next to her cousin, noting the way their dresses filled up nearly every inch of floor space in the tiny house. Hers a boring pink. Cassie's a sultry black that screamed seduction and showcased her curvy figure.

"Last time you smoked you ralphed all over the bathroom."

Feeling sick enough already, Kate didn't risk smoking. "You okay? You skipped out on prom pretty early."

"Yeah. I'm sure the gold-plated set missed me real bad."

Kate ignored the sarcasm. "I missed you. What happened?"

Cassie gave a bitter laugh. "Biff said we were going to a party. Turns out he had a two-person, naked party in mind."

"Perv."

"Total perv. Then he gets pulled over for drunk driving."

"You were drinking?" Kate raised a surprised brow, knowing Cassie thought alcohol made guys stupid and mean.

"No. He wanted to get beer, so we stopped at the store before the prom. He said I should buy it since I look older. Friggin' moron. Like the clerk wouldn't notice I was wearing a prom dress."

"What'd you do?"

"I pretended I couldn't. He found somebody else at the prom who gave him some." Cassie squashed out her cigarette and leaned her head against the wall. "Look, Katey, I don't want to talk about this. Why are you here? Shouldn't you and Darling Darren be celebrating as king and queen of Pea-Ville High right now?"

Kate told her everything, leaving out what had happened when she got home. "Guess we both had disastrous prom nights."

Cassie took Kate's hand. "Did I say Darling Darren? I meant Dickless Darren. I hope you told him to eat shit and die."

"I told him he deserved a girl like Angela, and took off." Frankly, she liked Cassie's comeback better. If she'd thought about it long enough, maybe she could have come up with it. But Kate was so used to being the sweeter of the Tremaine cousins, she generally refrained from mouthing off out loud, as she often did in her brain, or when alone with Cassie.

"Good for you."

Cassie opened an old, dusty Arturo Fuente cigar box in which they hid the stashes of stuff they didn't want the moms to find. It held candles, diaries, even a *Playgirl* they'd dug out of Flo's trash can a few years ago. "I hate this stinking town."

Remembering the way she'd felt as she watched Mayor Winfield and her mother, Kate completely understood. "Ditto."

"I'd give anything to get outta here. Make it big, make lots of money, then come back and tell them all to stuff it."

Kate had the same fantasy. Hours spent in the old Rialto Theater had introduced her to places she wanted to go, people she wanted to meet. Women she wanted to become. Far away from here. "Wouldn't that be something? The trashy Tremaine cousins coming back and stirring up some serious trouble," Kate said. "You know what I'd do? I'd open up a shop right next door to Mrs. McIntyre's Tea Room. And I'd sell…dirty movies!"

Cassie snickered. "Go all out, triple-X porn, baby."

"And sex toys. Darren's mom could really use a vibrator."

"You wouldn't know a vibrator if it fell in your lap. *Turned on.* So, first stop in the big city, we buy sex toys."

Kate giggled. "And when we're rich and famous, we come back here and shove 'em right up certain people's noses."

Cassie reached into the box, grabbing Kate's diary. "I've been sitting here listing all the things I'd do to get even with some people in this town. Why don't you make one, too?"

"A list?"

"Yep. We each list the things we'll someday do to the cruddy populace of Pleasantville, if we ever get the chance."

The idea made perfect sense to Kate. "Publicly humiliate Darren McIntyre and Angela Winfield," she said as she wrote.

As they wrote Kate watched Cassie's smile fade as she thought of something else. Kate couldn't stop her own thoughts from returning to her mother. John Winfield.

She ached, deep within, at the loss of her own childhood beliefs.

Tears blurred her vision as she secretly added one more item to her list. *For Mom's sake, get even with the Winfield family...particularly John Winfield.* She didn't know how, but someday she would do to that family what they'd done to hers...

Cause some serious heartache.

1

Present Day

As SHE PULLED UP in front of the Rose Café on Magnolia Avenue, Kate Jones took a deep breath and looked around at the heart of Pleasantville. Heart. Probably the wrong word. The town hadn't possessed that particular organ when she'd left ten years ago. Judging by what her mother had told her in their last phone call, she feared it hadn't grown one in the intervening decade.

The street appeared the same on the surface, though was perhaps dirtier, its buildings grayer than she remembered. Warped, mildew-speckled boards covered some of the windows of the once-thriving storefronts. Very few people strolled along the brick sidewalks. The cheerful, emerald paint on the benches lining the fountain in the town square had faded to a faint pea-green. A reluctant grin crossed her lips as she heard Cassie's voice in her head. *Welcome back to Pea-Ville.*

Hers wouldn't be an extended stay. She had a job to do, then she'd drive away forever. Reaching for the door handle of her SUV, she paused when she heard her cell phone ring. "Yes?"

"Kate, I'm going crazy. Tell me you're on your way home."

"Armand, I've only been gone one day," Kate said with a laugh, recognizing the voice of her high-strung, creative business partner. "Besides, you were crazy before you met me."

"Crazy and poor. Now I'm crazy and rich and I can't take this kind of pressure. You are going to pay for leaving me in charge. Nothing that happens at Bare Essentials while you're gone is my fault. Understood?"

"Nothing's going to go wrong in two or three days. Tell me what happened so we can fix it."

"The shipment didn't arrive from California. We're down to *one* Bucky Beaver. And he was featured in the ad this weekend."

Oh, yes, the world would indeed stop revolving without their bestselling special toy. "I don't think it's a problem of catastrophic proportions. We sell lots of other products."

"None that were featured in the ad. I can see an entire girl's college softball team coming in to stock up for an out-of-town game, and finding the shelves bare." She heard Armand groan. "I see riots. Stampedes. Ten-inch rubber dildoes lobbed at my head until I am knocked unconscious. Imagine having to explain that to the handsome young police officer in his tight blue suit with his jaunty black cap when he comes in response to my frantic call." He paused. "Hmm...maybe this isn't such a crisis after all."

"Definitely not, but just call the supplier anyway."

"Maybe I should ask your cousin to use her connections..."

"Cassie's still in Europe. I think." Kate wasn't quite sure where her famous model cousin was working this week. She'd tried to track her down after getting her mother's news and had left messages with Cassie's agent and publicist. So far, no word. Cassie almost seemed to be in hiding. Another worry.

"So how's business today?" she asked.

"As thriving as ever," he replied. "Two different bridal parties came in this morning, hence the shortage of Buckys."

"I do love those wedding showers."

"Dewy brides and do-me bridesmaids. A delightful, money-spending combination."

"Absolutely. Now, have there been any calls for me?" She wondered if Edie had tried to reach her again from her new home in Florida. Their last conversation had ended somewhat abruptly.

Edie hadn't told her all the details of what some people in this town had put her through during her last weeks of residence. What she did say had made Kate wince. She gave her full opinion on the matter, though never revealing she knew the truth of Edie's relationship with Mayor Winfield.

"None that matter. But I warn you, if Phillip Sayre calls again, I'm stealing him for myself. So you better hurry your pretty fanny back here to Chicago."

"You're welcome to him. One date was quite enough for me. The man has a huge ego."

"You know what they say, big ego, big…"

"I think you mean big hands. Or big feet. In any case, I don't have any interest in finding out when it comes to Phillip. Who needs a big, sloppy real one attached to an arrogant, untrustworthy man, when a small, clean vibrating one with no strings attached is sufficient?"

Armand tsked, though she knew he wasn't shocked. After all, he was one of the few people with whom Kate felt comfortable enough to reveal her occasional less-than-nice-girl qualities.

"Playing with the merchandise?" he asked.

"Ah, you caught me. How can I sell it if I can't attest to its effectiveness?"

"As long as you paid for it first and weren't sampling the wares then putting them right back on the shelves."

Yuck! Kate snorted a laugh. "Okay, you win, you nasty thing." Armand always won in games of sexual one-upmanship.

"Besides, small vibrating ones don't have hands or mouths."

"Some have tongues," Kate pointed out with a grin, remembering one of their more popular models of vibrator... a wagging tongue. Cassie had seen it during her last visit to the store in Chicago and had declared it the most disgusting thing she'd ever seen. When Kate had turned it on to show her what it could do, Cassie had bought two of them.

"I'm hanging up now. Be good," Kate said.

"Impossible. Don't you be good, either. It's bad for you."

Kate smiled at Armand's kissy sounds as she cut the connection. She remained in the driver's seat, missing Armand. He was the only man in her life she had ever completely trusted.

A shrink might surmise that it was because Armand was gay, and therefore not a romantic possibility, which allowed Kate to open up and trust him.

The shrink would probably be right. Trusting men had never been her strong suit. One more thing to thank Mayor Winfield for, she supposed. Not to mention the few men she'd dated over the years, who had never inspired thoughts of true love and Prince Charming. More like true greed and Sir Fast Track.

"So, do I get out or restart the car and drive away?" she asked herself, already missing more than just her friend and partner. She also missed her apartment overlooking the water. She really missed her beautiful, stylish shop with its brightly lit, tasteful decor, such a contrast to some of the more frankly startling products they sold.

Two stories high, with huge front glass windows, soft lemony-yellow carpet and delicately intricate display cases, Bare Essentials had done what everyone had sworn couldn't be done. They'd taken sex and made it classy and elegant enough for Michigan Avenue.

Yes, she wanted to be home. Actually, she wanted to be *anywhere* but here.

Could she really go through with it? Could she walk along these streets, enter her mother's house and go through her childhood things so her mother could list the place for sale?

Well, that was the one good thing. At least Edie had finally gotten out, too. Though Edie had taken frequent trips to the city, she'd resisted moving away from Pleasantville for good. No, it had taken Mayor Winfield's death, his subsequent will and some vicious gossip to accomplish that feat.

Kate thought she'd outgrown the vulnerability this place created in her. She wasn't the same girl who used to hide in the tree house to cry after school when she'd been teased about her secondhand clothes. She was no longer a trashy Tremaine kid from the wrong side of town. She and her cousin had bolted from Pleasantville one week after high school graduation, moving to big cities—Kate to Chicago, Cassie to New York's modeling scene—and working to make something of themselves.

Kate had long ago learned the only way to get what you wanted was to work hard for it. Being smart helped, but she knew her limitations. She wasn't brilliant. And as much as she hated to admit it, she wasn't talented enough to pursue her teenage dream of a career in theater, though she'd probably always fantasize about it.

No, common sense and pure determination had been the keys to achieving her goals. So she'd worked retail jobs by day and gone to school by night, taking business and accounting courses, sneaking in a few acting or performing credits when she could.

Then the fates had been kind. She'd met Armand, a brilliantly creative lingerie designer, at exactly the time when Cassie's career had taken off and she'd had the means to loan Kate the start-up money for a business.

An outrageous, somewhat *dramatic* business.

Combining her need to succeed, her innate business sense and her secret love for the flamboyantly theatrical, she'd dreamed up Bare Essentials. Though originally just designed to be an upscale lingerie boutique to feature Armand's creations, bringing in other seductive items—sexy toys, games for couples, seductive videos and erotic literature—had really made Bare Essentials take off like a rocket when it opened.

The fabulously decorated, exotic shop had taken Chicago by storm. With the right props, location and set design, what could have been a seedy, backroom store was instead a hot, trendy spot for Chicago's well-to-do singles and adventurous couples.

Coming back to Pleasantville should have been absolutely no problem for the woman who'd been featured in Chicago's *Business Journal* last month as one of the most innovative businesswomen in the city. Still, sitting in the parked SUV, she felt oppression settle on her like two giant hands pushing down on her shoulders. The long-buried part of her that had once been so vulnerable, made to feel so small and helpless and sad, came roaring back to life with one realization.

She was really here.

Taking a deep breath, she opened the door. "Home lousy home," she whispered. Then she stepped into Pleasantville.

As HE SAT gingerly on the edge of a plastic-covered sofa in the parlor of his childhood home, Jack Winfield considered committing hari-kari with the fireplace poker. Or at least stuffing two of the cow-faced ceramic miniatures his mother collected into his ears to block out the sound of her chewing out the new housekeeper in the next room. *Sophie, the luncheon salad was unacceptably warm and the pasta unforgivably cold.*

As if anyone cared about the food's temperature when its texture was the equivalency of wet cardboard.

"She'd never forgive me if I got blood on the carpet."

He eyed the poker again. Maybe just a whack in the head for a peaceful hour of unconsciousness? At least then he could sleep, uninterrupted by the prancing snuffle of his mother's perpetually horny bulldog, Leonardo, who seemed to have mistaken Jack's pant leg for the hind end of a shapely retriever.

"Sophie," he heard from the hall, "be sure Mr. Winfield's drink is freshened before you start clearing away the dishes."

"Sophie, be sure to drop a tranquilizer in his glass, too, so Mr. Winfield can get through another day in this bloody mausoleum," he muttered.

He rubbed a weary hand over his brow and sank deeper into the uncomfortable sofa. The plastic crinkled beneath his ass. Sick of it, he finally slid off to sit on the plushly carpeted floor. Grabbing a pillow, he put it behind his head and leaned back, wondering how long it had been since he'd relaxed.

"Three days. Five hours. Twenty-seven minutes." Not since he'd returned home to Pleasantville for this long weekend.

Jack didn't like feeling so caged-in. He needed to be home, in his own Chicago apartment, away from grief and the smell of old dead roses and talcum powder. Away from his mother's tears and his sister's complaints.

Actually, when he thought about it, what he really needed to bring about sleep and a good mood was a seriously intense blow job. Followed by some equally intense reciprocal oral sex. And finally good old, blissful, hot, headboard-slamming copulation.

He hadn't been laid in four months and was feeling the stress. It almost seemed worth it to call his ex and ask her to meet him at his place the next day for some we're-not-getting-back-together-but-we-sure-had-fun-in-the-sack sex.

Home. Chicago. Late tonight. And not a moment too soon.

Jack supposed there were worse places to visit than his old hometown of Pleasantville, Ohio. Siberia came to mind. Or Afghanistan. The fiery pits of hell. Then again…

"You're sure you have to leave tonight?" his mother asked as she entered the room. "I thought you were going to stay longer than three days. There's so much to do."

"I'm sorry, Mother, you know I can't."

Tears came to her eyes. If he hadn't seen them every hour or so since his birth, they might have actually done what she wanted them to do—make him change his mind.

Sadly enough, his mother simply knew no other way to communicate. Honest conversation hadn't worked with Jack's father, so she'd relied on tears and emotional blackmail for as long as Jack could remember. His father had responded with prolonged absences from the house.

Dysfunctional did not begin to describe his parents' relationship. It—and his sister's three miserably failed walks down the aisle—had certainly been enough to sour Jack on the entire institution of marriage.

Relationships? Sure. He was all for romance. Dating. Companionship. From shared beer at a ball game, to candlelight dinners or walks along the shores of Lake Michigan on a windy afternoon, he thoroughly enjoyed spending time with women.

Not to mention good, frantic sex with someone who blew his mind but didn't expect to pick out curtains together the next morning. Someone like his ex, or any number of other females he knew who would happily satisfy any of those requirements with a single phone call. Not calling any of them lately had nothing to do with his certainty that he wasn't cut out for commitment or happily-ever-after. It had everything to do with his father's death. Work and his obligation to his family had been all he'd thought about for several months.

"Why can't you?" his mother prodded.

"I've got to wrap up the mall project I'm working on. You know I've planned some extended vacation time in July. I'll come back and help you get things settled then." *Unless I get hit by a train or kidnapped by aliens…one can hope, after all.*

Nah. Trains were messy. And after watching the "X-Files" for years, the alien thing didn't sound so great, either. He really couldn't get into the whole probing of body orifices gig.

So, a summer in Pleasantville it would be.

Thinking of how he'd originally intended to spend his long summer vacation—on a photographic big-game safari in Kenya—could almost make a grown man cry. Pampered poodles instead of elephants. Square dances instead of native tribal rituals. The chatter of blue-haired ladies sitting under hair-drying hoods instead of the roar of lions and the crackle of a raging bonfire. Small town, pouting blond princesses with teased up hair instead of worldly beauties with dark, mysterious eyes.

He sighed. "I think I'll take a walk downtown. To walk off that great lunch." What he really needed was to escape the stifling, decades-old, musty-rose-tinged air in the house.

"Just be careful, J.J."

Jack cringed at the nickname that his mother refused to give up. No one but his parents had called him J.J.—or John Junior—in twenty years. Still, he supposed he could put up with it if it made her happy. She could probably use some happiness right about now; she'd taken his father's death very hard.

"And it looks like it's going to rain. Take your rubbers."

He almost snorted. If she knew how badly he wanted to use a few rubbers—though, not the kind she imagined—she'd faint.

Kissing her on the forehead, he shrugged away a pang of guilt. He needed a brief break from her sadness to deal with his own. Besides, he wanted to get out of the house before his sister got back. With the three of them together, the absence of the fourth became all the more obvious.

His mother would sob quietly. His sister would wail loudly. And Jack would remain strong and quiet. He grieved for his father, too. But always alone, always in silence.

No, they hadn't been on very good terms lately. His father had never forgiven Jack for accepting a scholarship and moving to California fifteen years before. Even after grad school, when he'd gotten a job with an architecture firm in Chicago, he'd managed to avoid all but a handful of visits. The most recent, four months before, had been to attend his father's funeral.

He'd always figured there would be time to mend that fence, to try to make his father understand why he couldn't stay here, couldn't continue the family tradition and become king of Nowhereville. He'd never said that, of course, knowing the old man would have been cut to the quick at an insult to his town. He'd reminded Jack at least once a week growing up about his ancestors, who'd lived here since before the Civil War.

His mother's roots ran even deeper, a fact she enjoyed bringing up whenever his father had started pontificating.

Funny. Walking past his father's study, eyeing the brandy decanter and the old man's favorite glass, he realized he'd have gladly listened to his father pontificate if it meant seeing him once more. Amazing how there always seemed to be time for one more conversation right up until time ran out. That realization had helped a lot lately in dealing with his emotional mother.

He considered it a new life's lesson. Tomorrow might not ever come, so don't put off what you want to do today. Grab it now or risk losing the chance forever. John Winfield, Junior...Jack to his friends...planned to stick to that mantra.

Starting today.

THE FIRST THING Kate noticed during her walk downtown was the absence of the pungent odors of the Ohio General Paper Mill. The unpleasant aroma used to hang over the town, which had once seemed appropriate to Kate and Cassie. The mill had closed three years ago, according to her mother. That had caused the town's bad economic situation. Kate couldn't even conjure up any satisfaction about it. She felt only a sharp tinge of sadness, particularly when she saw the sorry condition of the town square and the courthouse. Pleasantville might not have been pleasant for the Tremaines, but it had actually once been pretty.

As she walked, she got a couple of curious looks. No one recognized her, not that she'd expected anyone to. She was no longer the pretty-in-a-quiet-way, nice girl she'd once been. That was one good thing about her move away from Pleasantville. She no longer felt the need to always be the good girl. Without Cassie around to be so flamboyantly bad, Kate had become free to speak her mind. She sometimes went out of her way to shock people, even if it was really only a defense mechanism to keep others from trying to get too close, as Armand claimed.

There were one or two people she wouldn't mind seeing. Some of her mother's friends had been kind. And Kate's high school drama teacher, Mr. Otis, had been one of the smartest people she'd ever met. She imagined he was long retired by now.

Feeling hot, Kate went into the deli for a drink. She didn't know the couple who ran the place, and they were friendlier than she'd expected. She began to relax. Maybe ten years of dislike had created an unrealistic anxiety about her trip back here.

After the deli, she continued her stroll. Heavy gray clouds blocked all but a few watery rays of sunlight and kept the unusual spring heat close to the ground. The soda helped cool her off, but her sleeveless silk blouse still clung to her body, and her ivory linen skirt hung limply in the thick humidity.

A few buildings down, in what used to be a record shop, she noticed a new business. A nail salon, judging by the neon hand in the window, which beckoned customers inside. From an angle, the middle finger on the hand appeared abnormally long, almost as though it was flipping the bird to everyone on the street. Then she saw the name—Nail Me. "Well, now I've got to go in."

"Pull up a chair, angel face," she heard. "You want your fingers, your toes or both? I'm runnin' a special."

Kate had to grin in response to the welcoming smile of a skinny girl, who looked no more than eighteen, sitting on a stool in the empty shop. "Uh, I don't actually need a manicure."

The young woman, who had bright orange hair and at least a half-dozen pierced earrings in one ear, sighed. "You sure?"

Kate nodded and held out her hands, knowing her regular manicurist would throw a fit if she ever went to someone else.

The girl whistled. "Nice." She then pointed to some chairs in a makeshift waiting area. "Have a seat anyway. You're a stranger, I can give you directions to anyplace you need to go."

"I'm familiar with this town. I've been here before."

"And you came back voluntarily?"

Kate chuckled. "You're not a fan of Pleasantville?"

"It's all right," the girl said, shrugging. "Could be a decent place, if it would move out of the 1940s and into the new millennium. Just needs something to shake things up."

The return of a trashy Tremaine could do the trick...not that Kate would be here long enough to renew any acquaintances.

"I wanted to see how the place has changed. I really should go now, though." She'd seen enough of downtown. Time to stop putting off the inevitable and to go out to her mom's house.

Bidding the girl goodbye, she exited, crossing Magnolia Avenue to walk back to her parked SUV. She'd only gone a few yards when someone across the street caught her eye.

A man. Oh, without question, a man. A tiny wolf whistle escaped her lips before Kate could stop it. *Mister, you are definitely in the wrong place.*

No way did this blond god belong here. He should be in Hollywood among the beautiful people. Not in this Ohio town where some men considered changing from crap-covered work boots into non-crap-covered work boots dressing up for a night out.

She sighed as she realized even her thoughts had regressed. Kate Jones, successful business owner, did not generally think about crap-covered anything.

Unable to help herself, she looked across the street at the man again. He appeared tall. Of course, to Kate, most people appeared tall since she stood five foot four. The stranger's dark blond hair caught the few remnants of sunlight peeking through the gray clouds. It shone like twenty-four-carat gold. Though she wasn't close enough to determine the color of his eyes, she certainly noted the strength of his jawline, the curve of his lips. And a body that would moisten the underwear of any female under ninety.

Knock it off, Kate. He's going to catch you staring.

She couldn't stop herself. She had to look some more, noting the tightness of his navy shirt against those broad shoulders and thick arms. Not to mention the tailored khaki slacks hugging narrow hips and long legs.

They hadn't grown them like this when she'd lived here.

From behind her, she heard a man shout, "Hey, Jack!"

The blond man looked over, probably searching for the person who'd shouted. But his stare found Kate first.

She froze as he spotted her. So did he. Though several yards of black paved street separated them, she could see the expression on his face. Interest. Definite interest. A slow smile. A brief nod.

The person who'd called to him was a man, so she figured Mr. Gorgeous—Jack—was smiling and nodding at *her*. And staring just as she had at him. An appreciative stare. An I'd-really-like-to-meet-you stare. A totally unexpected stare, considering her frame of mind since she'd pulled into this place a half hour ago.

She smiled back, simply unable to help it. Damn, the man had dimples. Someone needed to come along with a big street sweeper and clean her up, because, unless she was mistaken, she was melting into a puddle of mush from one heartbreakingly sexy grin.

"Hi," he said, though she couldn't hear him. She could tell by the way his lips moved. Those lips... Lord save her, the man had to kiss like a sensual dream with a mouth like that. And those thick arms to wrap around her. The hard chest to explore.

An old, seldom-heard voice of doubt mentally intruded. *He must be talking to someone else. Why would he be talking to me?*

Once Kate had reached Chicago, it had taken her a while before she'd begun to accept that men might really want to look at *her*...even when her stunning blond cousin was in the room. She almost couldn't get used to it, even now. Sure, she knew she had always been pretty. Sweet Kate. Quiet Kate. Smart, dark-haired, petite Kate with the pale, delicate face and the boring chocolate-brown eyes who'd always been too easily wounded by the meanness of others. Nothing like show-stopping bombshell Cassie, who was every 36-24-36 inch a Tremaine, with a mile of attitude and a ton of confidence.

Yet this Mount Olympus-bound hunk had stopped to flirt with *her*? He tilted his head to the side and raised one eyebrow. When he pointed to her, then to the sidewalk on which he stood, she knew what he was asking. *Your side or mine?*

Remembering where they were, she stiffened and shook her head. *Forget it. No way are you going to even say hello. Do what you have to do and get outta Dodge, Katherine Jones. You've got no time to get all drooly over the local Don Juan.*

He stepped closer, toward the curb. By the time his feet hit the street, Kate realized he was coming over, though not to talk to the man who'd hailed him. No, his stare had never left Kate's face. She forced herself to move, hurrying down the sidewalk.

She peeked over her shoulder only once. A mixture of relief and disappointment flooded through her as she realized the man who'd hailed him had planted himself firmly in the path of the blond hunk. He couldn't follow her even if he wanted to.

Did he want to? *Doesn't matter.* She kept on walking.

A plop of rain landed on Kate's shoulder. She experienced an instant of déjà vu, remembering walking the streets of

Pleasantville on a rainy night when the raindrops had warred with her tears to wash away her makeup.

Seeking shelter, she turned toward the nearest doorway. Somehow, without realizing where her steps had carried her, she found herself standing outside McIntyre's Tea Room. "Oh, no."

The Tea Room, owned by Darren McIntyre's mother, had been the worst spot for any Tremaine ten years ago. The old guard of Pleasantville—the Winfields and the other Lilac Hill set, considered this "their" territory. Kate's mom and her friends had been more comfortable at the beauty parlor in the basement of Eileen Saginaw's house, so it wasn't until Kate had gotten friendly with Darren that she'd ever even been in the Tea Room.

"Still the same," she mused, looking at the small, discreet sign in the window. Next door, though, Mr. McIntyre's menswear shop was gone, closed, dark and empty.

Don't, Kate. Just don't. Casting one more quick look up the street, she saw the handsome stranger watching her from over the shoulder of his companion. He wouldn't follow her, would he? Well, he certainly wouldn't follow her into the Tea Room, a notoriously female establishment.

Knowing she must have some liking for self-torture, she walked up the wood steps to the awning-covered porch and reached for the doorknob. Once inside, she had to pause for a moment as sense memory kicked in and her mind identified the smells of her youth. Yeasty bread. Raspberry jam. Spiced teas. Some old lady perfume...White Shoulders? Lots of hair spray. Dried flowers.

She had to stop in the foyer to take it all in.

This place, at least, was hopping, every table full. She recognized some faces, though they'd aged. Physically, nothing had altered. From the white-linen tablecloths to the lilac-tinted wallpaper, the room looked the same as the last time she'd been in it. All it needed was a glowering, frowning-faced Mrs. McIntyre to flare her nostrils as if she smelled something bad whenever Kate walked in, to make her trip down memory lane complete.

No one paid a bit of attention as she stood watching. They were all, it appeared, engaged in a room-wide debate over some poor soul they kept calling shameless and shocking.

Things hadn't changed here at all.

Knowing there was absolutely nothing in this place for her, Kate turned to leave. Before she could walk back out the door, however, she heard the only word that could have stopped her.

Tremaine.

2

As Harry Billingsley, the town's ancient barber, engaged him in conversation, Jack watched every step the brunette took. She walked quickly, almost tripping once on an uneven brick, as if she wanted to escape the rain. He knew better. She wasn't running from the rain. When she peeked over her shoulder at him, he knew she was avoiding *him*.

Something downright electric had happened a few moments ago when their stares had met across Magnolia Avenue. There'd been an instant connection, a shared intimacy though they were complete strangers. It was like nothing he'd ever experienced before.

Obviously she had been just as affected. Only instead of intriguing her, as it had him, their silent, thirty-second exchange had bothered her, scared her even. Her feet had turned cold and she'd run off.

No matter, he'd be able to find her again. The woman stood out here like a bloodred rose in a bouquet of daisies.

A few months ago he might not have let the charged stare across a deserted street affect him. His new attitude toward life, however, made finding the brunette and talking to her a must. No more letting opportunities slide. Now, when Jack Winfield saw a good thing, he was going to go after it. He somehow knew the stranger could be a very good thing indeed.

Jack tried to brush off Harry as politely as he could. "Yes, but I really have to go now. Maybe we can talk in July when I come back for a longer stay."

Harry continued. "Your father made some mistakes. Stirred up a lot of gossip around here with his will and Edie Jones."

Gossip. His least favorite word, and it was used as currency in this town. Jack had never listened to it and never would. So his father had left his maid a small bequest. Only in a town like this could that be considered gossip-worthy.

Watching as the dark-haired stranger in the sexy green blouse went into the Tea Room, he cringed. Of all the places she could have picked, why did she have to go into that hen's nest?

"I'm sorry, I really have to go," Jack said, finally simply walking away in the middle of Harry's long-winded monologue. He didn't care to hear about any old town scandals, especially not if they involved his father, the former mayor.

Following a stranger down a public street wasn't Jack's M.O. In fact, he didn't think he'd ever done it. But something about this stranger…this perfectly delightful stranger…made him certain he could follow her anywhere. He simply had to see her, up close. To determine if her face was really as delicate and perfect as it had appeared from across the street. If her eyes were possibly the same dark, rich brown as her long hair.

Shrugging, he walked to the entrance of the Tea Room and stood outside the door. For a second he wondered if old lady McIntyre would come out and shoo him away. She used to shout at all the boys who'd plant themselves on the stoop, hoping a customer with a take-out bag would hand over some free sweets.

Never happened, as far as he recalled. The snob set of Pleas-antville was notoriously tight-fisted with their sweets.

Crossing his arms in front of his chest, he proceeded to wait. "You've got to come out sooner or later."

It took less time than he expected. Before he even realized what was happening, the door to the Tea Room opened and she barreled out, crashing straight into his arms.

Just as if she belonged there.

"Oh, I'm so sorry!" Before Kate could step away from the person she'd crashed into, she quickly reached up to dash away some angry tears blurring her vision.

That these people could make her cry infuriated her. Some-how, though, anger and sharp hurt for her mother had com-bined to bring moisture to her eyes while she stood in the Tea Room listening to her family being torn apart yet again by a bunch of small-minded, small-town witches. It was either turn and hurry out or throw a big screaming hissy fit telling them all to jump on their broomsticks and fly straight to the devil.

She couldn't have said which course of action her cousin Cassie would have chosen. But for Kate, who'd become quite adept at maintaining a cool and calm composure, it was think first, react second. Kate didn't believe in hysterical fits—par-ticularly not when she had tears in her eyes. She did, however, believe in well-thought-out retaliation. *Someday.*

Finally turning her attention to the person she'd nailed, she sucked in a breath. "You."

Mr. Gorgeous. Jack. *This is* so *not my day.*

"Nice to meet you too," he said with a sexy grin, as if they were exchanging handshakes instead of being practically wrapped around one another on the steps of the Tea Room.

He made no effort to move away, seeming content that her

hand was on his shoulder, her belly pressed to his hip and her leg between both his thighs.

Of course, Kate didn't move, either. Funny thing the sudden lethargy in her limbs. Particularly considering the sharp heat shooting from the tips of her breasts—which brushed against his shirt—down to her stomach. Lower.

"Did I hurt you?" she whispered.

"Only my ego when you ran away from me a few minutes ago."

Kate blinked, but remained still, somehow unable, or perhaps unwilling, to break their intimate contact. Her breaths grew deeper as she watched him stare at her. His gaze studied her long, dark hair, her face, her mouth. His eyes glittered and a smile played about his sensual lips, as if he liked what he saw.

As did she. Up close, he was even more devastating than he'd been from across the street. Tanned skin, square jaw, beautiful green eyes with lashes a cover model would envy. Her fingers tightened slightly into his cotton shirt.

Move, Kate. Put your hands in the air and step away from the hunk.

"Are you married?" he asked.

She shook her head. But before she could ask him why he wanted to know, before she could do anything—including disengaging their much-too-close-together bodies—he moved closer. Kate thought she heard him whisper the word, "Good," just before he caught her mouth in a completely unexpected kiss.

Kiss? A gorgeous stranger was kissing her, in broad daylight, outside Mrs. McIntyre's Tea Room?

That was as far as her thoughts took her before she shooed them away and focused on what was happening.

Yes, the kiss was unexpected. And unbelievably pleasurable.

She didn't try to step back, didn't shove him away and slap his face as she probably should have. Instead she let him kiss her, let this incredible stranger gently take her lips with his own. Soft and tender at first, then more heated as he slipped his hands lower to encircle her waist and pull her even tighter against his body. As if they weren't already so close together a whisper couldn't have come between them.

As the kiss went on, she briefly wondered if she'd fallen asleep, if she was still at the motel where she'd spent the previous night. Maybe she'd popped one too many nickels into the Magic Fingers and they'd gotten her all worked up so she was having an amazingly intense, erotic dream.

Kissing had never been this good in real life. Besides, no man this perfect could exist in this nightmare of a town.

So she could be dreaming, couldn't she? And if it was merely a dream, couldn't she, uh, kiss him back?

She softened her mouth and tilted her head. Feeling the flick of his tongue against the seam of her lips, she whimpered, continuing to tell herself that this couldn't be happening. The beeping of a passing car horn and the musty damp-wood smell of the old porch on which they stood were merely realistic elements of her dream. These weren't real lips now tugging gently at hers, tasting her, exploring her. She hadn't fallen into the arms of a complete stranger...and stayed there quite happily.

Feeling a few drops of rain plop down from the striped awning over the Tea Room's porch onto her face, she focused on their descent down her cheek. Cold water. Warm kiss. Gentle tongue. His clean, male scent. Hard chest pressing against hers. A thrilling bulge in his pants pressing firmly against her lower belly, which made her rise up on her tiptoes to line things up a little better. The sudden hot flood of moisture between her thighs. Definite car horn beeping. Nosy-faced old lady stepping around them to go down the steps to the sidewalk.

The clarity of detail assured her she was not dreaming.

Insanity. She didn't care. His breath tasted minty as his mouth caressed hers, gently, then deeper. She moaned slightly, deep in her throat, no longer able to pretend this wasn't real, knowing she had to either just go for it, part her lips and let their tongues tangle and mate, or else shove him down the steps.

Kate's rational side said to shove. For once she told it to shut the hell up.

Her entire body hummed with energy. She lifted her leg, sliding it against his, delighting in the friction of her stocking against his trousers. As he moaned and pushed closer, she considered how simple a thing it would be to lift her leg to his hip, to let him pick her up until she encircled his waist with her thighs. To slide onto the wonderfully hard erection straining against the seam of his pants.

She wanted to. Desperately. If only there were no car engines, broad daylight...and the minor fact that he was a complete stranger.

He finally pulled away and smiled gently at her. She shook her head hard and gulped, noting the slowness of a passing car, the curious stare of a face in the window of the Rose Café across the street. Finally she took a wobbly step back. "You're insane."

He stepped forward. Following her. "No, I'm Jack."

Kate shook her head, still bemused. "You kissed me."

"I'm so glad you noticed."

"You can't go around kissing strangers on the street. How could you do that? Just...just...kiss me?"

He shrugged. "You said you weren't married."

"What if I were engaged? A novitiate? A lesbian?"

"Engaged isn't married, so I'd say tough luck to the guy." Grinning, he continued, "Novitiate would simply be a crime against mankind, definitely worth ignoring." He glanced down at her trembling body, his stare lingering on the hard tips of her breasts, scraping so sensitively against her blouse. Then at her legs, which she had to clench together to try to stop the trembling. Not to mention the hot, musky smell of aroused woman.

"Lesbian isn't even in the realm of possibility," he finally said, his voice nearly a purr. "You want me pretty badly."

Her jaw dropped. He tipped it up with the tip of his index finger. "Now, introductions. Remember? I'm Jack. It's very nice to meet you. Who are you, and what in God's name are you doing in Pleasantville?"

She ignored the question. "You followed me."

He didn't try to deny it. "Guilty."

That stopped her. "Why?"

He shrugged. "Fate? Instinct?" Then he lowered his voice, almost whispering as he leaned even closer until his body almost touched hers from shoulder to knee. "Or maybe so I could see what color eyes my children are going to have?"

Kate opened her mouth, but couldn't make a sound come out.

The man was unbelievable. Outrageous. Sexy. Charming and heart-stoppingly handsome.

And still standing much too close. So close she could see his pulse beating in his neck and the cords of muscle on his shoulders. His upper arms were thick beneath the tight navy cotton of his shirt, so different from the Chicago health club addicts she sometimes dated. As if he didn't work out for his health, but because he was the kind of guy who just needed to pound something once in a while.

Her breath caught as she imagined his sweaty, hard body pounding something. Pounding *into* something. Into someone.

Focus!

"How do you know I don't already have a live-in guy and three kids somewhere?" she finally asked, hearing the shakiness in her voice. She took another step back, needing air, needing space, needing control of her own mind, which seemed muddled and fuzzy as she examined the tanned V of skin revealed by his shirt. Had she really been kissed by him? Held in his arms? And, damn it, why hadn't she thought to move her fingers to that V to tangle in the light matting of chest hair just below his throat? *Cool it, Kate!*

"Do you?"

Yes. Tell him yes. Then run like hell. "No."

He smiled. "I didn't think so. So, tell me your name, tell me your phone number, and let's go to dinner."

Dinner. Only a few hours till dinnertime and she hadn't even made it to her mother's house yet.

"No. I can't."

"You take my breath away, run right into me, ruin my pants and you won't even tell me your name? Cruel."

"Cruel. Yeah. Welcome to Pleasantville," she muttered.

"Ah, I suspected you weren't a native."

Remembering his other comment she asked, "What's wrong with your pants?" She glanced down, noting the rigid bulge in his crotch, and had to gulp. Yeah, she guessed their embrace had ruined the *fit* of his pants, anyway.

He obviously saw her stare and lifted a brow. Then he turned, pointing ruefully at his taut backside hugged close in the expensive khaki trousers. Expensive, wet and *dirty* khaki trousers. Somehow, during their embrace, he must have leaned back against the soggy wood porch railing.

"You're making it worse," she noted, watching as he tried to brush off the dirt, but only succeeded in smearing the stains around.

"You could offer to help."

Uh, right. Her hands. On his perfect male butt. Brushing against those lean hips. Trying not to squeeze his firm thighs. She swallowed hard. Glancing at him, she saw laughter in his eyes. Green eyes, dimples, thick blond hair, a body to stop traffic and what looked to be a good solid eight inches of hot and ready hard-on just waiting to be let loose.

On a public street. In broad daylight. In *Pleasantville*.

Sometimes life simply wasn't fair.

"Sure, take off your pants and I'll drop them off at Royal Dry Cleaners for you," she finally managed to say, striving for nonchalance.

"That'd cause some eyes to pop, wouldn't it?" he asked with a wicked grin. "You really want me to take them off now?"

She felt heat stain her cheeks. "I mean, you can…go somewhere and change."

He chuckled. "I was teasing you. It's not a problem. Besides, Royal closed several years ago. Pleasantville has no dry cleaner anymore."

"A shame, given this town's dirty laundry," she muttered.

He gave her a curious look, but she certainly wasn't going to elaborate.

"So, are you going to make it up to me?"

"I'm sorry if my running into you caused you to fall headfirst onto my lips and then back into the railing to ruin your pants," she said, crossing her arms in front of her chest.

"Apology accepted," he said succinctly, as if he'd had nothing to do with what had just happened.

She found herself almost grinning. Finally she admitted, "My name's Kate."

He brushed a strand of hair off her face, his fingers warm against her temple. Her heart skipped a beat.

"It's nice to meet you, Kate." He somehow made the simple

words seem much more suggestive than they were. *It'd be nice to have you, Kate.* And, oh, it'd be nice to be had.

Before she could reply, Kate heard the Tea Room door open. Three women emerged, eyeing them curiously.

"I have to go," she whispered, feeling the blood drain from her face. How this stranger could have made her forget the things she'd heard in the Tea Room, she didn't know. The memory of the vicious gossip came back full force now, though.

Gossip about her mother. Her aunt. And the men in this town who apparently had left them each money or property.

According to the harpies, Edie had been left a fortune by Mayor John Winfield. Which, they believed, had to have been a payoff for a secret, torrid love affair.

Kate mentally snorted. The man had left Edie a measly thousand bucks. As far as Kate was concerned, that didn't even cover the interest on all the late paychecks over the years.

It was almost laughable, really. The town in a tizzy, rumors of a scandalous affair. It could have been downright hilarious…if only it hadn't been true. Kate suspected she was the single person who understood that, just this once, the vicious, mean-spirited Pleasantville grapevine was spreading a rumor actually based in truth.

The old saying about the truth hurting had never been more appropriate. In this particular case, the truth made her ache. She'd never completely gotten over the shock and hurt of that life-altering moment when her childhood illusions had shattered and her mother's saintly image had become all too human.

"Don't leave."

She turned her attention back to the amazing stranger. He didn't plead, didn't cajole or coerce. He simply stared at her, all gorgeous intensity, tempting her with his smile and the heat in his eyes.

"I have to go somewhere. I'm only in town for today." She wondered if he heard the anger and hurt in her voice. Did he see her hands shaking as she watched the audience inside the doorway of the Tea Room grow and expand?

Then, perhaps *because* the audience in the doorway was expanding, or perhaps because she simply wanted to know if he'd really kissed as well as she'd thought, she leaned up on her toes and slipped a hand behind the stranger's—Jack's—neck.

"Thanks, Jack, for giving me one pleasant thing to remember about my visit back to this mean little town." His lips parted as she pulled him down to press a hot, wet kiss to his mouth. She playfully moved her tongue against his lips, teasing and coaxing him to be naughty with her.

He complied instantly, lowering his hands to her hips, tugging her tightly against his body. The kiss deepened and somewhere Kate heard a shocked gasp.

As if she cared.

Finally, dizzy and breathless, she felt him let her go. Somehow, a simple "Up-yours" to the occupants of the Tea Room had turned into a conflagration of desire. She found it hard to stand. Her whole body ached and she wanted to cry at the thought of not finishing what she'd so recklessly restarted.

"I'll be seeing you, Kate," he promised in a husky whisper.

And somehow, not sure why, she felt sure he was right.

AFTER SHE GOT IN her SUV and drove away, Jack stood on the porch for several moments. He ignored the people exiting the Tea Room—his mother's cronies who'd probably already called her. And the men staring unabashedly from the barbershop—his late father's buddies who probably wanted to change places with him.

They'd all watched while he'd done something outrageous. He'd seen a chance, seen something he wanted, followed his instincts and kissed a beautiful stranger. In his years playing the male/female sex/love game, he'd never done something so impulsive. Yeah, he'd probably had a few more women in his life than the average guy. But he'd never been as deeply affected by one, just from a heated stare across a nearly deserted street.

Jack still had the shakes, remembering the feel of her in his arms, the way she'd tilted her supple, firm body to maximize the touch of chest to chest, hip to hip. Man to woman. Her dark eyes had shone with confusion, but had been unable to hide the unexpected flare of passion. "Kate," he whispered out loud.

He felt no sense of urgency to go after her since he knew who she was. As soon as she'd said her name, he'd remembered her face from the picture in the Chicago paper a few weeks ago.

He hadn't read the article, and couldn't remember much— only that she owned some trendy new women's store on the Magnificent Mile. But he definitely remembered her face, and her name—Katherine…Kate—because, with her thick, dark hair she'd reminded him of an actress of the same name. Kate Jackson? No…but something like that. He couldn't place the last name yet, but he felt sure he would.

What on earth she was doing in Pleasantville he couldn't fathom. But tracking her down really shouldn't pose much of a problem at all. A scan of the newspaper's Web site archives and he'd be able to find the article easily enough.

His return to Chicago tonight couldn't come soon enough.

KATE DIDN'T PLAN to spend much time in her mother's house. Edie had packed up everything she really wanted when she'd moved to Florida a few weeks back. The place was immaculate, the cabinets emptied and the furniture covered. All Kate had to do was go through her own personal belongings and load what she wanted to keep into her SUV for the drive back to Chicago.

There wasn't much. Edie was a practical person, not an overly sentimental one. So there weren't scads of toys or Kate's first-grade papers to sort through. Just some precious items. Family pictures. Her first doll. The stuffed bear her father had given her for her sixth birthday—that was a month before he'd been killed in an accident involving his truck.

She carefully packed a carton with those things, rubbing the worn fur of the bear, remembering how she'd once been unable to sleep through the night without it curled in her arms. Leaving it behind when she'd left town had been an emotional decision, not a logical one. She'd left to escape her childhood, to escape the burden of her family name and the sadness over her mother's situation. She'd left everything that might connect her to this place, telling her mother over the years to feel free to get rid of her old stuff. Thankfully, Edie never had. She'd known exactly what to keep. And, judging by the absence of most of her high school junk—with the exception of the programs from plays in which Kate had appeared—what to throw away.

When she'd nearly finished, Kate noticed the old Arturo Fuente cigar box in the corner of her old room. Opening it, she felt a smile tug her lips as she saw two diaries, an empty pack of cigarettes, the stub of a burned-down candle. Even the tattered, musty *Playgirl*. Surely her mother hadn't opened this box—the magazine would have been long discarded, otherwise.

The memory of prom night descended with the impact of a boulder on her heart. That night had marked the end of teenage illusions. It had enforced adult consciousness, made her see her mother as a woman not merely a parent. Over the years she'd come to accept that moment as something everyone had to go through. While she'd been deeply disappointed, it hadn't affected her strong feelings for Edie. She loved her as much now as she ever had. And, deep down, she was thankful for having learned the valuable lesson about the fickleness of relationships and the heartbreak of love by seeing what her mother had gone through. It had saved her from ever having to experience it firsthand.

"Glad you got out, Mom. Now, find some great retired guy down in Florida and grab yourself some happiness."

Flipping idly through the *Playgirl,* she cast a speculative glance at the centerfold. "Not bad." She liked her men long and lean, though not hairless and smooth-chested like this guy. Though flaccid, he definitely had a decent package, reminding her that it had been a long time since she'd had sex. She'd been surrounded by fake penises of all shapes, colors and sizes for so long, she hardly remembered what a real one looked like.

"No big loss," she mused out loud, still staring. She hadn't been kidding when she'd told Armand a small, clean vibrating one was her preference these days. She enjoyed sex. But it seemed to be an awful lot of work for an orgasm she could give herself in five minutes flat. Okay, so she'd never stayed with a man enough to really fall in love and couldn't judge how "making love" compared to sex. Frankly, deep down Kate suspected she would *never* fall in love—since love would have to involve trust and vulnerability. She wouldn't allow anyone to make her vulnerable, not after seeing what it had done to her mother for a couple of decades.

So sex it was. And sex alone had suited her fine for some time now. As a matter of fact, her favorite new toy—and a hot seller at her store, Bare Essentials—was a tiny vibrator that snapped to the end of her finger and handled things quite nicely. Small enough to carry in a tiny case in her purse, it was safely hidden in a side pocket right at this very minute.

She might just have to dig out her small friend tonight at the hotel. An orgasm would help blow off some tension. Though it had been a long time since she'd had sex with a man—more than a year...okay, *two*—Kate certainly hadn't lacked for orgasms. "A woman owns her orgasms," she told the photo. "She can take them anytime she wants and doesn't need to be gifted with them by some guy with a big dick, a little brain and no heart."

Though, she had to admit, sometimes the real thing could be awfully nice. She closed her eyes, thinking of her day. Of Jack. Definitely not a little brain, judging by his quick wit and self-confidence. His friendly charm hinted at a man with a heart.

And, remembering the way he'd felt pressed against her body, he definitely had a big... "Snap out of it, Kate."

But she couldn't. Closing her eyes, she leaned against her old bed. She licked her lips, remembering how his tasted. She moved her hand to her breast, remembering how his chest had felt pressed against hers. She shifted on the floor, aroused again, her thoughts moving back to what she'd felt that afternoon.

She'd wanted him. Still did, judging by the hot dampness between her legs. Remembering she had brought her purse with her up to the bedroom, she reached for it, finding the zippered side pocket. Retrieving the vibrator, she snapped it onto the tip of her middle finger, and moved up onto the bed.

"Maybe it's been too long since the real thing," she said. There were benefits to sex with someone else. Touching. Deep, slow, wet kisses that curled her toes...like those she'd shared with Jack this afternoon. And she totally got off on having a man suck her breasts. Her nipples were hard now, just thinking about it. She envisioned a mouth. *His* mouth.

But her tiny friend would do for now. She moved her hand lower, down her body, under her skirt. Along the seam of her thigh-high stockings.

"Jack," she whispered as she brought the tiny, fluttering device to the lacy edge of her silk panties. "Who are you, really?"

3

A SHORT TIME LATER, after straightening herself up in the bathroom, Kate went back to work on her belongings. She grabbed the cigar box, snapped the lid closed and put it with the rest of her things. Loading everything in the car was a simple task, and she was finished a short time later.

Not even suppertime. In and out of Pleasantville in a matter of hours. A simple, unremarkable end to one long, painful chapter of her life. Well, unremarkable except for one thing. "Jack," she whispered. Did he live here in town? He must if the barber knew him. So he was best forgotten. She had no desire to get to know someone from Pleasantville. No matter how amazing a someone he might be.

Judging by what had happened in the bedroom, however, she imagined he'd be starring in her fantasies for a while. Her private interlude had done little to ease her tension. Orgasms were lovely. But she also found herself really wanting some hot and deep penetration. Unfortunately, she hadn't purchased any of the *larger* and more realistic-looking toys she sold at her store. "Might have to do something about that when I get home."

Before she left for the last time, she turned to look closer at the neighborhood. Her old street looked better than it had ten years ago. Obviously some new families had moved in. Most of the duplexes, which had once been considered the wrong side of the tracks, were neat and freshly painted. A rain-speckled kid's bike lay in front of a house up the block. Pretty flowers bloomed in the beds across the street. It appeared the lower-to middle-class residents here refused to give in to the apathy and depression that had sucked dry the downtown area. She smiled, hoping the kids growing up here walked with their heads held high.

Out of curiosity, Kate went back up to the porch to peek into the window of Aunt Flo's duplex. It was, as she expected, empty. Her aunt had hooked up with the rich man she'd always wanted and had gone off to live with him somewhere in Europe.

Good for the Tremaine sisters.

Kate got into her SUV and drove away, fully intending to drive straight out of town. There was nowhere else she needed to go. Yes, she might see a friendly face, such as Mrs. Saginaw or Mr. Otis. But, with her luck, she'd run into someone who'd greet her with a smile, then whisper about her family behind her back. As had most of the people she'd gone to high school with.

But Kate hadn't counted on one last tug of nostalgia. As she pulled off Magnolia onto Blossom, she spied the sign for the Rialto Theater. She sighed over the boarded windows and dilapidated sign. "Oh, no." The one spot in town she remembered with genuine fondness, and it had obviously gone under long ago.

Some demon pushed her right foot against the brake pedal and she brought the car to a stop. The cloudy, murky afternoon had actually begun to give way to a partly sunny early evening. Lazy late-day sunlight flickered off the broken bits of glass and bulb remaining in the old marquis. Casting a quick glance up the street, she saw no one else around. Obviously whatever was left of Pleasantville's prosperity lingered up on Magnolia. Only closed storefronts and boarded-up buildings framed the sad-looking, historic theater.

She got out of the car, telling herself she'd just glance in the giant fishbowl of a box office, but she couldn't resist going to the front door. Rubbing her hand on the dirty glass, she cleared away a spot of grime and looked in. To her surprise, the door moved beneath her hand. Reaching for the handle, she pushed on it, and the door opened easily. It seemed unfathomable to her that the graceful historic building should be left abandoned, but to leave it unlocked and unprotected was downright criminal.

She bit the corner of her lip. It was still light enough out that she could see clearly into the lobby. A ladder and drop cloth stood near the old refreshment counter, along with tools, plywood and paint cans. Someone had obviously been working.

"Curiosity killed the Kate," she muttered out loud.

Then she walked inside.

JACK WASTED A GOOD BIT of the afternoon walking around downtown Pleasantville, looking for pleasant memories. There weren't many. For a town where the Winfield family was considered royalty, he had to say he had few fond remembrances of his childhood. His father had been mostly busy. His mother had been mostly teary-eyed. His sister...hell, he barely recognized the smiling, sweet-faced toddler in the surly blond woman.

The only real ray of sunshine from his childhood, their *maid,* had recently left Pleasantville and moved away. He wished he'd had a chance to say goodbye to Edie. Maybe he'd ask his mother if she had her new address. Then again, his mother seemed awfully skittish whenever Edie's name came up. He hoped she didn't owe the hardworking woman back wages. His mother had no conception of careful spending and was usually in debt, part of the reason his parents' marriage had been so rocky.

While he walked, he kept his eyes open for a brand-spanking-new SUV. He really didn't expect to see her. Since he knew he'd be looking Kate up when he got back to Chicago, he didn't feel it imperative to find her today. Then he glanced down a side street and saw it. Her silver car. Parked right in the open in front of the old movie theater.

Another opportunity—one too good to pass up. He headed for the theater entrance. When he saw one door was slightly ajar, he figured she'd gone inside, so he walked in, also.

Hearing some loud, off-key singing, he followed the sound through the lobby area. His steps echoed on the cracked-tile floor, the only sound other than the top-of-the-lungs belting coming from the theater. He barely spared a glance at the lobby, beyond noting that someone had been painting and cleaning up.

When he pushed open the door to enter the auditorium, he paused, figuring it would be dark and his eyes would need to adjust. Somehow, though, probably because there was repair work going on, the electricity worked. The theater wasn't dark at all down in front where work lights washed the stage with light. In the audience area, a few side fixtures made things visible.

He could see the rows upon rows of burgundy crushed-velvet seats. The thin, worn carpeting in the aisle hadn't changed; its pattern remained virtually indistinguishable after decades of wear. A pair of vast chandeliers still hung suspended over the audience—not lit, obviously. Even fifteen years ago when he'd come to see movies in this place, the chandeliers had been strictly decorative. The town was too cheap to electrify them, so they remained a sparklingly dark reminder of another era.

Finally he turned toward the stage, at the bottom of the theater, where the organist had played in the silent picture days. And he saw her. Kate. Singing as though there was no tomorrow.

Jack began to smile. Then to chuckle. He approached the stage, remaining quiet. She still hadn't seen him, so he took a seat a few rows from the front, watching her performance.

Lordy, the woman could *not* hold a tune. But what she lacked in pitch, she made up for in volume. The rafters nearly shook and he finally recognized the song. Vintage Pat Benatar. She even had the rocker's strut.

No, she couldn't sing, but damn, the woman had some moves.

"I would *definitely* like to hit you with my best shot," he murmured, knowing she couldn't hear over her own voice.

Her legs looked impossibly long beneath her short ivory skirt as she gyrated. She was bent at the waist, holding an imaginary microphone and singing into her fist. Her thick, dark hair fell forward, curtaining her face. From here, he had a magnificent view of the curve of her ass and hips as she bent lower, with parted legs, rocking on her high white heels. Then even lower, until the hem of her skirt rose higher, revealing the top of one thigh-high stocking.

Jack swallowed hard, knowing another inch or two and he'd be seeing whether Kate favored bikinis or thongs. Deciding to alert her to his presence, he prepared to stand. Before he could, however, she tossed her head back, and stood upright to finish the song. She thrust her chest forward. He shifted in his seat, watching the silkiness of her sleeveless blouse brush against the pronounced curves beneath.

When she finally finished, he simply had to applaud. She

heard, obviously, and looked down toward the seats like a kid who'd been caught shoplifting bubblegum. "Who's out there?"

Jack rose to his feet, still bringing his hands together in a slow and lazy clap. "We meet again," he said as he walked down the aisle to greet her.

"Oh, no, did you hear me?" She looked thoroughly disgruntled as she narrowed her eyes and crossed her arms in front of her chest.

He climbed the steps leading up onto the stage. "Yep."

She cringed. "For your information, I know I can't sing. So don't even try to pretend you don't think I sounded like a howling female cat in heat."

Hmm. Interesting image—a female in heat. Particularly with the flush of color in her face, the sheen of sweat on her brow and the clinginess of her damp clothes against her amazing body.

She looked aroused. Sultry. Alive. He'd love to hear her purr. "You didn't sound like a cat."

"Well, then, a mutt braying at the moon," she continued with a surly frown. "Don't humor me."

"Not humoring you. Honey, you really can't sing. But, boy, you obviously know how to dance."

The compliment didn't ease her frown. Instead she practically glared. "So, are you following me? Should I worry I'm being stalked by the kissing bandit?"

"I wasn't stalking. I saw your SUV outside and came to investigate. Besides, I'm wounded. Here I thought you liked our kiss." Her cheeks flushed and she averted her eyes. *Gotcha!* He stepped closer until their bodies nearly touched. "I certainly did, and I've been thinking all afternoon about how much I wanted to see you again."

"You don't even know me."

"We could change that. Come have dinner with me, Kate."

"I'm really not hungry, thank you."

"Just coffee, then. Let's go sit somewhere and talk for hours while we pretend we're not both thinking about what happened this afternoon."

She raised a brow. "Oh, you've been thinking about that? I'd nearly forgotten all about it."

"Liar."

"If it helps your male ego to think so, go right ahead."

He laughed out loud. "I'm not an egotistical man, Kate. But I know when I'm being kissed back." He stepped closer, into her space, but she wouldn't back down. "Admit it. You *definitely* kissed me back."

"Only to give the old biddies something to chew on with their tea and crumpets," she said with a determined frown.

"Ah, ah, you're breaking my heart here." He held his hands out at his sides, palms up in supplication.

"I somehow doubt that. You're a complete stranger. One who accosted me in public this afternoon."

A definite overstatement. "Not accosted. Surprised."

"You surprised me all right. Don't guys like you usually wind up kissing a celebrity or streaking through the Academy Awards, then get committed to the funny farm sooner or later?"

He rolled his eyes. "Do you always keep your guard up? Except when you're singing your heart out in an old abandoned theater, that is?"

"Do you always go around kissing women you see on the street?" she countered.

He shook his head, becoming very serious. "Never. Not until today. Not until you."

She broke their eye contact first, suddenly looking nervous. "Look, this is probably not a great idea, us being here. I don't even know you."

"Would it help if I give my word I'm not a psycho serial killing…or serial kissing…nutcase?"

She shrugged. "If I'd thought that I woulda pushed you into the orchestra pit and run like crazy out of here."

"I'm glad to know you trust me. Now, about the coffee…"

"Don't you ever give up?"

"Not when I'm faced with something this important."

He didn't elaborate, and she didn't ask him to. They both knew what they meant. There was something happening here, something living and warm and vibrant flowing beneath them. She just wouldn't admit it.

"I won't say I'm not tempted. But I am on my way out of town," she said slowly. "Heading home."

"To Chicago?"

She paused. "How did you…"

"Well, I know there's no way you live in Pleasantville."

"True."

"And I recognized you."

"From where?"

"I'm from Chicago, too." He saw her eyes widen. In interest? Or maybe relief? "I saw the article in the business paper a few weeks back. You own some hot new women's store, right? The picture was striking." He looked down at her body, her chest still heaving as she brought her breathing back to normal. His mouth went dry. "But it didn't do you justice."

She froze as he looked at her, probably seeing the pulse in his temple as he stared. Beneath his gaze, two sharp points jutted against her silk blouse, telling him she was as aware of him as he was of her. "I liked that picture," she said, unable to disguise a shaky tremor in her voice.

"I did, too. For a businesswoman. A Katherine." He watched as she smoothed her skirt with her palms. She then checked the waistband to be sure her blouse was tucked in.

"But today, when you landed in my arms, you didn't look like a Katherine. Then…and now…you're Kate."

Almost as if she was unaware of her movements, she slid one hand up higher, up the smooth, soft-looking skin of her arm, until the tip of her finger rested in the hollow of her throat and her forearm on the curve of her breasts.

Her nipples jutted harder now, brought to tighter peaks by the scrape of her own arm across them. Did she realize it? Was she conscious of the silently seductive invitation she issued? As if she read his thoughts, she tapped her index finger against her throat. Lightly. Drawing his gaze there once again.

"So you read about me." She sounded breathless. Clearing her throat, she continued. "My store. Is that why you followed me? Why you kissed me?"

He shook his head, still watching the pulse tick away in her throat, right beneath the tip of her finger, wondering how she tasted right there. Wondering how she smelled. Wondering if she'd whimper when he gently licked the moist spot. And mostly wondering when he'd be able to take her in his arms again. Though, this time the decision would be hers. As much as she might believe otherwise, Jack didn't believe in *taking* what he wanted. It was much more pleasurable to be given such a gift.

"I followed you because of the way we looked at each other." Like they were looking at each other now. "I kissed you because you landed in my arms." As he wanted her to now. "What can I say? You were a beautifully wrapped present and I couldn't resist. Who could resist a beautiful woman so obviously in need of a kiss?" *Like now.*

She took a tiny, step back. He let her go. Not crowding. Not encroaching.

"You let me leave. You didn't try to stop me."

He smiled. "I let you go because after you told me your

name, I remembered your face and the article and knew I could find you again once I got home to Chicago."

Her eyes widened. Tap went the index finger. Tick went the pulse. Down went the heat—through his gut, into his groin.

"So you read the article?"

He shook his head, being honest. "Not really. I just remember your face, your first name and something about a store. You sell women's lotion and things?"

She chuckled, a warm and truly amused laugh that rose from her throat. "And things." Before he could question the naughty twinkle in her eye, she'd turned and looked out into the dark auditorium. "When did the Rialto close?"

He shrugged. "I'm not sure, really. I don't come back too often. But I think it was seven or eight years ago."

"You have family here?" She lowered her voice, betraying her keen interest. "You're from Pleasantville?"

Jack nodded, but didn't offer more information. He certainly wasn't about to reveal who his family was. If Kate had spent time in town, she'd know the Winfield name. The last thing he wanted was someone else bringing up his father's death. And whatever scandal the town gossipmongers had been whispering about any time his back was turned in the past few days.

Besides, he liked the anonymity of this night. It seemed right, especially here, in the old abandoned theater, so rich with atmosphere and antique glamour.

"Yeah. But, like I said, I got out years ago, as soon as I could. And I avoid coming back as much as possible."

Her rueful nod said she completely understood what he was saying. Then she smiled, a small, friendly smile that made him think for some reason she'd let down her guard. Because he'd admitted he didn't like this town?

"I used to love this building. It was my favorite place in

Pleasantville." She walked across the stage, her footsteps echoing loudly on the wooden planks. "I used to come for the first showing of a new movie, then hide in the bathroom to stay and watch it again and again."

"Ah, a daredevil," he said with a laugh.

A reminiscent smile curled her lips. "The ticket taker, the old one with the poofy black wig, caught me once."

"Miss Rose?"

She nodded. "Yes! That's it. Miss Rose. She was so funny, the way she'd talk about the movie stars, as if they were really here, living behind the screen."

"So what'd she do about you hiding?"

"From then on out I didn't have to hide—she always let me stay, but told me not to let on to anybody else." She looked down at her hands. "I'd forgotten about her."

Interesting. She looked happy and sad at the same time, as if it pained her to find positive memories about her years in Pleasantville. He could relate. Since his father's death, especially, Jack had tried to reconcile the kid Jack who'd left town with the man who'd come back.

Seeing a table right behind the partly open, red-velvet stage curtains, he pointed. "Anything interesting back there?"

Kate stepped between the curtains, and he followed her into the murky backstage area.

She picked up her purse, which was lying on the sturdy old wooden worktable beside the curtain. But, thankfully, she didn't immediately turn and try to leave. *"Flashdance,"* she said out loud, looking at a stack of papers lying on the table. "And *Dirty Dancing.* I think I actually saw that one in this theater."

"I could have guessed you liked dance movies."

She grinned. "What can I say? I can't hold a tune, but I can move to one."

"Did you take lessons?"

"Yeah, I started when I was really little, back in Florida."

"Florida? I thought you were from here."

"We moved here when I was six. After that, I took lessons when I could, before the only dance teacher in town got married and moved away."

He winced. "Don't remind me. My sister went into mourning and my mother wanted to sue the teacher for breaking her lease on the studio...just as a way to try to get her to stay."

As soon as he said it, he wished he hadn't. He still didn't want to get into any discussion about his family. Stepping closer to the table, he was easily able to distinguish the names on the old, crinkled, dusty advertisements. It wasn't completely dark back here—after all, the curtain remained open and the stage was brightly lit. Still, it felt very intimate. Almost cocooned.

"I wonder why no one ever took all these wonderful old movie posters. Look, here's Clint Eastwood."

He glanced at the title. "Don't think I've seen that one."

"*High Plains Drifter.* Not one of his most popular." She stared at the poster, looking deep in thought.

"Spaghetti western?"

"Sort of. He's a ghostly man who comes back to a horrid little town to get vengeance on the townspeople." Her eyes narrowed. "They think he's there to save them. In the end, he destroys them and rides away, disappearing into the mist."

He reached around her and pulled the poster away to see the next one. She didn't watch, appearing completely unaware of anything except the Eastwood picture, at which she still stared.

"Here's a James Bond one...from several Bonds ago."

She finally shook her head, ending her reverie, and glanced at the poster in his hand. "Sean Connery. He's still so hot."

"You have a thing for older men?"

She cast a sideways glance at him. "No." Then she studied

the poster again. "I think it's his mouth. He's got the kind of mouth that makes women wonder what he can do with it." She looked at Jack's lips, looking frankly interested.

"What he can *do* with it?"

She nodded. "Some men are strictly visual. While women might like being looked at, we're more elemental creatures. Some women like to be...tasted."

Jack dropped the poster, staring intently at her. "Are you one of them? Do you like to be...tasted?" He wondered if she'd dare to answer. If the color rising in her cheeks was brought about by sexual excitement, or simply nervousness.

"Yes, I do," she admitted, her voice husky and thick.

Definitely sexual excitement.

"And you? Do you like to *taste?*" she countered.

Yeah, he *really* did. Right now he wanted to dine on her as if she were an all-you-can-eat buffet and he a starving man.

Which was exactly the way she wanted it. She, the woman, in complete control. He, the drooling male, at her feet. He wasn't sure how he knew, but there was no doubt Kate liked being the one in charge when it came to sex. Perhaps that's why she'd kissed him the second time today. As if to say, "Okay, the first one was yours. Now, here's what *I've* got."

Two could play this sultry game. He shrugged, noncommittal. "I enjoy input from all my senses, Kate. Taste, of course. Good food. Cold beer. Sea air. Sweet, fragrant skin. The salty flavor of sweat on a woman's thigh after a vigorous workout."

She wobbled on her high-heeled shoes.

"And sight, of course. I think men are focused on the visual because we like to claim things. We like to see what we've claimed. Whether it's a continent, a car, a business contract. Or a beautiful woman in a red silk teddy."

She swallowed hard, then pursed her lips. "Some women don't want to be claimed."

He touched her chin, tilting it up with his index finger until she stared into his eyes. "Some women also *think* they don't want to be kissed by strangers in broad daylight."

She shuddered. "Touché."

"I'm a sensory man. I also enjoy subtle smells." He brushed a wisp of hair off her forehead. "Like the lemon scent of your hair, Kate. And sounds. Gentle moans and cries. Not to mention touch. Soft, moist heat against my skin."

Kate leaned back against the table, as if needing it for support. Her breathing deepened. He watched her chest rise and fall and color redden her cheeks.

"Yes, some men are definitely capable of appreciating all their senses." He crossed his arms, leaning against the table, next to her, so close their hips brushed. "So, Kate, tell me, a man who knows how to use his mouth. Is that really your *only* requirement?"

She licked her lips. "I suppose there are...other things."

"Other things?"

His fingers? His tongue? His dick, which was so hard he felt as though he was going to shoot off in his pants?

"His..." This time she ran her hand down her body, flattening her palm against her midriff, then lower, to her hip.

"Hands?" he prompted, staring at hers.

She nodded. "And one most important thing of all."

He waited.

"His brain."

Jack grinned but didn't pause for a second. "Did I tell you I graduated with honors from U.C.L.A. and have my masters in architectural design?"

She laughed again. A light, joyous laugh, considering they were having a heavy, sensual conversation about oral sex and other pleasures. He found himself laughing with her.

"I like you," she admitted, her smile making her eyes sparkle. Then she paused. Her smile faded, as if she'd just realized what she'd said and regretted saying it. A look of confusion crossed her face. It was quickly replaced by cool determination. As if tossing down a gauntlet, or trying to shock him into backing off, she tipped up her chin and said, "I mean, it's been a long time since I met a man who made me laugh and made me wet in the same sixty seconds."

Whoa. Yeah, definite challenge. Did she think she'd scare him off? Erect a wall that most men wouldn't have the guts to try to broach? He could have told her, had they known each other better, that he wasn't a man who was easily scared. And nothing turned him on as much as a woman who said what she wanted.

Holding her stare, he let a relaxed smile cross his lips, and let her have it right back. "I like you, too. It's been a long time since I've had to jerk off in the shower of my parents' house after meeting a beautiful, amazing, unattainable female."

Kate's heart jumped out of her chest and into her throat, then skipped two solid beats as she took in what he'd said. He'd answered her deliberate challenge with one of his own, without so much as a second's hesitation. Most men would have backed off, intimidated into retreat. A few would have thought about it, deciding whether or not they wanted a woman who knew what she wanted and said so. Some would have figured out a way to see if she really intended to put out. Played the standard game.

Not Jack. *He's too much. He's too much for you to handle.*

But, oh, my, how she wanted to *handle* him.

The realization surprised her. She'd thought she wanted him to back away. She'd figured her natural defense—that being a deliberately aggressive offense—would protect her as it had so many times in the past. It hadn't. Instead it had catapulted her right out of the frying pan and into the fire.

A seductive, intoxicating, all-consuming fire.

He didn't move closer, made no other suggestive comment, didn't try to kiss her or to persuade her in any way. They both knew what was at stake here. Good, hot, completely unexpected sex. A gift of pleasure from an attractive stranger.

She didn't think she'd had a more appealing opportunity in years. She'd never wanted anything so much in her entire life.

There really was no deciding.

"Now why on earth would you want to do something so terribly wasteful in your parents' shower?" His eyes widened as she reached up to touch his cheek, then pulled him close for a kiss. "And why would you possibly think I'm unattainable?"

She felt his shudder as he recognized her answer to his unvoiced invitation. To have him. To take him. To take this, now, to hell with what came afterward.

Yes. This wet kiss. This warm meeting of lips and tongue that stole her breath and rattled her senses. The touch of his hands, sliding around her waist, cupping her hip, then her bottom. He pulled her tighter against him and she ended the kiss, dropping her head back to moan at the feel of his rigid hard-on pressing insistently against the apex of her thighs.

"You're sure about this?" he asked, almost growling against her neck as he nipped at her throat, then lower, to press a hot kiss in the hollow below.

Her answer emerged from both her energized, aroused body, and also from a lonely, empty place in her heart. She wanted to be close to someone. Held by someone.

Taken by someone.

"More sure than I've been about anything in a long time."

He didn't ask again. Lifting her at the waist, he sat her up on the table and continued to feast on her neck. Her earlobe. Her collarbone. Tangling his fingers in her hair. She parted her legs, and he stepped between them, making her hiss as his big erection came directly in contact with her thin, wet panties.

He couldn't seem to stop touching her. Her arms, her thighs, her face. She was just as greedy, tugging his shirt up so she could slip her hands beneath. She felt his washboard stomach, the light furring of hair, then tugged the shirt off.

He was glorious—a woman's erotic dream, with the kind of long, lean body she'd fantasized about earlier that afternoon.

"Can I tell you something?" she asked in a hazy whisper.

"Anything," he replied, pulling her blouse free of her skirt. He began to slip the buttons open, one by one, his fingers creating intense friction as they brushed against her bare belly and midriff. She shivered, lost her train of thought and strained toward his hands. Her breasts felt heavy and full and if he didn't touch them soon, she'd go crazy.

"Tell me, Kate," he said, finishing the unbuttoning and leaving her blouse hanging from her shoulders. He glanced down at her, his eyes darkening with desire.

Kate had never felt such a fierce sense of satisfaction about her own body. She did now, though. She liked herself because of the appreciation in his eyes as he studied her. Her skirt was pulled all the way up to her hips, exposing her thigh-high stockings and her tiny white silk panties. And the curves of her breasts, barely contained in the skimpy lacy bra.

But he still didn't touch them. Didn't caress them as she wanted him to. She whimpered and leaned into his hands. Offering herself. Hissing as her nipples brushed his index finger.

He moved his palms to cup her around the ribs. With his thumbs, he lightly touched her nipples, easily visible behind the lace of her bra. Then he moved them again, a tiny flick, a taunting caress. Knowing why he waited, she admitted, "I wanted you so much earlier today, I had to…to…"

"Yes?" Another flick, too gentle. She wanted more, wanted

him to push the fabric away and take her nipples between his lips and suck deeply. Her breasts were ultra-sensitive; it wouldn't take much more than that for her to come.

"Tell me," he ordered.

"I had to touch myself," she admitted.

He rewarded her with a longer stroke, sliding two fingers into her bra and taking her nipple between them. Then he stopped again. "Where?"

"In my old bed."

He chuckled lazily and resumed the all too brief flicks of thumb against nipple, accompanying the touches with tantalizing love bites to her neck. "I meant where on your body?"

She groaned in frustration. "Where do you think?"

"Here?" he asked, covering her breasts with both hands, cupping their fullness.

"Oh, finally!"

"So you did touch your breasts?"

She shook her head, desperate for more. "No, but that's exactly where I want *you* to touch."

"You've got me curious, Kate." He kissed his way down her neck, pushing her back farther on the table until she was nearly reclining. Then he moved his lips down. Over the curve of her breast. Scraping his teeth along the lace, slipping his tongue beneath it to lick her nipple.

She jerked hard, her hot core grinding against him. "Curious? You've got me ready to sing the Hallelujah Chorus!"

"Hey, no singing," he scolded, lifting his mouth from her.

"I promise," she said between harsh pants. "No singing. But please, don't stop touching me or I'll scream."

"I want you to scream," he murmured, staring down into her face, his eyes lit with passion. "I want us both to scream because it feels so good there's no other way to express it."

Finally he deftly undid her bra, tugging it away and catching her fullness in his hands.

"Have I told you yet that I'm a visual man?" he asked as he moved lower to kiss her. "I love looking at these." Then he lifted her nipple to his lips and flicked his tongue over it with exquisite precision. "And feeling them."

"Thank heaven." She clutched his hair in her hands and pulled him closer, silently ordering him to stop fooling around and to get to some serious action. He complied, sucking her nipple deeply into his mouth as he caught the other between his fingers.

She had her second orgasm of the day a minute later. It made the first one in her old bedroom pale in comparison.

"I see we're well matched. You're very sensitive here, aren't you?" he asked, continuing his sensual assault on her chest. The pleasure began to build again, before she'd come down from her orgasmic high. "But we still haven't found the spot you touched yet, have we?" He reached around to unzip her skirt.

Okay. This was good. Her nipples still tingled, but now other parts—lower parts—were ready for some action. She almost purred as he followed the path of skin exposed by the zipper, trailing his fingers down her tailbone until he slipped a hand under her panties to cup her bottom.

"Are you going to show me, Kate, where you touched?"

She nodded wordlessly, wondering how he'd stolen all thought, all will. He eased the skirt down, waiting for her to lift up so he could pull it all the way off and toss it to the floor. Then he stepped back and merely looked at her, clad only in panties, thigh-highs and strappy sandals. He looked his fill. "I'm suddenly starting to hear strains of the Hallelujah Chorus myself. I think I've died and gone to heaven."

Kate twisted and shifted restlessly, loving the way he ate her up with his eyes. Then she reached for the belt of his trousers. "Well, angel, you're not going to get your wings, until you ring my bell."

Chuckling, he pushed her hands away, undid his trousers and pushed them down. Kate bit her lip, watching through a curtain of her own hair as he pushed off his boxer briefs. When she saw his thick, erect penis spring free of them, she moaned out loud.

Vibrating fingertips just can't compare.

She found her voice. "My purse. In my purse…"

He understood what she meant. He grabbed it, handing it to her while he shucked off the remainder of his clothes. Kate dug inside, grabbing one of the small foil packets in the bottom of the bag. She saw his curious expression. "Freebies from my shop. Some stores give away matchbooks. We give away condoms."

He looked as though he wanted to question her, but she wouldn't have that. Ripping open the condom with her teeth, she reached for his penis to put it on, but had to pause, to feel the pulsing heat in her hands, to test the moisture at its tip with her fingers. *It's definitely been too long.*

But what a yummy way to get back in the saddle.

"Let me," he insisted, his voice thick and nearly out of control with need.

She did, turning her attention to her now-in-the-way panties. Pushing them off, she watched as he groaned at the sight of her. Glistening. Open and ready.

"Kate?"

"Yes?"

"Remember the discussion we had about the senses?"

Remember? She could barely remember her own name.

"I don't think I told you…I'm a visual man. But taste really is my favorite."

She only understood what he meant when he bent down and licked at her glistening curls.

Welcome her third orgasm of the day.

Before she'd even recovered from it, he stood, took her by the thighs and pulled her to the edge of the table. "Now?"

"Now," she cried, still heaving from the feel of his tongue inside her. "And, Jack? Don't even think about being gentle."

She had one moment to suck in a deep breath before he plunged into her. No hesitation. No sweet, thoughtful insertion.

Thank heaven.

He was giving her exactly what she wanted. She was being well and truly...

"Faster?" he asked when she jerked her hips harder and tugged him down for another wet kiss.

She couldn't talk, just nodded, delighting in the fullness, in the thick, hard feel of him driving ever deeper into her body. And when he finally dropped his head back and groaned with the pleasure of his own fulfillment, she greeted orgasm number four.

Definitely a personal record.

4

IF THERE HAD EVER BEEN a time in Jack's life when he needed a bed, this was it. He wanted nothing more than to pull her body tightly against his, curl around her and languorously come back to earth after their pounding, exciting interlude. Instead he kept his hands on either side of her, holding himself above her, still connected below the waist. "You okay?"

Below him, Kate lay panting, with her eyes closed and her skin still flushed with pleasure. A sultry smile curved her lips, and he watched her pink tongue dart out to moisten them as she nodded. Though he couldn't imagine possibly having anything left in his body after exploding into hers a few minutes before, he felt a definite stirring of interest. God, she was glorious.

"Is that a gun in your condom or are you just happy to see me?"

She opened one eye and glanced down at their joined bodies.

He chuckled, again delighted by her wicked wit. "I can't seem to get enough of you. But, oh, I could use a bed. Or even a comfortable chair."

"Chaise longue," she said, a purr in her voice. "No sides."

Her suggestion definitely brought to mind some enticing images. Her, on top of him, straddling him and taking as much pleasure as she wanted. He held on to the mental picture, determined to one day make it a reality.

She wriggled beneath him, tightening herself deep inside and wringing a moan from him. "As flattering as this is, I don't think those things are reusable," she said, biting the corner of her kiss-swollen lip, trying unsuccessfully to hide a grin.

He gently pulled out of her. What he really wanted to do was grab another condom and go right back in. Make love to her slowly. Erotically. For hours. But this wasn't the time, place or soft flat surface for slow, sultry sex. *Chicago.*

"Any suggestions on where to, uh, dispose of the evidence?"

"I hadn't thought of that," she said with a giggle.

He chuckled, too. "It's been a long time since my teenage years in the back seats of cars, when this was a real issue."

"Teenage? Tsk, tsk. Don't tell me you were a bad boy."

"Actually, I was the golden boy," he replied, making no effort to hide his own disgust. "Which is why whenever I dated a girl, we'd have to go out of town if we didn't want a full report on our activities phoned in to our parents before our 1:00 a.m. curfew." Not wanting to get into a conversation about his family, he looked around backstage. "Now, I really should…"

"There." She nodded toward the workman's ladder standing in front of the partially drawn curtain. Jack followed her stare, seeing the big trash can standing nearby. Tugging his pants up to his hips, he said, "I'll be right back." He gave her a quick kiss on the lips before he walked away.

By the time he returned, after burying the used condom amid the remains of plastic, paint-speckled drop cloths and food wrappers, she was sitting up on the table, buttoning her blouse.

"So, wanna go see a movie sometime? I'm sure we could find something to do while we hide in the bathroom to sneak into the second show," he said with a grin.

She laughed again, not appearing at all nervous, having no second thoughts or regrets. He liked that, since he felt exactly the same way. Tonight was only the beginning. And he didn't regret one damn minute of it.

"I don't know if I'll ever be able to go into a theater again without thinking of this," she admitted, looking up from her buttoning to fix her brown-eyed stare on him. "I think we definitely made a memory tonight."

"Do you like making memories?"

She nodded. "I guess that's what my impromptu rock con-cert was all about. Throughout my childhood I'd wanted to get up on this stage. I always hoped somebody would buy it, forget about showing movies here and get down to business putting on some great plays in which I could be the star."

"Hopefully not musicals."

She responded with a light punch on his upper arm.

"I'm kidding," he said. "So, did that have something to do with why you decided to, uh, go for it with me? Not just a memory—but living out some childhood fantasy?"

"I don't know what kind of childhood you had, but I did not spend my third-grade year wanting to be stark naked, having the hottest sex of my life, on the stage of the Rialto."

He raised a brow. "Hottest of your life, huh?"

She looked away to reach for her skirt. "Well, hottest in the past year at least."

He crossed his arms. "Admit it. You haven't had sex in the past year. Have you?"

Her face flushed. "How could you possibly know?"

"Let's call it a lucky guess."

"Well, what about you?" she asked as she hopped down

from the table and slid her feet into her shoes. "Can I hazard a guess and say it's been a while for you, too?"

"I guess it *was* over pretty fast."

She laughed, low and sultry. "It was perfect. Exactly the way I needed it. One to blow off steam…"

"And the next one?"

She paused. Then, lowering her voice, she said, "I wish there could be a next one."

Her honesty did not surprise him. No coyness, no shyness, no flirtation, just fabulous, forthright, honest Kate. No question, she was the most intoxicating woman he'd met in years.

She bent to hook her sandals, her hair brushing Jack's naked stomach. He heaved in a breath.

"Unfortunately," she continued, apparently not noticing his sudden inability to think a coherent thought, "there can't."

That woke him up and he bent to look at her. "Why can't there?"

She straightened immediately, almost cracking the top of her head into his chin. "You want there to be?"

Seeing the look of uncertainty in her rich brown eyes, Jack immediately took her into his arms. "Yeah. I definitely want there to be. And you're right, I haven't been involved with anyone for several months. I guess you and I met each other at precisely the right moment for volcanic sexual eruption."

She raised a brow. "Lucky us."

"By the way, the movie idea, and my dinner invitation, were very real. I want to see you again, beyond more of…*this*."

She hesitated, leading him to wonder if she really was out for sex and nothing else. For some reason that thought didn't hold as much appeal as it usually would for Jack. Sex and no strings had seemed fine for him up until a few months ago.

Hell, up until today. When he'd met her eyes across a nearly deserted street.

"We'd better go," she said softly. "The workman who left this stuff might remember he forgot to lock up and come back."

Sensing her desire to change the subject, Jack let it go. The subject of what they each were looking for in a relationship could be left for another time. Kate was unlike other women he'd known. She obviously knew what she wanted and wasn't afraid—nor apologetic—about going after it. Her cool exterior and calm demeanor hid a passionate woman with a naughty streak.

"Hope he didn't come back a while ago and quietly watch."

A decidedly wicked grin curved the corners of her lips up. "Well, what's a stage for, if there's no audience?"

Yes, a *definite* naughty streak. He could hardly wait to get to know her better.

After they dressed, they left the theater and stood outside, next to her SUV. Jack hated to see her leave, though he knew he'd see her soon. "So you'll get home sometime tomorrow?"

She nodded. "And you fly home late tonight."

He wished he didn't have to go back to his mother's house to pack. The simple solution to his regret at parting from this amazing woman was to drive back to Chicago with her. But he didn't suggest it. He sensed Kate wanted some time alone to sort things out. He didn't need any alone time. He had not one single doubt about what had happened. He was fully prepared to ride out this incredible wave to see what might happen next.

"I'll call you the day after tomorrow," he assured her.

"We'll see." She turned away, looking down the silent, shadowed street. "You don't have to, you know. You didn't do anything I didn't want you to. So there should be no guilt."

"I'm not feeling guilty." He brushed a strand of hair off

her brow, wishing the streetlights around here worked so she could see the sincerity in his eyes. "I'm missing you already."

She shrugged, appearing unconvinced. Leaning forward, he pressed his lips to hers. Her hands snaked around his neck, and she deepened the kiss, as if making one of her memories—this time, the feel of him in her arms. He made one, too.

"I *will* call. So can you give me your number and save me from having to dig through my neighbor's recycling bins, trying to find a month-old newspaper with your name and store address?"

She chuckled. Reaching into her purse, she pulled out a small pink card and handed it to him. He palmed it. "Thanks."

She got into her car, then lowered the window. "I had a great time tonight, Jack. Thanks to you, from now on when I think of Pleasantville, I'll have much more pleasant memories."

He leaned in to kiss her one more time. "I'll see you in two days. I promise." He watched as she drove away.

Still holding the business card in his hand, he headed back to his mother's house. He hadn't even closed the door behind him when she waylaid him in the foyer. "Where have you been? And who were you kissing? Elmira Finley called this afternoon and said you and some stranger made a spectacle of yourselves outside the Tea Room!" She paused only long enough to take a long sip of her drink. Her favorite cocktail— a glass of vodka with a thimbleful of orange juice to turn the thing a murky peach color.

He walked past her. "I wouldn't call it a spectacle."

"How could you? And who was she? Nobody recognized her."

His sister Angela entered from the living room and gave him an amused look. "So, the golden boy gets a turn as black sheep."

"Who, J.J.?" his mother stressed, ignoring Angela.

Jack glanced at the business card, which he'd tucked into his pocket. Jones. Katherine Jones. Of course. Her thick, long, dark hair and name had made him think of Catherine Zeta-Jones when he saw the picture in the paper. "Her name's Kate Jones."

The glass slid from his mother's fingers and crashed to the tile floor, shattering into several sharp pieces.

"Mother?"

She shook her head, saying nothing. Angela, however, didn't remain silent. "You've got to be kidding. Kate Jones is back here? I can't believe she'd show her face in town now."

He narrowed his eyes and stared at his sister.

"You know who she is, Jack. For heaven's sake, she's one of those trashy Tremaine women."

Jack clenched his teeth. "I don't care what her connection is to this town. She doesn't live here now, and neither do I."

"You can't mean to see her again," his mother said, sounding on the verge of tears. "Edie, her mother…"

He instantly understood. Kate was Edie's daughter. He'd forgotten all about the fact that Edie had moved home to Pleasantville as a widow with a little girl so many years ago. He'd been only a kid of eleven or twelve himself.

His instant connection to Kate sure made sense. Edie was one of the nicest people he'd ever known. "Mother, it's fine. Kate's wonderful, honest and open, like Edie. You'd like her."

Angela stepped over the broken glass until she stood next to him. "Honest? Open? Get real. How can you call the woman who'd been banging our father for twenty years honest and open?"

He narrowed his eyes. "You're on dangerous ground, Ang."

"Come on, Jack, the whole town knows it," Angela said. "Including Mom, who, if I'm not mistaken, was happy about it. Free maid service because Edie felt so guilty, plus you got to avoid any icky sex with Dad. Isn't that what you said, Mom?"

Jack looked at his mother, waiting for her to deny it. He expected her to faint, cry or yell. She did none of these. In fact, there was only one way to describe her expression.

Guilty as sin.

"So, HE STILL hasn't called?"

Kate looked up from her office computer screen and frowned at Armand. "I don't know who you're talking about."

He waved an airy hand. "Remember who you're talking to."

Kate smirked. "Your sexual preference is showing." Armand hated to be thought of as flaming, though he occasionally was.

"I don't really care, because for the first time in forever, we're talking about your sex life, not mine!"

"No, we're *not* talking about it." She walked past him onto the sales floor. The overhead lights were on, though they wouldn't open for an hour. Pretending she needed to check the bondage section, she busied herself counting leather masks and handcuffs. Big sellers, particularly around the holidays.

"Kate, stop pretending you don't care this guy didn't call. You've been moping for ten days, ever since you got home from Tortureville. Track the bastard down and confront him about it."

"I can't. The last words I said to him were there's no guilt, no regret, and he didn't have to call."

Armand rolled his eyes in disgust. "Well, of course, but you didn't *mean* it. Darling, all men—including the heterosexual ones—know that speech is complete bullshit."

She ignored him. "Besides, I don't know his last name."

"Stranger sex. I still can't believe you went for it."

She wished she'd never told him. But Armand was a sexual bloodhound. He could smell naughty secrets, even days later.

"So, you see, I can't track him down, even if I wanted to."

Which she didn't. Jack's silence in the past ten days spoke volumes. He knew where to find her and he hadn't looked. She'd cared at first. Too much. Then she'd reminded herself she knew what she was getting into. She could have walked away at any time, but she wanted great sex, with him, then and there. And she got it. So she couldn't now hate him for not following up on his promise to see her when he got back to Chicago.

"Please, Armand, let it drop," she said, rubbing a weary hand over her brow. "It was great, now it's done. I'm over it."

"You're such a phony, Katherine Jones," he replied. Then he stepped closer and took her in his arms, hugging her close. Kate allowed herself to be comforted, burrowing into Armand's hard, masculine chest the way she would with an older brother.

"It's really a shame you don't like women," Kate said, looking up at him. "You're funny, loyal and a total hottie."

Armand smiled, a heart-stopping smile that could make women try to reform him and gay men sit up and beg. "I *adore* women. I just don't want to sleep with them. Besides, I wouldn't want to be one of those men you push away as you close yourself up in your prickly, tough shell, keeping out anyone you think could hurt you. This way we can love each other without any sex or commitment stuff getting in the way."

"I love you, too," she said with a gentle smile, not acknowledging his probably all-too-accurate description of Kate's views on trust, love and relationships.

Before they could get any mushier, the phone rang. Kate answered, smiling as she heard her mom's voice. The smile faded as Edie told her some bad news about her Pleasantville house.

"Vandalized? How? Did the Keystone Kops do anything?"

"Sheriff Taggart assures me he'll do everything he can to catch those who did it," Edie said. "Tag's a nice young man, you'd like him. He and your cousin have apparently already met."

Kate snorted, still unable to believe Cassie had gone to Pleasantville. "Yeah, the son of a...I mean, the sheriff, gave her a ticket last night, her first night in town. Sounds like Pleasantville's as pleasant as ever to the Tremaines."

"It's not the whole town, Kate. Only a few bad apples."

"Enough to fill Mrs. Smith's pies for a decade."

Her mother tsked. "Obviously your cousin disagrees with you, since she's decided to spend the summer there."

Kate could have told her the *real* reason Cassie had gone to Pleasantville. But the cousins had agreed not to. Edie and Flo didn't need to know that Cassie was, in essence, hiding out from a troubling situation. A possibly dangerous situation.

At least Pleasantville is better than dead. Kinda.

"In any case, the real estate agent is having a handyman re-paint," Edie said. "He also tells me he had a call asking if the house was available for short-term rental. What do you think?"

Kate, the accountant-at-heart, nodded. "Good idea. If you can rent it out to cover the mortgage until it sells, then do it."

After a few minutes' conversation she hung up and told Armand what had happened to her mother's house.

"What a horrid little burg," he said. "Who would paint graffiti on Edie's door? She's the nicest soul I know!"

Kate nodded, agreeing. Her mom was genuinely the nicest person she knew. Patient and understanding. Sweet-natured, helpful and modest. All the qualities Kate had wanted as a kid—which she now knew definitely had *not* swum across that gene pool from mother to daughter. She'd tried to pretend they had, while growing up in Ohio. But the sweet, modest, quiet genes had eluded her. She had to admit it…she liked herself better now that she was free to be herself. Prickly tough shell and all.

"I can't believe Cassie's vacationing there. Couldn't she have gone *anywhere* else but Nastyville?"

Kate shrugged. Yes, Cassie could have gone somewhere else, but fate and circumstance had pointed her to Pleasantville. There was Cassie's personal situation. Edie's departure. Flo's affair and decision to give Cassie several properties in their hometown—properties left to Flo by some of her more affluent lovers. That had amused Cassie to no end. And the diaries.

Kate had mailed Cassie's diary to her immediately after her return from Ohio, and the two of them had sat on the phone for two hours one night, talking about them. They'd relived all the slights, the hurts and their infamous prom night. They'd even read over their "revenge lists." Then and there, Cassie had decided the best place to hide out was in a town that had never really seen her anyway. It made sense, in a sad, twisted way.

THEIR DIARIES were still on Kate's mind late that night when her phone rang at home. Cassie, needing a friendly voice. They talked for several minutes about the pricey house on Lilac Hill, which Flo had given Cassie. Then Kate asked the inevitable. "So, did you go by Pansy Lane today?"

When Cassie went silent, Kate sighed. "You saw."

"Yeah. Your mom called, and I went to see how bad it was."

"And?" When Cassie hesitated, Kate said, "Come on, Cass, do you think I'll be shocked by anything the people there do?"

"It's pretty bad. Horrible, ugly words, spray-painted across the front of your mom's house." Cassie gave a humorless chuckle. "And a few for Flo's house, just for good measure."

Kate muttered an obscenity. "I'm thinking Pleasantville could really use a High Plains Drifter," she muttered. "Mom says the agent's going to have the damage fixed. Let's talk about something else. Tell me how it's going for you."

Cassie chuckled. "Did I tell you about the other building Flo gave me? It was Mr. McIntyre's shop on Magnolia."

Kate gasped. "McIntyre's? No way! I never knew Flo was involved with Darren's father. No wonder Mrs. McIntyre hated us. I guess that's why the men's shop closed down."

Kate should have expected what came next. Cassie had come up with the crazy idea to give Kate the building to open a store, a Bare Essentials, in Pleasantville! She laughed, loudly, as her cousin launched into reasons why it was a good idea.

They lightheartedly argued about it for a few minutes then Cassie said, "And besides, it's right downtown. Right next door to the Tea Room. Are you following me here?"

While they kept discussing it, Kate's mind was somewhere else. Thinking of Edie. Of the vicious words that day in the Tea Room. Of the spite. Of the silly Clint Eastwood poster. Of the big overstock she had piling up in the backroom of her store, because of the going-out-of-business sale of a sex toy supplier from Texas. Of a big empty building and store-front, which, Cassie said, needed only a little elbow grease to get it ready to open. Which Cassie wanted to provide, if only to keep from going crazy with boredom. She thought of the cute girl she'd met in the nail salon, who'd longed for something to happen.

Mostly, she thought of Cassie. Alone, a sitting duck, in a town that didn't care a rat's ass for any of them and wouldn't lift a finger to help if her trouble followed her to Ohio.

Cassie urged, "Come on, Kate. Opening a porn shop in Pleasantville. It doesn't get better than that."

Kate rolled her eyes. "Bare Essentials is not a porn shop.

But you're right, it sure would cross number one off my revenge list, wouldn't it?" Then she chuckled. "And some of the Winfields are still in town to get even with, right?"

Cassie obviously understood. She knew what had happened on prom night, just as Kate knew what had happened to Cassie. They'd shared their most anguished secrets one night a few years ago over a bottle of cheap tequila and an entire key lime cheesecake. Then Cassie gasped. "Oh, I can't believe I forgot. Did your mom tell you someone wants to rent her house?"

"Yeah. I guess *if* I come back to town, I'd better ask her not to so I'll have someplace to stay."

"Don't be silly. You can stay with me. It's too late, anyway, your mom told me she heard from the renter today. It's J. J. Winfield. He's renting her place in a couple of weeks."

Kate reeled. J. J. Winfield was going to be living in her mother's house? Why would he stay on the *seedy* side of town when his family lived on the sunny one? "Impossible!"

"Swear to God. Your mom seemed really touched by it."

Kate wasn't surprised her mother hadn't called her back to tell her. Kate had never admitted knowing about her affair, but Edie knew she couldn't stand the Winfields, anyway.

Kate suddenly saw an opportunity. Mayor John Winfield was gone, but there would soon be another John Winfield in Pleasantville. Could she possibly get vengeance on the late Mayor Winfield through his son? Seduce him, break his heart, get some serious payback on behalf of the Tremaine women?

She wondered if she could really go through with it. Physically, yes. Kate wasn't vain. But she knew something about sex and seduction. It was her stock in trade. So yes, she could do it. It was the emotional part she worried about.

But men did that kind of thing every day, didn't they? Look at what had happened to her in good old Pea-Ville ten days before. A man had taken what he wanted—admittedly giving her some pleasure, too—and walked away without a single word since. Hurting her. Though, damn it, she'd never admit that to anyone!

Her decision was easy. With a few shipments of goods, and some vacation time this summer, she could look out for Cassie, give a major screw-you to the old guard in Pleasantville…and seduce and break the heart of the son of the man who'd broken her mother's. Throw in a humiliating moment for Darren and Angela, and she'd make all her teenage dreams come true.

"Cassie," she finally said, knowing her cousin awaited her decision. "Do you think Flo would let me stay in her old place?"

5

JACK COULD HAVE CHOSEN the master bedroom when he moved into Edie Jones's house. Since he'd be in town for at least a month settling his father's tangled financial affairs, he probably should have made himself comfortable in the larger bed. He didn't, for several reasons, but mostly because of the image of his own father—and Edie—in it. He shuddered at the thought.

He still couldn't believe it. His father and Edie had been lovers for two decades. He hadn't just taken Angela's word; his mother had admitted it. That was when he'd decided he couldn't stay in his parents' house during his trip home this summer.

Most sons would probably have felt as much anger toward Edie as toward his father. Jack felt only pity and regret for the woman, who'd been the kindest part of his boyhood. His parents' marriage had been as convoluted as his father's finances, and Edie had been a victim more than anything else. Looking through his father's records, it became obvious the pittance he'd left Edie in his will didn't come near to covering her paychecks, some of which she hadn't cashed over the years.

His family owed Edie something. Staying here, fixing up her house, doing repairs and maintenance so she could sell the place and make a new life for herself, was the least Jack could do.

"Sleep, Jack." He glanced at the clock, which showed the hour had moved past one. Sleep proved elusive here, especially because Kate had told him how she'd spent her last afternoon in this house. Lying on her bed. Thinking of him. Touching herself. "Knock it off, moron," he said. He couldn't allow himself to think about Kate. Not until he'd figured out how to make up for the damage his parents had caused to her and her mother.

"God, I'm sorry," he muttered. Sorry for Edie, who, he'd learned, had been ridden out of town like a scarlet woman by the old guard of Pleasantville. Sorry for Kate, who'd grown up in this tiny house, on Edie's small income, made smaller by his parents' selfishness. Sorry for himself, because what he wanted more than anything was to find Kate and to tell her how hard he'd fallen for her on the day they'd met, just over a month ago.

But he couldn't. His family had done enough to hurt the Jones women. Until he could find some way to right the wrong, he couldn't let himself see Kate again.

It had been impossible to stay away from her. He'd been drawn to her, easily locating her store on Michigan Avenue. Twice he'd watched her from outside, trying to figure out how to go in and face her. The second time he'd had his hand on the door handle, prepared to go inside. Then he'd seen her in the closed shop in the arms of a tall, dark-haired man. He'd driven away, never finding out whether the guy had been friend or lover. But the image of her with another man had given him some long, sleepless nights.

Like now.

He closed his eyes again, determined to sleep, then opened them as he heard a noise through the wall. A bang. A low curse. Both came from next door, inside what should have been the *empty* half of the duplex, which belonged to Edie's sister.

"Son of a bitch." Jumping up, he grabbed some sweatpants and ran downstairs, figuring the vandals had returned.

Whoever the vandals were, they weren't very smart. The front door to the adjoining unit was wide open. He easily made out the beam of a flashlight moving around upstairs. Ready to transfer all his unexpended sexual energy into some violence against the intruders, Jack took the stairs two at a time. In the upstairs hall he turned toward the room directly beside the one in which he'd been lying next door. As he burst in, the beam of a flashlight, held by a dark-clothed person, swung toward him.

"Stop right there, you rat bastard," Jack snarled as he tack-led the person and took him to the floor.

"Ow, get off me!"

A female voice had spoken. Definitely a soft, curvy female body cushioned his against the hard floor. A mass of thick, dark hair spilled across his hands and brushed against his bare chest. Catching the achingly familiar sweet scent of lemon, he knew even before he saw her who it was. "Kate?"

The flashlight thunked as it rolled out of her hands, swinging around to shine on her face.

She stopped struggling beneath him and stared up, finally recognizing him in the shadowy darkness. "Jack?"

"I'm sorry." He rolled off her. "Did I hurt you?"

She sat up, sucking in deep breaths, but didn't answer. When Jack reached toward her, to make sure she was real and all right, she flinched away as if she couldn't bear his touch.

He probably deserved it. He couldn't imagine what she'd made of his silence since their meeting. "Are you all right?"

"I'm fine," she finally answered, her voice shaky and her breathing still shallow. "What are *you* doing here?"

"I could ask the same of you."

"This is my aunt's house. She knows I'm here, she told me I could stay for a while."

Kate staying right next door? Sleeping in this room, directly next to the one where he'd be sleeping? Moving around in this house behind one all-too-thin wall so he'd be able to hear her sigh in her sleep or step into the shower?

God help him.

"Now, answer my question, Jack. Why are you here in the middle of the night?" She glanced down, as if just noticing his bare chest and loose sweats. Her eyes immediately shifted away, but not before he saw her lips part so she could suck in a deep, shaky breath.

"I'm staying here."

She jerked her attention back to his face. "Staying? *Here?*"

"I mean, next door. I'm renting the duplex next door." He paused. "Your mother's place."

"My mother's...wait, you know my mother?" She paused. "You know who I am?"

"Yes. To both questions."

"How? And what do you mean, you're renting Mom's duplex? That's not possible. You can't be living in her house."

"You didn't know she'd rented it out?"

"Well, of course, but to J. J. Winfield..." Her voice softened. Even in the low lighting provided by the flashlight and the moon shining in through the bare front window, he saw her cheeks go pale and her mouth drop open. "Oh, no. Tell me your name is not J. J. Winfield."

He shook his head, sending a bolt of relief shooting through her body. "No, it's not." Her relief quickly disintegrated when he continued. "No one except my parents and your mother have called me J.J. since I was a teenager. I go by Jack now."

Kate couldn't breathe. Couldn't think. Certainly she couldn't speak. The man she'd had fabulous sex with in the theater several weeks ago was J. J. Winfield—the son of Mayor John Winfield? The man she'd come back to town to seduce and to destroy was the one who'd already hurt her so badly by breaking his promise to call after their amazing encounter? She covered her eyes. "This is a nightmare."

"Kate, I'm sorry, I had no idea you were coming back to Ohio. Your mother never mentioned it."

She didn't know which was worse. That he was here and she had to face her inattentive lover, or that he was John Winfield Junior. Somehow, the memory of all those long, silent, lonely weeks since she'd seen him last seemed the more devastating now.

"No, of course you didn't know I was coming."

Her mother couldn't have told him, because even *she* hadn't known. Kate and Cassie hadn't told Edie because Kate knew her mother too well. She'd be on the first plane back here if she thought Kate was coming to stay in town.

Cassie was one thing—everyone in the family knew Cassie could take care of herself. With her looks, brains and her self-confidence, Cassie had never really had to rely on anyone for anything. Except love and loyalty, which the Tremaine women were always quick to provide to one another.

But, to Kate's eternal annoyance, her mother seemed to think Kate was too easily hurt, too vulnerable, and in need of protection. Which really sucked when she wanted people to see a hardworking, intelligent, kick-ass businesswoman. Not the girl who'd cried into her teddy bear after so many childhood hurts, the girl who'd hidden in her tree house and made up stories about how her father hadn't really died and would one day come back.

Not the girl who'd been dumped on prom night.

Jack couldn't have heard about her return from anybody else, either. Kate and Cassie had been careful to keep their plans quiet, to avoid the inevitable protests and backlash. She was sure many people had known Cassie had been working in the old storefront for the past three weeks, preparing to open a ladies' shop, but not the exact *nature* of the ladies' shop.

"No, you couldn't have known I'd show up. You never would have stayed here, in this house, had you known," she said. "Because, you couldn't very well avoid me if we were practically roomies. And obviously, you had no intention of seeing me again. Right?" She couldn't keep the accusation out of her voice. She wondered if he heard the tinge of hurt there, too.

She waited for him to run the usual male line. *I meant to call you, babe, just lost your number…forgot to pay my phone bill… broke my dialing finger…was sent away on a deadly, top-secret government mission.*

"I should go," he said, not even acknowledging her justified anger.

His lack of response angered her even more. He couldn't even *attempt* to make up a lame excuse? He wasn't going to be courteous enough to give her the chance to tell him what she thought of him? Wasn't going to try to sweet talk her so she could tell him he could touch her again when hogs started flying over Pleasantville, leaving the appropriate droppings right down the middle of Magnolia Avenue?

That wasn't how the game worked. Uh-uh. No way was he getting off so easily. "Oh, sure, I know you must be a busy man. Too busy to even, oh, I dunno, pick up a phone once in a while?"

"Kate…"

"What, Jack? You expect me to be like your Lilac Hill girl-friends? Like your sister, *Angela?*" She spat out the name, not caring if he heard her dislike. "I'm supposed to be brushed off quietly, like a lady, not bring up the fact that I'm *unhappy* you lied?"

"I didn't lie…"

"You shouldn't have promised, Jack. You shouldn't have made a big deal out of swearing you'd see me in two days. I was willing to let it end right then and there outside the Rialto. But you had to be Mr. Noble, Mr. Good Guy. You made me think of what happened as something more than it was. You hurt me and, damn it, you have no business hurting me!" To her horror, she heard her voice break. If one tear fell down her cheek, she mentally swore she'd poke her own eye out.

"Kate, honey, I'm sorry. Listen…"

"Forget it," she snapped. "Forget I said anything."

"I thought about you all the time," Jack said, his voice low and throaty in the near darkness. "But things got…complicated."

She snorted. "Complicated. Uh-huh." She started to rise. "Look, I don't really care. You shouldn't have said you wanted to see me again if you didn't plan to, that's all." Swallowing hard, she continued. "We're both adults. We both knew it didn't mean anything."

Her words seemed to anger him. He grabbed her wrist and held her, not letting her get up beyond her knees. "Like hell. It meant a lot, Kate, and you know it."

His green eyes sparkled with intensity in the near darkness, and she could almost believe him. Then she remembered his name. His lineage. And knew she could never trust a word that came out of his heartbreaking mouth.

"No, *Mr. Winfield.* It didn't mean anything more than any

other sexual encounter between two strangers." She jerked her arm away, stood and brushed off her jeans, wincing as she realized he'd knocked her hipbone right into the floor with his tackle. It already ached.

"We're not strangers." He stood, as well, standing so near she could feel his warm breath against her hair. She bit her lip, trying not to look at him, trying not to remember the feel of his hot, hard chest pressing against hers. Trying to erase the mental picture of him standing above her, his face filled with need and passion, as he thrust into her while she lay on the table at the Rialto.

"We recognized something in each other from the minute our eyes met," he continued. "That's never happened to me before."

From out of the near darkness, she felt his hand move to her cheek. She pushed it away. "Back off, J.J. Don't touch me."

"Ouch. I don't know which is worse, hearing you tell me not to touch you, or hearing you call me J.J. Please call me Jack." His voice moved lower. She realized he'd bent to pick up the flashlight only when he brought it up and shone it on them both.

The light looked pretty damn good on him. His chest. His tousled, right-out-of-bed hair. His thick, muscular arms and broad shoulders. His green eyes, not twinkling with humor now, but dark and confused. His mouth…

She gulped, then crossed her arms in front of her chest, looking for a defense mechanism when there was really none to be found that could halt her physical attraction to him. Finally she said, "What kind of stupid nickname is Jack, anyway?"

"What?"

She knew she sounded like a belligerent kid, but couldn't help herself. Sarcasm was her only defense. "I mean, come on, aren't nicknames supposed to *shorten* your real name? Like Kate instead of Katherine? What genius decided to change a four-letter word like John into a four-letter word like Jack?" *Four-letter word being the operative phrase, here.*

She saw his lips turn up as he shook his head and gave a rueful chuckle.

"Oh, I amuse you now? You break in here, tackle me, almost break my back…" *Almost break my heart…* "And now you're laughing at me?"

"No, I'm actually agreeing with you. It doesn't make much sense, does it? But anything's better than J.J."

"So what's wrong with plain old John? It's good enough for your average, everyday toilet, isn't it?"

"Ouch. You're really pissed."

She clenched her jaw, mad at herself for letting him see her anger, which he would rightly assume had to have evolved out of hurt. She took a few deep breaths, trying to regain control. Where was her infamous control? *Gone, baby. Gone for weeks, since that kiss on the steps of Mrs. McIntyre's Tea Room.*

Finally she forced a shrug. "No, I'm not, not angry at all." A strained laugh emerged from between her clenched teeth. "I'm just tired and cranky from getting knocked on my rear by a six-foot-tall man in the middle of the night."

"I'm so sorry about knocking you down. I had no idea it was you moving around over here. I was afraid someone had come back to cause more problems for your mother. I told her I'd look after the house for her. Both houses, actually."

"Why would you do that?" she asked, still not able to comprehend him being here. "Why would you, a mighty Winfield, care what happens to your trashy Tremaine maid's house?"

He stepped closer, holding her chin and forcing her to look up at him in the semidarkness. She remembered, suddenly, how tall he was. How petite and feminine he'd made her feel.

Their bodies were only inches apart and she could smell his musky, clean scent, and feel warmth radiating from his hard, bare chest. Her body reacted instinctively, getting hot and achy. Her nipples felt incredibly sensitive against the cotton of her sleeveless tank top, and her jeans were suddenly uncomfortably snug. She wanted nothing more than to taste him. All over.

"Your mother was the nicest person I knew growing up," he said, his voice thick with emotion. "And I hated to hear what this town had done to her because of my father."

Kate's eyes widened. Did he know? Could he possibly know about Edie's affair with the mayor? She took a deep breath and carefully asked, "Your father?"

He let go of her face, walking over to stare out the undraped window at the shadowy front lawn. "My father left her a small amount of money, when by rights he owed her more." He cleared his throat and shook his head. "A *lot* more. As usual, the town looked for scandal and decided to crucify her with spite and innuendo because of it."

No. He didn't know. He didn't understand the truth. Kate, Cassie and Edie were still the only ones who knew the Pleasantville gossipmongers really had the story right.

And that's the way it was going to stay.

"Okay, you liked her. You wanted to help her. Why does that equal you living here, in her house, instead of with your mother and Angela at your family's place?" Her voice dripped dislike. "Don't tell me you're not one big, happy, rich Winfield family?" She could tell by the look in his eyes, and the way his jaw clenched, that he was mentally arguing over how to answer. "Come on, Jack, what's the story?"

Finally his eyes shifted away from her face and he muttered, "You know my father died only a few months ago."

She bit the corner of her lip, trying hard to remember

Mayor Winfield had actually been someone's father. Swallowing her dislike, she murmured, "Yes, I know. I'm sure that's been painful for you."

"It's been difficult. I never realized..."

"What?" she prompted.

"I don't know. How much I cared about him, I guess?" He gave a sad laugh. "How much I'd miss him, even as I find out day by day how very little I knew him."

Having lost her dad at a young age, Kate could understand that feeling of wishing she'd had a chance to know a parent. "I'm sorry, Jack. I know how it is to lose your father."

"I know you do. You were a kid when you lost yours, right?"

She nodded. "Six."

He shook his head. "Awful. Your mom was so young to be a widow." He lowered his voice. "And she never remarried."

No, Edie had never remarried. She'd instead wasted decades on a man who was married to someone else. Kate rubbed a weary hand over her brow. "No. But we're talking about your father."

"Yes, we are," Jack replied. "He left a mess behind him."

More than you could possibly know.

"I told my mother I'd come help her out this summer, sell some real estate, get some paperwork taken care of."

"And you can't do that on Lilac Hill?"

"I'm a grown man, Kate. Can you picture me living in my mother's house for a month, being scolded not to let my shoes scuff up her tile floor, and to be careful not to rumple the plastic on the sofa in the parlor?"

She couldn't help it. She burst into laughter. "She has plastic on the sofa?"

A faint smile crossed his lips. "Yeah."

"Does it ever come off?"

He shook his head.

"Not even if the First Lady came over?"

"Well, maybe the current one. But definitely not a Democrat. And certainly it wouldn't come off for me!"

Suddenly his childhood sounded less golden than she'd always imagined. "Sounds like you were the classic poor little rich kid."

"I did okay. Thankfully, your mother was around a lot."

Kate's smile faded. Yeah, her mother had been around the Winfields a lot more than he knew. She wondered what he'd think about that.

In her heart she knew it would hurt him, just as it had hurt her to learn a parent she loved really hadn't been perfect. Maybe if she were a vindictive person…or maybe if Jack weren't already mourning his father's death…she'd have told him. As it was, she simply couldn't. No matter what he'd done to her, no matter how much his broken promises had hurt her, she couldn't repay him with that kind of spite.

His sister was much better at that, she recalled.

"Anyway, I wanted to be on my own," he continued. "There aren't a lot of furnished short-term rentals around. Your mom seemed happy to let me stay here for a month. End of story."

Kate sensed it wasn't really the end of the story, but she was too tired to think about it tonight. She still hadn't quite absorbed the fact that she was here, back in Pleasantville, this time not only for an afternoon, but for weeks.

And Mr. Gorgeous was her next-door neighbor. Oh, joy.

"You need to leave," she finally said, wanting him out of here before she did something terribly stupid. Such as kick him, kill him. Or even worse, kiss him. "I'm tired and I want to go to sleep."

He looked around the empty room. "Uh, where?"

"I brought a sleeping bag for tonight."

"The power's not even on and it's hot as blazes in here. You'll roast."

"I'll be fine. Just go, please? I'm really beat, it was a long drive from Chicago."

He turned to leave, then hesitated. "Look, your mom's furniture is all still in her house. Why don't you stay over there tonight? It'll be more comfortable than the floor."

Stay there? With him? And give him another chance to use her again? *Do I have I'm A Sucker stamped on my forehead? No, thanks, mister.*

Then she thought about her revenge plan, one of her main reasons for coming back here. Hadn't she intended all along to get involved with J. J. Winfield? Seduce and destroy. Entice and evade. It appeared he was handing her the prime opportunity to do exactly that.

But that was with J. J. Winfield. The spoiled, weak, pale and pasty-faced J. J. Winfield she'd pictured in her mind for so long. Not Jack. Definitely not golden-haired, laughing-eyed Jack with the strong hands, the perfect mouth and the big...

"What do you say, Kate? Just for one night." He raised a brow and gave her a wicked smile. "It could be fun."

One night. One more night like the one they'd shared at the Rialto? She might never survive it. Though, there was no doubt in her mind she'd love every minute of it. Every deep, sweaty, hot, pounding, orgasmic minute of it.

Get your mind out of your pants, Kate! This man could hurt her. She was already too vulnerable to him, too attracted to him. Damn it, she already liked him too much. Or at least she had before she'd decided he was a creep and a user. Another interlude with Jack and she might find herself forgetting she wasn't allowed to like him anymore. She could be the one with the broken heart if she followed through on her seduction idea.

No, there had to be another way—a less dangerous way—to even the score with the Winfields. One that wouldn't risk her own emotions. Emotions she'd become quite adept at protecting over the years. After all, with the examples set by women in her family, emotional self-preservation was a requirement. Nobody else looked after a Tremaine woman... except a Tremaine woman.

"I'll be fine. I can open a window."

"What about the vandals?"

She shrugged. "My mother told me the sheriff caught the kids who sprayed her house. They'd apparently hit a lot of other houses in town with the paint cans, and now they're doing five hundred hours community service each."

"Good. Still, you don't need to stay here. Come on, it makes sense. Your mom's place is furnished, and lit. Aren't you achy from your drive? Don't you feel like taking a long shower?"

"I know what you do in showers," she snapped, remembering his comment from the theater.

He thought about it and chuckled. "I just moved in today."

"Doesn't take too long for some men."

"Zing. Was that another comment about how quickly it was over the first time?"

Quick? Ha! In her memory she could *still* feel him making love to her. Riding her, filling her, rolling orgasm after orgasm over her body. She'd felt him inside her for weeks.

"No," she finally replied. "And I think you mean *only* time. First implies there could be a second." *Or a twentieth.*

But there wouldn't!

He ignored her comment. "I promise the shower's clean, Kate. As for anything happening between us..."

She waited, wondering if he'd make some flirtatious, sexy

suggestion that they pick up where they'd left off weeks before. If he did, she'd have to kick him, she really would.

He shook his head. "Don't worry. Strictly platonic."

She found herself wanting to kick him anyway.

As if his silence in the past weeks wasn't bad enough, now he'd basically admitted he didn't want her even though she'd practically fallen right back into his arms? She hated to admit it, but her femininity took a definite hit.

"Well, maybe a shower would be nice," she mused out loud, suddenly wanting some payback, wanting to remind him what he was missing out on. She tilted her head from side to side to work out some imaginary kinks in her neck, then raised her arms above her head to stretch. Arching her back so her breasts pushed tight against the cotton tank top, she hid a look of satisfaction as Jack stared, long and hard.

"Okay," he finally said, his voice low and shaky. "Do you need any help with your stuff? A suitcase?"

"No, thanks. I'll only need my purse and my toiletry case." Some devil made her add, "I don't wear anything to bed, anyway."

He closed his eyes.

"It'll be funny, going back to sleeping in my old room for one night. At my place in Chicago, I have a huge California King bed." *Liar.* She had a queen. "With black satin sheets." *Double liar.* They were percale. And pink.

Rather than looking even more hot and bothered, as she'd hoped, Jack gave her an amused look. Finally he said, "Sorry, Kate, your room's taken. 'Fraid you'll have to take the master bedroom...or the foldout."

"You're staying in my room? Why?"

He nodded. "You're not the only one who remembers everything we talked about that night at the Rialto."

She didn't follow.

He stepped closer, invading her space again so their bodies were separated by only a bit of air and moonlight. "You might know what I do in the shower," he whispered, reaching out to scrape the tip of one index finger along her shoulder, playing with her bra strap, which had somehow slipped out. His touch made her shake and she could barely keep herself focused on his words.

"But I also remember what *you* did in your old bed."

By the time she understood, and felt hot blood rush into her cheeks, Jack had already turned and left the room.

6

OFFERING A SHOWER and a bed to a woman he couldn't have—
but wanted so much his nuts ached—had to rank up there
among the stupidest things Jack had ever done in his life.
Maybe not as stupid as the time he'd tried bungee jumping off
a bridge in California, or when he'd scuba dived with sharks
in Australia, but pretty stupid all the same.

The house had only one bathroom. It was upstairs, between
the two bedrooms, and he listened to every move Kate made
in there. He could swear he heard a metallic hiss as she unfas-
tened the zipper of her jeans, followed by a whoosh of air as
she dropped her clothes to the floor. Then the rustling of the
shower curtain as it opened, the water starting, her tiny gasp as
she tested the temperature and found it too hot. Or too cold.

Jack gave up trying to sleep. Sliding closer to the wall in
her small, twin-size bed, he listened intently. The gurgling
rush of the water from the faucet changed to a sizzling stream
emerging from the showerhead. She stepped into the tub, closing the curtain behind her. Then she dropped something—
the soap? As she retrieved it, her hand knocked against the tub
just inches from his head. He swallowed hard.

She began to hum. Off-key. Not Benatar now, but some other old rock tune he couldn't place.

Soon there was nothing but the pounding cascade of water, muted when her body was beneath it, harder as it struck the tub when she had stepped out of the stream to wash.

That was the hardest. Imagining her rubbing a soapy washcloth, or, better yet, her bare hand, over her skin. Easing the tight muscles of her neck. Kneading the kinks out of her shoulders. He closed his eyes and pictured the slide of her hands down her body. The way her fingers would look on her throat, her breasts, her thighs. And between them.

He shuddered. Probably the only thing he could imagine being as arousing as touching her himself would be to watch Kate's hands on her own body. Giving herself pleasure, the way she said she had here, in this very bed, a few weeks back.

He groaned and pulled the pillow over his face, dying for sleep...for release. Both thoroughly eluded him.

Her long shower continued. *Hurry up, would you?* He had a feeling he was going to need to take a cold one of his own.

Jack imagined sharing one with her. It would be incredible. He'd barely gotten to taste her at the theater and his mind flooded with images of sitting beneath her in the shower. Looking up at her. Holding her hips in his hands and tilting her soft thatch of dark curls toward his hungry mouth to taste her, indulge in her, positively inhale her.

Only after he'd had his fill would he stand up, turning her to face away while he stood behind her. She'd lift one foot, resting it on the side of the tub. He could picture her hand, flat against the tile wall for support, her red-tinted nails a stark contrast to the cream-colored tiles. Her fingers would clench then widen as he stepped closer and she felt his body press against her back, his hard-on slipping between her legs.

He'd have to touch her. He'd reach his hand around, caressing her breast, then her belly. Then lower, until he could slide his fingers into her slick crevice, testing her readiness. Pleased at how wet she was for him.

She'd bend forward slightly, arching her back, turning to look over her shoulder at him with wide, passion-filled eyes that screamed "Take me now." He'd tease her, not giving in to her demands yet, taking time to kiss the tiny little bones on her spine until he heard her whimper in anticipation.

Then he'd give her what she wanted, sliding into her from behind, slowly, until he was so deep inside her they couldn't distinguish their bodies from one another.

They'd pause, the hot water pelting them as they savored the connection. They'd be inundated with the scent of the soap and her lemon shampoo. And the thick, heady smell of sex.

She'd bend lower, tempting him with the curve of her hips and her perfect rear. The visual would join with all his other senses to overwhelm him and he'd have to move. Faster. Getting caught up in her tight heat, having to bend over her, holding her hips and driving them both into oblivion.

"Stop, you idiot," he muttered with a gasp.

He almost came in her bed. It took all his concentration to grab his last bit of control to prevent his body's reaction. Calling himself an asshole, he lay there for a few moments, thinking of prostate exams, Brussels sprouts and wrinkled geriatric patients. Anything unappealing.

It wasn't easy; it didn't help his erection subside, but he managed to avoid having to make a sneaky, middle of the night sheet change as he had a few times during puberty.

Jack couldn't remember the last time he'd come so close to climaxing just from thinking about a woman. Considering Kate was all he'd thought about for weeks, maybe it wasn't so surprising.

He still couldn't believe she was here, not only here in this house, but in Pleasantville at all. From some of the things he'd heard, Kate and the rest of her family hadn't been treated too nicely in the old days. He only hoped she wouldn't hear any of the rumors about her mother while she was in town. He knew she couldn't possibly be aware of the truth…if she were, she'd never have spoken to him once she found out who he was.

If she ever did find out, she'd hate his guts, thinking him just another snobby Winfield out to nail a trashy Tremaine.

Wrong. So wrong. He'd been fascinated by her, wildly attracted to her, dazzled by her, back when he didn't even know her name. He didn't remember another better sexual encounter in his life than the one they'd shared on the stage. Completely spontaneous, passionate, fulfilling. If her last name—or his—had been anything else, he would have spent every night since then in her bed. Guaran-damn-tee it.

And during each one of those nights, he would have worked to remove the sadness he sometimes saw in her eyes, and the anger he'd heard in her voice. Particularly tonight, next door, when her sarcasm hadn't been able to disguise her hurt.

He made it his goal, then and there, to do exactly that. But not here, not in her mother's house, in this town that sucked the soul right out of her. The only place he'd seen her truly happy, passionate and excited was at the Rialto. That was the Kate he wanted to seduce—but he had a feeling he wouldn't find her again until they returned to Chicago.

And until Jack wiped the slate clean regarding his father.

In the meantime he'd control himself, keeping his libido firmly in check. "Yeah, right," he muttered.

Just when he wondered if she was ever going to get out of the shower, he heard the water turn off. "Thank God," he muttered.

The plastic rings clinked against the metal rod as she pulled back the curtain. Then silence, for one long moment, until he heard her voice. "Jack? You awake?"

Was he awake? How could he *not* be awake when three-quarters of his blood supply was centered in his groin? It was a miracle he hadn't passed out from lack of blood flow to the brain.

"Yeah," he said. Realizing he'd spoken in a whisper, he cleared his throat. "Yeah, Kate, did you need me?"

"I don't have a towel."

No towel. Perfect.

Tempted to tell her to stay in there and drip dry—quietly—until he could get control over his raging libido, he sighed and sat up in the bed. Throwing back the sheet, which had felt cumbersome and heavy against his naked body anyway, he reached for his sweatpants. He couldn't find them.

"They're too hot, anyway," he muttered in disgust. Instead, he grabbed a pair of gray boxer briefs and tugged them on. It wasn't as if the woman hadn't seen him naked already.

They were uncomfortably tight. Too damn bad.

Walking out of the bedroom to the small linen closet out on the landing, he grabbed the top two towels on a stack and knocked on the bathroom door. "I've got two for you, just in case."

"Great. I don't have a robe, so I can wrap up in one."

Jack gritted his teeth.

"You can leave them on the counter," she continued.

Pushing the door open several inches, he reached in, intending to drop the towels and go. The shower was behind the door, no way would he see anything. He figured she was hiding in there, fully covered by the flowery plastic curtain, and certainly didn't consider trying to sneak a peek. He was already horny enough, thanks so very much. Even a glimpse at her naked body behind the curtain could have him coming in his briefs.

Jack hadn't counted on the mirror. As he dropped the towels, he glanced up and met her eyes in the reflection. The cold air from the hall had seeped in when he opened the door. Where it met the glass, the misty steam rapidly began to evaporate. She was *not* cowering behind the curtain, probably having assumed he couldn't see her from around the nearly closed door. But see her he did.

Her brown eyes widened in her creamy pale face as their stares met in the mirror. Her lips were parted, droplets of moisture falling down her cheeks toward them. She slowly licked one away. He had to clutch the doorknob for balance.

Swallowing and taking in a deep, shaky breath, he lowered his eyes, staring at the long, wet hair that hung over her shoulders. Jack couldn't have prevented his gaze from shifting even lower if someone held a gun to his head. So he looked, seeing a few strands of hair draping her breasts, though not completely covering them. Her dark, puckered nipples were easily visible. His mouth went dry as his pulse sped up.

She said nothing, didn't make a move, just watched him watch her. He kept looking, at the curve of her waist, that wet thatch of brown curls between her slim thighs.

Then his stare shifted to her hip where a purplish bruise marred the pale perfection of her skin. "What happened to you?"

She seemed to awaken from her daze. Snatching the edge of the curtain, she pulled it over herself, until only her face was visible. He wondered what she'd do if she knew he had a perfect view of one breast and puckered nipple peeking between the leaves of two roses on the plastic curtain. He thought it wise not to point it out. "Tell me."

"You can leave now."

"I mean it, Kate, what happened to your hip? You've got a horrible bruise." He clenched his fists. "Did someone hurt you?"

Obviously seeing he wasn't going to go away until she explained, she said, "You did, you big jerk. When you tackled me earlier."

"Oh, God, I'm so sorry." Pushing the door farther, he stepped inside and turned to face her. "I didn't realize I'd injured you. Let me see it."

She didn't answer. Her attention was firmly fixed low on his body. Her lips parted as she saw the erection he couldn't hide. "I think you should go." Her voice was thin and reedy.

Seeing her injury had nearly made him forget the almost painful urge between his own legs. He could only imagine what she thought. He thrust the concern away, not caring right now if she wondered what he'd been doing in her old bedroom while she'd showered. "Let me see your hip."

She shook her head, slowly, not saying anything. But she didn't resist as he gently pulled the edge of the shower curtain from her fingers and tugged it over a few inches so he could see the side of her body. She still said nothing as he dropped to his knees to examine the reddish-purple bruise on her hipbone.

The size of his palm, it must have hurt like hell. "I'm so sorry. Can I get you some ice for it?"

"No," she whispered. "I'll be fine. Thanks for the towel."

"Why didn't you say something?"

"It's not a big deal, Jack. I'm fair-skinned, I bruise easily." Her voice still sounded shaky. "I can barely feel it."

He touched the bruise with the tip of his index finger. When she winced, he yanked his finger away. "Liar."

Then, almost unable to resist, he leaned forward to place a gentle kiss on the bruise. When she moaned, he pulled back. "Did I hurt you again?"

"No. You didn't…hurt me."

He leaned forward again to gently kiss her skin. He avoided the tender bruised area. Instead he kissed her all around it, caressing her waist, her upper thigh. Unable to resist, he moved to that vulnerable hollow of flesh between her pelvic bone and the still-concealed dark thatch of curls hiding her feminine secrets. The curtain shifted slightly, as if she'd let go of it. When he glanced up, he saw her eyes closed, her head tipped back and her hand on her throat.

"Better?"

She groaned. "You're trying to kiss it and make it better?"

He nodded, his lips still brushing her skin as he inhaled her, breathing in the smell of her clean skin. And the unmistakable, musky scent of aroused woman. "Is it working?"

"I can't tell yet."

He chuckled, knowing she wanted more. He gave it to her, now kissing her more deeply, flicking his tongue over her moist body, licking the water off her hip and thigh. She shuddered and he moved his hand up to steady her. He held her leg, then higher, to cup her rear. Her scent filled his brain, drawing his mouth closer to the edge of the plastic curtain, which barely concealed her curls. He remembered the hot, sweet taste of her on his tongue, the tenderness of that beautiful pink flesh between her legs. He wanted to taste her again. Wanted to feel her, touch her, have her. He pulled her tighter against him, unable to resist the feel of her skin against his cheek, fighting a battle deep within himself.

His mind told him no even after his body had decided yes.

When she hissed, he realized he'd pressed too hard against her bruise. "I'm sorry, you really are in pain." He looked up and saw her flushed face, her parted lips.

Well, she didn't look *entirely* pained. She also looked very aroused, very…*close*. Hot satisfaction at having brought her to the brink swept through him. He'd seen her this way in his dreams. Every night since the night they'd met.

Shit.

Unless he was prepared to forget all about his decision to be a decent guy and not make love to her again while they were here in Pleasantville, he needed to exit stage left. Immediately if not sooner.

He stood, trying not to notice that the curtain had moved farther to the side, completely baring one perfect breast and delicious puckered nipple. Remembering how sensitive she was there made his feet freeze and his hands clench.

"I'm going to get you some ice," he finally said tightly. He somehow found the strength to turn and walk out of the bathroom.

Kate watched him leave, then let out a long, shuddery breath. "Not one of your brightest ideas, Kate Jones."

No. Not smart. She'd come into the bathroom knowing full well there were no towels. She'd had one thing in mind. Okay, two, if she counted washing away the grime of several hours' worth of driving. Even more than cleanliness, however, she'd wanted payback. Just a tiny bit of satisfaction by way of some brief shower exhibitionism. The way Jack had walked away from her next door—after commenting on how she'd had to pleasure herself in her bed the day they'd met—had pricked her ego. Not to mention her libido.

Damned if she hadn't wanted to prick his, too.

Hence the naked-in-the-shower-without-a-towel bit. Okay, so it was sneaky, though, she really hadn't intended for him to see her reflection completely. She'd figured there would be only a foggy image to get his imagination racing and give him some sleepless hours tonight.

Once their eyes had met and she'd seen the heat in his stare, her will had fled as quickly as the steam on the mirror.

She'd certainly been repaid in full. Because, man, oh man, she'd been the one left shaking and unfulfilled. Yes, she'd brought him to his knees, literally. But looking down, seeing him with his mouth and tongue on her body, so warm, so tender, so *close* to where she'd wanted him to be—had been agony.

"I can't believe you just left," she whispered angrily as she got out of the tub, grabbed one of the towels off the counter and began drying off.

His quick departure rankled. No, she wasn't going to sleep with him, she'd already decided. Getting further involved with him would be about as stupid as sitting in a tub full of water and turning on the hair dryer.

Good analogy. He could fry her brains and she knew it.

Of course, that didn't mean she didn't want him to want her. She had to admit, if only to herself in the quiet bathroom—it bugged her that he'd walked away, that he'd been *able* to walk away. If the fit of his briefs was any indication, he had not been physically unaffected by her.

Which meant he didn't want her mentally.

"Well, doesn't this suck eggs," she muttered. The first guy she'd had sex with in two years, and it wasn't even good enough to make him want seconds, not even when she had been wet and naked right in front of him.

Frowning, she moved faster, drying her body in quick, almost rough strokes. She winced as the cotton scraped across her bruised hip. Biting her lip, she looked at it in the mirror and winced. *Okay, yes, an ice pack would be good.*

Tucking the towel around her body, sarong-style, she reached for the other one and used it to dry her hair.

"I can think of a better use for an ice pack," she muttered. If she truly wanted to feel better, she should put the damn thing between her legs to try to cool herself off where she was *really* aching.

But cold, hard ice wasn't what she wanted between her legs. She wanted hot, hard man. One big, hot, hard man.

"No way, Kate. It's a Hugh Jackman fantasy and a vibrating fingertip for you tonight," she muttered as she bent to wrap the towel around her hair.

"Vibrating fingertip?"

Still bent at the waist, she winced, hoping those weren't Jack's sexy bare feet she spied right outside the partly open doorway. Praying that hadn't been his voice and he hadn't heard her comment about needing to get herself off with an actor fantasy and a vibrator.

She squeezed her eyes shut. When she opened them, the feet were still there. And she was still bent in front of him like some kowtowing servant. He'd heard.

Kate knew she had three choices—ignore him, pretend he'd misunderstood or be bold and shameless about the whole thing. Knowing what Cassie would do—what any self-respecting Tremaine woman *should* do—she took a deep breath. *Brazen it out.*

"Yeah, a vibrating fingertip," she said, standing and twisting the towel so it would stay on her hair. Her upraised arm caused the towel wrapped around her body to loosen. As it began to slip, she caught it at the tip of her breasts, and tucked it back together. Then she risked a glance at Jack. His chest was moving rapidly, as if he had to struggle to breathe.

She had a feeling it wasn't the lingering steam in the bathroom making him gasp.

Thank heaven.

"It's actually a clever little vibrator that slips over your finger and feels...mmm...so good." She licked her lips. "I have it right here in my purse, and can take care of myself anytime I want," she added, not knowing how she could be stupid enough to step even closer to the fire in which he could consume her. But step she did. Then even closer. "Would you like me to show it to you?" She lowered her voice. "I remember you're the kind of man who appreciates visual images."

Jack's jaw clenched and his eyes narrowed. "Sit down."

"Excuse me?"

"You heard me," he said, his voice low and thick. "Sit down, Kate."

He stepped closer. Not waiting for her to obey, he instead pushed her with the tip of his index finger until she backed up against the bathroom counter. Sliding up to sit on it, she held her breath, wondering what he would do next, wondering what she'd begun…and if she dared to finish it.

Had she gone too far? Her intention had been to taunt, to arouse, then to walk away leaving him to imagine her touching herself in another room in the house. Somehow, though, things had changed. He'd taken control of the situation.

She didn't pause to evaluate why she didn't care.

He reached for her thighs, tugging her closer to the edge of the counter. Then he gently eased her knees apart.

She shuddered. "Jack, I…"

"You don't have to take care of yourself."

Her eyes widened and her heart pounded with the primal rhythms of a tribal drum in her chest.

"I'm going to take care of you this time," he whispered.

She held her breath as he reached for her towel, tugging it open at the bottom, exposing one thigh all the way up to her hip. The other flap of the towel remained over her lap, caught almost coyly between her thighs. He made no effort to tug it free, instead trailing his fingers on her flesh in a slow, gentle caress.

Kate closed her eyes, waiting for a voice to scream in her head, telling her to stop, to not be taken in by him again.

Great sex and a whole bunch of earth-shaking orgasms won't cancel out the hurt of his disinterest later.

Who the hell was she kidding? Right now, at this very moment, great sex and a whole bunch of orgasms would be worth just about anything, including a kidney or her firstborn child.

It was only when she felt the frigidly cold water splash on her leg, and the colder ice pack connect with her aching bruise, that she realized what he'd meant by *taking care* of her.

"You're taking care of my hip."

He nodded. Only a tiny twitch of his lips told her he knew what she'd been picturing him taking care of.

Touché. Score one for Mr. Gorgeous. She almost groaned out loud. But she didn't. This game wasn't over yet. Especially because he did not simply leave the pack in her capable hands and walk out of the room. No. He stayed, holding it against her skin, still standing between her knees. His jaw remained rigid as he sucked in deep breaths, as if he were trying to control himself by sheer force of will.

She dared a quick glance down. *Those tight briefs can't lie, sweetheart.* She almost purred with satisfaction at the sight of his immense hard-on. A small spot of moisture on the gray cotton tempted her beyond belief. She wanted to touch it, taste it with her tongue. Wanted to have him explosive, hot and wet in her hand. Her mouth. Her body. *All three.*

Smiling slightly, she murmured, "Thank you for the ice."

"I really am sorry I hurt you," he rasped.

Her hip? Her heart? Her feelings? He didn't clarify. She didn't ask.

"Funny thing, ice. So cold, it's almost painful. Yet it's… pleasurable in a way. Makes me feel tingly."

"Tingly?"

"Yeah. Almost…hot. As strange as that sounds."

"Shut up, Kate, you're breaking my concentration."

She grinned. "Uh, sure. I know it takes a lot of concentration to hold an ice pack on someone. I mean, I'm sure that's why there's such a high turnover rate in the candy striper field…all that ice pack holding. Sheer torture."

His bare shoulders—so thick, broad and toned—shook as he chuckled. Darn, he'd succeeded in distracting her. The laughter hadn't changed the way she felt, though. She shifted, not feigning her discomfort on the hard surface of the small counter. She was wet and throbbing, sensitive and needy, and the countertop didn't help things. "This isn't the most comfortable place to sit. It's almost as hard as that table at the Rialto."

His eyes narrowed as he continued to stare at the ice pack, holding it steady. Now and then, though, she'd feel his fingers shift, feel him touch her, just the tip of an index finger on her hipbone. So light and fleeting at first she thought she'd imagined it. Now she ached for it.

"So, you never answered my question, Jack."

"What question?"

"About whether you want to see my little toy."

"I thought you were joking."

Reaching for her purse, she unzipped a side pouch and pulled out the small carrying case.

"You weren't kidding," he said, staring at the plastic pouch. His stare never wavered as she flicked the snap open with her thumb.

"One of the hottest sellers at Bare Essentials."

"Your store?"

Nodding, she ran her fingers along the tip of the vibrator, knowing he paid very close attention.

"You *sell* vibrators in your ladies' shop?"

She tsked. "You never did go back and find that article, did you, Jack? If you had, you'd know that Bare Essentials isn't a typical ladies store. We sell intimate items for women."

"Like that," he said, nodding toward the vibrator.

Smiling lazily. "Like this. And other things. Lots of delightful…other things."

He raised a brow. "So, you own a porn shop?"

She sniffed. "Bare Essentials does not sell pornography. We have lots of fun, sexy toys for ladies and couples. People come from other cities to shop for our lingerie, which is designed by my partner. We have a media section, with tasteful, instructional books. Plus erotic videos geared for women and couples. But nothing X-rated."

"I'm not criticizing, Kate," he said, obviously sensing her defensive reaction. "I'm fascinated. You have obviously made a big success for yourself. It's not often you see the owner of a sex shop on the cover of the Chicago *Business Journal*. You should be very proud."

Sensing he really wasn't being judgmental, and finding herself refreshed by his attitude, she relaxed slightly. "We found a niche. A clean, tasteful, brightly lit place for women and monogamous but adventurous couples—who are our biggest client base—to shop for special items. Bringing sex out of the seedy dark rooms or brown-paper-wrapped catalogs, and into the bright light of Michigan Avenue." Some demon made her add, "Complete with guest sex therapist lecturers, and the best selection of dildoes and cock rings in the state."

"Oh, so we're back to that, are we?"

"What?"

"This game of up the ante again. Trying to shock and tempt me some more."

Heat rose in her cheeks. "I don't know what you mean."

A slow smile spread across his lips. "Sure you do. The way you're running your fingers over that thing, like you don't know I'm watching, as if you don't think I'm picturing you touching yourself like that." His voice lowered. "Turning it on and moving it over every sensitive inch of your body."

Taking in a shaky breath, she pulled the vibrator out of the pouch. "Are you?"

"You know damn well I am."

She clipped it onto her middle finger.

He continued. "Just like you knew how I'd react to you naked in the shower. The forgotten towel. The vibrating finger comment."

"I really didn't know you were there when I said that," she murmured. Turning the vibrator on, she ran it across her shoulder to her collarbone, then her throat. Lower, over the curves of her breasts. Goose bumps rose on her skin. Beneath the towel, she felt her nipples grow even harder, until they scraped almost painfully against the cotton fabric.

Heat, stark and intense, flashed in Jack's eyes as he watched her. He silently dared her on, and she answered his challenge. Running the tiny device down the edge of the towel, she followed the seam down to her stomach. Lower. Until her hand rested on her lap and the vibrator kissed the inside of her thigh. Its hum was the only sound in the room, other than the faint rasp of Jack's labored breathing. And her own.

Pausing, she curled her lips into a sultry smile, warning him that she wasn't going to stop. Not unless he stopped her.

He didn't move a muscle.

Kate slid her hand beneath the towel.

"Mmm." She moaned as she scraped her fingertip across the curls between her legs.

"Enough." He dropped the ice pack and caught her wrist in his hand, clenching it tightly.

"I've barely started." She knew he could hear both the challenge and the promise in her voice.

He shook his head. "You've done what you set out to do, Kate. Hell, you did that the minute I saw you next door earlier." He let go of her wrist and took a step back. "You want me to want you. You want me crazy with wanting you."

Well, yeah!

"Mission accomplished."

He didn't try to do anything about it. He'd admitted it, but made no move to kiss her, to touch her.

"You've won. I concede. Now you need to stop."

His lips said stop. His eyes begged her to proceed. She moved her fingertip, letting her lips fall open in a pleasureful sigh as the vibrator skimmed across her throbbing clitoris. She knew he was going crazy, imagining what she was doing, but not really able to tell because of the discreet draping of the towel over her hand. "You're sure you want me…to stop?"

He closed his eyes. "Yes."

Liar. With a quick glance down, she saw that his body was still raring to go.

"The timing's bad on this, Kate," he said. "Really bad."

Obviously his mind was *not* raring to go.

"Bad timing. Right. There's a good reason for me not to give myself the orgasm I'm dying for," Kate said. "This has nothing to do with you, anyway."

"It has everything to do with me." He stepped closer, putting both his hands flat on the counter on each side of her hips. Leaning in until his face was inches from hers, he admitted, "I want to take you right here and now, fast and hard and furious, just like you're *begging* for…like it was that first night." His gaze dropped to her lips, to the towel, which had loosened again and barely clung to her body. As if he couldn't resist, his hands moved closer, until they touched her thighs. His fingers were cold from the ice pack, but it wasn't cold that made her gasp. It was the heat of his touch.

"Then I want to take you to bed, kiss away the pain on your hip, spend hours exploring your body and make love to you in ways you've never even dreamed of," he finally said, his voice ragged and full of need.

His expression told her he could, too. *So do it.*

"But not tonight, Kate. Not now." He straightened and stepped back. "Definitely not *here.*"

Once she was able to think again—once her heart started beating again—she told herself it didn't matter, that she had never planned to have sex with him tonight anyway. And he was right, she couldn't imagine a worse place to have sex with Jack Winfield than in the same house where their parents had probably spent intimate time together.

She flipped off the vibrator. "Sure." After tightening the towel around her chest, she slid off the counter. "Look, maybe I wasn't playing nicely. Maybe I was being unfair, trying to pay you back a little for not calling."

"I figured as much. And I'm sorry."

He didn't try to explain. Made no effort to tell her what had happened, what had changed between that night in the theater and two days later when he *hadn't* called her.

She couldn't ask him, of course. She instead relied on false bravado. "It really doesn't matter. I got what I wanted. A little payback." She glanced down at his body, making them both fully aware of his need for her. Then she smiled seductively.

"You go back to bed. Alone." Stepping closer to walk around him and out the door, she continued. "While I go back to bed, too. With the mental image of a shirtless Hugh Jackman." Holding up her hand, she glanced at the vibrator.

"And this."

7

JACK SLEPT LATE the next morning. That wasn't a big surprise since he'd lain awake in her bed until at least 5:00 a.m., wondering what she was doing. If she was touching herself. If she ached, the way he did. He'd listened for hours, torturing himself, waiting to see if she'd cry out when she came, as she had the night in the theater.

He wasn't sure if he ever heard her cry out, or if he just imagined the cries of ecstasy throughout the long night hours.

Enough of that.

Rising, he pulled on some jeans, then walked down the short hallway to the master bedroom. Though the door was partially open, he knocked quietly in case she was still asleep. When there was no answer, he glanced in and saw the stripped bed.

Kate hadn't slept in her mother's old room.

Curious, he went downstairs and saw the pile of folded linens and a pillow on the living room sofa. Hearing a voice through the thin wall, he stepped out onto the patio and walked over to the open door of the adjoining duplex.

Kate was inside, talking on a cell phone, sounding more than a little irritated. "Look, the power was supposed to be turned on yesterday. I have my confirmation numbers, you already charged my credit card, so why am I sitting in the dark, sweaty, and unable to take a shower this morning?"

He couldn't imagine how she could be dirty after the endless shower she'd taken the night before. She looked fresh and chipper, dressed in tight jean shorts and another of those flimsy, sleeveless tank tops. Red and wicked, it hugged her curves and made his heart skip a beat. There'd obviously been no sleepless night for her. She'd probably slept like a baby with her play toy clipped to her finger, her hand curled in her lap.

"Yes, I know it's a Saturday," she continued. "But please try to get someone out here this morning."

Jack would be willing to pay any after-hour fees the company might charge if it meant getting her into her own place by that night. No way could he take another night like the previous one.

"Problems?"

She almost dropped the phone when she heard his voice. "Hi. Yes, problems. The power company's as efficient as ever around here. They lost the work order to get the electricity back on for me before yesterday."

Without waiting for an invitation, he entered the living room of the small house. It was a mirror image of the one next door, though it held not a stick of furniture. "You never did tell me why you're here, anyway. I had the impression visiting Pleasantville isn't your favorite thing to do."

"I suppose it's better than being buried up to my neck in a red ant nest," she muttered.

He chuckled. "So why're you here?"

"Business."

Interesting, given her line of work. "*Your* kind of business?"

"The private kind."

"Okay," he said with a shrug. "Is this business going to keep you in town long?"

"A few weeks at least."

Weeks. Damn. He'd really hoped she was making a quick trip. If she stayed, he'd be in for lots of long, sleepless nights. Even worse, it would be nearly impossible for her to avoid hearing the gossip about Edie and his father.

Jack suddenly found himself willing to do just about anything to prevent that. As sorry as he felt for Edie, he knew she'd made her choices. She'd dealt with them in her own way.

Kate hadn't chosen to be the target of gossip, scorn and spite from this town. Yet that was about all she'd gotten here as a kid. And, he feared, about all she'd find here now.

If his sister Angela's comments were anything to go on, Kate and her cousin hadn't had the best time in high school. Kate hadn't let that stop her in the least. She'd gotten out, made a life for herself, created a new world where she had the power, the money and the upper hand.

Much as he had done.

No wonder he liked her so much. After all, in spite of their dissimilar childhoods, they had a lot in common. Hadn't they each been put into a mold by this town, and done whatever they could to break out of it? They'd both left after high school—her opening a sex shop and him focusing on career and casual relationships with a lot of different women. And they'd both come back, still wanting to rebel and shock, until they'd found each other and fallen headfirst into a hot kiss on a public street. Not to mention what had happened in the theater.

"Do you want something to eat?" he finally asked, figuring she couldn't possibly have any groceries in the house.

"I already had a donut and a warm diet Coke, thanks."

"How nutritious."

"It's not exactly the breakfast of champions, but it will do."

Glancing toward the floor, she bent to get something out of her purse. Jack tried not to notice the way her shorts hugged her ass, the way they rode up on her thighs until he could see the hem of her panties.

Well, no, he didn't really try not to look. He just tried not to let it affect him. Which was impossible.

After grabbing a brush, she straightened and gathered her hair into a ponytail at the back of her neck. Her shirt pulled tighter against her curves as she lifted her arms. Jack again wished he'd stayed in bed, avoiding her for the day.

"Did you sleep okay? I noticed you stayed downstairs on the couch. You could have used your mom's room."

She looked away, busying her hands putting the brush back into her purse. "The couch was fine."

"Sure there was enough room for all three of you?"

"Three of us?"

"You know. You, Hugh and your little friend?" he asked, wondering what demon made him bring the subject back to what had happened last night when they'd parted.

She laughed softly.

"So what is it with Hugh Jackman? A mouth, like Connery? Dangerous glint in his eye, like Eastwood? Or that schmaltzy chick-flick-time-travel with him and Meg Ryan?"

She shook her head, licking her lips. "Wolverine in *X-Men*. I just love a lean-looking man who can kick ass." She shrugged, obviously being honest and not trying to torment him sexually as she had the night before. "What can I say? I like men who can move their bodies gracefully while being seriously dangerous."

If he were going to pursue a sexual relationship with her—which he absolutely was *not*, not *yet* anyway—he'd have contemplated inviting her to one of his Tae Kwon Do classes, which he taught three nights a week. Instead he changed the subject. "So, are you planning to sleep on the floor for weeks?"

She glanced around the empty room. "Some of my aunt's old furniture is stored in the garage of her new place. My cousin, Cassie, is going to help me load some up and bring it here."

"Cousin? Your cousin's back in town, too?"

She shot him a look from half-lowered lashes. "She's been here in town for several weeks already. Do you know her?"

He shook his head. "No, I don't remember her at all. But I know the two of you lived here, in these houses. Is she going to stay here with you?"

"No. Her mom owns some other property around here. Cassie's staying at Aunt Flo's other place up on Lilac Hill."

Jack raised a questioning brow.

"Aunt Flo had a lot of admirers in this town. Male admirers. A couple of them liked to give her presents."

He understood. "Someone *gave* her a house on Lilac Hill?" At her nod, he whistled. "Some present. Who was it?"

"Mr. Miller, the banker."

A grin tickled the corners of Jack's lips. "He was old as dirt when I was born."

"Flo's not age discriminatory."

"He was a widower with no family for as long as I can remember." Jack thought about it. "I'm glad your aunt gave him a little bit of happiness. He was a nice old guy. You know he lived only two doors down from us."

Her chuckle was decidedly wicked. "There goes the neighborhood."

Knowing how his mother and sister felt about the Tremaine family, he had to wonder why he hadn't heard anything about this latest insult upon the glory that was Winfield.

"So, Cassie stays on the hill and you're staying here."

"Right. Is there a problem?"

"I'm wondering why you're not staying there with her."

"Let's just say the snob set's not exactly my cup of tea."

"But they are your cousin's?"

Kate shrugged. "Cassie fits in anywhere. She's very successful. You'll probably recognize her when you see her."

"Why?"

"She's a lingerie model. Poses in sexy underclothes for catalogs that pretend they're for women, but which men swipe from their wives and hide in the bathroom to look at."

He shrugged. "And you're a super successful store owner who makes front-page news. Sounds like both of you got away from here and made good." He glanced around the room. "I'm sure you have more expensive tastes these days, too."

"This is fine for me." She raised a hand, gesturing to the small room. "Part of Cassie's reason for staying up there was out of her innate need to be as outrageous as possible."

"I somehow think your cousin hasn't cornered the market on being outrageous in your family."

Rolling her eyes, she sat on the floor, draping her arms on her upraised knees. "No, I'm the smart, quiet, *sweet* one." She sounded thoroughly disgusted.

He couldn't help it—he let out a loud bark of laughter. Her glare told him she didn't appreciate his amusement.

"Honey, I can think of a lot of words to describe you, but something as insipid as sweet definitely isn't on the list."

She frowned at him. "You're saying I'm not sweet?"

"No, you're definitely not sweet, Kate." Stepping across the room, he bent to sit directly in front of her. "Smart, yes. Quiet—well, only in the way that smart people are because they're always thinking. Deciding their course of action before they act on it. Like you did at the theater."

Her jaw tightened. "Get back to the part where you tell me why I'm not a nice person."

He wagged an index finger at her. "Uh-uh, I didn't say you're not a nice person. You're a fascinating, charming, *nice* woman, Kate. But not anything as simple as sweet. There are such depths to you…." He stared intently at her face, losing himself again in those dark brown eyes, wondering what was going on in that beautiful mind of hers. "I'd like to know what makes you tick," he admitted softly.

Color rose in her cheeks and her lips parted. He'd gone too far, treaded back into personal, intimate territory. He backpedaled. "So, tell me, why do you think you're sweet and quiet?"

"Because my family has told me I am for twenty-eight years." She blew out a frustrated breath. "Cassie was the wild, tempestuous child. I was the sweet, good girl. The little ballerina, the straight-A student."

"I imagine you got quite a reaction with your store."

"My mother left during the grand opening reception. Never came back again until after I started sending her copies of my bank statements." She paused. "Of course, my aunt Flo sent a huge bouquet of orchids and told me she never thought I had a wicked streak in me. I guess they thought Cassie and I were destined to be exact replicas of them. They expected it even before we were ever born."

Knowing how difficult it was to break out of the position in which every family tried to paint its members, he nodded in agreement. "I would be willing to bet Cassie is not nearly as wild as she's said to be." He leaned closer to her. "And I know you're not exactly a good girl."

"Really?" She looked at him so hopefully he almost laughed. He didn't, though, not wanting to hurt her feelings.

"No, I don't think good girls own sex shops or carry tiny vibrators around in their purses. Nor do they often go for it when offered the chance to do something as wildly impulsive as what we did at the theater."

He waited for her to look away, to break the stare, but she didn't. Her eyes looked softer, dreamier, as her lips parted. A tiny sigh preceded her reply. "Thank you."

"For?"

"For seeing the Kate I see…not the one everyone else sees. For letting me be myself, not who everyone thinks I am." She paused. "Even if who I am is sometimes a not-so-nice, not-so-sweet person."

Jack leaned close and pressed a kiss to her temple, then brushed her hair away. He saw her pulse ticking in her throat as she looked up at him. "Sweet is boring, Kate," he whispered. "I much prefer spicy…even if I know I'm going to get burned."

Her moist lips parted and she tilted her head back as she took in a deep breath. He'd never seen a more clear invitation to go further. Kissing her temple wasn't enough for either of them. He had to taste her, just once more, or else he'd go crazy wondering if her mouth was as soft as he remembered. He leaned closer, brushing his lips across her temple again, then her cheek, and her jaw. She sighed, but didn't pull away.

"I take it back, Kate," he murmured as he moved lower, to kiss her earlobe and the side of her neck. "You taste very sweet." Then, unable to resist, he moved his mouth to hers. Their lips met and parted as instinctively as the beating of a heart. He licked lazily at her tongue, dipping his own into her mouth to taste her more thoroughly. She kissed him back, curling against him, tilting her head, inviting him deeper.

When they finally pulled apart, neither spoke for a moment. Then she narrowed her eyes. "Don't you do that again."

Her shaky voice held a warning and a challenge. He wondered if, as usual, she was trying to scare him into backing off. He mentally tsked. Obviously she didn't remember what had happened when she'd tried that at the Rialto.

Finally, Jack smiled. "Yeah, there's definitely both sweet and spicy to you, Kate Jones. I can't decide which side I like better."

Before she could reply, he got up and left the duplex.

WHEN KATE ARRIVED at Cassie's house up on the hill that afternoon, her cousin greeted her with a big hug and a humongous margarita. "A pea-green drink in honor of your return to Pea-Ville." Cassie held up her salt-rimmed glass to clink a toast.

Kate clinked back, then sipped deeply. The electric company still hadn't gotten her power on by the time she'd left the house, and the drink went down like a powerful blast of air-conditioning. Besides, she'd been all hot and bothered ever since Jack had kissed her then walked out. "Ah, perfect. I'd forgotten how hot it is here in the pits of hell in the summer."

"I guess I'm getting used to it."

Hearing an unexpected note of warmth in Cassie's voice, Kate raised a brow. "The heat? Or the town?"

Cassie shrugged. "Maybe a little of both."

"Well, I can see you don't have a scarlet letter on your shirt, so maybe things aren't as bad as I'd expected."

"Believe it or not, I haven't heard one person call me a tramp since I got here." She winked. "At least not to my face."

Her cousin led Kate into the house, then gave her a quick tour, including a stop in Flo's outrageously decorated boudoir.

Going back downstairs, they sat in the kitchen, drinking their margaritas and gabbing for an hour. Kate didn't like the tired, dark circles under Cassie's eyes—though, they certainly didn't distract from her beauty. Since Cassie never brought up the trouble she was in, trouble that involved an over-amorous man who hadn't taken her rejection too well, Kate didn't, either. There would be time enough to talk about it, and to give Cassie her mail, which had been forwarded to Kate in Chicago while Cassie hid out. Kate wanted to put off handing over the dozen or more letters. "So the store's really coming along okay?"

"Absolutely. I've got a couple of high school boys who've helped with the painting and repairs. The shelving units and cabinetry were already there from when the men's shop was open. Carpet goes in Monday, and the stock you sent arrives daily."

"Well, I'm here now to help with the inventory, at least, now that you did the hard stuff. The permit was approved, right? I still don't know how you pulled it off."

Cassie gave her an evil smile. "It's called boobs. A low-cut shirt and a pair of breasts leaning on the desk of a city worker's office can accomplish a lot. Including rubber-stamping an application for a business license."

"Boobs and brains. Cassie Tremaine Montgomery, you're a force to be reckoned with." Kate sipped her drink.

"It's only fair I got the bigger boobs, since you got the bigger brain," Cassie pointed out.

Kate sighed. "But we both got the big hips."

Cassie gave her a Cheshire-cat smile. "Most men who look at my pictures in the catalog like curvy hips."

Kate agreed. "I'll bet the permit guy is a fan."

"Even if he's not, I didn't lie on the business app. We *are* going to open a lovely, tasteful little ladies' shop…."

"With King Kong Dong featured prominently in the front display window," Kate interjected with a snorty laugh.

They clinked their glasses again.

Cassie got up to make them a couple of sandwiches for

lunch. "Speaking of King Kong Dong, or dongs in general, have you met your new neighbor yet?"

Kate didn't answer right away, drawing a curious stare from Cassie. In spite of how close they were, Kate hadn't told Cassie about her interlude with Jack at the Rialto. So she couldn't exactly explain what had happened the night before when she'd discovered he was really J. J. Winfield. "We've met."

"And?"

Kate got up to wash lettuce for the sandwiches.

"Come on, what gives? Aren't you going to make him your love slave, then trample all over his heart with the heels of your six-inch-high, slut-puppy boots?"

"I don't own slut-puppy boots."

"You sell them."

"I sell a lot of things that I don't own or use myself," she said as she sipped.

"Aw, gee. Here I figured you gave a personal testimonial with every dildo, clit ring and butt plug you peddle."

Kate laughed so hard some of her margarita spilled from the corner of her lips. "You are as bad as Armand."

"So tell me about the Winfield prince," Cassie said.

"I don't know about Jack—J.J. He's not what I expected."

"Meaning?"

"Meaning he might be more than I can handle."

Cassie lifted a brow. There probably wasn't a man alive who her cousin couldn't handle. But Kate wasn't Cassie.

"Maybe I'd better start out a little easier. Focus on some of my other goals. Like the shop. Or Angela and Darren."

"Hmm, yeah, I forgot about them. I saw Angela one day, walking out to her car. She and her mom live up the street."

"Please tell me she's fat."

"Sorry, hon. She looks pretty good. Still looks like a total bitch, but not a Jenny Craig-bound one."

Rats.

"What about Darren?"

"Works at a car dealership and lives downtown in an apartment over the Tea Room. Did you know he and Angela were married for a while right after high school? The rumor mill says she got knocked up on prom night. They married that summer. Then when she lost the baby, he divorced her and went into the army."

Kate winced. "Maybe I should thank her for stealing him on prom night." She couldn't imagine how her life might have ended up if she'd been the pregnant teen. Probably she'd be living here, bitter and sour with a poochy belly, saggy breasts and four kids who looked like moon-faced Darren clinging to her skirts.

Kate met Cassie's eye, knowing she was thinking along the same lines. They exchanged shaky smiles. "Here's to what *didn't* happen to us on prom night," Kate said softly.

Cassie nodded. "Hear, hear."

JACK LUCKED OUT and arrived at his mother's house after she'd left for her Saturday hair appointment. Closing himself in his father's office—to the chagrin of Leonardo the bulldog—he spent two hours balancing bank statements, sorting out documents. He heard his sister Angela moving around, once stopping to have a long phone conversation in the next room.

He didn't get his sister. Angela was pretty and had been given every advantage. She'd been the apple of their parents' eye, and had once had a genuine sweetness to her personality. Sure, she was spoiled. She'd shown signs of that, even as a toddler. But at least before, when she'd been a kid, she'd had an infectious laugh and a beautiful smile. In the fifteen years he'd been gone, she'd lost them both. Probably three failed marriages and two miscarriages could do that to a person.

Resolving to get along better with her, he forced a look of welcome to his face when she walked into the office. "Hi."

"You busy?"

He nodded and rubbed his weary eyes. "Dad left a mess."

Her laugh could only be described as bitter. "Yeah. As usual." She sat on a chair next to the window. "I don't suppose you've changed your mind and plan to stay here."

He shook his head. "I'm sorry, Ang. I don't know how you can stand it. I can't breathe in this place."

"Even after he died Dad still managed to drive you away."

Jack pushed his chair back. "What are you talking about?"

"I mean, you took off fifteen years ago because of him. Because of how he pressured you to follow in his footsteps."

"Most fathers do."

Angela continued as if he hadn't spoken. "And as soon as it looks like you're going to come back, you find out about his dirty little secret and won't stay here now, either."

Jack shook his head. "It's more complicated than that. How did you find out about Dad and Edie, anyway?"

She glanced out the window. "I saw them kissing once. Not long after you'd gone away to college."

She'd been thirteen. He swallowed, hard. "What'd you do?"

"Nothing. I didn't confront him, or tell Mother, or anybody else. I was afraid if she found out, they'd get a divorce and I'd be shuffled back and forth between them forever."

A wave of guilt washed over him as he acknowledged he'd left her here without an ally in his hurry to escape from home. "I'm sorry, Angela. But maybe now it's time to move on. Have you thought about getting out of here, too?"

"I've been dying to move out, get my own place downtown, but Mother plays the guilt card whenever I mention it."

"I meant, maybe it's time to get out of Pleasantville."

"I can't. I don't want to leave him…I mean, leave here."

Him? He didn't think Angela was seeing anyone, though she'd been divorced from her third husband for over a year.

She stood abruptly. "I have to go. I have a nail appointment. Be sure to lock up when you leave, okay? Mother doesn't trust Sophie to secure the house." Her jaw clenched.

"After all, she's not nearly as trustworthy as *Edie* was."

Judging by the way she spat out the other woman's name, Jack surmised his sister had not been able to forgive and forget.

As Angela left the room his parents' ever-hopeful dog, Leonardo, slunk in and strolled over to the desk. At Leonardo's longing glance at his jeans-clad leg, Jack shot him a suspicious glare. "Dog, how many years is it gonna take for you to figure out you've got no balls?"

Leonardo gave him a sheepish glance from his wrinkled face. Walking around in circles once or twice, he appeared to be looking for something—or someone. He finally curled up at Jack's feet and looked up at him with sad eyes.

"Okay," Jack said with a sigh. "I guess you miss him, too."

A half hour later he straightened up to leave, determined to get out before his mother got back. After making sure the mutt had enough water, he locked up and headed for his father's pickup truck, which he'd been driving during his stay.

As he drove down the street, he glanced toward old Mr. Miller's house and saw a shapely brunette in a red tank top trying to drag a big mattress across the driveway.

He immediately stopped the truck. "Kate, are you trying to break your back? Put that down."

She dropped the end of the mattress and frowned at him. "You distracted me. Do you know how long it took to tug that thing out of the garage?"

He trotted across the driveway to her side. "I thought your cousin was going to help you."

"She is. She's had a bunch of phone calls to deal with. Problems with her agent."

"And Miss Have-To-Do-It-Now can't wait for her?"

"I'm not helpless. I've gotten a bunch of other stuff by myself." She gestured toward her SUV, which already held a couple of chairs. And, judging by the upraised legs that nearly reached the interior roof, a small kitchen table.

He couldn't believe she'd done it all alone. "I suppose you plan to unload all this stuff without help when you get back home, too?"

She scuffed the toe of her sneaker on the driveway and mumbled, "Well, I kinda figured you'd be back sooner or later."

"Back to help you unload it, or to make you another ice pack and take care of you again after you slip a disc?"

Wrong thing to say. They both instantly remembered how he'd taken care of her the night before. Awareness hummed between them, as always, now not below the surface, but right out in the open again.

She bit the corner of her lip. "Look," she finally said, "I'm almost done, are you going to help me or criticize me?"

He glanced at the open hatch and the mattress. "Honey, I hate to tell you this, but you've got a size problem here. I don't think something this big is going to fit in there."

"You sound like a conceited teenage boy about to get laid for the first time."

Not recognizing the sultry voice of the woman who'd spoken, he turned and saw a shapely blonde standing just behind them on the driveway. She had her head cocked to the side and her hand on one hip, smiling wickedly. With her eye-popping build, sunny-blond hair and outrageous words, he immediately assumed she was the cousin.

Frowning, he ignored her comment. "I hope your call was

important, since your cousin nearly gave herself a hernia out here."

The blonde's brow shot up. She immediately turned to Kate. "Katey, I told you to wait for me. Good grief, how'd you carry all that stuff by yourself?"

Kate didn't answer. She was too busy looking back and forth between Jack and Cassie, a confused frown scrunching her brow.

Jack grabbed the end of the mattress. "Let me throw this in the truck and take it for you, Kate. I'm going home anyway."

"Home?" the blonde—Cassie—asked. Then understanding crossed her face. "Oh, my, you're J. J. Winfield, aren't you?"

He swallowed a groan. "Jack. Jack Winfield."

The blonde didn't reply, just looked him over, head to toe, very intently. Smiling, she extended her hand. "Hi, Jack. I'm Cassie. The truck's a great idea. Can you take a few other things, too?"

"Sure," he said, still wondering why Kate looked so befuddled and hadn't said a single word since her cousin had come out of the house. "Is that all right with you, Kate?"

After she nodded, he hoisted the queen-size mattress up with both hands. He saw Cassie's eyes widen as she stared at his arms, chest and shoulders. As he walked away, he heard her whisper, "Too much to handle, indeed. But oh, Kate, wouldn't you have fun trying?"

They loaded up his truck with the few remaining pieces of furniture and were finished within a half hour of his arrival. Cassie disappeared into the house again, after thanking Jack once more for his help.

"Are you heading back now? Or do you want me to drive this stuff back, then wait for you to get there to unload it?"

"Let me say goodbye to Cassie and I'll come back so we can unload it this afternoon." She turned to go into the house, then paused. "Jack? Thanks a lot for stopping to help. I really do appreciate it."

He shrugged. "Just being neighborly."

She glanced up and down the block, at the manicured lawns, the gated driveways that were filled with expensive cars. "Yeah. Right. I'm sure there were bunches of other neighbors lacing up their deck shoes to come out and help when you stopped. I bet they're still peering out their windows, waiting for the chance to lend a hand."

He followed her stare, figuring she was probably right, but not admitting it. "It's not all bad here."

"I guess Cassie likes it. But I wouldn't be able to stand the quiet sense of knowing everyone on the block is watching every move you make." She brushed an errant, damp strand of hair off her brow. "It'd be like living in a goldfish bowl, some big fat cat always waiting to pounce on you if you leap out of the safe waters where you belong."

"Yeah, that's exactly what it was like growing up."

Their eyes met. She looked surprised that he agreed.

As for Jack, he thought it remarkable how quickly Kate had nailed what his childhood had been like on this block. In this town.

"Can I venture a guess that living on Pansy Lane was something like a fishbowl, too?"

Her slow nod was his only answer.

He reached out to brush away the blowing strand of hair again. His fingers connected with her temple, sending heat through his body. Heat that had absolutely nothing to do with the blazing sunshine overhead.

"Then I guess it's a good thing we both like to live a little dangerously."

WHEN THEY GOT BACK to the duplex, Kate first went inside to check the power, then leaned out to give him a thumbs-up. "Yes! Houston, we have ignition."

"Good, now you can take a shower in your own bathroom tonight," he muttered.

They unloaded the truck, making several trips.

"So," she asked as they carried some chairs into the kitchen. "Did you get a lot done at your mother's house today?"

She seemed to be making an effort to be polite, social and absolutely impersonal. He followed her lead. "Barely made a dent. My father had accounts all over the state, with at least a dozen banks. He owned property I didn't know about, held mortgages my *mother* didn't even know about. I haven't even gotten to the stuff in a file marked Private that I found in his desk drawer."

"Well, if you need any help, I do have some accounting background." At his look of surprise, she hurried on. "What? I mean, I do owe you one for helping me today."

"I'll keep that in mind," he said with a smile. "Though, maybe I'll choose the way you repay me."

They left the queen-size mattress for last. It would be the trickiest, since it had to go up the narrow staircase to the bedroom. "Hope you sleep really well to make it worth lugging this thing all over town," he said as they hoisted the thing through the doorway. They dropped it right on the floor as Kate hadn't bothered with a bed frame.

"At least it's not a twin," she said with a smile, obviously referring to the way he spent his own nights. "Nice and roomy."

He frowned. "You're not planning on sharing it, are you?"

"Huh?" She looked truly puzzled and he felt like an idiot for his instant of jealousy. "Wait a second." She pointed an index finger at him. "You want to know if another man is going to be staying over here occasionally."

He crossed his arms, not saying anything. She chuckled. "Uh, I don't think so, Jack. In spite of what you might think, given the way I acted on the day we met, I'm not a bed hopper." She paused. "I don't think I could even be called a bed crawler, these days."

Good.

"Not that it's any of your business."

"No, of course not." *Damn right it was his business.*

"If I did choose to bring someone here, you'd have absolutely no say in the matter," she continued, almost challenging him to deny it.

He stepped closer, tipping her chin up with his index finger until she met his eye. "I wouldn't say a word." Her lashes lowered as she tried to look down. "I can promise I wouldn't say anything to him as I threw him out the window, Kate."

She bit her lip, looking both confused and a little bit pleased. Unable to resist, he bent to kiss her mouth. Lightly. Playfully.

"What was that for?" She brought her shaking fingers to her mouth when he ended the kiss and stepped away.

"Just to remind you."

"Remind me of what?"

He walked toward the door, but glanced over his shoulder. "That I'm the only man you want."

8

KATE DECIDED to spend her first few days in Pleasantville devoting all her thoughts to the new store. And none to
her love life, such as it was. That didn't count her dreams, of
course, over which she had no control.

Jack starred in them every night, damn it.

On Saturday night, after Jack had helped her unload some
furniture at the duplex and given her the playful kiss that
had left her reeling, she went downtown to see the shop for
the first time. Cassie and her high school helpers had done a
great job. Sure, there were some lighting problems, but the
old dressing room area was perfect, with lots of mirrors so
customers could get addicted to Armand's luxurious lingerie. And the store had adequate air-conditioning and plenty
of display shelves, with discreet alcoves for some of their more
risqué items. If this store were in some other town, she could
envision it thriving.

Kate and Cassie enjoyed eating pizza, listening to loud
music, drinking wine and examining sex toys until late Saturday night. At least until the sheriff, Sean Taggart, showed up.

As soon as Kate saw him, she understood why Cassie got
such a strange look on her face whenever his name came up.

The man was pure, rugged manna from tough-guy heaven. Maybe not movie-star gorgeous, like Jack, but with his lean body, thick brown hair and dangerous smile, she could see why Cassie might find him distracting. So distracting that Kate immediately decided to leave the two of them alone. After all, it wasn't often she saw her cousin nearly blushing around a man.

It also wasn't every day she came across a man who did not turn into a tongue-tied, drooling idiot around her cousin. Jack hadn't. On Saturday, when Cassie had been at her Cassie-est, all blond, leggy and saucy, he'd barely glanced in her direction.

She hadn't known whether to kiss him or to take his pulse to see if he was still alive and breathing. In any case, she could almost love him for it. "Love him?" Insane. She barely liked him.

Well, she conceded, that was a big lie. She did like him, she'd liked him from the minute they met, in spite of who his father had been. He was charming and sexy, playful and self-confident. She liked that he didn't swagger, and he felt no need to play tough guy. He was a flirt, a man who liked women. Right now he liked her, she knew it, in spite of his failure to call. She could see the heat in his eyes when he looked at her. He wanted her every bit as much as he had their first day. But something was holding him back.

If his last name were different, and if he'd come up with a reasonable excuse for not calling her, she might have tried to find out what was stopping him. And maybe she would have tried to change his mind.

The realization floored her. How strange that for the first time in nearly forever, she'd found someone who tempted her to let him get closer. She could conceive of lowering some of her guard, taking a chance on what could be a fabulously erotic, exciting relationship. But he'd erected barriers even taller than her own.

She supposed it was just as well there were insurmountable walls between them right up front. Jack obviously liked to play. A lot. He wasn't the stick-around type and she knew it. While Kate believed if there ever did come a time when she found that one right guy—her true love—she'd be a goner for life.

Much like her mother had been, unfortunately.

Over the next couple of days Kate refrained from pumping Cassie about her problems—either her old ones, or her new one, in the form of the hunky sheriff. Somehow, while they priced, ordered and set up displays, she found herself getting excited as she had before the opening of her shop in Chicago.

Knock it off, this isn't the same thing at all!

Nope, it definitely wasn't. In Chicago, she'd wanted her shop to be a wild success. Here, she fully expected it to be a grand failure. But at least they'd have fun failing, doing it publicly, right on the main street of Pleasantville. And, as they failed, she'd be right here in case Cassie needed her. She knew her cousin too well…if Kate had stayed in Chicago, Cassie would never have come to her if things got bad. Here, she couldn't very well avoid it!

She managed to avoid Jack for the most part—not an easy feat considering their close living quarters. But he was usually gone during the day, and so was she. That suited her fine.

Nights were tougher. They slept mere inches apart, separated only by the width of one slim, interior wall. There were times when she thought she heard his hand brush the wall behind her head, when he'd roll over in her old bed next door. She knew from childhood experience that at times she and Cassie had heard each other's late-night bad dream cries.

On Wednesday morning she stepped outside on the porch as soon as she got up, glad for the fresh early-morning air. Down the block, a mother rode a bicycle, with a toddler in the child seat. The woman waved as she rode by.

A nice, peaceful morning. She didn't remember those from when she'd lived here, though, she supposed there must have been some. At least for Edie. Otherwise, why would her mother have ever come back here when Kate's dad died?

Hearing sounds coming from next door, she stepped closer and peered into the front window of her mother's duplex. She wished she hadn't. Jack stood in his living room, bare-chested, wearing only a pair of loose white pants. He was stretching, moving his body with fluidity and grace. And power. It took a second for her muddled brain to realize that he was running through some type of karate moves.

He had no idea she was there. So she watched for several minutes. The sweat gleamed on his bare chest and thick arms as he swung and kicked and arched. He moved his body like a sleek animal, a finely tuned—but dangerous—machine.

Walk away before he sees you. She couldn't, though. She couldn't turn and walk into her house. Just one more moment of watching…. One moment stretched into five or ten minutes until finally, inevitably, he glanced up and saw her there.

He immediately stopped. They stared at each other through the glass for a minute, then Jack lifted his hand and pointed toward her with his index finger, wagging it back and forth like a parent to a kid who'd done something naughty.

Act innocent. She gave him a "Who me?" shrug.

He crossed his arms and raised his brow, waiting for her to admit she'd been spying on him.

"Oh, all right," she muttered. As she entered the front door she immediately launched into an explanation. "I didn't mean to watch you working out. I just stepped out for some fresh air, and couldn't help noticing."

"Uh-huh," he said as he began to stretch his arms out, slowly rolling his shoulders as if cooling down from his workout.

"I mean, the curtains were open. I just caught a glimpse."

"Right."

His one-word answers did nothing to hide his amusement.

"Really, Jack, I do respect your privacy."

He finally stopped moving all those yummy muscles long enough to meet her eye. "Kate, you've been standing there for almost ten minutes."

She fisted her hands and put them on her hips. "You saw me?"

"No," he admitted. Then he grinned. "But I heard your front door open, and that board on the front porch really creaks."

She was surprised he'd been able to hear anything except his own churning pulse as he'd flexed and stretched all those lovely, hard muscles. She forced herself to look away, wondering if she'd been drooling while she'd watched from the window. She surreptitiously lifted her fingers to her chin to check.

"So, uh, were you doing some kind of karate?" she finally asked, wanting to fill the charged silence. "I've thought about taking some self-defense courses."

"Tae Kwon Do. If you're serious, I teach at a studio in Chicago. I can give you the address."

That implied they'd see one another after they left Pleasantville, something Kate hadn't really allowed herself to consider. "Well, I don't know...."

"If you don't feel comfortable in a class," he said with a cajoling smile, "I'd be happy to work with you one on one."

Work with her. One on one. How about one you on one me?

She gulped. "I'd better go."

He grabbed a white towel and draped it over his shoulders. "Don't go. I'll make you some breakfast. I can't promise gourmet food like diet Coke and donuts, but I can do a decent omelet."

Considering she hadn't bothered to do a grocery shopping trip, and had been living off fast food and 7-Eleven burritos for the past few days, Kate's stomach overruled her brain. "Great."

"Lemme change."

You don't have to on my account!

While he was upstairs, Kate went into the kitchen, glad to see Jack was keeping the place spotless, just as it had been when her mother had lived here. Kate, unfortunately, was more the slob type. And the world's greatest chef—or even a competent one—she was not. She did, however, know how to crack an egg and was hard at it when he returned, dressed in jeans and a T-shirt.

"So tell me why you want to take self-defense courses," he said as he began making their breakfast.

"I dunno, I live in a big city and run a rather infamous store. I got a few wacky phone calls after that article."

Jack's shoulders stiffened. "Did anyone threaten you?"

"Oh, no. I just got asked on some unusual dates—to strip clubs, S and M hangouts and the Circus."

"Circus sounds pretty normal."

"I thought so, too, at first. Turns out there's a sex show called the Circus where the animals are all people in costume who offer rides to members of the audience."

"I think I'd rather not have known that," he said with a groan as he diced some ham for the omelets.

"Me, too." She made herself at home, finding his coffee supply and filling the coffeepot. "I guess some people heard about my shop and instantly thought the worst of me."

He put the knife down to study her. "You've had to deal with that before, haven't you?"

She knew he meant here, in Pleasantville. "Ancient history."

"So how does it measure up now? How has the town treated you these first few days?"

So far, she had to admit, things had been okay. Then again, she hadn't been out too much, staying mostly at home, at Cassie's place or at the store. "Fine, actually. How about you? Has the red carpet been rolled out for the return of the prodigal son?"

"I'm keeping a low profile, though one of my father's friends asked me to move back and run for mayor next year."

"Will you?" She held her breath waiting for his answer.

"Not on your life."

She nearly sighed in relief. *Why would it matter to you if he came back here, married the local big-haired town princess and stayed forever?* She didn't know why, she only knew it would matter.

Somehow, even though she'd told herself nothing was going to happen between them, Kate couldn't imagine being in Chicago, knowing Jack wasn't there somewhere, in that big bustling city, stopping traffic on the street with his smile and teaching his Tae Kwon Do classes. Tackling intruders and doing fix-it work on a needy woman's house.

Their eyes met, and somehow Kate knew Jack had read her thoughts. He knew she liked him, and she felt drawn to him.

Kate's eyes widened as Jack stepped close, until she was backed up against the kitchen counter, and he pressed almost neck to toe against her body. "I'm looking forward to a lot of things changing when I get back to Chicago, Kate." He lifted a hand to her face, softly caressing her cheekbone, then touching a strand of her hair. "Changing for both of us."

Before she could ask him to explain, he'd turned back to the stove. Kate clutched the counter and sucked in a few deep breaths, trying to regain her composure. By the time breakfast was ready, she felt completely calm and relaxed, or at least she thought she looked that way—no point in wondering if he knew she was still edgy and aware, and now very curious about what he'd meant about things changing between them.

"So, Jack, what else do you do in your real life. You're an architect. Ever designed anything I've actually heard of?"

He answered with a question. "Like to go shopping?"

"Does Imelda Marcos like shoes?"

He chuckled. "My firm designed the new Great Lakes Mall. I managed the project."

She gave a little whistle of appreciation. "Nice. Anything else?"

He named a few more buildings Kate instantly recognized, particularly the stores and shopping centers. "Sounds like retail's your niche."

"Mmm-hmm. If you ever decide to open a new Bare Essentials, let me know."

If only you knew…

"How'd you get into architecture? Didn't Daddy want you to follow in his footsteps and become a lawyer?"

"I prefer to build things, not tear them apart, which is what lawyers seem to spend a lot of their time doing." He flipped their omelets onto two plates and carried them to the table. "I really built things when I was going to college. I worked for a construction company in L.A. every summer."

"I somehow pictured you surfing your way through college."

"Ha! I tried it once and the damn board almost tore my ear off. After I wiped out, it hit me in the head. I still have the scar." He turned his head, pushing his hair up with his fingers. Kate bit her lip. Unable to resist, she stepped closer, until the toes of her sandals nearly touched his bare feet.

His hair was still slightly damp with sweat from his workout, and his skin still glowed with energy. She gulped, trying to ignore her response, and examined the thin scar that ran from just under his earlobe into his hairline.

If she wasn't mistaken, she might have kissed that spot during their interlude at the theater. Her heart skipped a beat.

"Ouch," she murmured.

He seemed to notice her sudden intensity, and her closeness. Her face was inches from his neck, and she inhaled deeply, smelling his musky warmth. She closed her eyes briefly, remembering what it had been like to kiss him. To touch him.

Lord help her, she still wanted him so much she could barely stand up. She wanted to nibble on his neck, to taste his earlobe, to feel his body get all sweaty again—preferably while it was on top of hers. Inside hers.

"You ready?" he asked, letting his hand fall to his side.

She nodded dumbly. "Uh-huh." Ready for just about anything.

"Do you like it spicy?"

Spicy? Oh, yeah, she loved it spicy. "Yeah. Real spicy."

"I think there's Tabasco sauce in the fridge."

Tabasco? Kate shook her head, hard, and realized Jack was watching her with an amused, knowing look on his face.

He'd been talking about hot and spicy eggs.

She'd been thinking about hot and spicy sex.

Please, floor, open up under me and swallow me whole.

"Kate?"

She raised a brow, trying to pretend she hadn't been picturing some of the spicy things the two of them could do on the kitchen table. Or counter. Or floor. "Huh?"

He reached for her, his hand brushing past her hip as he touched the handle on the refrigerator door. She jumped out of the way, noticing the way his hand tightened on the handle, as if he were exerting some great effort. Possibly for control? Was he as affected as she by their closeness?

There was only one way to find out. She reached out and touched the thin scar on his neck. He flinched and glanced at her. "It must have hurt," she said softly.

Jack didn't pull away as she moved closer, standing on tip-toes until her lips brushed his neck. Remembering the way he'd kissed her hip in the shower, she couldn't help kissing that hot, damp, male skin. Slipping her tongue out, she savored the faint salty flavor of sweat from his workout. She sighed at how good he tasted to her. Her touch elicited an answering groan from him, but he didn't move away. "I'm sorry I wasn't there to kiss it and make it better," she murmured as she moved her lips higher, kissing a path up to his earlobe. She stepped closer, for better access, sliding one foot between his, until his thigh was nestled between her legs. Kate closed her eyes briefly at the very intimate contact.

He muttered a soft curse, as if he could take no more. Catching her around the waist, he lifted her higher, pressing his leg tighter against her sex as he lowered his mouth to hers. Their kiss was explosive. Hot and wet. Deep and hungry. Kate met every thrust of his tongue, loving the way he tasted, the way he explored her mouth as if he couldn't get enough of her. She jerked her hips, needing the strength of his hard thigh against the crotch of her jean shorts.

When they finally broke apart, Jack stared down at her, warmth and tenderness shining through the passion of his gaze. "I invited you to breakfast. I didn't intend to leap on you at the first opportunity."

To be honest, she'd done the leaping. But she didn't point that out. "I wasn't playing any get-back-at-you games," she admitted softly. "Like Friday."

"Good. I wasn't playing games, either. But I think we should probably sit down and eat."

Nodding, she took a few deep breaths, trying to forget the way he'd kissed her, the way the strong muscles of his thigh had felt against her still-aroused body. She was too thankful that he wasn't going to tease her about her momentary lapse into mindless lust to argue.

As they sat to eat, Jack apparently looked for a quick way to change the subject. "Hey, I know what I forgot to tell you. I heard some news about the Rialto yesterday."

"Really?"

"Apparently the city now owns it, due to a loan default. It's sat there empty for years, but now a group of concerned citizens has announced they're going to work on renovating it, then open it as a public playhouse."

She smiled. "Wonderful."

"It gets better. Rose Madison is leading the effort."

"Miss Rose?"

He nodded. "She's the one who told me about it. I ran into her. I mentioned we were both happy to see some work being done on the old place."

"Did she remember me?"

"Yes. She said if you want to pay for those free movies, you're welcome to come down anytime with a paintbrush."

"I think I can wield a paintbrush."

"Hopefully better than you can crack an egg," he said with a grin as he picked a tiny white piece of shell off his tongue.

"You got me. I'm a lousy cook. But if you want me to tell you how to save money at the grocery store, I'm your woman."

"Absolutely," he said softly.

Absolutely? What did that mean? Absolutely he wanted to learn how to save money grocery shopping?

Or…absolutely, she was his woman?

Too chicken to ask which he meant, since she wasn't sure

what she wanted his answer to be, Kate finished her breakfast, thanked him and then left.

But she wondered about his comment all day long. Not to
mention their kiss.

Jack spent the afternoon out of the area, visiting some of
his late father's properties in nearby towns. They were mostly
rentals, small tract houses for young families. His father hadn't
been a slumlord, but some of the buildings were old and in
need of repair. The agent who was handling the sales told him
he'd take care of it.

When he got back to Pleasantville that afternoon, he found
the duplex empty. Kate's SUV was not parked outside. She'd
probably gone back to her cousin's place on Lilac Hill, which
was the reason Jack decided not to go to his mother's house.

He told himself he wasn't avoiding *her*. No, he was just
trying to avoid temptation. He hadn't been kidding in the
kitchen when he'd said he wanted things to change between
them once they got back to Chicago. That day couldn't come
soon enough for him, particularly after that kiss they'd shared.

He had also been fully aware of her desire for him. Hell,
she'd worn it as if it were perfume, oozing from her every
pore. So staying away from her seemed to be the smart choice.

Needing something to do, he remembered Rose's request
for help at the Rialto. He'd developed a real affection for the
old theater, particularly since the day he'd met Kate. Changing into some old clothes, he drove downtown and pulled up
outside the Rialto.

Right behind a silver SUV.

Drive away. Of course he didn't. Seeing her might be foolish, since he already spent way too much of his time thinking about her, but he parked and got out of his truck, anyway.

As he entered the building he heard loud music blaring

from a boom box and saw a pair of bare legs, complete with paint-speckled sneakers, dangling from a scaffold. "What do you think you're doing?" he asked, recognizing the curve of Kate's calves.

He realized he probably should not have startled her only after he saw her drop the paintbrush. Right toward his head.

A quick step back saved his skull, but not his shorts.

"Jack," she cried as the brush careened down his leg, leaving squishy beige marks in its path.

"I'm really sorry," she muttered. She shimmied on her hands and knees across the wood plank of the scaffolding, doing very interesting things to her black gym shorts. Well, black and beige gym shorts, considering all the paint stains.

She reached the built-in metal ladder on the side of the scaffold and swung around to it. Not wanting her to drop anything else—including herself—Jack went over and steadied her as she descended.

"Did you get any paint on the walls?" he asked her, looking down at her speckled clothes. And her skin. Not to mention her face and hair. "You are a complete mess."

"That's what long showers are for."

Oh, great. Kate was taking another long shower. Maybe he should just shoot himself now.

Looking around the empty lobby, he said, "You here alone?"

She nodded. "Miss Rose and her brother were here when I arrived. They were just getting ready to go for a dinner break, but said if I wanted to I could keep working on this wall."

Jack followed her gaze and looked at the interior wall that she'd been painting. It extended up all the way to the top of the open, two-story lobby. Where Kate had been working, he saw a big circle of paint. "Didn't anyone teach you to do the trim first?"

"Since you're the construction genius, why don't you do it?"

She bent, grabbed another brush and tossed it to him. Though not paint covered, the brush was wet and as he caught it on the bristle-side, it oozed beige-tinged water between his fingers.

"Nice," he said as he shook the moisture off. "I think you've been selling body paint at your store too long. This kind doesn't come off so easily."

She stepped closer, a laugh on her lips. "Oh, so you're saying I shouldn't do…this?" She lifted her completely white hand and cupped his cheek.

He cringed, then realized he didn't feel moisture against his skin. "If that paint on your hand had been wet, I'd be turning you over my knee and spanking you right now."

Her eyes widened. "Oooh, sounds kinky. I didn't know you were into that sort of thing."

"I'm not," he replied. He had to know. "Are you?"

She turned her head slightly and peeked at him through lowered lashes. "Light S and M? Well, lots of my customers are."

He couldn't resist asking, "*Light* S and M? How, exactly, would that differ from the heavy variety?"

She shrugged. "It's more playful, not for seriously weirded-out people. We don't sell whips, belts or paddles. But some couples enjoy the occasional black leather dominatrix outfit."

He had a sudden mental picture of her wearing black leather and clenched his jaw.

"And, of course, there's also light bondage. Handcuffs, silk scarves, blindfolds. It's all part of the fantasy."

"Fantasy?" God help him. Even though it might give him another long, sleepless night, he really wanted to know her fantasies. "Like?"

"Like being overwhelmed," she admitted softly. "Letting yourself be overcome by passion, even made helpless when you're with someone you can trust." She bit the corner of her lip, as if deciding to continue. "Exploring every possibility, going as far as your body can go, without being able to stop, because someone you know would never hurt you is in complete control."

Kate was nearly covered with paint from head to toe. Her thick, dark hair was pulled haphazardly into a ponytail at the back of her neck. She wore no makeup and she held a drippy paint roller plopping little drops of paint on the plastic drop cloth every time she moved it.

He'd never wanted her more.

Jack had walked hip-deep into this conversation, so he had no one else to blame. And he couldn't quite find a way to get out of it. Nor was he sure he wanted to.

"Is that your fantasy?" He heard the thick tone in his voice. "Being overwhelmed? Letting someone you trust give you pleasure without any mental barriers, any restrictions, taking because you have no other choice but to take?"

"I think so," she murmured. "Being free to wring every ounce of gratification you can because it's beyond your control to stop it."

In twenty seconds Kate had just made him understand the appeal of silk scarves and handcuffs.

"You must be really good at your job," he said softly. "Though, I still don't get the whole spanking thing."

She gave him a wicked grin. "Well, I don't particularly care for pain, but I have to say you are *very* good at kissing and making all better."

Remembering kissing her hip in the shower the other night, he knew exactly what she meant. His body reacted instinctively, another sudden rush of heat rushing southward from his gut to his groin. "Now, I *could* take that the wrong way and be offended," he said, stepping closer.

"Oh?"

He nodded. "You just basically told me to kiss your ass. I could take it as an insult." He lowered his voice to a whisper. "Or a really tempting invitation."

Her lips parted and her tongue snaked out to moisten them. "Which do you think it was?"

Unable to resist, he lifted a hand to her throat, running his finger down and touching its hollow. "I think if this were a week ago, it'd be an insult. Today, I'm not so sure."

She closed her eyes, tilting her head back as he traced a path around her neck, to her collarbone, touching her only with the tips of his fingers. "Me, neither," she admitted.

Needing to feel her in his arms again, Jack tilted her chin up and caught her mouth with his own. She moaned, parting her lips, inviting him deeper, and he accepted her invitation.

He loved kissing Kate. Every time was better than the last, hot and sweet, carnal and tender. He made love to her mouth, tasting her, drinking of her, making no effort to step away to disguise his body's reaction. She pressed against him, moaning again as he moved his mouth to press kisses on her jaw. "It's hard to find a clean spot," he said with a chuckle.

"Here's one," she whispered, pushing the sleeve of her tank top, and her bra strap, to the edge of her shoulder. A naughty invitation, which he immediately accepted. He kissed down her neck, to her collarbone, and right below it.

"Where else?" he asked, nudging the cotton top down even lower. She answered with only a soft sigh and an arch in her back, telling him to proceed. He did, scraping his tongue down to the top curve of her breast, then sliding it lower to flick at her pebbled nipple.

She quivered in his arms, and leaned back against the old refreshment counter. Appropriate. He wanted to completely gobble her up. But first he wanted to see her.

As if he had no control over them, his hands moved to the

waistband of her shorts and tugged her shirt free. He lifted it up, slowly, watching as the toned, creamy-colored skin of her stomach was revealed inch by inch. Until finally he saw the lace of her bra and the bottom curves of her breasts. His mouth went dry with hunger. "You are so beautiful," he whispered as he moved his hands higher. She didn't reply, just arched into his touch, twisting until he slipped his fingers beneath her bra. She hissed when he touched her nipples, tweaking them lightly, stroking and teasing the way he knew she'd liked when they'd made love before.

"I have to taste you," he muttered.

Before Kate responded, Jack heard the front door of the theater open. Footsteps echoed on the tile floor. Acting instinctively, he yanked Kate's shirt down, and turned to shield her behind him while she put herself back together.

"Get a lot of work done?" someone called. Wincing, Jack watched as Miss Rose and her grinning brother entered the lobby. The older woman gave Jack and Kate a pointed glance. "If Jack wants to be covered with paint, he's welcome to get on the scaffold and make a mess of himself, just like you have," Rose said with a chuckle. "There was no need to share yours, Kate."

Kate scrunched her eyes closed, obviously embarrassed as hell. Jack chuckled and reached for a paint tray. "Okay, Kate, you were good enough to teach me one or two things this afternoon." He winked. "How about I teach you how to paint?"

THROUGHOUT THE NEXT DAY, as Kate worked in the store with Cassie and some high school boys who followed her cousin around like puppy dogs, she kept wondering if she should move and stay with Cassie up on Lilac Hill. Even after everyone else left, leaving her alone in the shop to finish up some paperwork and cleaning, she thought about it. Cassie's house would be safer. Having Jack next door was impossible, especially now, after what had happened yesterday. Their kiss in the theater had been intoxicating. If Miss Rose hadn't come back when she did, they might have ended up rolling around on the floor, covering their naked bodies with the specks of paint littering the drop cloth.

She should move. Jack was simply too tempting. Too disturbing. Sooner or later they were going to end up back in bed together, and she didn't know if either of them was prepared for the consequences of that.

One other thing disturbed her about being back in town.

"Hiya, Kate! How's the store coming along?"

Friendliness. Damn, she really couldn't get used to that.

Pausing with her hand filled with the paper towels she'd been using to clean the front window of the store early Thursday evening, she turned around. Diane. New owner of the Downtown Deli, whom Kate had met during her one-day trip to town, then again when she'd gone in for lunch Monday. "Good, thanks."

"I remember when we were gearing up to open," the sweet-faced strawberry-blonde continued, as if not noticing Kate's less-than-welcoming reply. "We got a chilly reception from some of the other merchants, let me tell you." She cast a critical glance toward the Tea Room. "You'd have thought we murdered Mr. Simmons, instead of just buying the deli from him."

"I can't believe he finally decided to retire. He was as crusty as his sub rolls." Kate chuckled. "I bet he wanted you to promise never to put mayonnaise on an Italian sub, didn't he?"

Diane's eyes widened. "Yes, he did!"

"He called it a sacrilege whenever I ordered one for Mom."

"Well, I waited on your mother more times than I can count, and I never once deprived her of her mayonnaise," the other woman replied. "How's she doing down there in sunny Florida, anyway? We sure do miss her at the Bunko Club."

Kate's eyes widened. They missed her? At the Bunko Club? And what the hell was a Bunko Club? "I didn't realize you knew her."

Diane snorted. "Darlin', you've been gone a long time if you've forgotten that everyone knows everyone here. Edie was the first one at my door with a homemade apple pie when me and Will moved into the apartment above the deli. She's a real doll."

From behind Diane, Kate heard another voice. "Edie? You bet your life she is. Although, it sure was a nightmare getting her raggedy nails fixed all up. The woman worked too hard!"

Kate looked past Diane to see the young woman she'd met her first day in town. The friendly one from the nail salon. She looked different—her hair now being purple instead of a reddish orange. And the number of earrings had increased. But the welcoming grin was the same.

"Hi, again," Kate offered, unable to resist the smile.

"I sure never expected to see you here washing windows. Get in there and get some gloves on before you ruin that manicure."

Kate glanced down at her hands.

"On second thought, don't. Come by my shop after you're done and we'll fix you right up. And we'll have a long gab. Okay?"

"This is Josie," Diane interjected. "Don't make any pussy-cat jokes or she'll use too much glue on your acrylics then refuse to fill 'em. You'll have to pry them off with a crowbar."

Josie stuck her tongue out at the other woman, then turned her attention to Kate. "And you're Kate Jones. Edie's long-lost, super-successful daughter, cousin of the supermodel who has Sheriff Taggart going around in circles."

She talked so fast Kate had a hard time keeping up.

"Oh, really?"

Diane nodded. "His ex-girlfriend, Annie—she's the dispatcher—says Tag starts acting like a grizzly bear with a burr in his butt whenever he has a run-in with your cousin."

He hadn't looked like a grizzly Saturday night when he'd come to the shop at 1:00 a.m. No, he'd looked more like a panther. Dark and dangerous. She hoped Cassie knew what she was doing.

"Uh, can I ask a stupid question?"

"Anything," Diane replied.

"What's Bunko?"

The other woman linked her arm in Kate's. "You've never played Bunko? It's the woman's version of poker night. The Lilac Hill types have their bridge club. We prefer Bunko. A dice game, rotated among the homes of the club members. Twice a month we meet to talk, laugh and play. The hostess provides the prizes."

"The members provide the bourbon," Josie added helpfully.

Kate laughed out loud. "Sounds like fun." Surprisingly, she meant it. She could see how her mother would have enjoyed something so simple yet charming.

"Then it's settled, you come to our next game, which happens to be tomorrow night at Eileen Saginaw's house."

Kate's smile widened in genuine pleasure. "Eileen is my mom's best friend. I'd love to see her again."

And as easy as that, Kate found herself committed to a social event with some of the women of Pleasantville.

What is wrong with this picture?

"Now, tell us what you're going to sell in your store," Diane said. "Pretty please? Nobody knows anything more than it's a ladies' shop, and everybody's going crazy trying to find out."

Kate bit her lip. These two were the nicest people she'd met so far in Pleasantville, but that didn't mean they were going to welcome sex toys on the main drag of town.

"It's gotta be something good," Josie said. "Tell me it's real shoes. Real, decent shoes that don't have rubber soles and plastic uppers. If you say you're gonna carry Dr. Martens I'll get down on the ground and kiss your toes. And I'll give you a free pedicure while I'm down there."

Kate shook her head. "Sorry. Not shoes."

"Clothes. Oh, please let it be clothes," Diane said. "The closest store to buy a decent dress is twenty miles away. And that's not even one of those new super Wal-Marts, it's just a plain old regular one."

Kate bit her lip and shook her head at Diane's genuine consternation. "Sorry. Not clothes." *Not unless you counted crotchless panties and leather bustiers!*

Josie bounced on the toes of her chunky black boots like a kid waiting in line for Santa. "Then what?"

"You'll have to wait until our grand opening to find out."

"Grand opening?"

She recognized that voice. Wincing, Kate turned around to see Jack standing right behind her. The man was quiet as a cat—she'd never even heard him approaching.

Obviously neither had the other two women. Because she felt sure she'd have noticed those matching holy-cannoli-take-me-big-boy looks on their faces.

"Hi, Jack," she murmured. Her voice didn't even shake. Amazing, since her heart had started racing like an out of control freight train speeding toward heartbreak junction.

The man was too handsome. His smile too adorably sexy to be real, the twinkle in his brilliant green eyes too charming. He made women want to hug him. Then *do* him. Including Kate. Especially Kate.

Diane and Josie spoke in unison. "Introduce us."

After she'd made introductions all the way around, and listened to Josie and Diane pump Jack for information about why on earth he'd waited so long to come back for a visit to Pleasantville, she tried to slide away. Evening was approaching, though it was still light out. She wanted to get inside and lock up. Mainly she wanted to get away before Jack started asking any more questions about her store.

Just when she thought she might make a clean getaway, however, an old, beige Cadillac pulled up on the street and parked one building down, in front of the Tea Room.

"Great," Jack muttered. "It's my ex-brother-in-law."

"Which one?" Josie said under her breath, her voice holding a definite note of sarcasm. Obviously she knew Angela.

As Kate watched the man emerge from the Cadillac, she answered softly, "Darren."

9

DARREN HADN'T CHANGED a great deal, though his face was rounder and his hair thinner than it had been in high school. His belly was rounder, too. He wasn't fat, just soft and mellow-looking. Like a salesman.

He nodded to Diane and Josie, barely glanced at Kate, then noticed Jack. His face paled and for a second Kate thought he was going to get back in his car and drive away. Then his shoulders straightened as he locked the car and walked around it to the sidewalk.

Okay, so the jerk wasn't a complete wimp. He wasn't going to try to avoid his ex's brother.

"Hello, Jack, Josie. Diane." Then he glanced toward Kate, as if waiting for an introduction. His eyes narrowed as he tilted his head. "You…my God, it's Kate Jones."

"Hello, Darren."

"I had no idea you were back in town."

"Well, you know what they say about bad pennies."

"You look…wow, you look *great*," he said, his eyes wide as he stared her up and down.

Next door, the door to the Tea Room opened. Darren glanced past Kate, his face growing red. She knew darn well who stood there. "It was *so* nice seeing you, Darren. Be sure to say hi to your mom for me, okay?"

She turned around. Mrs. McIntyre stood on the porch next door, all stiff-necked, righteous indignation. Another woman, one Kate didn't recognize, stood with her. The two of them immediately started speaking in low voices. She couldn't hear their words, but she got the message loud and clear.

Kate gave them a forced but saccharine-sweet smile as she strode inside her store, as if she hadn't a care in the world.

Jack watched Kate leave, and made no attempt to stop her. He'd seen the silent exchange between Kate and Darren's mother. The glassiness in her eyes and the quiver of her lush, beautiful bottom lip, said she was holding on by a thin thread.

He'd also read the tension between his ex-brother-in-law and the woman he now considered his. He didn't stop to evaluate that, knowing Kate would resent the hell out of him thinking that way. Particularly since he'd wondered if it was best to stay away from her, for his own sanity and reproductive health. He'd come to the conclusion that walking around with a hard-on eighteen hours a day could really be bad for his future children.

Josie and Diane seemed to notice the tension in the air, as well. Telling Jack how nice it was to meet him, they both walked down the street, their heads close together as they talked.

Once they were gone, Jack eyed his sister's former husband. "How's it going, Darren?"

Darren was still looking at the door to the building that had once belonged to his father. "I can't believe Kate came back. I haven't seen her since graduation."

"You knew her in high school?"

Darren nodded. "We dated for a while, during senior year. She was my prom date."

Prom night. The night, if he wasn't mistaken, when his kid sister had gotten pregnant by this little prick, who'd walked out on her as soon as she'd miscarried their baby. Jack's teeth clenched. "I thought Angela was your prom date."

"Oh, no, we just left together afterward..." Darren seemed to realize who he was speaking to, because his face went redder. "I mean, well, Angela and I had dated the year before. And we kind of got back together that night at prom."

"What about Kate? You know, your *date?*"

Darren stood there looking hopeless, helpless and regretful. He finally shrugged. "High school, man. I was a kid."

Jack shook his head. "Some people don't have to wait till they grow up to become dickless assholes." He prepared to walk away, but paused. "Darren?"

Darren finally looked him full in the face.

"If you like breathing, you'll stay away from Kate." Not waiting for an answer, he turned to follow Kate into her shop.

The doorknob didn't jiggle in his hand, she'd obviously flicked the lock when she went inside. He knocked, figuring she wouldn't answer. To his surprise, the door moved. Pushing at it, he watched as it swung open. The lock was apparently broken, lucky for him.

After he got inside, and closed the door firmly behind him, Jack noticed the smell of paint and new carpet. The overhead lights in the shop were off, but recessed ones above the shelves cast illumination throughout the shadowy store. A bit of late-afternoon sunlight peeked in through the sheers on the windows.

He didn't see Kate. He did hear a voice, however. Following the sound of a radio, he walked through the sales area and back to the offices and storage rooms. He found Kate sitting in the center of a cement-floored room, surrounded by boxes, staring mindlessly into the air.

"Kate," he said softly. "Are you okay?"

She slowly nodded. "How'd you get in? I locked the door."

"Something's obviously wrong with the lock. You should have someone look at that. Are you all right?"

A small smile widened her lips, and surprisingly, no tears marred her cheeks. "I'm fine, Jack. Just wondering…"

"Wondering what?"

She hesitated, and he thought for a moment she wouldn't answer. Finally she admitted, "Wondering whether it's right to go on resenting someone for doing only what you yourself have done for much of your life."

He waited but she didn't explain. He somehow suspected she had no intention of talking about whatever it was she was thinking. "So you're really okay?"

She nodded. Rising, she brushed some dust from the floor off her butt, calling his attention to the miniscule white shorts she wore. He closed his eyes briefly. No wonder Darren had been unable to stop staring. Kate looked amazing. "I see you got all the paint washed off."

She nodded. "For now. Though I promised to go back and help some more tomorrow at the Rialto."

"Me, too," he admitted. "Now, you want to tell me what grand opening you were talking about." He glanced around the storage room at all the boxes. "Are you going into business here?"

"Yep," she replied as she grabbed a box and moved past him, exiting the storage room.

He followed her through a short hallway, into the store area. She continued, through an arched doorway toward the dressing rooms and a mirrored alcove. She dropped the box near several others already lined up beneath rows of shelves.

"Your kind of business?" he asked, repeating his question from Saturday.

She tilted her head and gave him an arched glance out of the corner of her eye. "What do you think?"

When she bent and retrieved a filmy white bra from one box, then what appeared to be a black leather bustier from another, his eyes narrowed. "I think you've decided to play Clint Eastwood."

He'd nailed it. He saw by the shock in her eyes, and the way she gasped as she dropped the two pieces of sexy lingerie, that he'd hit the truth dead-on.

"You're out for a little revenge."

"How could you possibly…"

"Come on, Kate, opening a new Bare Essentials right here in Pleasantville? Next door to the Tea Room?" He paused, letting the concept sink in, then reluctantly began to chuckle. "Damn, you really are something."

"You…you're not shocked?" she whispered.

Shocked? No. He'd already learned that Kate Jones was like no woman he'd ever known. He shook his head. "Not shocked. I think you're crazy, and you're going to lose your shirt." He cast a heated glance at her body. "I mean figuratively speaking. Literally, I wouldn't mind in the least."

She rolled her eyes.

"If you ever open your doors, that is. I'm sure there'll be a protest from certain quarters. You could lose everything you've already put into this place."

"Which wasn't much. It cost only some sweat equity— mostly Cassie's—and shipping charges to ship stuff here." She shrugged. "Besides, it's not about money."

"Of course not."

She stepped closer and her smile faded. "It's not some silly revenge plot, Jack. I had to be here…I needed to come back to town this summer."

He couldn't imagine what could possibly be important

enough to bring Kate back to a place she quite obviously hated, and told her so.

"I can't really talk about it," she said. "A lot of things happened all at once." She crossed her arms in front of her chest and rubbed her hands up and down, as if chilly.

"Kate, whatever is going on, whatever this is about…"

"Yes?"

"Just be careful. Sometimes things don't work out the way you think they will."

"I somehow think this will," she said, "because I don't have unrealistic expectations. I fully expect to fail here."

He raised a brow.

"We'll open, we'll cause a lot of chest-clutching, a lot of scandalous whispering, and then, when Cassie's safe…" She cleared her throat. "I mean, when Cassie's ready to leave… we'll close and go away. Cassie will sell this building and everything else she owns here and we'll never come back. No ties, no bad memories, just a laugh when we think back on our one last hurrah."

"Cassie's in trouble?"

"No. Forget it, okay? Cassie's fine." She looked at her nails, obviously feigning nonchalance. "Did you like her?"

"Like her? I barely spoke to her."

"Most men don't have to *speak* to her to form an impression."

Jack shrugged. "She's beautiful, of course. Flamboyant and probably too sexy for her own good. She'll drive any man who loves her to the verge of insanity."

She waited. When he didn't continue, she prompted, "That's all? You weren't…interested?"

He shook his head. "Do you think I'm a total scumbag? What kind of guy would lust after the cousin of the woman he's involved with?"

"We are not involved."

"Bullshit. We are very much involved," he admitted, confirming that not only to her, but to himself.

He waited for her to deny it. She couldn't. Who could deny the inevitable? They might not have done much about their relationship since they'd been back in town, except for a few hot kisses and that one close encounter yesterday. But there's no question they would. Sooner or later.

Judging by the look in her eye, and the expectancy in the air, he suspected it was going to be sooner.

He waited for a mental voice to tell him no, waited for his feet to instinctively turn toward the door. Waited to hear from the nice-guy voice of reason who'd been whispering in his ear for weeks.

That voice had been growing weaker as each day passed. He'd been listening to her from the other side of the duplex, seeing her shining, dark hair as she left in the morning, hearing her off-key singing as she showered. Every day another chunk had disappeared out of the wall of willpower he'd tried to erect between them. And after yesterday, it had come down like the last remnants of the Berlin Wall.

Sure he'd had good intentions, but all the good intentions in the world couldn't stop what was happening between them. No more than a surfer could stop a wave on which he was riding.

Sometimes he had to ride it out to see where it took him.

"So are you going to tell me what's wrong? Is your cousin in some kind of trouble or not?"

"Jack, let it go, okay?"

He didn't press her on the Cassie issue, sensing she wouldn't tell him what was going on, anyway. "So, back to your shop and your revenge plan. Anything else on the agenda?"

"No, I think I've summed it up."

"Not much revenge there. I mean, you're not having the population paint every building red?"

She chuckled. "You rented *High Plains Drifter*."

He nodded.

"Okay, so it's not the greatest revenge." Her smile was mischievous and it made her brown eyes sparkle. "Must be that rotten sweetness everybody says is somewhere inside me. I'm great at fantasizing, just not so great at execution."

Hearing her laugh at herself, Jack found her as captivating as she'd been the day they'd met. As if here, in a shop like the one she owned in Chicago, she was free to be herself. She'd let the negative elements of Pleasantville—her hurts, her misgivings, her sarcasm—disappear.

He found himself doing the same. As if nothing outside the building mattered. They could have been meeting for the first time in Chicago, as far as he was concerned.

She sighed. "Our plan seemed a lot more dramatic and outrageous when we fantasized about it as teenagers."

"You fantasized about opening a sex shop in Pleasantville?"

"Yep, we even wrote it down in our diaries on prom night."

His smile faded. "I heard about your prom night."

"It's fine. Water under the bridge," she insisted. But she wouldn't meet his eye.

"Should I even ask who else was on that revenge list you made that night?"

She pursed her lips. "No, you probably shouldn't."

As he'd thought—his own sister had probably been a pretty large target. Not to mention Darren.

"So, can I assume this shop will satisfy your need for revenge? I mean, I don't have to worry bodies are going to start flying out the upstairs windows over the Tea Room, right?"

She sidestepped the question. "Oh, look, the store's not even revenge at all. It's more…I don't know…like the old song.

They talked about us throughout our childhoods, well, now we'll *really* give them something to talk about! And they'll never forget the Tremaines."

"What if you fail to fail?"

"Excuse me?"

"You know, what if the store's a big fat success? What then?"

Her laughter echoed in the small alcove. "Not a chance. That'll never happen."

"You never know. Your store is a big hit in Chicago."

"This is *so* not Chicago." She bent, opening a box at her feet. "Can you see Mrs. McIntyre buying one of these?"

She pulled out what looked like a foot-long hot dog. Then he realized it was a dildo. "Now, there's something you don't see every day in Pleasantville," he mused out loud, not at all shocked, as she'd obviously intended.

"Gee, ya think?" She giggled like a kid as she grabbed something else out of the box. "I'm thinking of these in the display case right by the cash register."

He raised a brow. "Anal beads?"

Holding the strand of beads between her thumb and index finger, she swung them around, a wicked look in her eye. When he said nothing, she dropped them, reached back into the box and pulled out something else. He instantly knew what the black, rubbery circle was for.

The playful laughter faded as she caught the heat in his eyes. It was answered by her own aware expression.

His groin tightened as he imagined using the item during sex with Kate. The way she'd slide it down his dick, her cool hand holding his balls as she tightened the cock ring around him. Then climbing on top of him and riding him, letting the ring keep him engorged and rock-hard. Building the pressure until he'd have to grab her by the hips and thrust up into her until they both came together in one strong, fiery blast of sexual pleasure.

"Ever used one?" she finally asked.

He wondered if she'd be shocked by his reply, and decided to find out. "Yeah. Have you?"

Her lips parted as she sucked in a deep, shuddery breath. She obviously hadn't expected that, hadn't been prepared for him to answer with blatant honesty. Even from several feet away, he could see the goose bumps on her chest, and the sudden jut of her nipples against her tight blue T-shirt.

"No," she finally answered. "I, uh…don't try everything we sell in the store."

His stare shifted to the huge dildo.

She shook her head slowly, as if dazed.

He reached over and picked up a pair of handcuffs from a pile on a nearby shelf. Remembering their conversation from yesterday, he asked, "What about these?"

She shook her head again.

"Just as well," he murmured as he put them back. "They'll chafe your pretty wrists when you thrash around on the bed."

He wasn't speaking in general terms. And felt sure she knew it. This wasn't an *if* conversation—it was a *when*.

The inside of the store began to feel steamy hot.

"We do sell faux-fur-lined ones," she admitted, her voice shaky and breathless.

Did she even know she'd issued him a blatant invitation? Of course she knew. This was Kate, after all.

"What *have* you tried?" he asked, unable to stop this sensual self-torture. "I know you've got your little finger vibrator. But what else can you personally recommend for your shoppers…based on your own experience?"

She hesitated.

"Come on, Kate," he said as he stepped closer and dropped his voice to a whisper. "Show me your wares."

He wondered if she'd leave, if she'd back away from the sultry atmosphere into which they'd once again fallen together.

He should have known better.

"There's a nifty vibrating tongue…"

He groaned softly.

"It's not wet enough, though," she continued slowly, obviously knowing full well what she was doing to him. "Not like a real one. But powerful. It doesn't get tired, doesn't veer off at the last second and ruin everything just before climax."

Neither had he. Not that he reminded her of that.

"What else do you like? Any other replicas of body parts?"

She shook her head. "Not really. My favorite thing we sell is probably the lingerie. My partner has real talent. Bare Essentials goes well beyond your average teddies, thongs and push-up bras."

He managed not to come in his pants at the image of Kate in any or all of these seductive items. "Oh?"

Nodding, she pointed to a stack of folded cloth. She picked up something off the top and shook it out. It took him a moment to realize what it was. "Crotchless tights?"

"A big hit in Chicago in the winter. It's too cold for thigh-highs, or even regular panty hose. And, for some reason, men seem to get off on women in tights." She shrugged. "I think it's the same reason men like blondes on trampolines."

He understood. "Or cheerleaders. It reminds them of that whole teenage thing where boys are one six-foot-tall pile of testosterone and the girls know it."

She laughed.

"So, do you wear them?"

She gave him a coy look out of the corner of her eye. "Maybe. Most women who do like the naughtiness of it. They like knowing that even if it's twenty degrees outside, they can go for something outrageous in the back of a limo if the right man happens to be around."

His smile tightened. "Speaking from experience?"

She didn't try to lie. "No." Raising her hands, palms up, she shrugged. "What can I say? I live a pretty boring life in Chicago, in spite of being the sex toy queen of Michigan Avenue."

He was damn glad of that. He hated even thinking of Kate with another man. His own possessiveness surprised him. Jack had been involved in enough casual relationships to know women had as much sexual drive as men. Where they chose to fill that need had never been any of his business, once they'd left his bed.

Kate was a different story. He had a feeling he could get damn near violent thinking of her with anyone else.

Which completely floored him.

"There are some pieces of lingerie I've used." She bent at the knee, almost kneeling at his feet. Looking down, seeing the top of her head about level with his groin, Jack had to fist his hands to try to gain control.

She hunted around in a box, then said, "Aha." Standing, she showed him what she'd found. "My favorite."

She held a pretty, lacy, pale blue bra. It had straps, underwire, a satiny strip of material to go beneath a woman's breasts—but nothing to cover the rest. A front-less bra.

"You, uh, wear those things?"

"Sometimes. Especially when I'm wearing cotton or silk."

They both glanced at her cotton T-shirt.

Though almost afraid to ask, he had to. "Why?"

"The different textures of fabric feel amazing against my nipples," she admitted, something dark and erotic flashing in her eyes. "It's empowering to give yourself a thrill throughout the day, without anyone ever being aware of it. Like the tights."

He swallowed. Hard. Then he stepped closer, until their bodies nearly touched from neck to knee. Looking down at the sharp points of her breasts, he finally managed to ask, "Are you wearing one of those bras now?"

"Maybe." She didn't step back. Instead, she reached for his hand and pulled it toward her body. Dropping her voice to a purr, she said, "Why don't you see if you can tell?"

Dangerous. Like reaching out to touch a blazing red burner on a stove...you know you're going to get burned, but you just can't shake yourself out of the spell.

Jack didn't care.

He touched.

10

"YES, I THINK YOU MIGHT be wearing one now," he murmured.

Kate didn't reply, couldn't even speak as he traced the tips of his fingers across her sensitive nipple. Then he moved his hand lower, to cup her breast. Stepping even closer, until their hips brushed, he brought his other hand up. When he passed his open palm against her other breast, making the fabric of her top scrape the other distended nipple, she shuddered.

"Jack…"

"Shh," he whispered, his mouth so close to her hair she felt the warmth of his breath. "I'm not sure yet. I think I need to test some more before I decide if you are."

"Please do," she said with a tiny whimper.

He did, cupping, squeezing lightly. He caught her nipples between fingers on each hand, tweaking them, making sparks shoot from there straight down to her crotch. Her legs shook as heat and moisture flooded her shorts.

"Yes, you are," he finally said. Thankfully he didn't pull his hands away.

"So, Kate, let's recap. You wear seductive lingerie for your own pleasure. You carry a vibrator in your purse and use a battery-powered tongue whenever you want an orgasm."

She nodded mindlessly, agreeing, anything as long as he continued the stroking of her breasts.

"There's one thing you haven't mentioned. Something I know you like."

She instantly knew what he meant and whimpered.

"Penetration," he continued, dragging out the word as if it were a caress. "Deep, hard, erotic penetration."

"Yes." She arched her back, offering more of herself, her fingers itching to grab the bottom hem of her shirt and lift it so she could get even more of his intimate attention.

His hands moved away, caressing her waist, her back, her hip. "Can you get that from your toys or playthings?" he asked, as if he didn't know she was about to crawl out of her own skin out of sheer, undiluted need.

"No." Aroused to the point of pain, she shifted, pushing her pelvis toward his and grinding against the huge erection she could easily feel against her body. The moisture between her legs doubled, the electric awareness thrumming through her body quadrupled. Not questioning the impulse, knowing she had to touch him or die, she slipped her hand between their bodies to cup him through his jeans. "Nothing compares to this."

He hissed as her fingers tightened around him.

He suddenly got serious, obviously realizing she wasn't playing sexy games anymore. "You're sure?"

"Oh, yeah."

"Here?"

"Uh-huh. But there's no table," she said as she continued to caress him.

"Floor'll do," he muttered before catching her mouth in a wet, carnal kiss. She melted against him, rapidly refamiliarizing herself with the taste of his mouth, the sweetness of his tongue. The feel of his long, hard body pressed against hers.

One hand slipped from her breast down to the waistband of her shorts. He tugged it free, stroking her belly, her waist, then higher until his fingers were inches from her nipples. No cloth barrier this time, she knew it wouldn't take much and she'd be coming right then and there.

That would be lovely. But this time she didn't want to be the only one completely out of control, brought to ever higher peaks of ecstasy by Jack.

She wanted to be the one turning *him* into a raging, living, breathing hormone.

"I love kissing you," she said with a whimper when their lips parted. "I want to kiss you *everywhere*."

His eyes widened in understanding as she dropped to her knees in front of him. "Kate…"

"Hush."

Her hand trembled as she unbuttoned, then unzipped, his jeans. He wore white boxer briefs, which did little to hold back his erect penis. Her mouth watered, then went dry as she savored that long moment of anticipation that probably lasted no longer than a few erratic beats of her heart.

Finally, once again, she would see him. Touch him. Taste him. Working the briefs down, she held her breath, watching as his hard-on was revealed. She moaned at the sight, remembering how it had given her such pleasure their first time. Knowing he'd give her more pleasure tonight.

But not yet. Not until he was completely out of control.

Jack didn't want her to proceed. He'd been walking around in a state of arousal for weeks, and as she leaned closer to his cock, her lips brushing the sensitive skin at its tip, he nearly lost it. "Kate…" he said with a moan as her tongue flicked out, just a touch, a tiny caress to taste the moisture there.

"Remember what you said that day on the stage, Jack? Well, fair's fair. I like taste, too."

Then she moved her lips over him and took him into her mouth. "Ah, Kate." He moaned, dropping his head back. He clenched his fists, let her suck him, surrounding him with hot, wet sweetness and gentle pressure. When he felt her hand slide between his legs to cup his balls, his eyes shot open and he looked down at her.

Her head moved slowly, back and forth, sucking him deep, then pulling away until she'd almost released him completely.

"Kate, please, you've got to let me…"

"Watch," she murmured between one smooth stroke of her mouth and the next. When she tilted her head and glanced to the right, toward the mirror, he followed her gaze.

And nearly lost his mind.

Feeling her wet strokes. Hearing her coos of pleasure that said she really *liked* what she was doing. Seeing part of his body disappearing between those beautiful lips of hers.

He couldn't take another second.

"Enough," he growled, taking her by the shoulders and pushing her back.

Their clothes—with the exception of Kate's front-less bra—were gone within twenty seconds. He was between her up-raised legs ten beyond that.

"Condoms are in there," she muttered, pointing to a box near his hip.

Jack didn't even look as reached for it, feeling around with his hand while he kissed Kate senseless. "You knew what that would do to me," he whispered against her lips.

"I kinda hoped," she said with a sultry chuckle. "I wasn't ready to stop."

"Not now," he told her. She panted as he sucked her earlobe, and hissed when he caught her breast in his hand. "Our first time back together...we'll go at the same time."

She gasped and arched up, grinding her hips into him. "Go at the same time? Do you mean...in the *numerical* sense?"

It took him a second to grasp her meaning. When he did, the image she suggested—giving each other oral pleasure at the same time—flooded his mind, making him even harder. Even more frantic.

"Hate to have to break it to you, but you're definitely *not* sweet, Kate Jones," he said with a ragged laugh.

"Thank heaven."

He ran the flat of his palm down her body to her hip. Then he slid his fingers into her curls, into the slick, hot crevice, knowing she was ready. "Except maybe here," he whispered as he slid his finger into her.

She tightened around him, moaning and bumping against his hand. He gave her what she wanted, flicking her tight little clit with his thumb until she cooed, then inserting another finger into her, stroking her G-spot from within. "Yeah, you're very sweet here." He could tell by her cries she was within seconds of climaxing.

"No fair. We're supposed to go together this time," she said with a whimper.

Before he knew what she was doing, she'd pushed him, rolled him over so she could straddle him on the floor. "Better."

Looking up at what had to be the most glorious sight on the planet, he had to agree.

Kate stared down at him, seeing the passion and admiration he could never have feigned. He was hard beneath her bottom, and close to where she wanted him. She shifted slightly until his penis slid into the wet folds of skin concealing her opening.

He growled.

"What? Not good?" She knew damn well it was.

"You know it's good. It's just not enough."

"Anxious, are we?"

He ripped open the condom with his teeth, showing her how anxious he was. She took a glance at their reflection, amazed at the sensuality of the moment. She slid back and forth over him, using his hardness to stroke her clitoris until she gasped.

"You like watching, too." Jack's stare met hers in the mirror.

She nodded. Then, knowing he watched her every move, Kate slid her hands up her body, until she cupped her own breasts.

"Keep going."

She did, catching her nipples between her fingers. "Mmm. But not as good as your hands."

He complied, replacing her hands with his own, then leaning up to suck one nipple deeply into his mouth.

Kate had her first orgasm instantaneously. She was still shuddering from it as she plucked the condom from his fingers and moved out of the way to roll it down over him.

When he was fully sheathed, she held herself above him. She caught his stare and held it. Then, with aching precision and slowness, she slid down on him, taking him completely into her body, inch by endless inch, until he'd filled her up so much she felt complete for the first time in ages.

"Yes," she said with a contented sigh.

"Yes," he echoed.

She didn't move at first, just sat there, absorbing him, stroking him with muscles deep within her body. She saw him clench his fist and tilt his head back in pleasure.

"More?"

He nodded, reaching for her hips. "Definitely more, Kate." Then he started to move below her, thrusting upward. She met every stroke with one of her own, amazed at how quickly their bodies synchronized to one another.

It was hot. Energetic. Frenzied.

But also something else. There were moments when they'd meet each other's eyes and smile. When he'd reach up to brush her hair off her sweat-dampened cheek. Or he'd rub his thumb across her lower lip, then tug her down for a slow, wet kiss that somehow felt even more personal than the mating of their lower bodies.

He'd slow the pace, drag out the pleasure, until Kate felt her legs tremble with near exhaustion.

"Let me," he said as he held her around the waist. He rolled her over, staying inside her, his face inches from hers. Another kiss. Another stroke.

She turned her head and saw them in the mirror. Saw him holding his beautifully hard body above hers on his thick, strong arms. Saw his shoulders flex, his back strain, his gorgeous, tight butt move up and down as he pumped into her over and over again, so deep she had to gasp for breath. She clutched his shoulders, wrapped her legs around his hips and met him thrust for thrust.

She sensed the minute he'd gone too far to hold back. And as soon as he had, he braced himself on one arm, bringing his other hand between their bodies. "Come with me, honey."

And, of course, Kate did.

"I'M SORRY I didn't call," he whispered a few minutes later. They lay together on the newly carpeted floor, wrapped in each other's arms, exchanging lazy kisses and slow caresses.

He felt her stiffen against him. Then she asked, "Sorry because you had to wait for this?"

"No, I'm not sorry that way. I mean, I *apologize* for not calling you, Kate. I thought I had good reasons—and maybe I did. But I thought about you constantly and I never stopped wanting to see you again."

She tilted her head back to study his face. "Good reasons. And that's all you're going to say?"

He nodded once, knowing he couldn't elaborate. The truth of the long-term relationship between his father and her mother was tough enough for him to deal with. He didn't want to burden Kate with it. Her mother was still alive—the past needed to die.

"Just tell me one thing, okay? Tell me it wasn't because you're involved with someone else. If I find out you're married, engaged or engaged to be engaged, I won't be responsible for my actions."

He chuckled. "No. I'm completely unattached. Or, rather, I was until I met you."

She smiled languorously and leaned over to press a sweet, wet kiss on his mouth. He held her tighter.

"Can I ask you something?" she asked.

"Anything." Knowing the way Kate's mind worked, she was probably about to ask him something sexual and intense, getting them both hot and ready to go again. His mouth went dry in anticipation, knowing they could play sensual games here all night long. He definitely wanted to try some different positions in front of the mirrors.

"Do you know how to play Bunko?"

"I've never heard of it." He raised a hopeful brow. "Is it some kind of sex game?"

She bit her lip as she giggled. "I certainly hope not." He felt her shoulders shaking as her laughter increased. "Good grief, a sex game. Can you imagine? The women of Pleasantville gathering every other week to play a sex game in someone's living room? Complete with prizes and bourbon?"

"I think you could stock the prizes from right here at Bare Essentials."

She giggled even more. "Oh, my, I can just imagine Eileen Saginaw trying to choose her prize from between the strap-on vibrator or the two-headed dildo."

He rolled onto his back, tugging her with him until she lay on his chest. Her hair blanketed his stomach, flowing all the way down to his groin. He ran his fingers through its silkiness as he caressed her back, hip and bottom.

"So why are you asking about it?"

"It's some kind of dice game. I've been invited to come over to play with some of the women tomorrow night. I don't know much about it. The friends I hang out with in Chicago are more into lunch dates, shopping trips and cocktail parties than Tupperware gatherings or Bunko nights."

Her mention of cocktail parties reminded him of something. Knowing it was a long shot, given Kate's dislike of the Lilac Hill set in town, he asked anyway. "Speaking of parties, I've been asked to attend one at city hall Saturday night. A welcome reception for the new mayor."

She stiffened in his arms.

"I'd like you to come with me, Kate."

He could have predicted her answer. "I don't think that's such a good idea."

"Come on, what's the big deal? You're obviously getting involved with some of the townspeople, anyway. With your big Bunko orgy and all."

She laughed, probably in spite of herself. "It's not the same thing. Those are not the same type of townspeople."

He narrowed his eyes. "Oh, so you're a snob? You choose to associate only with *your* kind of people?"

When fire flashed in her eyes, he knew he'd said just the right thing. He prodded further. "Come on, you know you're every bit as good as any other person here. You're probably worth more than anyone who lives on Lilac Hill. Don't let childhood hurts affect the decisions you make today."

She sucked in a deep breath, staring at his face. He saw a variety of expressions rush across her face…hurt, confusion, then acceptance. "You're right," she whispered.

"That's my girl. The party is at eight."

"I'm sure I have something in my closet I could wear."

"Crotchless tights?" he asked hopefully.

She lightly bit the skin just above his nipple. "It's a little hot for that." As he sighed in disappointment, she whispered, "But probably perfect for crotchless panties."

THE NEXT AFTERNOON, as she stood in front of her closet trying to figure out what one wore to a Bunko night, Kate's cell phone rang. When she heard Cassie's voice, she told her about her plans for the evening.

"Are you sure it's a game, and not some swinging women's party with male strippers and livestock?"

Kate snorted. "Why, would you like to come?"

"Nah, can't do it. I'm on my way outta town."

Pausing with a jean skirt and a red peasant blouse in her hand, Kate said, "Where do you think you're going?"

When Cassie explained she was making a quick weekend trip to New York for her agent's birthday, Kate tried to talk her out of it. Cassie was not to be dissuaded. She was sick of hiding out like a victim. She was going. Period.

"All right, Cass, but please promise me you'll be careful. And call me when you're leaving Sunday afternoon so I can drive up to the airport to get you."

Kate cut the connection before she remembered to tell Cassie about tomorrow night's cocktail party. Just as well. She still couldn't believe she'd agreed to go, and wasn't sure she could make Cassie understand why.

Hell, she barely understood why herself. She only knew something had changed within her. Somehow, from the time she'd seen Mrs. McIntyre outside the Tea Room the day before, Kate had been unable to stop thinking about everything that had happened.

She'd been angry for years because Mrs. McIntyre hated her without reason. Now she wondered—was she any different? Darren's mother hated the Tremaine family because her husband had taken up with Flo. Kate had hated the Winfields because John Winfield had strung her mother along for two decades.

Yes, she had reason to resent Angela because of Darren, and prom night. But, really, who the hell cared what had happened in high school, ten years ago? No, she and Angela would never be friends, but there wasn't any reason they should be enemies, either. John Winfield was dead. His family wasn't responsible for his sins…they didn't even know about them! So what kind of hypocrite would she be to keep blaming them?

The thought rankled.

"And Jack." She had no reason to dislike Jack. Yes, she'd been hurt when he hadn't called her, but she sensed he was being truthful when he'd said he thought he had good reason.

She didn't want to put herself at the same level as Mrs. McIntyre—an angry, bitter person who blamed the wrong people for hurting her. Had she become so focused on self-protection, on not letting herself be hurt or abused, that she'd also denied herself the chance to build genuine emotion with a man?

Maybe it was time to rethink a *lot* of things.

Kate was still mulling over the whole revenge plan when she arrived at Eileen Saginaw's house that night. The older woman, who'd raised five kids and now had ten grandkids, gave Kate a hug and immediately asked her a bunch of questions about Edie.

"Last time we talked, she was determined to learn how to play golf so she could join a club in the retirement village," Kate said, pleased at the fondness in the other woman's voice.

Every woman at the party sounded just as regretful that Edie had left. There were no whispers here. No one acted as though some deep, dark scandal had forced Edie out. Not one person made Kate feel—in the three hours she stayed—the way the biddies in the Tea Room had made her feel in three minutes during her first visit back to town.

These were the real women of Pleasantville. And she was shockingly grateful she'd found them.

"Kate, I'm telling you, stop shaking the dice so much. That's why you keep getting snake eyes," Diane informed her as Kate prepared to take another turn late in the evening.

Kate blew an impatient, frustrated breath as she reached for her drink. Not bourbon—she didn't do bourbon. But thankfully someone had brought beer. "How can it be called snake eyes when there are three dice?" she muttered as she lost yet again, with all ones. "Snakes have two eyes, not three."

"Well, don't forget, there *are* snakes with one," Josie said with a suggestive wagging of her eyebrows.

When Kate gave her a confused look, Josie explained, using a bad Australian crocodile hunter accent. "I'm face-to-face with the deadly, one-eyed trouser snake, known to lead men into dark, dangerous places, and to enslave women with its potent power."

After a five-second pause all twelve women seated at the three card tables in Eileen's living room whooped with laughter.

It was, of course, inevitable that with each roll of the dice, the conversation degenerated into some outrageous sex talk.

Kate figured it was standard operating procedure, given how freely the women spoke to one another, though, she had a really hard time picturing her mother here as part of it.

"You know, it'd almost be worth it to test that Viagra stuff, just to see if it'd be noticeable if I put it in Hank's coffee every morning," one woman introduced as Viv said.

"You mean, slip it to him, like a mickey? But how would you know if you gave him enough?" another asked.

Eileen reached for the dice. "Just keep pouring until the kitchen table starts rising off the floor right over his lap."

Josie snickered. "Yeah, I can see you explaining it to the doctor when Hank has a heart attack 'cause all his blood's trapped in his winky."

"At least he'd die happy," Diane pointed out.

"Please don't tell me I have to wait till my husband's a corpse before I can see him with a decent hard-on again." Viv poured herself another drink.

When the laughter died down, Kate spoke up. "Have you tried seducing him? Letting him know you're interested?"

Viv grunted. "Sure. Unfortunately, after he drinks the six-pack of Bud I've bought him to warm him up, he doesn't notice I've shaved my legs and I'm not wearing my period underwear."

Kate chuckled. "I mean it. Sexy lingerie, candles, scented massage oils. Then you tell him you've rented a special movie."

"The only thing he likes is Arnold Schwarzenegger blowing up stuff. Which isn't exactly my idea of romance."

"I meant something a little more…titillating."

"Oh, sure," Viv said with a groan. "I'll drive over to Emmitsburg to the Triple-X video store, fight off all the winos hanging around near the nickel booths, and rent some big-boobed-lesbians-in-love flick. Sounds like a real romantic evening."

"I didn't mean porn," Kate explained patiently. "There are erotic videos made for women and couples."

Hot sellers at Bare Essentials.

"Yeah, but I bet they don't show penises, do they?" This from Josie who sounded indignant. "I mean, every erotic movie for couples I've seen—back when I lived in a town that had heard of such things—is camera-shy below the waist on the guy."

Kate shrugged. "Is that so surprising? Isn't the point to get your man worked up—not yourself? I don't think many men are into seeing the competition, and women don't need as much visual stimulation, which is why adult movies are geared toward men."

The women all thought about it. Then Viv sighed again. "You may be right, Kate, and if this were Chicago, I'm sure I could stroll to the neighborhood store to stock up on erotic movies. But this sure ain't Chicago."

Her disappointed sigh was echoed by every woman in the room. Right then and there, Kate started wondering if maybe Jack had been right. Maybe, just maybe, opening a Bare Essentials right here in Pleasantville wasn't such a crazy idea after all.

As the evening drew to a close, Kate found herself one of the last women there. She'd tried to leave earlier, but Eileen had put a quiet hand on her arm and asked her to stick around. Finally, after Diane and Josie exchanged hugs and one last round of man jokes, they said goodbye and left.

"Let me help you clean up," Kate said, though the room wasn't too bad. Part of the rules of Bunko night—hostess's house didn't get left in a shambles.

Kate helped Eileen take the tablecloths off the card tables and began to fold them. "I can't tell you how much I enjoyed tonight. I appreciate all of you making me feel so welcome."

Eileen gave her a sweet smile, which made her gray eyes

twinkle. "Katey, I am so glad you're here, even if you don't plan to stay—and I guess you don't."

She shook her head.

"Anyway, I wish you'da come back sooner. Not that I'm criticizing. Three of my kids left, too. This town can be awfully hard on its residents sometimes."

"Yeah." She wondered if Eileen knew how hard. No, Eileen didn't live on Lilac Hill, but she was married to a nice, well-liked gas station owner, and her beauty parlor, down in the basement, was a hot spot for most local women. So she probably hadn't experienced the worst Pleasantville had to offer.

"I guess you know it was hard on your mom and that's why she left. I wish she hadn't, it wasn't but a few nasty people."

Kate laid the folded tablecloth on Eileen's dining room table. "I'm sure you're right."

Eileen held her eye, gauging how much to say. Then, obviously seeing something in Kate's expression, she said, "You know, don't you. You know about Edie and John."

Kate's jaw dropped. "I'm surprised you do."

"Oh, darlin', your mom and I have been friends since eighth grade. I was there the first time she saw him, the first time he asked her out. Heck, we double-dated to our senior prom."

"Wait…you mean Mom dated John Winfield in high school?"

"Well, sure. Didn't you know that? The two of them were quite the talk of the town in those days, what with your mom being a Tremaine and all. He didn't care a bit. The two of them were crazy about each other."

Shocked, Kate leaned against the table. "What happened?"

Eileen sighed. "They had a fight about something stupid. John went and did something even *more* stupid with Pat Pickering. She told him she was pregnant the day after graduation."

Pregnant? With Jack? She quickly calculated—no, couldn't be right, that would make Jack close to forty.

Eileen ushered her into the kitchen, putting on the kettle to make tea. "Edie found out, broke it off with John and left town. John married Pat. When there was no baby several months later, he came to me asking where Edie was. I told him the truth. She was happy with her new life in Florida. He stayed married to Pat and they made a go of it, I guess."

"Years later, Dad died and Mom came back," Kate whispered.

Eileen poured some tea, then sat. "First loves never die. John was so sad, trapped by Pat, his job, the town." Eileen shrugged. "Edie made him happy...they made each other happy. But she would *never* have let him leave Pat and those children."

A half hour later, after one of the most shocking and revealing conversations she'd ever experienced, Kate hugged Eileen goodbye and headed home. She wanted more than anything to call her mother, just to hear her voice. Edie seemed so different to her now, not a victim anymore, but a woman in love who did the best she could with what she was dealt.

Kate didn't know whether to applaud her or to cry for her.

When she arrived home, she immediately looked toward Jack's side of the duplex, to see if any lights were on. He'd told her he'd wait up, saying he wanted the full scoop on the Bunko orgy. Judging by all the lights, he'd kept his word.

She pulled into the driveway, surprised when she saw a rental car parked there. Unsure who would be visiting at this late hour, she walked up to the porch and glanced in the window.

When she saw the dark-haired person sitting on the couch, and realized who it was, she hurried into the house and launched herself into his arms.

11

If Jack hadn't already figured out that Kate's business partner was gay, he might be feeling seriously concerned right now. The two of them hugged and chattered with the easy camaraderie of longtime companions. They acted as if they hadn't seen each other in months, rather than a week.

"Armand, what are you doing here? I can't believe you came all this way," Kate said.

"I missed you. I had a fabulous new design I wanted to show you, and since we seem to have a decent staff for a change, I figured we could both be gone for a day or two." Armand sat on the couch, pulling Kate down to sit beside him.

Jack, who'd taken a seat on the other side of the small living room, couldn't help smiling at Kate's obvious excitement.

He hadn't quite known what to think when he'd seen this tall, dark-haired man knocking on Kate's front door an hour ago. When Jack had stepped outside to see what he wanted, the other man had asked about Kate. Jack's first instinct had been to tell the guy she'd left town and had left no forwarding address. Then, when he'd recognized the stranger as the one who'd been hugging Kate at her Chicago shop all those weeks ago, he'd invited him into his place to wait for her.

The first rule in any battle—know your competition.

He'd figured out the man's sexual preference within five minutes. Not that Armand had tried anything—if he had, he sure as hell wouldn't still be sitting in his living room, friend of Kate's or no friend. No, what had tipped Jack off was Armand's reaction upon learning his name.

He'd acted just like one of Kate's gal pals.

"Oh, so you're Jack." He'd looked at Jack's arms and hands, raised a falsely surprised brow and said, "Hmm, no broken arms or fingers, did your building simply lose phone service for a month? Is that why you never called her?"

Yep. Definitely gay.

Once they'd gotten past those first awkward minutes, with Armand trying to punish him for not calling Kate, and Jack trying to change the subject, they'd actually enjoyed an interesting hour of conversation. The guy had even brought a six-pack of beer, two-thirds of which they'd already killed off.

Armand was part of Kate's other life. Her Chicago life. The life Jack fully intended to share when they both finished up what they had to do in Pleasantville and closed this door behind them. He wanted to see her through Armand's eyes.

Most of what he learned did not surprise him.

She loved the theater and saw nearly every touring production that came through town. A given.

She hated snow. Unusual, considering her Chicago address. But she did like long walks on windy days.

She'd put herself through college at night while working any job she could get, not finishing up her bachelor's degree until a few years ago. That reinforced what he already suspected—everything she had, she'd worked damn hard for. Nothing had been handed to her; she relied on her talent and her perseverance to succeed.

Her cousin Cassie had financed their Chicago shop, but,

mostly due to Kate's excellent management, Bare Essentials had already earned enough to pay off the loan.

One more intimate little detail Armand let drop—Kate hadn't dated any man more than twice in over two years, and he doubted she'd slept with any either. *Well, praise the Lord and pass the ammunition.*

"So, how was Bunko night?" Jack asked when he could finally get a word in edgewise.

Kate grinned. "Wonderful. I loved it. And, I tell you, there might actually be a client base in this town for Bare Essentials."

Armand raised a surprised brow. "Get *out!*"

She told them about her evening, then said, "I know a woman named Viv who would probably adore seeing your new designs."

"It sounds like Tortureville hasn't quite lived down to your expectations," Armand said.

She didn't answer for a moment, looking deep in thought. Something seemed different about Kate tonight. She looked less pensive, much more relaxed. Jack didn't think it was only because of her friend's visit. Nor did he think it was entirely because of what had happened between them last night.

And again this morning in her bedroom next door.

"I think we both had a few surprises from our returns to Pleasantville," Jack murmured.

She looked up and met his eyes, a soft smile curling her lips. Next to her, Armand looked back and forth between the two of them. "Okay, it looks like somebody has forgiven somebody for his telephone-itis."

"Not *entirely* forgiven," Kate said.

Jack raised a questioning brow.

"But he's getting closer."

Seeing warmth in her gaze, Jack gave her a slow, steady

look, telling her without words that he'd keep doing whatever he had to earn her forgiveness.

"I'm suddenly feeling very third wheel here. Kate, I do hope you have room for me to crash at your place, because I didn't make a hotel reservation or anything."

"I think the hotel in Pleasantville only rents by the hour anyway," Kate said with a grin. "Of course you'll stay with me. I don't have an extra bed, or very much furniture at all. But I do have a sleeping bag."

"You can stay here." Jack's tone allowed for no argument. "There's an extra, fully furnished bedroom." Two, really, since Jack fully intended to sleep in Kate's bed, anyway.

"Wonderful, thank you." Armand turned to Kate. "And tomorrow you take me downtown to show me the new store. Plus all the horrible places you remember from your teenage years. Your high school, the predictable barbershop, movie theater and fire station where they host pancake breakfasts. And you must introduce me to Viv. Does she have poufed-up blond hair, tacky plastic shoes and like to crack bubblegum?"

Shaking her head, Kate chuckled. "Nope. Sorry to disappoint you, she's a pretty, forty-something housewife with an uninspired husband. I think you've been watching too many movies about small-town life."

"I was raised in a town just like this, by my father the fire chief and my mother the former dairy princess."

"Interesting background, considering your name," Jack said.

"Arnold Dettinger didn't work for me in Chicago," Armand explained with a shrug. "And since I haven't been home in twelve years, I'll consider this my trial run. Who knows? If no one starts dragging out the tar and feathers, I might follow your lead and plan a trip back to Milltown for Christmas."

Jack saw Kate squeeze her friend's hand. "I'm sure your parents would like that."

Armand gave a resigned shrug. "My mother, maybe. My father would be too busy ordering me not to embarrass him in front of the guys at the fire house to have time to be pleased."

Jack cleared his throat. "He might surprise you." Seeing Armand's doubting expression, Jack continued. "I have to believe that deep down fathers always want their sons to come home. Just don't wait until it's too late to find out."

LATER, with Armand settled into Kate's mother's old room, Jack followed Kate into the other duplex and up to her bedroom.

"So, you going to tell me the truth about the Bunko orgy?" he asked as she reached for the bottom of his shirt.

"You really want to hear?"

"Uh-huh."

"Well," she said, her voice a sultry whisper. "All the women were blondes except me, and they all had *really* big breasts. When we got there, we all took off our shirts and compared."

He snorted with laughter.

"Then, we squirted each other up with scented oils and gave each other massages, until we were just rolling around on the floor, one big mass of naked, squirming female bodies."

"You're evil."

"Isn't that every guy's fantasy orgy?"

"Well, no, actually he'd need to be there. Preferably on the bottom of the pile of naked, squirming female bodies."

"Men are so weird." She rolled her eyes. "What is the attraction of more than one woman at a time?"

"I have no idea," he explained, trying hard to retain a serious expression. "I personally find that type of thing shocking and sordid."

She punched him lightly in the stomach.

"Oh, come on, you're buying into the male stereotype. It's

at most a fantasy—the old 'me Tarzan, you Jane, you Janet' thing. Caveman-must-propagate-the-species genes rearing their persistent heads." When she crossed her arms impatiently, he continued. "Most men don't know what the hell to do with one woman and certainly couldn't handle two and they know it."

"True."

"Besides," he continued, "don't women fantasize about being with two men, too?"

"Not this woman. I would never want to be in bed with a naked guy who didn't mind being in bed with another naked guy."

Jack's shoulders shook as he laughed.

"Besides," she continued, "if a man likes other men enough to be naked with them, then there's one or two things I'm lacking that he's bound to notice."

"I'd rather notice the one or two very nice, feminine things you have," he said with a definite leer.

As he reached out his hand and traced the tip of his fingers along the top hem of her loose blouse, she gave him a languid smile.

"One is more than enough for me," she murmured. "Though, two yous might be nice."

He paused, giving her a mock frown. "Did you say two Hughs?"

She rolled her eyes and shoved him onto the mattress, falling on top of him. They rolled across it, wrapped in each other's arms exchanging laughter and hot kisses.

"I said two *yous*. Two Jacks. Two sets of these amazing hands." She brought his hand to her lips, kissing the tips of his fingers and sliding her mouth over his pinky. "Two perfect mouths on my body." She leaned up to press her lips against his. "Two tongues to taste me."

He tasted her, nibbling, kissing and licking his way down her neck, across her collarbone, to the hem of her shirt. She lifted up so he could tug it out, and Jack tossed it over his shoulder to the floor. "No bra at all this time," he murmured, his voice thick with appreciation as he saw her beautiful breasts and pert nipples. When he moved his mouth over one, flicking his tongue across the puckered tip, she jerked against him and groaned.

"Two mouths would be useful here," he murmured as he went back and forth, from one breast to the other, sucking, nibbling and stroking her into a frenzy beneath him.

Sitting up long enough to yank off his clothes, he helped her unfasten her jean skirt, then pulled it off her. Her flimsy panties followed, then he had to pause, to look at her naked body, bathed in the soft glow of the hallway light. She looked at him, as well, her eyelids heavy, her lips parted as she took in deep, ragged breaths.

"Would you prefer two of anything else, Kate?" he asked, as he bent to kiss her again, letting her feel his hard-on against her thigh. She instinctively arched toward it in an age-old signal of welcome from female to male.

"Hmm, no, I think I can stay quite busy playing with this one," she whispered as she reached for him.

She proceeded to play. Stroking him, cupping him, running her hands up and down his dick as they exchanged lazy, wet kisses and he fondled her breasts. He didn't think he'd be able to stand it when she bent to take him into her mouth. He had to lift his arms over his head and press his fists against the wall to try to hold on to his sanity. The way her long, thick hair spread across his body, draping between his thighs to caress his balls, felt almost as good as her hot, wet mouth wrapped around him. Almost.

After a few moments she kissed her way up his body to his

lips, then slid one leg across his hips. She rubbed against him, letting her juices spread over his erection, and it felt so good, so damn good to be close to her, without the barrier of a condom, that he nearly came right then. He would like for there to be no barriers between them, of any kind. Ever.

"You amaze me," he admitted as he stared up at her.

"Even though there's only one of me?"

"One's all I want, Kate," he murmured. "One you."

She leaned down to kiss him, their tongues swirling languorously. Her breasts brushed his chest and her warm mound remained tantalizingly close to his penis.

"Not yet," he told her when she retrieved a condom from her purse on the floor next to the mattress.

Raising a curious brow, she stared at him. He smiled as he cupped her hips. Tugging her forward, he slid down to meet her. She watched him, her eyes wide and excited as she understood what he wanted. What he had to have.

"Are you sure you…"

"Oh, yeah," he replied as he positioned her bottom on his chest and her beautiful, sweet, wet opening right in front of his hungry mouth. Then he tasted her, holding her hips as she bucked in delight at the intimate contact.

The position gave him the perfect access to pleasure her, and himself. He licked, stroked and suckled her until she came right in his mouth, her body trembling and hot as she leaned against the wall above his head for support. And that wasn't enough. He kept tasting her, sliding his tongue into her, demanding that she give him more until she cried out as a second orgasm ratcheted through her body.

Only then did he let her go, rolling her onto her back and reaching for the condom she'd dropped.

"I guess two *is* better than one sometimes, isn't it? Twice the pleasure?" he said with a chuckle, referring to her orgasms. Sheathing himself, he plunged into her even before she'd stopped panting from her orgasms.

"Oh, yes," she cried.

He didn't move at first, just savored the wet heat in which he was enveloped. Looking at her face, he saw her parted lips, the flush in her cheeks, the long lashes on her lowered eyelids.

She began to move beneath him, her body telling him what she wanted. He gladly gave it to her. Slowly, with deep, steady, sure strokes, he moved in and out of her until she began to moan and roll her head back and forth on the pillow.

"More, Jack, please," she whispered, bending her legs even higher and tilting her hips up, inviting him deeper inside.

He knew what she wanted and how she wanted it. Faster. Harder. Mind-numbing and scream-inducing.

Kate didn't want sweet. Kate wanted hot.

He complied with a groan, tugging one of her legs over his shoulder and plunging harder than before. Her eyes flew open.

"Good?"

"God, yes," she muttered through choppy indrawn breaths. "I want you so deep inside me that I don't know if I'm feeling your body or my own."

"Oh, I think I can guarantee you're going to know it's mine," he said with a chuckle as he ground against her.

She hissed and met his every move, smiling as he gave her what she wanted.

He watched as she moved her hands up her legs, reaching for her own breasts. She plucked at her nipples with her fingertips, sexy little pants still coming from between her lips. "Four hands might be good right now," she said.

Remembering her incredible sensitivity right there, and wanting to give her everything she desired, Jack slid out of her.

"What are you…"

"Shh," he whispered, giving her a smile that said *Trust me.*

She watched, wide-eyed as he reached for her hip and gently rolled her onto her belly. He heard her moan into the pillow, obviously realizing how he wanted to take her.

"Oh, yes, absolutely," she said as she lifted her curvy bottom and hips, offering herself. The most tempting offer he'd ever had.

"Up, baby," he whispered, pulling her to her knees.

She complied, rising to all fours, moving back to meet him as he slid into her from behind, then leaned forward until his chest touched her back.

Perfect. The position left his hands free to pleasure her, to tweak her sensitive nipples, to stroke the curves of her breasts and the soft flesh of her belly. Then lower, to play with her sweet little clit as he rocked into her until she came close. Damn close, judging by her cries.

"Now," she ordered. *"Now."*

He knew what she wanted—she wanted him to come with her. Straightening, Jack took her hips in his hands and drove into her with a few powerful, body-draining thrusts.

"Now," he agreed.

The moment she screamed in climax, his own overtook him and they both collapsed to the mattress. He instantly rolled onto his side, tugging her close to nestle against his chest. He pressed a kiss to her brow, then to her cheek. Then to her mouth, still open and panting.

"That was amazing," she finally managed to whisper between deep, shuddery breaths.

He nodded.

"But, you know, Jack, now you've got me spoiled."

He lifted a brow.

"I suddenly want two of everything."

Smiling, knowing by the way his body began to react to her

all over again, he whispered, "Let's not set any limits, okay? Why stop at two?"

He caught her mouth in a deep, slow kiss as they began all over again.

ON SATURDAY, Armand took Pleasantville by storm, chatting easily with each person he met and seeming to really enjoy the small-town atmosphere.

He raved over the shop, and gave Kate some good suggestions on layout. He also helped her straighten up the dressing room area, asking once why there were crotchless tights strewn all over the floor. Thankfully, he hadn't questioned her blush.

Nor did he tease her too unmercifully about the thinness of the walls at the duplex, other than to say he'd heard some wild animals howling in the middle of the night, and wondered if there were coyotes in Pleasantville.

Later, during lunch at the Downtown Deli, he'd met Diane and Josie, charming them both completely. Josie had enough innate street sense to recognize his preferences in spite of his sexy charm. She seemed to like him all the more for it.

But the real highlight of the afternoon came when they walked out of the deli and straight into a couple, who stood exchanging heated words on the sidewalk.

"Angela and Darren," Kate whispered, instantly recognizing Jack's sister. "The banes of my teenage existence."

Surprised she hadn't run into Jack's sister before now, she forced herself to take a deep breath and to remember that she was completely over any childhood hurts.

"High school tormentors, hmm?" Armand whispered as they walked within a few feet of the two.

"Hi, Kate," Darren said. He looked at Armand, then stood a little straighter. Armand, with his height and elegant sophistication, had that effect on men.

Angela's face turned red as she stared at Kate, her mouth opening but no sound coming out. She looked not only flustered by Kate's appearance, but also annoyed at the interruption of her conversation with Darren.

"Hello, Darren. Angela," Kate replied, her voice sounding much calmer than she'd have expected.

Darren gave her a big, friendly smile. "I'm sorry I didn't get to talk to you much the other day. It's great to have you back, Kate. I'm really glad things have gone so well for you."

Surprisingly, he sounded sincere.

Angela didn't speak to her; she was too busy glaring at Darren as he talked to Kate. Then, when the other woman finally noticed Armand, an appreciative expression lit up her face.

Funny, when she actually smiled, Angela didn't look quite so much like a cast-iron bitch.

"Introduce us to your friend," she murmured.

After the introductions Armand stepped into his role as if it had been created for him. He flirted with Angela until the woman was practically melting into a puddle on the sidewalk. Once or twice Kate tried to tug him away, knowing he was trying to get a little payback on her behalf by stringing the other woman along. He'd probably be dashing off some scathing rejection at any moment now. The second time Kate tried to hurry him away Angela shot her a dagger-sharp glare. *Well, to hell with helping you, lady!* She stopped trying to lead Armand away.

"So, you're here visiting your *friend* Kate?" Angela asked.

Armand shrugged. "We're business partners. We own a store together on the Miracle Mile in Chicago."

Angela's eyes widened. "Really?" She glanced at Kate.

"Is it the same kind of store you're opening here?" Darren said, stepping not-so-casually between Angela and Armand. Kate noticed and wondered if things were heating up again between the ex-spouses. It would explain why Darren looked anything but pleased about Angela's interest in Kate's partner.

"Yes, but now, we really have to go. I have things to do before tonight's party."

Angela frowned. "The party at city hall? You're coming?"

"Yes." Kate couldn't resist adding, "As Jack's date."

The other woman's face paled. "How…nice." Turning toward Armand, she said, "And you must come, too."

"Will you be there?"

Angela nodded.

"Then I wouldn't miss it for the world," he said, looking at her with a sexy, promising grin.

Kate kicked his ankle.

"Okay, I guess it's time for us to go," he said with a grimace. If he bent to kiss Angela's hand or anything, Kate swore she'd shove him in front of the next oncoming car.

As soon as they were out of earshot of the other two, Kate said, "That was really bad of you."

"Oh, come on, I know something about high school tormenters, babe. You're telling me you never fantasized about getting a little payback?"

If only you knew!

"Just don't, okay? Angela is Jack's sister!"

Armand whistled. "Whoops."

When they got back to the duplex, Armand insisted on helping pick out something for Kate to wear. She'd brought a few nicer dresses and was now glad she had.

"Red," Armand said as he pulled out a tight spaghetti-strapped cocktail dress with a band of glittering sequins right above the breasts. "Perfect. And it'll match. Wait here."

When he returned, he was carrying a bundle of tissue paper. "My latest design. Here you go."

Kate opened the packet, seeing a tiny pair of red, lacy panties. She dropped the paper and held them up, looking for the trick. No zipper. No slit. Not a thong. And they had a crotch.

The only thing unique about them was their weight. They felt heavier than they should, given the minute amount of fabric.

"Very pretty, and you're right, they will match."

He rolled his eyes at her lack of enthusiasm. "Go into the bathroom and try them on," he said, shooing her out.

Following his orders, she went into the bathroom and took her shorts and underwear off. As she pulled the new underpants up, she noticed the extra weight seemed centered in the crotch area. When she pulled them into place, she realized why.

"Oh, my God," she whispered with a shocked laugh.

The panties were padded with a spongy, soft middle, covered with a feathery fabric that cupped her private area quite deliciously. A firmer, ridged section toward the front pressed against her clitoris. "You've got to be kidding me," she yelled.

"Walk in them," Armand ordered through the door.

The bathroom was too small, so she wrapped a towel around her waist and walked out into the hallway. Armand stood there, waiting for her reaction. As she walked, she had to admit it, the little ridge felt pretty damn good. Not to mention the soft middle, which made it feel like wispy, downy kisses were being pressed all over her opening.

"Nice?" When she nodded weakly, he practically bounced on his toes. "Try the stairs."

She did. "Oh, very nice," she admitted, almost purring at the pleasure of it.

"Good. You're wearing them tonight. And every time some pissy small-town matriarch wrinkles up her nose in your direction, you stroll right by her with a secretive, delighted smile on your face."

Sounded like a pretty good plan to her.

12

As he pulled Kate's SUV into the parking lot outside city hall, Jack could tell by the look on her face she was still uncertain about this evening's party. She wasn't frowning, but she looked deep in concentration, as if thinking of something else. Every once in a while, she even wriggled in her seat. "You okay? You're awfully fidgety."

From the back seat, he heard Armand snort a laugh.

She gave Jack a quick guilty look. "Uh, fine. I'm fine. Why do you ask?"

He shrugged. "You just seem distracted." Taking her hand, he squeezed it and said, "But you also look amazing."

She did. Her body turned the red fabric of her dress into pure solid sin. Though petite, Kate had curves men dreamed about. Curves *he'd* dreamed about many nights since they'd met.

Not to mention the fullness of her lips, the sparkle in her deep brown eyes. Her confidence, intelligence and attitude appealed to him even more now than the day they'd met. Especially since they'd become so intimate.

He got the shakes just thinking about the things they'd done together the night before in her bed.

He simply couldn't get enough of her. Kate was the woman he'd been casually seeking and had never really thought he'd find ever since he'd left home fifteen years ago. How funny that he found her right here in Pleasantville, the very place he'd been trying so hard to escape.

She'd pulled her hair back, letting cascades of curls drop over her bare shoulders. The dress was not too short, ending a few inches above the knee, but below it her legs were bare. Her strappy, red high-heeled sandals had caught his eye several times during the short drive from the house.

"I'm fine. Now, who is going to be at this thing? Should I have worn body armor?"

He shook his head. "My mother's not coming. She wasn't feeling well. Frankly, I think it's driving her insane to give up the title of First Lady of Pleasantville. She doesn't want to see her replacement holding court."

Kate chuckled. "But your sister will be here."

"Yeah."

"Ah, your sister, such a charming little thing," Armand murmured from the back seat.

Jack saw Kate shoot her friend a warning glare, but didn't have time to question it.

They made their way into city hall, blending into the crowd of people in the atrium. In a far corner a band played jazzy music and an area had been cleared for dancing. A bar had been set up on what was usually an information desk. Armand immediately beelined for it, offering to get a round of drinks, leaving Kate and Jack to circulate.

He felt her tension, the stiffness of her body. Her hands were like ice, though she maintained an expression of complete calm. Jack wondered again what it must have been like for her growing up here, if it could still make her so anxious all these years later. But she never flinched, never let anyone see a single sign of nervousness, not even when one of his mother's cronies glanced at her, sniffed rudely, and turned away.

He saw Kate's face grow pale. Leaning close, he brushed a kiss against her temple and whispered, "Ignore the old bat. Did you know she wears a wig?"

At Kate's surprised expression, he continued. "My mother told me years ago. Seems she's got a nervous habit and pulls her own hair, so she thought it would be easier—and less painful—to just buzz-cut it and wear wigs."

Kate giggled. "That's her story and she's sticking to it, huh? I think she was rude to the wrong person and someone just snatched her bald."

"That's my girl." Right there in the middle of the crowd, he pressed a soft kiss to her mouth. Her tension seemed to ease as he took her arm and continued to lead her through the crowd.

Finally they came face-to-face with the new mayor and his wife. Kate's eyes widened in shock. "Mr. Otis?"

The elderly mayor, who, Jack remembered, used to teach drama at the high school, squinted and looked at her more closely. "Why, Kate Jones, how you've grown up!"

The mayor then proceeded to sweep Jack's date in his arms and give her a tight hug. "You've gone off to the big city and done quite well for yourself, haven't you?"

"Yes, I have. I had no idea you were mayor. I figured you'd retired from teaching and were off fishing somewhere."

"Fishing for trouble at city hall," he said with a wink.

While Kate and Mr. Otis chatted, Armand returned, carefully balancing three drinks. Jack took his beer, and Kate's wine, holding one glass in each hand.

"By the way," Armand said, speaking in a near whisper, "I meant to give you something before we left the house."

"What?"

Instead of answering, Armand removed what looked like

a small black box from his jacket pocket. "You don't have the hands, I'll drop it in your pocket." He did so, then said, "Just something fun to ease Kate's tension."

Since Jack's hands were still full with the drinks, he couldn't reach in to see what Armand had put there. "You going to explain this?"

Armand shook his head then grinned. "Remember, roll the dial slowly and never take your eyes off her."

Then he strolled away, leaving Jack very curious.

Kate had never actually conceived of enjoying this evening, but as she chatted happily with her favorite high school teacher—now interim mayor of Pleasantville—she realized that she might. When she spied Diane walking around with a tall, red-haired guy who tugged at the collar of his suit as if it was itching him, she felt more certain of it.

"Well, I suppose I have to mingle," Mr. Otis finally said as someone tried to lead him away for a photo op. "It's so nice to have you back here, Kate. I hope you'll visit more often."

"Wow," she said to Jack when they were once again alone in the crowd of elegantly dressed people. "I never imagined Mr. Otis would be the new mayor."

Diane and her husband joined them. "He's been on the city council for a few years," she explained. "So's Will." She introduced her husband. Kate instantly liked the man, who looked as though he'd rather be anywhere but here, dressed in anything but his plain brown suit.

Jack, on the other hand, looked delicious in his dark blue one. Elegant, expertly tailored, it showed off his hard, lean form to perfection. With his thick, blond hair, vivid green eyes and sexy grin, he had the attention of every woman in the place.

He fit in with this crowd easily. But he was just as at ease with Will and Diane, who obviously lived far from Lilac Hill.

Throughout the next hour Diane introduced them to several other newer members of the town's business community, all of whom went out of their way to tell Kate how happy they were about her opening a new store in the downtown area. Kate began to feel torn. Yes, she'd decided to open the store as revenge. But if that were the case, she'd be punishing these nicer people she was meeting, too.

Or maybe not. Ever since last night at Eileen's house, she'd had to wonder if maybe her store wasn't exactly what this town needed. New, fresh, daring—like a lot of these younger people circulating amid the old highbrow set.

The highbrow set increased by one when Mrs. McIntyre walked into the room. Kate, standing close to the door, had turned to throw away her cup, and nearly ran into her.

The woman's face went rigid enough to crack. She made a sound that was a cross between a groan and a harrumph before she turned her back on Kate and walked away.

Taking a deep breath, Kate glanced around to see if anyone had noticed the snub. Jack stood several feet away, pretending to listen to an older woman chatting his ear off, but his attention was focused directly on Kate. His sexy smile was conspicuously absent, his eyes tender and concerned. She felt his silent support as though he'd put his arm around her.

She gave him a little nod, trying to assure him that she was okay, knowing he'd never believe it. He murmured something to the woman, who walked away, then gave Kate a slow smile. His green eyes shone with interest as he reached into his suit pocket.

Before she could step closer to see what he was up to, Kate's panties came alive. "Oh," she said with a sharp gasp.

She froze, her mouth falling open as she focused on the sudden, completely unexpected sensations in her private area.

"Good Lord," she said with a breathy sigh.

Armand had outdone himself.

The spongy middle slowly undulated against her rapidly swelling and quickly aroused mound, while the harder nubbins began to flicker against her clitoris with incredible friction.

She closed her eyes, taking deep breaths, quite unable to move. Around her, the crowd chattered. Someone asked her a question, and she nodded dumbly. Someone else handed her a drink. She lifted it to her lips and gulped without even looking at it, only realizing it was champagne when she felt a tickling sensation in her nose and throat. Of course, that couldn't match the tickling sensation between her legs.

The slow vibration picked up its pace, increasing in speed. She even swore she could hear a tiny hum and almost gasped as she wondered if anyone else heard it. As she cast a quick glance around to see, she met Jack's eyes. His pleased, boyish grin told her he was responsible for what was happening. "More?" he asked, though she couldn't hear him. She read the word on his lips.

She shook her head and gave him a scolding look, unable to believe he was doing this to her in a huge crowd of people.

The look in his eyes as he reached into his suit pocket could only be called wickedly anticipatory. She shook her head again, not able to take any more, but not able to stop it. His hand kept moving, slowly, as he dragged out the tension. And, if she were to be honest, the anticipation.

Kate shot a quick look around the lobby where the party was being held, gauging the distance to the ladies' room. Too far. No way could she make it when her legs were already weak, her breaths choppy and her heart racing out of control.

Jack's hand had finally reached his pocket and as it slipped inside, she sent him one more pleading glance. At this point, she really couldn't have said what she was pleading for.

If the vibrations got much stronger, she'd go right over the edge and have a shattering orgasm in the middle of this crowd of elegantly dressed people.

If they stopped, she'd die.

The heat in Jack's stare as he cranked up the pressure was almost enough to make her come anyway. She shuddered as the intensity of vibration rose yet another notch. Reaching blindly for support, she found herself grabbing the corner of an information desk and her fingers sunk into some creamy substance. A quick glance down told her it was a slice of cheesecake topped with strawberries, but she couldn't bring herself to care.

The waves of pleasure began to roll through her, signaling her climax, and she leaned her hip against the desk. She heard someone say her name, but couldn't even turn her head. Her eyes were glued to Jack's and he nodded with encouragement, knowing even from several feet away that she was close.

"Yes," she whispered, closing her eyes as an intense bolt of pleasure shot through her. Her hands clenched, oozing strawberries and cheesecake between her fingers. Dropping her head back, she gasped for breath as the orgasm sent electric pleasure racing through her body.

Finally the vibrations between her legs slowed, then stopped. When she opened her eyes, she saw Jack watching her, looking hot and ready, as if watching her reach her climax had pushed him close to the edge, too. She was about to walk over to him when she heard Diane's voice.

"Good God, I've eaten cheesecake I'd consider orgasmic, but I never got off just from *touching* one."

"THAT WAS REALLY BAD of you," Kate whispered as Jack curled her tighter in his arms in the back of her SUV an hour later.

They'd escaped the party as quickly as they could, after ensuring Armand could get a ride home with Diane and her husband. By silent consent, they'd avoided going back to the duplex, instead driving up to a popular lake on the outskirts of town. Their clothes had come off a minute after Jack had engaged the parking brake and they'd barely made it over the back seat into the cargo area before he was inside her.

They'd been frenzied and ravenous. Now they lay quietly, exchanging slow, lazy kisses and caresses that were going to lead to sweet, long lovemaking. Jack didn't know how he could want her again, already, but he did.

"I thought it was your fantasy," he finally answered.

"My fantasy?"

"Being made helpless. Having to accept pleasure because you are powerless to stop it."

She laughed. "Yeah, but I meant something more along the lines of being tied to the headboard, not being brought to a shattering orgasm in a room filled with a hundred people. I can't imagine what Diane must have thought."

"I think she went to look for the chef to ask for the recipe for that cheesecake."

She giggled. "Maybe we should sell it at Bare Essentials."

He stretched to work a kink out of his neck. "I haven't had sex in the back of a car in years."

"This is my first back seat experience ever."

"Uncomfortable, isn't it?"

She nodded. "But exciting. I keep picturing a cop knocking on the window and telling us to get our clothes on." She arched closer, sliding her arm around his waist. "Or an ax-maniac with a hook. You know, the kind who always slaughters the teenagers when they run out of gas on lover's lane?"

"I'm fairly certain the parents of a teenage girl made up that story the night before her first date."

"So, was this your make-out spot when you were a teenager?"

He shook his head. "No way. Everyone in town knew my father and I never dared to bring a date out here."

He felt her tense in his arms at the mention of his father.

"I know what it's like to have everyone in town know your family," she admitted.

Leaning down, he pressed kisses on her temple, her cheekbone, then her lips. He kissed her lazily, gently coaxing her mouth to open. When it ended, he whispered, "I'm sorry I didn't know you then. I'm sorry I wasn't around to stop it when you were being treated so badly. By my sister or anyone else."

He wished he had been. He hated like hell to think of anyone hurting her. Ever.

"It was a long time ago, Jack. And you know, being back here has made me remember some of the better times, too. I guess I should be thankful for that. I'd been angry for a long time and let that anger color my memories. It's good to have some of those nicer moments back."

He believed she meant it. Hopefully, no matter what else happened, Kate wouldn't regret this time spent in Pleasantville. Seeing the town through adult eyes had evened out her feelings, much as it had his. "So you think you might come back someday? For a visit?"

She shrugged. "Anything's possible."

Before he could reply, they heard the sound of crunching gravel. The bright sheen of headlights washed through the windows of the SUV.

"Oh, my God, someone else is here," she cried.

They scrambled for their clothes like a couple of kids caught making out by their parents. He tossed her the magical little red underwear she'd worn at the party, watching as she shimmied into her dress. She was giggling hysterically. "Please be the cops and not a guy with an ax and a hook."

408   *Leslie Kelly*

"You got your wish. It's the cops," he replied.

Jack was having as hard a time containing his laughter as Kate appeared to be. His first time going parking in more than a decade and they get caught by the town sheriff. Thank heaven it hadn't been ten minutes before or he doubted they'd have even noticed the approach of the other car.

He'd just zipped his pants when he heard a knock on the driver's side window, Thankfully, it was tinted. Recognizing Sean Taggart, with whom he'd gone to high school, he slid into the back seat, then opened the door. "Hi, Tag," he said as he jumped out. He shut the door behind him, giving Kate more time.

"Jack," the other man said with a nod. Tag pushed his sheriff's hat up on his head with the tip of one finger, trying unsuccessfully to hide a grin. "You out for a late-night drive?"

"Yep. Enjoying the view over the lake."

"Well, I can see why you felt the need to take off your shirt. Musta been awful hot with all that steam on the windows." He glanced at the lake. "But wasn't it hard to see the view considering you're parked facing the road, instead of the water?"

Before Jack could reply, Kate stepped out. "Hi, Sheriff," she said, her face awash with color.

Tag's eyes widened as he obviously noticed her crooked dress, bare feet and wildly tangled hair. "Kate, isn't it? Cassie's cousin?" When Kate nodded, Tag said, "Where is she? I heard a rumor she left town for a few days, which I couldn't believe since that'd be so incredibly stupid."

Sensing Tag knew about whatever trouble Cassie was in, Jack waited for her answer, as well. When Kate admitted her cousin had gone to New York for the weekend, and would fly home the next day, Tag swore under his breath. "When does her plane get in?"

"She's supposed to call me and let me know when she's leaving New York so I can go pick her up at the airport."

"Tell you what," Tag said, his calm tone not hiding his obvious anger. "You call me in the morning and tell me what flight she's on so I can go pick her up, and I won't arrest you both for public indecency."

"We weren't exactly in public," Jack said.

"Maybe not. Then again, I've just heard an interesting rumor about some mighty strange behavior by the two of you at the mayor's party, which was *very* public. Now, do we have a deal?"

Kate nibbled on her lip, then finally nodded. "Cassie's gonna kill me."

"Not if I kill her first," Tag muttered as he turned on his heel and strode away. He got into his car, but before leaving, he rolled down his window. "Next time, cut your lights before you pass by old lady Millner's place. She's a quarter mile up the road and calls every time a car comes down here late at night."

Then he drove away, leaving them standing alone.

"Sounds like he's speaking from experience," Kate said with a chuckle.

"Tag never had much problem with the girls back in high school."

"With those looks and that body? I can definitely see why he'd cause a sigh or two." She gave him a look out of the corner of her eye that screamed mischief.

Okay, Kate wanted him jealous. No problem. He grabbed her arm and tugged her close. Lowering his voice, he whispered, "I'm surprised you can sigh, or even talk at all, considering the way you were screaming ten minutes ago. Your throat must be sore."

Then he caught her mouth in a hot, wet kiss designed to

drive the thought of any other person on the planet out of her mind. Her gentle moans and pliant body told him he'd succeeded.

When they parted, she sucked in a few deep breaths. "You're definitely scream-worthy, Jack," she said. "And you certainly know how to show a girl a good time." She started to giggle, then to laugh out loud. "Oh, my gosh, if Tag tells Cassie about this, she'll never let me live it down. We made a pact to never go parking with guys when we were in high school. We pinky swore and everything."

"You mean I was good enough to break a pinky swear for?" he said with a pleased grin. "Wow. I don't know if anyone's ever broken a pinky swear just for me."

She lightly elbowed him in the ribs. "Don't go getting a swelled head." She leaned back against the car, crossing her arms and letting out an audible sigh. "I'm going to be dead meat when I'm not the one who shows up tomorrow to pick Cassie up at the airport."

"Something's going on between your cousin and the sheriff?"

"I think so."

"Tag's a nice guy. And a patient one, which is good, since I suspect your cousin could try the patience of a saint."

"Good thing that doesn't run in the family," she said, giving him a deceptively innocent look. When he raised one skeptical brow, she rolled her eyes. "Okay, okay, I guess I can be a pain in the butt, too."

"Nah," he said with a deliberate shrug. "In spite of a deplorable lack of sweetness, you're not so bad."

Her grin widened. "Do you know how nice it is to be with someone who doesn't expect me to be sweet?" She straightened, stepped away from the SUV, and put her arms out to her sides. Spinning around, she almost yelled, "God, tonight was *fun*. Outrageous and naughty, and definitely not sweet!"

"Yeah, it was," he admitted, remembering how aroused he'd been by her at the party. He loved watching her again now as she almost danced in the moonlight, her hair swinging wildly around her face. "But I hate to break it to you, babe. I suspect you really are kinda sweet, deep down."

She stopped. "Keep that up and you'll be walking home."

He jiggled his pants' pocket. "I've got your keys."

She stepped closer, laying her hand flat on his bare chest and giving him a limpid look. "Wanna place a bet on how fast I can get into your pants and get them back?"

He shook his head. "I think we've already proved you hold the world's record on getting into my pants, Kate."

"Ditto," she admitted, trailing her hand across his bare chest to his stomach. "So does that make us both cheap and easy?"

"Only with each other." He swallowed a groan as her hand moved lower, brushing across the front of his pants.

"Fair enough."

Jack liked the humor on her face and the sparkle in her eyes. He liked seeing Kate happy. He'd seen her that way much more often lately. The angry, mistrustful woman who'd come back to Pleasantville for revenge had been erased.

He hoped he'd had something to do with that. Because there was no question in his mind Kate had changed him. For the better. He doubted she'd believe it, he had trouble believing it himself, but he was falling in love with her. Falling hard and fast.

He'd started the slide the first time he'd laid eyes on her across Magnolia Avenue. Making love to her that same day had strengthened the feeling. Every day they'd spent together since then had been better than the one before.

"Come on," he said, tugging her by the hand. "Let's go down to the lake."

Though she wore an obviously expensive dress, Kate didn't hesitate. They walked hand in hand down to the edge of the lake, moving across the cool sand until they reached the shore. The warm water, lit by the bright, star-filled sky, lapped at their bare feet in a gentle rhythm. Not caring about his pants, he pulled her in deeper, until they stood almost knee-deep. He tugged her close, sliding his arms around her waist. She came into them easily, curling against his chest, tucking her head beneath his chin.

"I used to come up here to swim late at night," he said as he gently slid his fingers into her hair.

"It's warm enough," she replied. "But I don't really want to swim."

"Me neither. I'd rather stay just like this."

With Kate wrapped securely in his arms.

That seemed to be exactly what she wanted, too.

THE NEXT DAY, before Armand left to go back to Chicago, Kate asked him if he'd had a good time at the party after they'd left. He'd simply smiled and said, "It was a night that won't be forgotten for a long time."

Thanking him for the panties, she'd admitted she felt the same way.

The night before had been magic. Not only the party, not just the frantic sex in the back of her car. But standing there, wrapped in Jack's arms as they stood in the moonlight, simply enjoying each other's closeness. They'd exchanged long, languorous kisses, sweet, delicate touches. They hadn't talked much, nor had they made love again. Somehow, though, the night felt like the most intimate one they'd shared.

At some point Kate had even been able to admit the truth

to herself. Not only did she no longer distrust Jack, she was falling in love with him.

Not intentionally, probably not wisely, but there it was. She loved the son of the man who'd broken her mother's heart.

"Maybe it's fate," she told herself. "Maybe we can have the happy ending in this generation."

She told herself not to hope too much. After all, she'd gone through most of her adult life not believing she could ever trust someone enough to experience real love. Somehow, though, he'd worked past her defenses and captured her heart. She was simply unable to help it.

Cassie called Monday morning, and, to Kate's complete surprise, didn't even scold her for not picking her up from the airport. She did act very strange, though. Something had obviously happened between her and the sheriff after he'd picked her up, but Kate wasn't about to pry. After all, Cassie didn't question her about being caught having sex up at the lake with Jack. Kate had to figure it was because Tag hadn't told her. Cassie would never have let something that juicy go without comment if she knew. She'd instead been much more interested in hearing all about the Bunko party and the mayor's reception, seeming surprised to hear about the friendliness of so many of the women Kate had met.

When her cousin called again at noon, Kate instantly knew Cassie was in one of her wild moods. She sounded ready for something to happen. From experience, she figured that meant Cassie wanted something *dangerous* to happen.

Still, she had to admit, Cassie's idea was a good one. "You're saying we should have a pre-opening, private party for women only in the store tomorrow night?"

"Think of it as a very naughty Tupperware party."

It sounded ridiculous, outrageous and impossible.

And Kate loved the idea.

Their store would open in exactly one week. How better to test the waters than to invite some of the women Kate had met recently for a test run? They'd seemed modern and open about sex and relationships, and also starved for the type of products the store would carry. Deep down, she suspected they'd welcome Bare Essentials. The party would be the perfect time to find out.

That didn't mean she wasn't a nervous wreck. She liked these women, she really did, and she hated to imagine how she'd feel if they couldn't look past the titillation factor and see the potential for the store.

She wanted them to like Bare Essentials.

More importantly, she didn't want them to *dislike* her.

Kate did not pause to wonder when her goals had changed—she only knew they had. She no longer wanted only to cause controversy. Damn it, she wanted to succeed. She wanted the women of Pleasantville to be glad the Tremaine cousins had come back.

Thirty-six hours later, standing in the middle of a crowd of laughing women, she realized she needn't have worried.

"Oh, my God, Kate, no wonder you know so much about seduction!" Viv said as she greedily dug through the racks of erotic movies in the store.

"I never thought I'd say this, but these might be even better than Dr. Martens." This from Josie as she stood in front of a mirror, holding a jade-green silk teddy up against her body.

Diane went for the sex toys. "Anyone know which end is up?"

Crossing her arms and nodding in satisfaction, Kate met Cassie's eye from across the room. They exchanged a long, knowing look, each realizing that in spite of the way they'd started out, they were witnessing the birth of a bona fide success.

Who'd have ever believed it?

Soon the store was overflowing with chattering women. All the Bunko players came, and they brought friends. Cassie had also invited one woman, Stacie, who was a relative newcomer to town herself and seemed thrilled to meet all the others. Cassie and Kate could barely keep up with the sales, chatter and laughter. They passed around wine and hors d'oeuvres, and as the evening wore on, the sales added up.

"Well, all I know is, I want to buy whatever it was Kate had on under her dress at the party Saturday night," Diane said, fisting her hands and putting them on her hips. "Come on, show me. No cheesecake in the world is that good."

"Sorry," Kate said with a rueful shrug. "It's still in the testing phase. Armand is working on it, though, and I'm sure the store will be carrying them before too long."

"Armand," Diane said with a snicker. "He cracked me and Will up the other night. I don't know what he said to Darren and Angela, but I thought they were going to shit bricks."

Not knowing what she was talking about, Kate raised a brow.

"Oh, gosh, you and Jack had already left, hadn't you?"

"I know where they went," Annie the dispatcher said with a grin. "We got a call about a silver SUV at the lake."

Cassie jerked her head around to listen, giving Kate a curious stare. Feeling a blush stain her cheeks, she ignored the question in her cousin's eyes. "Get back to Darren and Angela."

"I don't really know what happened, just that Angela was dancing with Armand, getting all grabby and touchy-feely. Darren came up, Armand said something to them both, and they took off like bats outta hell in two different directions."

Kate winced. She had a feeling she knew what Armand had said. Probably something along the lines of, *Sorry, Angela babe,*

Darren's much prettier than you and he's the one I want. Kiss me, big boy. Armand specialized in cutting down homophobics.

Suddenly very glad they'd left the party early, she made a mental note to strangle Armand when she got back to Chicago.

Well, maybe she'd kiss him first. Then, for sure, she'd strangle him.

13

"SO THE PARTY WAS A BIG success and the rumors are already spreading throughout town about how fabulous your store is. Tomorrow's grand opening will be a hit, I guarantee it. What'd I tell you? You're going to fail to fail." Jack couldn't keep the smug tone out of his voice as he and Kate brushed another coat of varnish remover on the old concession counter at the Rialto on Sunday afternoon.

She stuck her tongue out at him. "Anyone ever told you it's not nice to say I told you so?"

"Anyone ever told you it's not nice to stick your tongue out at people? Unless, of course, you're issuing an invitation." He caught her mouth in a quick, hot kiss that left them both breathless.

When they reluctantly parted, she looked down at the plastic drop cloth beneath their feet, which was splattered with liquid. "Paint washes off. I think varnish remover would sting, though."

"There's no work going on down on the stage," he whispered. "And our table's still there."

"Miss Rose will be back from the hardware store any minute now." She sounded disappointed. Just like he felt.

They couldn't seem to get enough of each other. No matter how many times he made love to Kate, it was always exciting, always amazing. Like that first time had been, right here in the theater all those weeks ago.

Jack had a hard time believing how much things had changed since then. In the past several days he and Kate had spent hours and hours in each other's company. He'd told her about his plans to open his own firm, she'd talked about her desire to expand her store. They'd gone through the past relationship comparisons, each trying to one-up the other with stories about some really bad first dates.

They'd even talked about their families a little. She'd told him what it was like growing up without a father. He'd told her of his regrets at leaving Angela alone in a house with his very unhappily married parents.

She'd grown uncomfortable when he mentioned his parents. "I think we ought to change the subject."

Though he knew she was right, he wished he could tell her what he'd discovered Friday. He could hardly believe it himself and had no one with whom to discuss it.

Dealing with his father's bank records had been nearly impossible from the beginning. But suddenly, the other day, he began to make sense of things. For the first time in weeks, Jack started to realize that his father had, in his own way, tried to do right by Edie.

For each and every month when there had been an uncashed paycheck made out to Edith Jones, Jack had found a subsequent payment to a mysterious account at a state bank. Some digging had revealed the truth. His father had made several sizable payments against Edie's mortgage. He doubted she'd even realized it was happening.

No, his father hadn't wiped the slate clean by any means, but it was nice to know he had not completely taken advantage of Kate's mother. He'd obviously cared about her, enough to help her even when she refused to take his help.

It didn't make things right. But at least it made them better. It also made Jack wonder if he would ever really understand the truth about their relationship. It seemed now it had been more about emotion than just sex. Sex wouldn't have taken the older couple through nearly two decades. There had to have been love.

Somehow that made it a little easier to deal with.

"So, what are you going to do now that your store's on the road to success? You can't just shut it down," he asked.

She shook her head. "I've been thinking a lot about that. Cassie and I have worked there a lot lately and we've been discussing some options. At least she'll be here until the end of the summer. And who knows what she'll want to do then."

He laid his brush down and stared. "No way would Cassie stay here long-term."

She shrugged. "I don't know if she actually would, but I don't think it's a bad idea. I kind of suggested it to her."

He raised a brow. "I can only imagine how she reacted."

"After she stops laughing, maybe she'll really think about it. She's got a great house. And she seems to have found some things she likes about Pleasantville." She snickered, obviously thinking about Tag.

"So you really think she'd stay?"

"I honestly can't say. But it's a possibility. We'll see how tomorrow's grand opening goes."

"Then in a week or two you'll go back to Chicago."

"Right. And you will, too."

He nodded.

"I'm going to miss having you right next door," she admitted. "Who'll nearly kill me when he bursts in to tackle me in the middle of the night?"

"I only hurt you the *first* time I tackled you in the middle of the night. Admit it, every other tackle since then has been painless." He gave her a suggestive look, telling her he meant their more amorous tackles. "Don't forget, I did kiss it better that first time."

"Oh, yeah, you definitely did."

Though he hadn't planned to bring it up, figuring Kate might not have realized yet that she was falling in love with him, he couldn't help himself. "Besides, we don't have to give up on having each other around once we get home. I have a big apartment. And if it's not big enough, I can design us something better. Closer to your store."

Her eyes widened. "What are you saying? You mean, you want us to…"

"Move in together," he said. "I know it's kinda fast, but we're practically living together now. Why don't we just make it official when we get home?"

She lowered her eyes, looking away. Jack called himself ten kinds of fool for bringing it up. *It's too soon.* Hell, he knew they hadn't been together long enough to start talking about cohabitation. But he was already picturing little dark-haired Jacks and blond-haired Kates! Marriage, happily-ever-after, all the stuff he'd once sworn wasn't for him.

Now he understood. He simply hadn't found the right woman yet. Until Kate. His future. The woman he wanted to spend the rest of his life with.

The one who'd gone silent and white as a sheet at just the mention of them moving in together. If he told her he wanted to marry her someday, she'd probably faint face-first into the bucket of varnish remover.

Kate was an unusual woman and she wouldn't approach things—including her love life—in the usual way. A complicated mix of modern vixen and smart businesswoman, she'd wanted the sex first, then the relationship. He couldn't forget that, because she might never have even thought about the future or long-term plans. Talk of those things might scare her off.

It killed him to wonder if she'd figured their involvement would end once they left Pleasantville behind. Because it wouldn't. It *couldn't*. He was never letting her go. Though she might not be ready to admit it, he knew damn well she felt the same way.

She couldn't hide the way she looked at him, particularly when he held her in his arms. There was love in her eyes.

"Let's talk about it later, okay?" he said, quickly backtracking. "We still have some time here, and I know you need to focus on the grand opening tomorrow morning."

She looked troubled; her eyes were bright, as if she had tears in them. He silently cursed himself again for putting her on the spot, pressuring her too soon.

Before he could say anything, or even think of what to say, a woman's voice intruded. "Speaking of the grand opening, Kate, I need you to set something aside for me tomorrow morning."

They both looked up as Rose joined them, her arms loaded with bags of supplies from the hardware store.

"I want one of them Kama Sutra sheet sets, so I can honestly say my bed has had every sexual position known to man performed on it."

Kate's worried expression faded as she ruefully grinned. "You got it, Rose."

KATE FIGURED the grand opening of Bare Essentials in Pleasantville would be discussed by its residents for years to come. Old-timers would reminisce about it the way they did the big snowstorm of '73, the high school girls' state championship team of the early eighties. Even Flo Tremaine's striptease and skinny-dipping session in the town square fountain thirty years back would take a back seat to this day.

The newest generation of Tremaine women were definitely giving them something to talk about.

The line to get into the store Monday morning wound down the cobbled sidewalk, blocking the entrance to the Tea Room. That obviously ticked Mrs. McIntyre off royally, because she'd posted a snippy little sign saying Do Not Block Stairs on her porch railing.

Kate heard later that a few of the Tea Room biddies had made rude comments about the store. They'd been overruled by the people in line, including Mayor Otis who declared Kate and Cassie worthy of a civic award for their efforts to revitalize Pleasantville's downtown shopping district.

A neighboring city had even sent in a news truck. Sure, it was a teeny cable station, with a viewership of about eight, but it was exciting, nonetheless. The reporter conducted interviews with the customers, many of whom were the Bunko women who'd come to the pre-opening party last week. Their husbands were even more enthusiastic in their support of the new shop.

Singles, couples, young and old, the populace of Pleasantville chatted and laughed, lauding the store as an asset to the town while they shopped their hearts out.

Armand's lingerie was a huge hit, with sexy books and fun-and-naughty gifts doing well, too. Kate suspected the hotter items—dildoes, vibrators and the like—would sell better when there were no throngs of townspeople present. Or TV cameras.

If Kate hadn't already changed her mind about wanting this store to fail, she might be feeling pretty upset about its obvious success. Now, since she wanted it to succeed, she should be feeling at least triumph, if not downright jubilation.

Depressed better described her mood.

Stupid. It was stupid, juvenile and girlish, but she was depressed about Jack asking her to move in with him yesterday.

The modern woman who carried a vibrator around in her purse should have been thrilled, recognizing Jack had really been offering a sort of commitment in today's day and age.

A deeper, more vulnerable part of her had been very hurt.

Did he want her to serve the same function as her mother had? The woman who was good enough to mess around with, but not the one you married, not the one you had children with?

Men from Lilac Hill didn't marry trashy Tremaine women. They had sex with them in secret and left them stuff in their wills, but they certainly didn't introduce them to their mothers or give them wedding rings.

She knew her reaction was unfair. She'd seen motives and desires he might never have intended. And it wasn't as if Jack knew about his father's relationship with her mother, so he couldn't possibly have realized how she might take it.

Kate was intelligent enough to know her own deep-down insecurity had made her tense up when he'd asked. That didn't lessen the feeling, though.

At the end of the day, a few minutes before closing time, Kate found herself alone behind the cash register. Cassie had run an errand, most of the shoppers had left. There were one or two people in the dressing rooms, she believed. She was ready for them to get out so she could go take a long, hot bath. When the bell jingled over the door, she glanced up and saw, to her surprise, Darren McIntyre.

"Still open for business?"

She glanced at the clock. "You've got two minutes. Tell me what you're looking for. I'll point you in the right direction."

He shrugged. "How about the apology area?"

Kate dropped her pencil. "Huh?"

Darren walked over to the counter, not able to disguise his interest as he studied the various items on the shelves. He chuckled. "Bet my father never pictured this display case being used for *those* when he had it installed." When Kate didn't reply, he said, "Look, Kate, I came to apologize. I know it was years ago, and I'm sure you've forgotten, but I was a jerk to you in high school and I'm sorry."

Well, indeed, a day of surprises. "That's nice of you, Darren. I appreciate it. I know it's probably not easy for you to walk in here, remembering your dad and all."

He shrugged. "My father had every right to do with this building whatever he wanted to. I'm sure he'd rather see it open as a ladies' shop than sitting here moldering away. My mother on the other hand..."

Kate snorted. "Yeah, I can imagine."

"Divorce can be tough." He glanced away. "On everyone. You marry someone you think you know, think you love, then you find out you don't really know them at all."

She figured he was referring to his marriage but didn't ask. After a minute of small talk Darren said, "I'd better go. I just wanted to wish you luck and to say I'm sorry. Your, uh, *friend* Armand reminded me the other night that you might have a score to settle."

Kate shook her head, putting aside not only Darren's doubts, but any of her own. "No, Darren, I don't." *Not anymore.*

Darren had no sooner left, shutting the door behind them, when Kate heard someone emerge from the dressing room area. She sensed her long, hot bath was going to be further delayed when she recognized Angela. "I didn't know you were here."

"Stay away from Darren," the woman said. "You got your

revenge. Your friend made a big fool out of the both of us the other night, so leave him alone."

Seeing tears in the other woman's eyes, Kate had to wonder whether Angela had ever given up on her first marriage. Any sympathy she felt for Angela evaporated when she saw the book she held. Her diary. The last time she'd seen it, it had been in a drawer in a desk in the storage room. "Snooping?"

Angela didn't even have the grace to flush. "Stay away from my brother, too. I won't let you hurt him in some nasty plot."

"You don't know what you're talking about." Suddenly so tired, Kate rubbed her eyes. She didn't want to have this conversation. Ever.

Angela slammed the diary on the counter, open to the page with Kate's revenge list. "Yes, I do. Didn't you write this? 'For Mom's sake, get even with the Winfield family,'" she read. "'Particularly John Winfield.' My father isn't around to hurt anymore, so you've decided to focus on my brother. A different man, but who cares, the name's the same, right?"

Kate took a deep breath, trying to remain calm enough to deal with Jack's sister, trying to have sympathy for her, given the way Jack had described her childhood. "Angela, that was years ago. I don't have any intention of hurting Jack."

The other woman crossed her arms. "Just like you didn't want revenge on me and Darren, by setting us up to look like fools at the mayor's reception the other night? Like you didn't want to hurt the town by opening up this shop? Don't give me that. You want to hurt my family the way your mother did."

Then it hit her. Angela didn't seem the least bit surprised her diary had spoken of Edie and John. She tilted her head and stared at the woman. "You knew. About their affair."

Angela nodded. "Of course I knew. I've known for years. Everyone knows, even my mother."

Everyone? Including Jack?

"The point is, Kate, your secret's out. I'm going to tell Jack all about this little revenge list of yours, which you've been crossing off since the day you hit town."

Kate shook her head. "You're wrong. I care about Jack."

She smirked. "Won't matter. Jack doesn't care about you. You've been about one thing to him from the very beginning. He doesn't love you. Winfields don't marry trashy Tremaine women who own sex shops or work as maids. He won't marry you any more than my father married your mother."

Kate's anger made her reply so quickly her mind barely registered the ringing of the bell over the front door. "Thanks to *your* mother." At Angela's puzzled look, Kate said, "She made sure of it. Trapping him into marriage with a fake pregnancy just to get him away from *my* mother, who was his girlfriend throughout high school! That's probably just what you did to Darren, only he didn't stick around like your father did after he found out. So don't talk to me about families being hurt. If anyone deserves some payback, it's the Winfields."

Angela had grown pale and looked utterly shocked. Kate regretted the words as soon as she said them, angry with herself for letting the woman goad her so. Kate regretted them even more when she realized who had walked into the store.

Seeing the late-afternoon sunlight shining through the front windows onto a familiar—and very dear—blond head, she felt the blood drain from her face. "Jack."

"Do I even want to know what's going on here?" Jack forced a note of calmness in his voice as he walked across the store to the counter, where Kate and his sister both stood. They looked equally as disturbed by his appearance.

"This is a misunderstanding…"

"She came here for one reason. To get revenge," Angela said at the same time. His sister thrust a small book in his hand, obviously a diary. "She's been plotting it for years. Against me and Darren—we were both totally humiliated by her gay friend the other night. But she's not satisfied yet, she's out to get the whole town, including *you*."

He didn't look at his sister, focusing all his attention on Kate. "Angela, would you please leave?"

He thought she'd argue, but she didn't. Looking confused and upset, more than angry, Angela grabbed her purse and hurried out of the store. As soon as they were alone, Jack put the diary back on the counter.

"It's not like she said…"

"I know about your revenge list, remember?" he interrupted softly. "You don't have to explain it to me."

She looked relieved. For a moment, anyway.

He continued. "I once asked you if it would be bad for me to see the list. When you said yes, I figured it mentioned Angela. Was she right? Was there more to it than that?"

Kate took a slow, deep breath, then nodded.

"You knew about my father and Edie."

She crossed her arms tightly. "I found out on prom night."

He absorbed her words and said a silent curse. Both Kate and his sister had learned as teenagers of their parents' affair. He again kicked himself for leaving town, for not being around when he might have been needed.

"When did you find out?" she asked softly.

"The night I met you," he admitted. "*After* I left you at the theater. I had absolutely no idea who you were until then. I didn't even know your last name, remember?"

She glanced away, her face growing even paler.

As a heavy, uncomfortable silence fell between them, Jack mentally replayed what he'd heard of the conversation. He still had trouble believing it. Not that Kate had written a revenge list, he'd known about it before, after all. He just hadn't known his entire family was part of the plot. Somehow, it had been easy to imagine she'd gotten over any high school hurts, so he'd accepted her assurances that she really wasn't opening her store for revenge. Now, however, he had to wonder.

"I have to know," he finally said, "was your list on your mind when you came back here? When we got involved?"

She stared at him, not answering.

"Tell me, Kate. When you decided to come back to Pleasantville, did you think about a little payback? Getting involved with me, then breaking my heart, like you thought my dad did to your mom?"

She countered with a question of her own. "You tell me something, Jack. The night we met, when you found out who I was, that Edie *Tremaine* was my mother…is that the reason you never called? The reason you decided we couldn't get involved?"

He answered easily. "Of course."

She stiffened, as if offended by his honesty, though he didn't know why. He opened his mouth to elaborate, to tell her how hurt he'd been for Edie, how he'd wanted to make it up to her and not take advantage of Kate.

Before he could say a word, however, she picked up her purse and keys. "Thanks for being honest. Now, you want the truth? Here it is. I came back here with every intention of seducing J. J. Winfield." Stepping around the counter, she met his stare steadily with her own. "I planned to get him to go crazy over me, then stomp his heart into the dust with the heels of my six-inch-tall slut-puppy boots."

Without another word, she turned and walked out of her own store.

14

WHEN NURSING A BROKEN heart, it really sucked to live next door to the person who'd done the breaking. Kate found that out late Monday night when she lay on her mattress bed in Aunt Flo's duplex, listening to Jack arrive home next door.

As soon as she heard his truck outside, she bit her lip to stop her tears. She definitely didn't want him to hear her through the wall.

She'd been crying for hours. Whimpering like a sissified baby. Wishing she had someone to talk to, but knowing there was no one. Cassie would be too pissed on her behalf to be of any help. Plus, the last thing she wanted to do on the day of the triumph at the store was to tell Cassie someone she thought she loved still looked at her as unworthy.

When Jack had admitted he'd decided to end their involvement because of who she was—a Tremaine—Kate had wanted to die. All she'd heard were his sister's angry words, the echo of taunts of her childhood, the deeply-buried-but-not-erased voice of her subconscious that had told her she would always be just a trashy Tremaine. Never good enough for decent people. Worthy of sex but not love, fun but not commitment.

Living together, but not marriage.

Even though her heart was breaking, she'd still almost gone back to apologize, to tell him she might have first intended to get involved with him for revenge, but knew she could never go through with it. Because like a colossal fool, she'd fallen in love with him. And it had hurt her to see the pain on his face at her confession.

Pride had kept her walking out the door the same way it had sustained her on prom night when she'd walked home in the rain.

She didn't sleep more than one straight hour all night long. Kate knew she looked and sounded like hell, so when she called Cassie the next morning, told her she wasn't feeling well and would be late coming in to help in the store, her cousin hadn't protested. She felt like a heel leaving Cassie holding the bag at Bare Essentials. Still, she doubted their day would be anywhere near as busy as yesterday had been.

Jack left the house early—before eight. She watched him from the upstairs window, careful not to let him see her. She needn't have bothered. He never spared a glance at her half of the duplex as he got in his truck and drove away.

Once he'd gone, she cried some more. Ate some donuts. Took a shower. Finally, sick of feeling sorry for herself, she pulled her cell phone out of her purse and called the one person she knew would understand.

Her mom.

JACK DIDN'T WANT to see anybody Tuesday. He had no interest in being anywhere near his mother or sister. Nor could he stay at the duplex, knowing Kate was right next door.

Sleeping there the night before had been sheer torture. He had lain awake most of the night, thinking about what had happened, replaying the scene at the store. He'd tried to find some explanation, but couldn't deny the truth. She'd said the words herself. She'd fully intended to get involved with him for the express purpose of hurting him as some kind of whacked-out revenge on his father.

Mission accomplished.

Damn, it was almost easier when he thought he'd never fall in love.

After driving around for a while, he went downtown and parked outside the Rose Café. Across the street, Bare Essentials remained dark, not yet open for the morning. When he went inside the café for breakfast, he took a seat away from the front windows. He really didn't want to see Kate arriving for work.

After he ordered, he tried to figure out just how much more he had to do for his family. There were one or two more legal issues, but the real estate situation was taken care of, as were the banking problems. At this point, all he wanted to do was to wrap things up and go home to Chicago. He frankly didn't care if he never saw Pleasantville again.

Just as the gum-chewing waitress deposited a plate full of artery-hardening breakfast on the table in front of him, the café door opened. As Darren entered, Jack looked away. He did not want to talk to anyone, particularly his ex-brother-in-law.

Unfortunately, Darren had other ideas. "Can I sit down?"

"Do I have any other choice?"

Darren took the seat opposite him in the booth. "I need to talk to you. About Angela. She came to see me last night and told me what happened with Kate."

Jack raised a brow, practically daring Darren to make one slimy comment about Kate. "And?"

"Apparently Kate said something to Angela that made her do some serious thinking. About us."

"You and Angela?"

"Yeah. She asked me if I'd left her because I thought she faked being pregnant to get me to marry her."

Jack calmly took a sip of coffee. "Did you?"

Darren answered with a slow nod. "I was convinced she'd made it up, that there had never been any baby. Because I'd overheard your parents arguing about it one night. Your father accused Angela of being like your mother, who'd done the same thing to him."

Jack could only shake his head. Kate had been right about that much of the story, it seemed.

Before Darren said anything else, the door to the café opened again and Angela came in. Her face was lit up by a huge smile, and her eyes sparkled as she looked around the room. She spotted Darren and walked toward them. Her steps slowed when she realized he was sitting with Jack. Squaring her shoulders, she sat opposite him, sliding easily under Darren's outstretched arm. The two of them might as well have started cooing like doves.

Jack raised a brow. "I see you've worked things out."

Darren nodded. "Angela made me realize how wrong I'd been."

Angela had the grace to admit, "I had no idea, Jack, about Mother and Dad. It never occurred to me what Darren thought until Kate accused me of it last night. I had to make sure he knew the truth. I wanted to be sure Darren understood how much I grieved for our very real baby." She swallowed hard. "I guess I owe Kate one."

Well, let's give a round of applause for Kate, matchmaker and revenge seeker extraordinaire.

"You should probably know," Angela continued, "Darren confirmed what Kate told me. About Dad and Edie being together before he married Mother. I guess...well, it doesn't make it right, what they did, but I think I can see Kate's side a little better now." Angela cast a quick, nervous glance at Darren. He smiled and nudged her, obviously trying to give her courage. "I also, uh, should tell you, I know you only heard part of our conversation. Kate wasn't the only one who said nasty things, Jack. I was pretty mean to her first."

Angela expressing regret? He could hardly believe it. "If it's any consolation," Jack said, "whatever happened with Armand, whatever revenge you think he got on you? I don't think Kate was involved. He's just very loyal to her."

Angela stared at him. "You're in love with her."

He gave her a rueful look. "Crazy, huh?"

"Wow." His sister bit her lip, looking more nervous. "Jack, one of the mean things I said to her was that you, uh…"

Starting to feel very anxious, Jack leaned closer. "What?"

Darren took her hand, squeezing it to give her courage. "Come on, Ang. New leaf, remember?"

Angela spoke in a rush. "I told her you could never love her. And that you'd never marry a trashy Tremaine woman any more than our father ever would have."

Jack sat silently for a minute, beginning to understand, to make sense out of what had happened yesterday.

Probably without even realizing it, Angela had pushed exactly the right button to hurt Kate the most. Because in spite of how put-together, confident and successful a woman she was today, there was still that vulnerable, defensive, wrong-side-of-the-tracks kid lurking underneath Kate's beautiful exterior.

Kate's childhood had molded her into the striking mix of sweet and tough, gentle and outrageous, smart and self-doubting.

Jack had fallen in love with all of her.

But she didn't believe that.

"I've got to go," he said. Dropping cash on the table for his uneaten breakfast, he barely spared a glance at his sister.

"I'm sorry, Jack," she called as he walked away. "I'm sorry I hurt her."

Not as sorry as he was.

RIGHT AFTER Kate's long telephone call with Edie, she hung up, hearing her mother's words again and again in her mind.

"Oh, honey, don't you think for a minute I regret loving the man I loved. And don't think I didn't know how much he loved *me*. Heavens, John asked me to marry him more than a dozen times over the years, starting all the way back in tenth grade." She'd laughed softly, as if remembering something warm and tender. "After Angela grew up and got married, I started to think we could really be together. Then her marriage failed. As did her second. And her third. Pat blamed John for his bad example and guilt made him stay. But we still loved each other. Why do you think I had to leave Ohio when he died? Do you think some narrow-minded people could have forced a Tremaine out?" Her voice had broken and Kate had somehow heard the silent tears she knew were rolling down her cheeks. "It was too painful to stay, Katey. Knowing he was gone."

After she hung up, Kate shed more tears. This time not for herself. But for Edie.

A short time later she grabbed her purse and keys and went to find Jack. One thing her mother had said rang true…if she loved the man, pride had no place in the equation. Any chance for happiness was one worth grabbing.

She took a deep breath as she slowly drove by the Winfield house on Lilac Hill. No truck in the driveway. Thank God. She needed to see him, but she wasn't ready to face his family.

She tried the downtown area next, cruising along Magnolia, looking for his golden hair shining in the bright morning sun. She still didn't see him. Finally, thinking hard about where he might have gone in this town, she turned down a side street toward the Rialto.

Bingo.

Parking her SUV behind his truck, she walked to the front doors and entered the lobby. The overhead fixtures were off out here, but she saw a sliver of light from the main auditorium area. Pushing through the swinging doors, she paused in the back of the theater, looking around in the murky shadows of the cavernous, dimly lit room.

Jack sat in one of the old plushly covered seats in the back row. She saw him there at the same instant he saw her.

"What are you doing here?" she asked.

"I was looking for you. I went to the house, and the store. I finally figured you'd show up here. So I sat down to wait."

He was right. Eventually, even if she hadn't gone looking for him, she would have shown up here.

He remained seated, while Kate stood. She didn't know what to say, now that she had finally found him. There didn't seem to be an easy way to apologize for admitting what had once been the truth. She really had thought she could set out to hurt this man. This amazing man who'd captured her heart and soul.

It now seemed almost inconceivable.

Finally, as if realizing she couldn't find the words to begin, Jack stood and extended his hand. She stepped closer, taking it, letting him pull her into the seat next to his own.

Finally she heard him say, "I'm not J. J. Winfield, Kate."

She bit her lip.

"Maybe J. J. Winfield was someone you once wanted to get even with. But that's not me."

"I know," she admitted. "Jack, as soon as I saw you, as soon as I realized who you were, I dropped any idea of revenge. I knew I was too vulnerable to you." She lowered her voice.

"I already liked you too much. I knew from the beginning I could care for you."

"I knew it, too," he said. "I never would have believed it if it hadn't happened to me, but I knew from the first time I saw you something amazing was going to happen between us. I started to fall in love with you before I even heard your voice or knew your name."

Her name. Yes, back to the issue at hand. Kate thrust away the thrill of pleasure that had raced through her body at hearing the word love on Jack's lips. "My name. Who I am. That's the issue, right? The reason you didn't call."

She felt his level stare as he carefully answered. "Kate, finding out your name, learning you were a member of the *infamous* Tremaine family, had absolutely nothing to do with me staying away from you." He sighed, shaking his head. "You want the truth? Here it is. I couldn't handle the guilt. I really thought my father had used and abused your mother, and I wasn't about to follow in his footsteps. In case you didn't know it, I don't have a great reputation as a stick-around kind of guy."

There was no question of doubting him, the sincerity in his voice was matched by the look in his eyes.

"So, when you asked me to live with you..."

He cocked his head. "You were upset about that?"

She glanced at her fingers. "I just figured it was history repeating itself. Tremaines are good enough to live with..."

She almost expected him to react in anger, but instead he laughed, long and loud. "God, have we ever been at cross purposes." Turning in his seat, he grabbed her around the waist and lifted her over the armrest, pulling her onto his lap. "I'm crazy about you, Kate. I want the whole nine yards. Marriage, kids, P.T.A. meetings."

Marriage? Kids? She choked on a mouthful of air and had

to hack into her fist. When she could breathe again, she said, "P.T.A. meetings?"

"We'll go together, unless, of course, you're busy peddling sex toys at your store."

She couldn't even laugh, still too amazed to see what she wanted was truly within her grasp. "You're serious? You want all that?"

He brought her hands to his lips, kissing her palm. "I absolutely want all that." He pulled her closer, until her head rested on his shoulder. "I figured you'd laugh in my face if I started talking about that kind of stuff, though. You, Miss Lusty Vibrating Fingertip, seemed to not only enjoy doing things backward, but you seem to want to make them as outrageous as possible. I kinda figured love and marriage stuff would turn you off…make you think I thought you were sweet or something."

She sat up and punched his shoulder. "I am sweet, damn it."

He gave her a hopeful smile. "Hopefully not too sweet for those slut-puppy boots."

She lowered her lashes, giving him a coy look. "If you're good. But in the meantime, get back to the L word you mentioned."

"Lusty?"

Their laughter faded as Kate stared intently into his fine green eyes. "Love. Did you mean to use that particular word?"

He reached up and slipped his hand into her hair, caressing her gently as he tugged her mouth toward his. "Yeah. I meant to use that particular word. I love you like crazy, Kate."

Just before her lips touched his, she whispered, "I love you, too, Jack."

Epilogue

Six Months Later

LYING IN THE UNFAMILIAR king-size bed in their hotel suite, Jack listened to Kate get up and go into the bathroom. He'd thought she was asleep. Heaven knew, she should be after their strenuous evening. But maybe she was still too keyed up to sleep, too happy, excited and relieved that they'd actually made it. As he was.

Jack waited for her to come back, then smiled in the darkness as he heard the sound of the faucet turning and the gush of water in the tub.

A late-night shower.

What a way to start off married life.

He didn't get up to join her right away, content instead to listen to her from the bed. He waited for the pulling of the plastic curtain, the clink of the rings on the metal rod. The gurgle turning to a hiss as the shower jets came on. Kate's light, off-key humming.

Remembering lying in bed at the house in Pleasantville, listening to her all those months ago, he had to laugh. They'd come a long way. Physically and emotionally.

Unable to hold out any longer, he got out of bed, almost

tripping on Kate's white sundress and shoes, which he'd tossed to the floor earlier that evening in his rush to make her his wife in every sense of the word.

Her wedding dress. And the flip-flops she'd worn for the small beachside ceremony.

They'd had a perfect sunset wedding with two bartenders at the couples-only resort serving as official witnesses. A beach vendor had made Kate her bouquet and a housemaid had caught it. A steel drum player had riffed in the background, competing with the sound of the surf and the low, lyrical voice of the island minister who'd married them.

Considering their two mothers couldn't stand one another, they'd thought it best to fly to the Caribbean for the ceremony. Maybe someday they'd all have to be together—probably when he and Kate started having kids. But for now, long-distance family relationships seemed the wisest solution.

Their families certainly wished them well, for which they were both grateful. Edie and her new boyfriend had thrown them a big engagement party at the retirement community in Florida at Thanksgiving. And his own mother—who had decided to give Mayor Otis a run for his money and seek her late husband's seat—had done the same on New Year's Day a few weeks ago in Pleasantville.

Jack still cracked up remembering the expression on Kate's face when his sister Angela had hugged her, telling her how sorry she was her pregnancy would prevent her from being maid of honor. He'd had to cover his mouth so Darren wouldn't see him snort with laughter.

The best party of them all, however, had been the bridal shower at Bare Essentials, hosted by Armand and Cassie. He hoped to God Kate had packed some of the gifts they got *that* night.

Unable to wait any longer, Jack walked into the bathroom.

Seeing several conveniently placed candles and matches, he lit a few, then turned out the light. Kate's silhouette shimmered through the shower curtain in the soft glow of candlelight.

She said nothing, obviously waiting for him in the semi-darkness. When he stepped inside the tub, pulling the curtain closed behind him, she leaned back against his body and turned her head to look up at him. "I thought you were asleep. I didn't mean to wake you."

"I wouldn't have missed this. Our first married shower."

She was hot and wet, slippery and lithe. Jack wanted to touch her everywhere. Pulling her closer, he knew she felt his hard-on slipping between her thighs. He groaned as she rocked back on it, rubbing her curvy backside against his groin. Sliding his arms around her waist, he held her tight as he bent to press his mouth to hers for one long wet kiss after another.

"Hope they paid the hot water bill," she said when their lips finally parted.

Remembering some of the other showers they'd shared over the past few months, he hoped so, too.

"I love you, Kate," he said as he pushed a long, dark strand of wet hair off her brow.

She rubbed her cheek against his palm, whispering, "And I love you."

He kissed her again, sweetly, cherishing her tonight as his wife as much as he already cherished her as his mate. Finally, spying a bottle of body wash on the edge of the tub, he reached for it. "Want me to wash your back?"

She nodded, giving him a look of sultry heat. "And my front."

Oh, without question.

"It's a deal." He grinned. "Just remember the rule…"

She rolled her eyes and gave him a disgruntled look. "Okay,

I know. No singing in the shower." Then she raised a brow. "Just don't you forget your rule, either, *angel*."

Remembering their first time together back on the stage at the Rialto, he chuckled. "No wings until I ring your bell."

Their laughter, their loving…and their shower…lasted long into the night.

★ ★ ★ ★ ★

Looking for more *red-hot* reads like the ones you just read?

Harlequin Blaze stories sizzle with strong heroines and irresistible heroes playing the game of modern love and lust. They're fun, sexy and always steamy.

Enjoy four *new* **Harlequin Blaze** stories every month!

Available wherever books and ebooks are sold.

Also by *New York Times* bestselling author Jill Shalvis:

Time Out

The Heat Is On

Storm Watch

Aftershock—Coming July 2014

And *New York Times* bestselling author Leslie Kelly:

Lying in Your Arms

Waking Up to You

Blazing Midsummer Nights

It Happened One Christmas

Terms of Surrender

Connect with us to find your next great read, special offers and more!

Facebook.com/HarlequinBooks

Twitter.com/HarlequinBooks

HarlequinBlog.com

Harlequin.com/Newsletter

Love the book you just read?

Your opinion matters.

Review this book on your favorite
book site, review site, blog or your own
social media properties and share
your opinion with other readers!

Be sure to connect with us at:
Harlequin.com/Newsletters
Facebook.com/HarlequinBooks
Twitter.com/HarlequinBooks

H HARLEQUIN®

A *Romance* FOR EVERY MOOD™

Stay up-to-date on all your
romance-reading news with the
Harlequin Shopping Guide,
featuring bestselling authors, exciting new
miniseries, books to watch and more!

The newest issue will be delivered right to you
with our compliments! There are 4 each year.

Signing up is easy.

EMAIL

ShoppingGuide@Harlequin.ca

WRITE TO US

HARLEQUIN BOOKS
Attention: Customer Service Department
P.O. Box 9057, Buffalo, NY 14269-9057

OR PHONE

1-800-873-8635 in the United States
1-888-343-9777 in Canada

Please allow 4-6 weeks for delivery of the first issue by mail.

ml   2-14